ALSO BY ENID SHOMER

Tourist Season

Imaginary Men

Stars at Noon

Black Drum

This Close to the Earth

Stalking the Florida Panther

The TWELVE ROOMS *of the* NILE

ENID SHOMER

Simon & Schuster
New York London Toronto Sydney New Delhi

Simon & Schuster
1230 Avenue of the Americas
New York, NY 10020

First Simon & Schuster hardcover edition August 2012

Designed by Nancy Singer
Map by Paul Pugliese
Illustration by Laura Levatino
Calligraphy by William Lung

Manufactured in the United States of America

10 9 8 7 6 5 4 3 2 1

Library of Congress Cataloging-in-Publication Data
Shomer, Enid.
The twelve rooms of the Nile / Enid Shomer.
p. cm.
1. Nightingale, Florence, 1820–1910—Fiction. 2. Flaubert, Gustave, 1821–1880—Fiction. 3. Friendship—Fiction. 4. Nile River—Fiction. 5. Egypt—History—1517–1882—Fiction. I. Title.
PS3569.H5783T94 2012
813'.54—dc23 2011037151

ISBN 978-1-4516-4296-4
ISBN 978-1-4516-4298-8 (ebook)

In memory of William Magazine

and for my family

—Nirah, Mike, Oren, and Paula

Is discontent a privilege? . . . Woman has nothing but her affections,—and this makes her at once more loving and less loved.

—Florence Nightingale, *Cassandra*

The future is the worst thing about the present. The question "What are you going to do?," when it is cast in your face, is like an abyss in front of you that keeps moving ahead with each step you take.

—Gustave Flaubert

To speak the names of the dead is to make them live again.

—The Book of the Dead

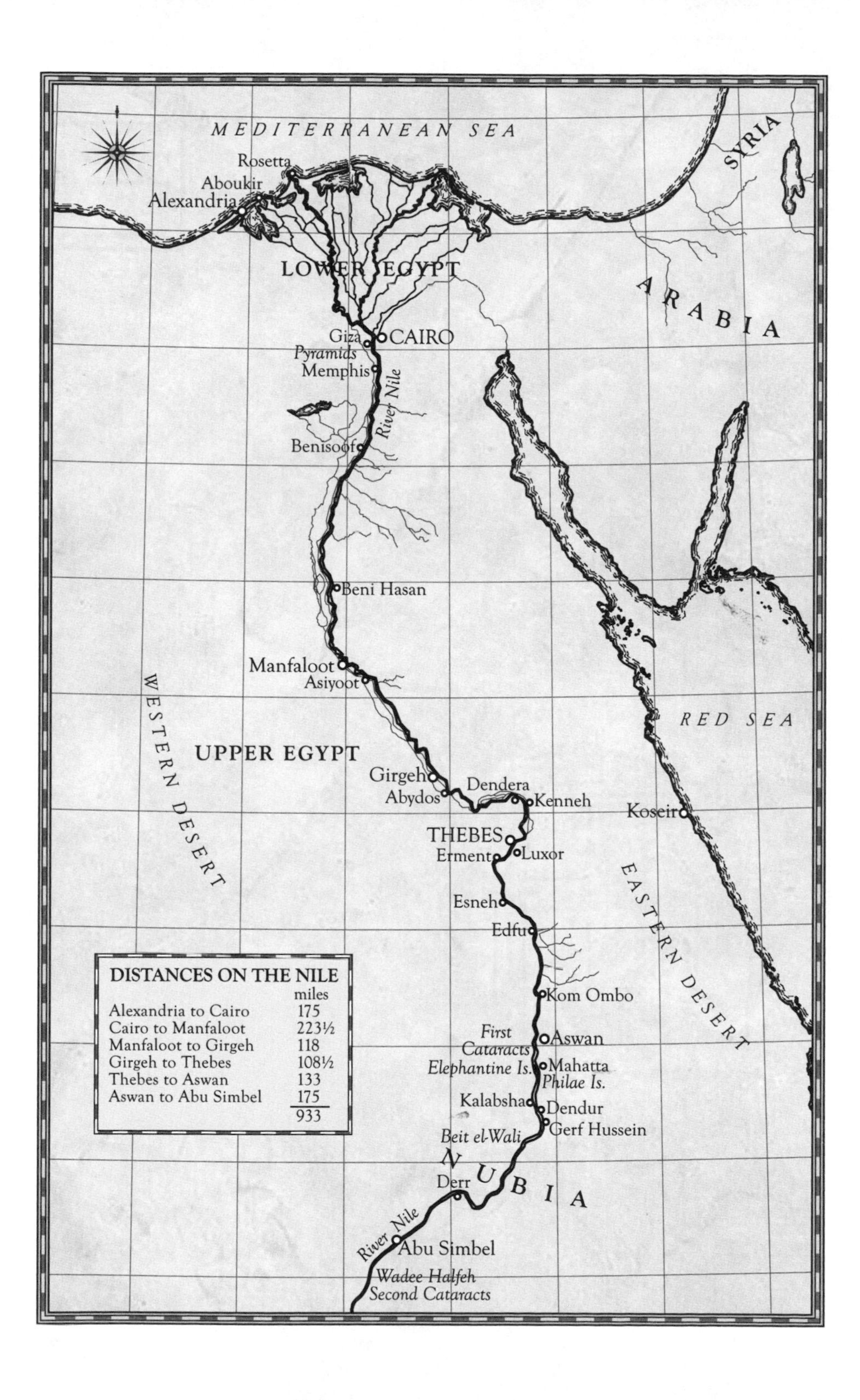
MEDITERRANEAN SEA
SYRIA
Rosetta
Aboukir
Alexandria
LOWER EGYPT
ARABIA
Giza
CAIRO
Pyramids
Memphis
River Nile
Benisoof
Beni Hasan
Manfaloot
Asiyoot
WESTERN DESERT
RED SEA
UPPER EGYPT
Girgeh
Abydos
Dendera
Kenneh
Koseir
THEBES
Erment
Luxor
EASTERN DESERT
Esneh
Edfu
DISTANCES ON THE NILE
miles
Alexandria to Cairo 175
Cairo to Manfaloot 223½
Manfaloot to Girgeh 118
Girgeh to Thebes 108½
Thebes to Aswan 133
Aswan to Abu Simbel 175
933
Kom Ombo
First Cataracts
Aswan
Elephantine Is.
Mahatta
Philae Is.
Kalabsha
Dendur
Gerf Hussein
Beit el-Wali
NUBIA
Derr
River Nile
Abu Simbel
Wadee Halfeh
Second Cataracts

The TWELVE ROOMS *of the* NILE

1

FATHER MUSTACHE AND THE FATHER OF THINNESS

Had the young Frenchman not been lost in thought, he might have caught his Baedeker as it jostled free of the gunwale and slipped into the river. Bound in red morocco with gilt lettering and gilt-edged pages, it was a costly gift from his dear mother.

At first the book floated, spread open like a bird with small red wings. But as the waters of the Nile darkened the onionskin pages already stained with Oriental sauces and cup after cup of Turkish coffee, they swelled like the gills of a drowning fish. His dragoman, Joseph, reached for it with an oar, but the attempt served only to push the guidebook farther under and soon it disappeared into the murky wake of the *cange*. The gentleman frowned.

The crew set about mooring the vessel on the riverbank. The Frenchman took a deep breath and realigned the incident in his mind, turning it the way you might a newspaper the better to scissor out an article. If he had to lose his guidebook, what better place than the Nile, that great liquid treasure pit? Let it molder in the deep, among shepherds' crooks and shards of clay oil lamps, or be heaved ashore with the river's yearly inundation of silt. He pictured a workman or scientist retrieving it in the future, reading the inscription he'd written on the fly page in indelible ink: "G. Flaubert, author of the failed novel *The Temptation of Saint Anthony,* 1849." Maybe he would be remembered for something after all! But the thought only made him frown again. Ambition was a dull pain, like a continually broken heart.

The crew prepared to serve the midday meal. Egyptian cleverness extended not only upward to the immense, immovable majesty of the Pyramids, the Sphinx, and the gargantuan colonnades at Karnak, but also downward to the practical and portable, to folding stools, chairs, and tables, expandable fishnet sleeping hammocks, and sacs for foodstuffs. Where moments before the crew had trafficked the broad central planks of the deck, there now appeared a dining nook, shaded by muslin hoisted on poles and tied at the top like a fancy parasol. He watched Achmet float a white damask cloth onto the table, then lay pewter chargers and pink porcelain plates, and finally, neatly frame each table setting with utensils and drinking vessels. A ewer of red wine and two full wineglasses in the dead center of the table reminded him of a floral arrangement trailing two spilled roses.

On the foredeck, a Nubian crewman was chopping and cooking, while leaning on the mainmast of the skysails, Rais Ibrahim, the captain, haggled with a fishmonger. Soon enough a phalanx of tin trays laden with dolma—all manner of stuffed vegetables—would appear to rise unaided, levitating on the heads of the crew.

Gustave and his companion, Max, had left France four months earlier. They were sailing south to Abu Simbel, after which they would turn around and follow the current back toward Cairo, visiting more monuments at their leisure. Upon the completion of their river journey, now in its eighth week, they would tackle Greece, Syria, Palestine, and all of western Turkey from Smyrna to Constantinople. Later, perhaps Persia and India.

Most of their itinerary lay within the borders of the Ottomans, who cared nothing, Gustave knew, for the connection to the classical past that so thrilled him. Genuflection at the altar of Graeco-Roman and Egyptian antiquity was to their thinking probably amusing if not idiotic. Their holy shrines lay farther east, in domains marked by a fastness of sand and abstinence. When, four decades earlier, they'd allowed the Elgin Marbles to be removed to England, it had ignited bidding wars among curators, archaeologists, and wealthy collectors for every torso, ossuary, and water jar. To the Turks this was not vandalism, but an opportunity to sell off useless debris. With their prohibition against the graven image, he imagined they might even be disgusted that a human form fetched up in stone could excite such ardor.

Though his hosts ruled a large chunk of the world, historians seemed to agree that a golden age based in raw courage and gallantry was behind them, that they now lived by collecting in tribute what they had once secured with the bloody scimitar. He admired the fact that unlike the Europeans, who were prone to wars of ideas, the Turks reigned benignly, ceding to their conquered peoples great latitude in the practice of religious and national customs. Or were they benign out of inefficiency? The sultans, caliphs, viceroys, emirs, sheiks, and pashas—they had countless names for grand and petty offices—ruled from an ornately disorganized web of bribery and corruption so bloated with excess that the empire had grown unwieldy as an elephant balanced on a ball. Someday it would tumble in an earth-shaking, ruined heap.

In the meantime, both he and Max entertained fantasies of returning home with a marble bust or two, possibly a mummy. For they had learned the secret to a successful tour of the Orient: baksheesh. A handful of drachmas or piastres opened the doors of private estates to the two young Frenchmen. Obscure ruins were lit by torchlight if necessary for their inspection, and skilled cicerones were assigned to guide them to hidden corners of antiquity. With the right attire, a modicum of financial resources, and a pouch bulging with documents adorned with diplomatic wax and ink flourishes, Europeans traveling the Orient enjoyed the privileges of nobility. Lord knew that made for a stampede of them everywhere in the cities of the delta, if not yet on the river itself. Egypt was on the verge of becoming an industry. They would be among the last to see it before it was entirely corrupted by foreigners.

To burnish their air of importance, Max, the more savvy of the two, had secured official missions for them from two different ministries of the French government. Unpaid missions, to be sure, but nonetheless effective in connecting them to diplomats and commercial agents in the East. Gustave's collection of gaseous bureaucratic prose commended him to the world beyond the Tuileries as a gentleman in the employ of the Ministry of Agriculture and Commerce with the task of collecting in ports and caravansaries information of interest to chambers of commerce in France. He had planned to dispense with his official designation upon arrival, but soon grasping its value, instructed his mother and friends to address their letters to *"Gustave Flaubert, chargé d'une mission en Orient."*

Max's mission was substantive, and Gustave envied him it, though he was too lazy to have undertaken it himself. The Ministry of Public Instruction had charged Max with compiling a catalog of the ancient monuments. With the latest camera, Monsieur Du Camp could efficiently replace corps of savants and artists who in Napoleon's day had performed this task. He was also charged with making life-sized facsimiles of the inscriptions, similar to stone rubbings, but producing an actual relief. These molds, or "squeezes," made using wet paper, were simple but tedious to produce, and Max depended upon Gustave to assist in their manufacture. Much to his disgust, Gustave often wandered off or fell asleep precisely when he was needed.

The truth was that Gustave had never considered himself anything but a writer. He pictured his study at home, an airy consortium of books and flowered chintz, thriving potted plants, a bearskin rug and massive desk where he had devoted the last two years to his first novel. While other writers poured out their tales or allowed them to trickle forth like seasonal streams, he had carved *The Temptation of*

Saint Anthony from the very mountain of the French language. Then, after reading it aloud to them, his best friends Max and Bouilhet had pronounced it inferior, unworthy of publication. The recollection sent a sharp pain through his chest and arrested his breathing. The reverie of the writer's life he would return to in his study at home vanished, like smoke on a wind.

He turned his attention to the crew approaching single-file amidships. On either side of them the waters of the Nile lapped like molten pewter touched with rivulets of gold. Hasan lowered a tray of delicacies, while above his shoulder, a gull's wing fluttered like a feathery epaulet as the bird swooped onto the bow of the *cange*. I'm traveling in the world of Byron! he thought, surrounded not by shopkeepers and prim demoiselles, but men wearing fezzes, bare-chested under fancy red vests. Nota bene: trimmed with soutache and black silk embroidery, one of these vests would make the ideal gift for Louise. In the past few months, the memory of her infuriating possessiveness had faded somewhat, and he had begun to ponder her charms. Just now, as he sipped his wine, he recalled the disarming way on their first rendezvous she had turned to him and said, "Shall we kiss awhile, my darling?"

Each man had spent the morning in solitary chores, Gustave composing in his journal, Max readying the camera for the afternoon excursion.

Max appeared at the table and greeted him. "I will need your help," he said. "Today we scout the temple of Derr."

"Yes," Gustave muttered. "I'm sure it will be grand." He was remembering the Sphinx, that sublime surprise. He had seen drawings of Luxor, Giza, and Abu Simbel at an exhibition in Paris. The Sphinx, though, had existed only in his imagination until the instant he came upon it, a ferocious giant perched on the desert floor, its nose smeared flat as if bloodied in a brawl.

"There will be many inscriptions, many squeezes to be made."

Gustave savored his wine, letting it trickle into the back of his throat. "How many?"

"Hundreds. I don't know. Thousands. Too many to do. There are hieroglyphs, demotic Egyptian, Greek, and something called Carian, a language no one can read."

Gustave scratched his whiskers. "In that case, we will have to bring an extra pack donkey." He served himself a second helping of rice flavored with cinnamon and cumin. The first thing he had noticed about the Orient was its parade of exotic spices, the bazaars smelling of coffee and sandalwood oil; the prostitutes of rosewater, balsam, and musk.

Max thought for a moment. "A litter will do, I think, dragged behind us Indian style."

Usually, he and Max rode donkeys or horses, but now Gustave imagined himself tugged along on the pallet, reclining like a minor grandee. Save for the dust. And the smell and sight of the animal relieving itself. A veritable shit caravan.

"Joseph, of course, will go with us," Max planned aloud, "plus two of the crew, Aouadallah and Hadji Ismael, as usual."

"Yes, Hadji Ismael, for scale."

Gustave hated being within range of a camera, so Max used Hadji Ismael in his photographs to establish the implausible size of Egypt's monuments. Perched on a gigantic toe, lounging inside a mammoth doorway, Hadji Ismael was not only reliable but also photogenic—a one-eyed, well-muscled fellow who spoke a strange pidgin in the considerable gaps of which he remained always courteous and sweet. On the ship, he acted the wife to Big Achmet. Bardashes all, the crew. That was something sexual he'd not yet tried. He was just waiting for the right opportunity. At a Turkish hammam, perhaps, where the young attendants were willing and the steam would leave him open-pored and pliant . . .

"Not just for scale—to represent the human enterprise," Max said for perhaps the fifth time in two weeks. "Even the stars mean nothing without a steaming hovel beneath them."

Such grandiose talk was the result of the photography apprenticeship in Paris that the ever-industrious, energetic Max had completed to prepare for the trip. Upon their return, his photographs would likely be the subject of an exhibition, and serve as illustrations for the travelogue he was writing. Gustave disliked this aspect of his friend—the pragmatist who readily lowered his nose to the grindstone to advance himself. In this regard, Gustave was something of a snob, deeming useless knowledge (of beauty, truth, love, etc.) preferable—indeed, superior—to more practical information. If he were ever to publish a book, ideally he wanted it to be about *nothing*.

"You and Aouadallah will work on the squeezes," Max said, wiping a spot of red sauce from his chin with his napkin, "and I will join you when I can." He pushed back his chair as a crewman began to collect the dishes.

Gustave scoffed at this idea. "But you will be photographing all day, and then the sun will be down. You can't help to make squeezes in the dark. Besides, I have my own mission to accomplish. Who knows what commercial secrets I may uncover? I may find a mirage that is *real,* for example."

Max began packing his bulky and fragile photographic equipment into sheepskin cases he'd had custom-tailored for the trip. "We have a deal," he reminded Gustave. "Let's stick to it."

They did have a deal, struck in the sixth week when Gustave announced he could not bear to make one more squeeze; the process was driving him mad. He no longer felt like a man, but an automaton, a mold machine. Max was sympathetic; nonetheless, he needed Gustave's labor as well as his supervision over any Egyptian apprentices. And so, in exchange for Gustave's help, he had promised to make a formal photograph of Gustave's favorite prostitute. It was a strong enticement: in the damp cold of Normandy, Gustave would have his sun-drenched whore in crisp black and white and silky grays, every eyelash sharp as a pin. Not even Madame Flaubert would object to an artful rendering of an Oriental woman on the wall. The following week he had chosen Kuchuk Hanem, the dancing girl of Esneh, with whom he and Max had spent a satisfying day and night. But the photograph was spoiled by a mistake in the exposure. Max planned to remake it on their trip back down the Nile. What, though, if Kuchuk Hanem were not at home when they called? What if she had moved or was occupied or had fallen ill? Heraclitus was right—time was a river you couldn't step into twice. Gustave thought of nothing so much as the return visit to her quarters.

Their deal—exchanging squeezes for photographs—was a polite and simplified version of the complicated alliance between them, about which they never spoke. Max loved literature and had literary aspirations, and it was in the fire of that mutual passion that their friendship had been forged and was continually annealed. But Gustave was deeply indebted to Max on several counts, for without him there would have been no trip. And while Max graciously acted his equal, he was in fact the senior partner in the venture. As the more experienced traveler, he was willing to sort out the tangle of logistics. He was wealthier, which put the burden of keeping within a budget on Gustave. But most important, it was Max who had swayed Madame Flaubert into subscribing to the near-mythic healing powers of the Mediterranean. In service of this, Max had all but sworn to be the guardian of her delicate younger son. In this web of obligation and kindness, only one question sometimes nagged at Gustave: had Max cynically manipulated his dear mother, playing her for a fool, or did he actually care for her (and him)? Perhaps Max himself did not know. That would be like him, Gustave thought. Nevertheless, out of gratitude for Max's many beneficences, Gustave had agreed to make squeezes, and though he found it insufferable at times, he intended to keep his word.

Gustave would have napped after lunch, but Max insisted they leave immediately. Gustave donned his heavy boots and pulled up the hood of his burnoose, which framed his face with a fringe of black pompoms that bobbed with the slightest movement, adding a dimension of merriment to his guise. With the help of the crew, they collected their belongings and arranged the donkey packs. Joseph had three horses waiting on the bank. They set off at once. Neither man had shaved or barbered in weeks, and with their ragged beards and soiled clothes, they looked neither European nor Egyptian but altogether alien.

They rode small mares trained to neck-rein. Compared to the colder-blooded European horses, the Arabians appeared scraggly and weak; in fact, Gustave had discovered, they were fine mounts of excellent endurance and temperament, accustomed to the grueling sun and sand and the merciless onslaughts of the *khamsin*. Hadji Ismael and Aouadallah rode donkeys, hurtling alongside them.

The road from Aswan to Derr was crowded, being the only overland route south of the cataracts on the eastern riverbank. Aside from the monuments, Gustave had observed, little in Egypt stayed still. In the desert's dry sea, the Bedouin lived as nomads; on the great Nile, commerce from all of Africa moved to market, whether slave girls from Nubia or rice from Luxor. The Bedouin took their houses on their backs; the Nubians lived in mud huts that could be rebuilt in a day elsewhere.

The stream of traffic reminded him of the sugar ants that invaded the house at Croisset in early summer. With no laws or rules of etiquette for the road, people traveled on both sides and in the middle. Every manner of conveyance and beast moved together—camel caravans, flocks of sheep and goats, asses, horses, and the occasional richly draped palanquin with, presumably, a notable personage within. The ubiquitous cudgel flashed out from robes and saddlebags like a lightning bolt. Public beatings were an everyday occurrence. It seemed to Gustave that everyone in clean clothes routinely beat everyone in dirty clothes. Where baksheesh ended, the cudgel began. Between the two, commerce moved at a brisk clip. Arguments were short, ending with much begging and quivering before punishment was meted out and all protest resolved by a quick blow to the back or thighs. He had witnessed an official bastinado in Cairo—fifty strokes delivered unhaltingly to the soles of the feet. The poor fellow was no doubt crippled for life.

They skirted a shallow lake as calm and bright as a sheet of steel. What had appeared from the distance as clumps of snow on the surrounding trees were revealed at closer range to be rookeries of white ibis, herons, egrets, brown pelicans, and other birds he had not yet identified in his Baedeker and now never would.

"Look up, Du Camp Aga," he called to Max, pointing at the birds. "Are these edible?" Their horses were walking slowly, unable to get up any speed in the crowd.

"Your highness, O sheik Abu Dimple, it would seem so."

They'd taken to this kind of chitchat during their hiking tour in 1846, although then they had affected the bourgeois accent of Brittany, and had been, instead of sheiks, two irreverent adolescents. "I feel like shooting something now, effendi," said Gustave, "don't you?"

"Well, I am a lower sheik than you, so I would have to say I only want to if you do."

"Indeed. Let's get the guns out," Gustave said.

Hadji Ismael took the rifles from the donkey and passed them to his masters. "Gustave Bey," he muttered as he handed over the gun, "who shall be the most fortunately blessed one to pick up the birds when they fall?"

There was a shortage of gun dogs in the Orient—none, to be exact. Arabs apparently considered canines too filthy and profane to domesticate, though they didn't mind sleeping alongside their sheep, goats, and camels. "You and Aouadallah will go out for them," he said, looking at Max. "Right, Sheik Max?"

"No heroic efforts, though."

The crewmen looked puzzled as Joseph translated.

"Don't worry if you don't find them," said Max. "We will buy dinner somewhere else."

Joseph bowed slightly. "Captain is buy fish for dinner, effendi." It had taken Gustave weeks to adjust to Joseph's strange French, which had Italian and Arabic elements and a completely mongrelized grammar, made up as needed. Genoa-born, he was a self-effacing, diffident man. Though he had an encyclopedic knowledge of Egypt, he rarely volunteered information, preferring to be asked for it. He had made the voyage up and down the river sixty times.

"Then this will be the *first* course, should we have any luck," Max said.

The Frenchmen slid down off their mounts and took aim in the distant trees. Gustave fired first at a tall white bird standing on a dead snag, while Max aimed at a brownish clump on a nearby branch. As the shots rang out, every human being on the road dropped to the ground in terror. The two servants trotted off in search of the shot quarry, and the ersatz sheiks stared up at the circling flocks. "Beautiful sight," Max said. "Makes me long for quail."

Gustave was not particularly fond of birds. He preferred animals with fur, and was considering bringing back a monkey to France. *A monkey, six meters of Dacca cloth, stones from the Parthenon, maybe a mummy, the photograph of a whore, a red vest . . .* the list was starting to sound like an incantation. He tinkered with the order. *A monkey, six meters . . . a mummy, stones, a photograph, a red vest.* That was better—more musical, more memorable.

The crowd began to right itself, among its members three Europeans traveling in the opposite direction, one of whom now approached, a woman wearing a dark blue dress and pink bonnet. Gustave couldn't help noticing her neck, which was unusually long, slender, and, despite the unrelenting sunshine, pale. "I say, I think it's bad form," she announced in a firm voice, "*very* bad form."

Gustave knew only a little English. *"Je ne comprends pas l'anglais,"* he said, staring sweetly at her, his eyebrows a question. Her hair was a plain, honest brown, but so clean, despite the dusty air, that tiny rainbows danced along the strands about her face. Her eyes were gray and her gaze direct, without the habit of looking away as she spoke that, to his mind, made so many women look insincere.

She encircled the stock of his gun with one hand. *"Ça, ce n'est pas bon. C'est mal. C'est malheureux."* The woman appeared to be groping for French words to launch a jeremiad against the discharge of firearms in public places. *"Je suis malhereuse!"* she protested, jabbing at her chest with an index finger as she repeated, "I am *unhappy*!" and awaited a reply.

"Aha!" Gustave said, nodding with dawning comprehension. All women are unhappy, he wanted to reply. He understood women to be powerless and therefore demanding, and had confided to his mother that he would never marry. Besides, how could he give up his darling prostitutes? He could not imagine being loved so thoroughly in a domestic arrangement where he would have to worry about offending a proper dame. His mother concurred in his determined bachelorhood, eager to keep her delicate son with her rather than sanction a union with some *petite bourgeoise* and be reduced to the status of infrequent visitor.

"Allow me to make the introductions," the ever-unflappable Max said, stepping forward to offer her his hand. "May I present M. Gustave Flaubert? And I am Maxime Du Camp." He paused and added their official designations. *"Chargés d'une mission en Orient."*

"Florence Nightingale." The woman curtsied as she took Max's hand. "From England." She acknowledged Gustave with a nod.

He would have known her for English anywhere in the world, his friends, the Collier sisters, having been his University of English Womanhood. Miss Nightingale had, for one thing, the typical English prepossession. "Much charming," he said, continuing his struggle in the language, *"très charmante. Enchanté."*

"How do you do?" She paused, sucked in a little air, then switched back to her tentative French. "I hope you won't mind if I say you shouldn't be shooting here." She gestured toward the stream of humanity once again toiling down the road. "Stray bullets, women and children, livestock, innocents all."

"We aimed at the birds," Max replied.

"It is inconsiderate. And very dangerous. Loose bullets kill."

"We will be happy to oblige you, then, *mademoiselle,*" Max said, switching back to French. He doffed an imaginary hat and swept it before him in a broad arc. "No more shooting on this road. Where are you headed, by the way? You are the first white woman we've seen in these parts."

"I am touring the Nile," she replied in French. "Visiting the monuments. *Nous trois.*" She gestured toward a couple on the far side of the road. The woman waved back. The man saluted. There was not the nick of a doubt in Gustave's mind that this pair was English too, though they were surely too young to be her parents. An aunt and uncle perhaps?

"So are we," Gustave said. "Max is making photographs, and I am recording the inscriptions."

For the first time she looked pleased. "I, too, am sketching and reading the inscriptions."

"You can read them?" Max asked. "The hieroglyphics, I mean?"

"Oh, yes, most of the time, with the help of my good friend Herr Professor Bunsen." She paused. "That's a *book,*" she explained, smiling quickly. The two men nodded.

"And of course you read Greek," Max said.

"Yes, Father taught it to me and my sister. We were very fortunate."

"What is your itinerary?" Max asked. "Perhaps we may assist you in some way."

As she and Max talked, Gustave thought about the Collier sisters and decided that it was the eyelashes that distinguished English- from Frenchwomen. Englishwomen were not inclined to show theirs off, while the French used them as semaphores, signaling with quick blinks and flashes, like peacocks in a courtship dance. Miss Nightingale blinked only when necessary. She was like an English sparrow, short of wing, busy with purpose; not, by a mile, the flirtatious, feathery bird of paradise. All her delicacy, which was considerable, was contradicted—indeed, canceled out—by her commanding voice and pragmatic eyes.

It soon became clear that Miss Nightingale's itinerary on the river was nearly identical to theirs. She was also traveling by houseboat, in a splendid *dahabiyah,* a bigger, more deluxe version of their *cange.* She, too, planned a long stay at Abu Simbel, after which she would float downriver touring select monuments. She had spent the previous few days visiting four temples just south of Aswan at Kalabsha,

Dakkeh, Beit el-Wali, and Gerf Hussein, the last by moonlight with the entire village hooting at her heels. Today she and her companions had bought dates in Derr. She would return home via Europe by late summer. They all agreed it was confusing that the Nile insisted on flowing north to the Mediterranean, and that Upper Egypt lay to the south and lower Egypt to the north. "It always seems backwards when I look at the map," Max said. "Yes," Miss Nightingale replied with a nod, "I believe most rivers flow south." They chatted for a while about the Blue and White Nile, the mysterious sources of the river.

"Did you *adore,*" Gustave took her hand, *"comment ça se dit en anglais?"* He switched to French. "Did you like the crocodiles and the hippopotami at Kalabsha? But the people, you must have been as shocked as we were. They wore no clothes."

"Oh," she said, as if someone had pricked her with a needle. "Yes, we saw the poor creatures." Her expression turned grave.

"Don't tease our new friend," Max said, elbowing Gustave.

"We must remember," Gustave said, recalling the bouquets of naked breasts and buttocks—some of the women had worn little more than beads around their waists—"they are all innocents."

"Women and children living in such squalor," Miss Nightingale opined, her voice grim. "One wishes one could intercede on their behalf."

"Yes," Gustave agreed, noticing that her French had improved. "Sometimes one does, one must enter their lives. It seems too tragic to refrain." He could sense Max stifling a smirk. He loved to torture him this way. Max would reprimand him later for the double entendres. They'd have a good laugh.

"Baksheesh, always baksheesh." Miss Nightingale's voice rasped in imitation of the beggars. She shook her head in disapproval, though whether of the constant request for money or the deplorable condition of the beggars was not clear.

Suddenly she straightened up and her demeanor changed. "How are you sleeping then?" she asked, her voice edged with eagerness, as if she had a secret to share.

Max and Gustave shot brief glances at each other. "Well enough," Max said. "Why do you ask?"

Miss Nightingale drew a little closer. "I am sleeping with a new invention."

Obscene images tumbling through his mind, Gustave pasted a smile on his mouth and blinked, waiting. Max grew more animated, not from bawdiness, Gustave knew, but curiosity—Max could turn serious in an instant. Another trait of his that Gustave did not altogether admire. Laughter, after all, was far too rare. One could be serious all night while one slept.

"What *sort* of invention?" asked Max.

Just then, Aouadallah returned with a lifeless, nearly obliterated egret dangling by its waxy yellow feet from his fist. Gustave turned to him. *"Alors?"*

"Do you wish to cook it, effendi?"

He picked up the bird by its neck and examined the long, lacy breeding feathers sprouting from the wings and the fancy tufts at the skull and belly. "No, we will keep only these long plumes and a few wing feathers. The big ones." He splayed the wing to point them out. *A monkey, six meters of Dacca cloth, a mummy, stones from the Parthenon, the photograph of a whore, a red vest, and egret feathers.* He handed his gun to Hadji Ismael to stow on the donkey.

"It's called a *levinge,"* Miss Nightingale replied. "It keeps out insects and promotes sleep." Cheerfully, she described its construction and design. "Once I'm inside"—she hugged herself and stood on tiptoes—"I tighten the tapes and then I'm like a butterfly in a cocoon. We all have one, on the boat. We call it 'levinging.'"

Gustave tried to picture her in the contraption. "Do you cover your face?" he asked. For it was to her face and small, pale hands that he was drawn, the hands in particular, which seemed vulnerable and pure, as if they had not yet touched much of the world. She was so earnest!

"Yes, of course. To keep the mosquitoes off, but you leave room for breathing."

"You must be bandaged like a mummy," Gustave said.

"Yes!" Miss Nightingale agreed. "Exactly! I expect that's where M. Levinge took the idea. But it's very comforting to be so tightly wrapped."

"I'm certain," said Gustave, recalling Kuchuk Hanem's body warming his in the chill of her rock-walled room.

"If you give me your address," Miss Nightingale said, "I shall send you the plans so that you can make one for the rest of your trip. I am sure you shall need it in Damascus and Constantinople. The insects will be frightful. You'll be there in the summer."

"No doubt," Max said. He took out his card and wrote out their mailing address in Cairo. *"Merci beaucoup."*

"I thank you in advance for the good nights of sleep," Gustave added.

After the threesome shook hands, Miss Nightingale crossed the road and returned to the couple who had dismounted and stood patiently waiting. Pink and plump, the woman of the pair reminded Gustave of a drawing exercise in art class—the human body as three circles set on top of each other, with a round face, a larger, rounder bosom, and a bell-shaped bottom. Only a belt defined her waist. So much roundness suggested a warm and generous nature. The man was likewise corpulent. He embraced Miss Nightingale, patting her repeatedly on the back before supervising her climb onto a donkey. In the saddle, her feet nearly touched the ground. The asses in Egypt were bred to be small and desert-hardy.

Gustave waved good-bye as Miss Nightingale's donkey bounced forward, responding to a leather quirt in the hands of an African behind it. She and her party went north, returning to their houseboat. He and Max set off in the opposite direction, the dead bird flapping from the saddlebag. Joseph had said not to pluck the feathers yet. They must blanch the bird as if to eat it; otherwise, the quills would be damaged.

Half an hour later, they reached the rock temple of Derr, a rather crude structure built by Ramses the Great. Max spent the afternoon photographing while Gustave made squeezes of the hieroglyphs on the columns. The temple was not as impressive as he had expected, but it was old and important, Max said, most likely a rehearsal for the magnificence farther south, or possibly an afterthought.

The next morning, they left Derr for Abu Simbel in the wilderness of Nubia. There, Gustave calculated, he'd be five hundred kilometers and three weeks distant from Kuchuk Hanem on the last tame section of the river. South of Abu Simbel at Wadi Halfa, it devolved into an unnavigable 750-kilometer stretch of sunken rocks and rapids. The Nile was a long, skinny prick of a river.

2

CHATELAINES

There was something of the trickster in Florence Nightingale, a trait she'd reluctantly put aside as she reached womanhood, but which she had never completely outgrown or forsworn. This is why as soon as she'd determined that the two Egyptians discharging firearms on the road were, in fact, French, she had chosen to speak a halting, stilted, schoolgirlish français. She hadn't known exactly why she did this, only that she could not resist the pretense. Perhaps she had hoped to overhear a shocking tidbit? The men might have commented on her appearance or manner, for instance, feeling as free to speak about her as they would to talk treason in front of the family cat. But nothing scandalous in their conversation had ensued.

Florence bent her head to peer through the small windows that ran the length of the cabins on the dahabiyah. The sleeping chamber where she sat floated just above the waterline, and if she lay on her divan with her head alongside or out the window, she could see both river and sky. The previous night, she'd watched the moon pave the Nile with silver. Now the sky was split in two: above, tufts of cotton drifted high in a gray patch, while closer to the horizon, the sun blurred into an aura of pale yellow behind cloud cover.

She pulled her traveling desk from a nearby compartment and set it upon her knees. Perhaps she'd felt free to mislead the Frenchmen because they themselves were so clearly involved in a deception. In their burnooses and caftans, they were literally draped in a lie—obviously in hopes of gaining access where it would otherwise be denied. Abbas Pasha, the ruler of Egypt, did not hesitate to enforce the death penalty for even minor offenses against Europeans. Abandoning Western garb might bring them Egyptian secrets but it also entailed risking their safety. At any moment, they could be mistaken for natives and robbed or even bludgeoned. To her mind, this bravery, though foolhardy, bestowed on them a dashing air. A grin stole across her face. Lying had its advantages. Aside from producing results unavailable by honest means, in a strange way, it built character—at least audacity.

Florence decided to write them in her usual polished French. If they crossed paths again, which was likely given the similarity of their itineraries and the paucity of Europeans on the Upper Nile, she hoped they'd forget her pitiful French of the first encounter.

Opening the mahogany traveling desk she had used since the family jaunt to Europe twelve years earlier, when she was seventeen, she withdrew her pen, inkpot, and a sheet of fine rag.

13 Février 1850

Chers Messieurs,

Quelle chance que de vous avoir rencontrés hier! On a si peu l'occasion en Egypte de voir des Européens que c'est un réel plaisir que de bavarder un peu ensemble. Comme nous le dit Homère dans L'Iliade *"pour se sentir chez soi, on n'a besoin que d'une seule personne et d'une langue en commun . . .*

I love French, even more so when I hear it spoken. No other tongue makes such a lovely music or conveys so well the spiritedness of its people. (Our French servant, Mariette, is as patriotic as any Parisian I have met, wears a locket with a likeness of Napoleon, and mourns the Battle of Aboukir Bay, though she was not yet born when Egypt changed from French to English hands.)

I am enclosing my calling card as well as one from my companions, Charles and Selina Bracebridge. Our families write to us in care of the British consul, who then dispatches local runners for delivery. I trust that being chargés of the French government, your post will travel by diplomatic pouch. However it arrives, I hope you will let me know that this letter has reached you.

As I mentioned on the road, were it not for my levinge, my journey in Egypt would be listed among the great victories for their side in the annals of the insects. (What tiny ledgers those must be, inscribed on leaves or carved on daubs of mud to make petite earthen tablets. First commandment: Bite. Second commandment: Bite again.) English bugs are no match for the fleas, flies, mosquitoes, and other unnamed creatures that would feast on our poor hides the instant the sun sets.

I found this gadget, invented by a traveler to the East named M. Levinge, in my Murray guidebook.

It's easy to make. All you need are two bedsheets, a piece of thin muslin to serve as a mosquito net, strong sewing thread (waxed twist is best), caning in three pieces to make a hoop, cotton twill tape, and a nail to suspend it from the ceiling. (I'm going to sketch it for you on a separate page.)

After entering the levinge through the opening at c, you pull the tape tight and tuck it under the mattress. You can sit or lie in this contrivance. Be advised: tight fastening is essential, if initially uncomfortable. You will soon accustom yourselves to the confined space and enjoy it like swaddled babes.

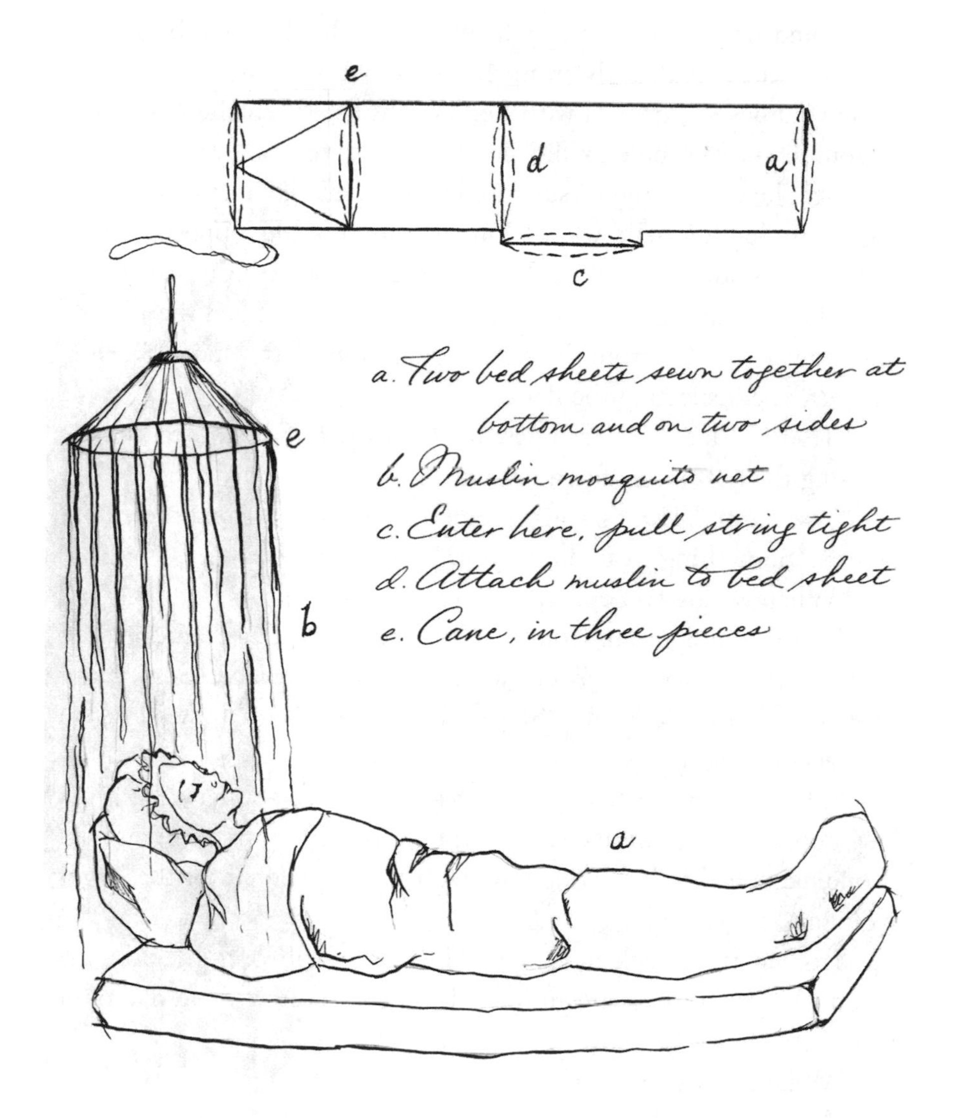
e
d
a
c
a. Two bed sheets sewn together at bottom and on two sides
b. Muslin mosquito net
c. Enter here, pull string tight
d. Attach muslin to bed sheet
e. Cane, in three pieces
e
b
a

Florence withdrew a six-inch ruler from the desk and began her facsimile, copying directly from the Murray book, one of the forty-some volumes she carried with her. As always, when she wrote, her surroundings vanished, as did her body and the sensation of time passing. She was, therefore, surprised when she looked up from drawing to see that her maid was no longer resting on the opposite divan. Trout's backside, encased in floral chintz like a cushion one might find plumped up in the corner of a horsehair sofa, filled the narrow passageway that led from the sleeping quarters to the stairs. She appeared to be inspecting the floor.

"Trout?" Florence exclaimed uncertainly. It felt odd to be addressing the bottom half of a person.

"Yes, mum?" Trout's voice seemed to emanate from the floorboards. "Something I can do for you?"

"Whatever are you doing?"

At this, the figure in front of Florence straightened and pivoted toward her, the upper portion taking its rightful place. "Something dropped off my chatelaine." She reached forward to show Florence the vacant dangling chain. "It must have rolled away."

"Oh, then let me help you find it." Florence set her desk aside and stood. But the passageway was too narrow for both of them, even if one happened to be a willow withe. Florence waited for the larger woman to move aside.

Trout stepped back and lowered herself wearily onto the portside divan. "Maybe my eyes are going bad." She sighed. "My dad had poor sight by my age."

"What exactly did you lose?"

"A key, mum. Black key."

Florence knelt in the passageway. Trout was never without her chatelaine, which, with its many implements, comprised a small hand manufactory. Florence knew well what hung from each chain: scissors, a needle case, a bodkin, a brass-capped emery in the shape of a strawberry, a crochet hook, pin safe, thimble, buttonhook, another strawberry made of beeswax, and spools of black and white thread.

Trout wore the chatelaine pinned at her waist, its parts dangling down, or else pocketed in her apron, like a watch. Florence had never noticed a key.

Her own fancier, gold version lay in a drawer at home, a gift from her mother, Fanny, with items befitting a country lady: a dog whistle embossed with spaniels, a diminutive magnifying glass, a telescoping pencil, and a vinaigrette stuffed with cotton wool soaked in French perfume. With her chatelaine, Florence could make or repair nothing, as was proper for a fashionably helpless young woman who moved in society, while Trout's was a portable wonder.

The wooden floor of the dahabiyah was smooth, Florence noted, as she ran her fingers over its grooves, worn from the tread of so many feet, she imagined. She pictured its owner, a prosperous Ottoman functionary named Hasan Bey, standing barefoot on the very spot where she knelt. He used this boat, she knew, to ferry the veiled, bejeweled wives of his hareem and their children on pleasure cruises up the Nile.

Florence felt the key with her fingers before she saw it. Lodged behind a wooden post, it was heavy, made of iron, and vaguely industrial. She was certain she'd never seen it among the shiny brass dangles on her maid's chatelaine. Why had Trout never worn it before, and what did it unlock? It was too big for a diary, certainly. A desk drawer? But Trout didn't have a desk. A lockbox?

After teasing it from its hiding place, she stood up and offered it to Trout on the palm of her hand.

"Thank you, mum. You can be grateful for your good eyes, Miss Florence."

"Perhaps I should take on the mending."

"Well, that wouldn't do, would it?" Trout reattached the key and dropped it in her pocket. "No, I can manage the buttons and seams, though a body hardly wants to wear clothes in this heat. Oh, what a climate."

"Indeed. But it will be nightfall soon, and the heat will subside, as it has every evening."

"Not *every* night, no—that first evening in Alexandria I liked to go blind from the sweat pouring into my eyes."

"Well, then," Florence said, patting the sides of her legs briskly, "I've letters to finish. Have you done with your nap?"

"Not yet, mum, my mind keeps going round and round like them waterwheels on the riverbanks. I'm not used to so little work. Don't know what to do with myself, seems."

"Oh. Then perhaps you can have a lie-down now . . . or read." *Just do be quiet,* Florence thought in some desperation.

"Yes, mum." Trout stretched out on her divan and turned toward the wall, her back to her mistress. Sitting on her divan, Florence placed her desk on her knees but did not yet take up her pen.

Trout had been miserable since they arrived in Egypt. She complained constantly of the heat, though this was the cool, dry season. She griped about insect bites, too, as well as stomachaches, headaches, and her deteriorating eyesight.

Trout would never have spoken so freely in England. And sympathetic as Florence was to suffering, she couldn't help wondering how a strongly built woman of forty-three years and Teutonic ancestry could suddenly turn so frail. Or how it was that the ailment jumped around so variously. For no sooner had a headache subsided than a muscle cramp or skin rash would crop up in its place. It was as if an ill wind had been trapped in Trout's body, battering part after part in its attempts at escape. Florence suspected hypochondriasis, which she had read about in her medical books, an illness that the Greeks believed began in the hypochondrium, the soft area below the ribs, but that modern medicine understood as a case of overactive nerves. Whatever the cause, Trout was clearly a valetudinarian, creating ailments from thin air through the weakness—or was it the power?—of her mind. The continual whining was driving Florence mad. Since Trout was not only her maid and chaperone but also her roommate, she never had a moment alone. Even as she turned back to her writing, Trout began to snore, a rattling intake and exhalation that filled the room like the fluttering of a panicked hen.

If only Mariette could have accompanied her to Egypt. She could speak French with Mariette, for one thing. And no one did her hair as well, or made her look more glamorous and à la mode. But Mariette had gotten pregnant, and since the trip would last nearly a year, had to stay home. Might she not have done this on purpose? Flo suspected that Mariette had not wished to travel in a land that her countrymen had lost so ignominiously to the English and that was hardly likely to meet her standards of good taste. Only the year before, in Italy, Mariette had found fault with some of the hotel food and furnishings. She would have hated the backwardness of Egypt.

Trout, alas, had little experience as a lady's maid. But her references painted her as steady, honest, and hardworking. Certainly there had been no mention of time spent in bed in a state of "green as the trees" nausea, or foot pains which, she claimed, made her life "a walking crucifixion." Well, nothing to be done now except bear it. A hand mirror borrowed from Charles's naturalist's kit had improved Flo's hairdressing. By holding a mirror in front while Trout held another in back, she could avoid a coiffure that flapped like turkey wattles.

Flo watched the Nile through the window. She thought of the river as a male presence, a creature of long, sinuous muscles strong enough to lift and rearrange the littoral each July when it flooded. Her Nile shone in the sunlight like a bronze shield. At night, with the dahabiyahs and feluccas moored along its shores illuminated by oil lanterns and the occasional candle, her Nile was a London street fair, its goods lit up by paraffin flares. The river had not only currents and tides but also mysterious eddies that whirled at the surface as if Poseidon himself were stirring it from below with his trident. Now, though, it was calm, steadily and smoothly rocking the dahabiyah.

Trout continued to snore in a sleep so heavy she lay unmoving as a clod of earth, while Florence finished her letter. Some time later, the door creaked open and Selina Bracebridge leaned her head into the cabin. "Flo?"

"I'm awake."

"Come up to the foredeck, dear." The door clicked shut again.

Florence gathered herself together, stepped out of the room, and mounted the narrow stairs, emerging onto the deck to see a band of orange and navy at the horizon, and above it a single star. Venus. It was childish, but she always made the same wish on the first star. *Please, God, tell me what to do.*

Selina sat in a chair made of plaited palm leaves. She was fanning herself languidly, as if from habit rather than intention. Two letters lay on the table beside her. Charles had just returned with candles, Selina said, and was belowdecks, resting. "The consul's runner delivered the post to Charles in the village. Isn't that something?"

"Perhaps he was the only European."

"Yes. Anyway, you have a letter from home." She handed an envelope to Florence.

Whatever hostilities had been brewing among Fanny, Flo, and her sister, Parthe, all was forgiven when it came to letter writing, everyone in the family being reliably voluble. Since her trip to Italy the year before, Florence had become a celebrated correspondent. The whole family cherished her letters. Parthe had taken to making copies to send on to the grandmothers, aunts, and cousins.

"I've had a note from Fanny myself," Selina said, tapping an open envelope on the table. "Your father's eyes are still bothering him. They are considering consulting a specialist in Germany, at Carlsbad."

Flo reflected that Fanny never omitted troublesome developments, feeling no particular need to spare Florence or Selina worry.

"Any outgoing letters?" Selina glanced at a basket on the foredeck, the captain's makeshift depository. It was empty.

"Nothing just yet." It took Flo days to compose a proper letter. She kept a diary of quick notes but liked to ruminate on events and ideas, especially anything to do with Egyptian religion, which intrigued her.

Florence opened the butter-colored envelope. The handwriting was Parthe's—careful, well-formed letters that never varied in size or shape, nor rode up and down the page. First: expressions of affection. They missed her. Oh, they always missed her. They missed her if she was gone for an hour, especially an unaccounted-for hour spent in what Fanny regarded as "improper" visiting, such as comforting an ailing villager near Lea Hurst, the Nightingales' summer home, or teaching the poor boys at the Ragged School in Wellow.

Parthe reported on the weather at Embley, and then on the park. The rhododendrons and azaleas were in bloom, the hillsides around the house a feast of pink, white, fuchsia, and rose, more flowers than usual, perhaps because of the heavy rains the previous autumn. Parthe was learning a new Beethoven sonata on the pianoforte, while her worsted work was progressing slowly, in shades of green that were easy on the eyes.

The mere phrase "worsted work" inflamed Florence, automatically registering in her mind as "worst work," a pun that always fell flat on the ears of a disapproving Fanny. How Flo deplored that fashionable waste of time! Was there anything more pointless than the relentless embroidery of articles that needed no further decoration? It was Fanny's way of keeping Flo's hands in a state of busy idleness and away from worthier pursuits. Surely, Parthe had included the reference to goad her.

Flo looked up for a moment. The dome of the sky had darkened; the lavender trails through it had faded to a dusty pink. More news: Fanny had recovered from her ague and was feeling fit. Father had joined a new society considering revisions to the Poor Laws. Flo set the paper down wistfully. She loved her father, a tall, gangly man with an air of innocence, despite his age. Such an idealist; such an independent thinker. How many fathers, after all, took pains to teach their daughters Greek and Latin? But his marvelous intelligence was too scattered to be of real use. How she wished he could have found a focus for his genius. Fanny said his defeat in 1834 for a seat from Derbyshire had deeply wounded his ambition.

Oh, and there was something else, Parthe announced, something "ENORMOUS." Gossip, actually, since Fanny had heard it secondhand, but still, news that would greatly interest Flo: Richard Monckton Milnes (whom they both called the "Poetic Parcel" behind his back) had announced his engagement to the Honorable Annabelle Crewe!

Oh God. She felt her lungs deflate and then fill up again. In and out, her breath, her life, a meaningless exchange of air. It surprised her that the pain was so sharp and immediate. This must be what Richard had felt on that afternoon last October when she refused his proposal.

Was Selina still talking? Florence had been nodding and offering monosyllabic assent as she skimmed the letter and Selina spoke of home, but now a heavy silence fell upon the two women. "I'm sorry—what was that you said?" Flo asked. "Was there a question?"

"I haven't said anything, dear. Are you all right? Your face has gone quite white."

"News from home."

"Nothing troubling, I hope?"

Selina Bracebridge had one of the sweetest faces in the world, Flo thought, and now she turned it toward her, the eyes softened by concern. More than once Selina had rescued her from Fanny's smothering. Selina was unselfish and devoted to anyone sheltered under her wing, but kindest of all to Flo, whose anguish she seemed innately to grasp. Being barren, Selina had had to endure the pity of relatives and strangers for decades. Flo thought this might be what had made her so compassionate.

"No, no . . . *good* news, I suppose." Flo felt like crying—blubbering like a child—but the last thing she wanted Selina to think was that she had a broken heart. She stanched the tears, swallowed them back, throat burning. "Perhaps troubling only to me." She would cry later, but where? Sharing the cabin with Trout, she never had any privacy. In fact, her whole life seemed but a miserable catalog of togetherness designed to deprive her of solitude. To be alone, Fanny believed, was the worst of social blunders, an offense to civilized society, of which one must always partake, no matter how infantile and boring the talk, how insipid and without merit the activity of that darling blood mob known as one's *family.*

"Oh, my dear." Selina reached over and stroked Florence's hand. "Is there anything I can do?"

"Perhaps in a bit. . . . My apologies—I don't mean to be rude or mysterious."

"Well then, may I ask what this news is?"

Of course she would have to say the words. She straightened up, her neck lengthening with determination. "Richard Milnes has announced his engagement to Miss Crewe."

"Oh." Selina looked worried. "I shall have to tell Charles."

"Of course. It's no secret."

"I just meant he may mention it to you, too. Will it bother you to talk about it?"

"No, it will be fine." Flo caught the worry in Selina's voice. "They are to be married in a year's time."

"But you *did* refuse him," Selina said softly, placing Flo's hand in her own.

"Indeed." And Fanny had hated her for it; not that she would ever have used so coarse a word. Flo loved her family, but she was unwilling to marry simply to please them. It was a painful stalemate, for her parents seemed to believe that by refusing to marry, Flo was refusing their love for her and hers for them. And Parthe? What had she felt? A woman who, at thirty, had not entertained a single proposal, and who would have been content to live vicariously through her younger sister's successes had her sister the grace to grant her that. Why was it that all of Florence's decisions inflicted pain on those she loved?

"Then you must not regret it now."

"I felt I had no choice."

"Yes, I remember your saying that." Selina picked up her own letter as if to reread it. Flo understood this as a loving ploy on Selina's part to allow her to sit silently if she wished. Selina never insisted on conversation. Indeed, silence was one of her greatest gifts to Flo. She understood how much strength could be gained from the simple presence of a friend. Unlike Fanny, who had always been politely overbearing, beginning with naming her daughters after *cities*. Fanny claimed she chose "Parthenope" and "Florence" to commemorate the travels of her early married life. But Flo believed that like a benevolent witch in a fairy tale, Fanny sought to cast a spell over her two infants. She didn't care that "Parthenope" was obscure and difficult to pronounce or that "Florence" was traditionally a man's name. She expected her daughters to inherit enough of her own good looks and charm to convert their burdensome names into one of many fascinations for which they'd be known in society. It seemed never to have occurred to Fanny Nightingale that her daughters might be different from herself.

Florence did not want to think about Richard, though the news swarmed in her chest like bees around an intruder. Tomorrow, perhaps, she would arrange to be alone. She could go to some minor temple and find a haven in one of the inner sanctuaries where Trout wouldn't wish to follow. Only the day before, in Kalabsha, the maid had preferred to sit beneath a tree and crochet a baby's bed jacket rather than ponder a single antiquity.

A spit of land she'd noticed earlier alongside the boat was now much enlarged by the receding tide, rising up from the river like a misplaced island, a geological mistake. Deep channels, perhaps the very ones that had carved it, ran swiftly on every side. A surge of pity replaced the ache in her chest. How sad the little island was, orphaned from the earth of which it was a part. The riverbank altered with each annual inundation. She wondered how many years or decades or centuries must pass before it reunited with the shore.

3

DANCING THE BEE

"There are even more Ramses than there are kings named Louis," Gustave observed, "though this Ramses is in a select group—he has a speaking role in the Bible."

Max did not reply. He lifted his binoculars and scanned the horizon, where vultures floated on the updrafts in slow circles.

"It's thought he's the hard-hearted pharaoh of Exodus."

Max passed him the binoculars. "It's there, in the distance, I think. You can just make out the top of the mountain."

It had taken a week to sail the sixty kilometers south from Derr, but now the sandstone cliff of Abu Simbel lay in the distance, a hazy golden-white prominence that pushed against the sky.

They rounded two more bends and came upon an impressive sight: a pair of temples separated by a steep ramp of sand. As the crew moored the boat at a ramshackle wooden pier, the larger temple disappeared into the perspective and the smaller one into the distance behind them. The magnificent view could only be appreciated from the far shore of the river, midway between the two. Max pointed out that he'd have to scale the opposite mountain to get both monuments in the same frame.

Followed by Joseph and two crewmen, Gustave and Max jumped

ashore and slogged up the enormous ramp, which resembled nothing so much as an artificial ski jump. As they approached the huge monument, the vista became more difficult to assimilate. Everything was so outsized.

The great rock temple at Abu Simbel, built by Ramses II, was in the middle of a mountain set back from the river. Unlike the pyramids at Giza, assembled brick by massive brick, it had been hewn from the native stone in a magnificent feat of subtraction. Inside it, Gustave had read, soared a hypostyle that dwarfed any European concert hall. There, the ancient Egyptians celebrated their rituals.

Having seen an exhibition of drawings by Napoleon's savants, he expected to be stunned by four colossi of Ramses seated on thrones—two on either side of the temple entrance. The pharaohs would be in full regalia, brandishing the imperial flail and crook, wearing the beard of divinity and the crowns of Upper and Lower Egypt.

What greeted him instead was an accumulation of silt that had nearly buried the statues. Sand reached to the nose of the highest one. Farther down the slope, the figures were more exposed, until entirely visible. But the first was a toy buried in a giant's sandbox. Gustave began to howl with laughter. The servants cowered behind him.

"Mon Dieu, mon Dieu," Max bellowed, raising his arms to the heavens. "Do these people care nothing for their own magnificent history? Can you imagine Notre Dame in such disrepair? Even the humblest village church?"

Still chuckling, Gustave said, "Perhaps we've come at the wrong season of the year."

"No, effendi," Hadji Ismael offered, "it has been this way since I am a boy." Joseph nodded in agreement.

"My God," Max repeated. Sighing, he regarded his boots for a time, then straightened up and planted his hands on his waist. "We shall have to dig them out."

Gustave did not believe his ears. "What?"

"At least to their necks. They look so . . . unregal. The first photograph of Abu Simbel cannot present them to the world in this condition."

The world? At moments like this, Max taxed Gustave's patience. For an orphan with a fortune at his disposal and no relatives to please, he was grindingly diligent. What Gustave wouldn't give for such freedom! Madame Flaubert doled out his portion of his father's estate in spoonfuls. "That, my dear friend, will take forever," he complained. "Do we even have the implements? The manpower?"

But Max was already instructing Hadji Ismael to unpack the shovels from the *cange*. "We'll excavate the first head completely—at least *that*. I don't care if it takes a week." He ordered Joseph to engage laborers in the nearest village and buy the necessary provisions; also to inform the captain that they would be staying put for several days.

Prone to acrophobia, Gustave peered gingerly down. He couldn't see the river directly beneath the temple, but in the distance, two boats glided, hugging the opposite shore. The *cange* was hidden by the declivity.

He sat on a flat outcrop. He could not engage in such work. Though he hadn't had a nervous episode in seven months, heavy exertion could trigger one. Surely Max grasped this possibility; it was he, after all, who had persuaded Madame Flaubert, with the help of Gustave's brother, Achille, that the balmy climate of the Orient would be salutary. But excavating? No doctor would sanction that. "I'd better start on the squeezes then," he told Max. "I shall work in the smaller temple with Aouadallah." The farther away from Max just now, the better.

He and Aouadallah set off on foot down the steep sand ramp, carrying their equipment with them. They passed a party of tourists camped below the temple façade. English, he guessed, from their clothing and the clipped intonations of speech ricocheting off the rocks in the dry air. The gentlemen poked with walking sticks or stood soberly gesturing under parasols, while a quartet of women sat on folding chairs at easels, busily reducing antiquity to squares of paper. He pulled up his pom-pommed hood to discourage conversation.

The small temple appeared to be a variation on the large one, with four shorter, flatter likenesses of Ramses standing rather than seated at the entrance. He imagined the Virgin and Child raised up in multiples at the nave of a cathedral: unthinkable. It would cheapen the effect, the very sanctity of the figures. Yet four Ramses, or eight, or sixteen, perfectly suited the pharaoh's majesty.

Aouadallah brought the water jug, brushes, and paper. Gustave had decided to try a new technique, shredding a ream of paper into bite-size pieces in a trough while Aouadallah trickled water over the tatters. For glue, he added the flour he'd nicked the night before from the galley. Together they kneaded the mixture until it was as smooth as the papier-mâché from which he and Caroline had fashioned the heads of marionettes for their childhood plays.

They began inside, at the base of an interior wall. There, clad in breastplates, pleated kilts, and intricate wigs, the ancient Egyptians waged war, issued proclamations, hunted lions and stags, and worshipped their animal gods. Royalty and slaves, animals and furnishings alike were depicted in profile, never frontally. Those at a distance were portrayed as doll-size figures floating in the ether. The art historians of the Academy had already sunk their teeth into the ancient Egyptians, pronouncing them ignorant of perspective. Arrogant cads! Shitheads! Pressing the paper mash into the crevices, he was certain of it: the inscriptions resulted not from a limited but a deliberate aesthetic. The Egyptians preferred profiles not because they were easier but because they considered them more beautiful.

He and Aouadallah worked until late in the afternoon, then packed their equipment and sat down to enjoy the sunset. As the shadows lengthened, a breeze blew down from the heights. He watched the orb of the sun hover in the western sky above the temple, a molten disk turning from yellow to copper and finally a luminous red etched by the silhouetted palms and ragged brush of the hillside. Then, like a giant eye blinking shut, it sank below the world. In the pearly dusk, they returned to the *cange*.

• • •

The Frenchmen decided to camp onshore the first night, Gustave in the open air and Max in a tent. After a supper of flat bread, tomatoes, garlic, and a salty white cheese, Gustave smoked two pipes as he sat on his blanket and stared at the sky, while Max recorded the day's events and updated the concordance of photos in his tent. Max had high hopes for his pictorial travelogue. With photography all the rage, he said, even people who didn't like to read would buy his book. And what, Gustave wondered, might his dear friend be writing about *him*? Nothing, probably; he doubted that Max would wish to share credit or glory with anyone. Since Max was not one to read his work aloud to friends, the book would remain a mystery until it was published.

Max gave the impression that he had already lived his life and had returned merely to perfect a few flawed performances. Nothing caught him off guard or disturbed his calm authority. Not that he was without passion. His lechery was more expansive than Gustave's. He had had sex with women, men, adolescents, and animals. A week before at Derr, while Gustave limited himself to flirting with the whores lounging about in flimsy blue and white gowns, Max partook. He always partook. He simply fucked more. It wasn't a question of stamina. Gustave was more discriminating.

Nevertheless, Max was an excellent—no, the *best*—brothel companion. A tall, slender fellow, all angles and little flesh, the whores had dubbed him *Abu Muknaf*, "the Father of Thinness." He moved like a wolf—stealthily and quickly, with no wasted motion. A wolfishly cunning rationality ruled his writing, too. His philosophy was not Art for Art's sake, but art with a lowercase *a*, for audience. Everything he wrote was undertaken with particular readers in mind. And like any good pragmatist, he was supremely *organized*, the instrument of his control being the list. He made reading lists, shopping lists, packing lists; lists of literary critics, of dramatists, of whores. Upon Max's advice, they had brought seventy trunks to the Orient and most likely would return home with a dozen more brimming with trophies and treasures purchased from a list. It was hard to argue with this strategy. Gustave himself sometimes made lists, though rarely wrote them down. *Dates from Derr, a monkey, a mummy . . .*

They had packed up nearly all their possessions, as well as a great number of items bought for the trip. As government chargés, Max had explained, they required the finest suits and cravats, linen and silk shirts, waistcoats, the best fur felt hats and cloaks as well as four pairs of boots, two saddles, journal books, botanicals, and medicinals, all kinds of tapes, gauzes, and bandages, essence of orange to make flavored water, fifty kilos of confectioners' sugar for same, rifles and ammunition, lye and lemon soap, drawing and painting supplies, surgical tools, sheets, coverlets, two featherbeds, grooming and smoking paraphernalia, traveling desks and drafting boards, books, enough whiskey to last two years, laudanum and opium balls in case of injury or illness, whistles, dictionaries, daggers, ceremonial swords, tricolor bunting, woolen underwear, and, of course, the photographic equipment. Max knew precisely where in the seventy trunks each item lay, though at the moment, sixty-five trunks were sweating in storage at the consul's warehouse in Alexandria. Max was a stranger to self-doubt. He was as sure of himself as a bird is of flight.

But was he always right? Was he right, for instance, about *The Temptation of Saint Anthony*? Could both Max and Bouilhet be wrong? Gustave winced at the memory of that sickening night. He had read it to them over the course of four days. Afterward, they had rested and dined, then sauntered down the terrace with lanterns to the tenebrous banks of the Seine, its liquid fringe unraveling at their feet. "Consign it to the flames!" Max had shouted skyward, as if the stars would quake at the news. Bouilhet had been gentler. He had taken Gustave's arm, his voice motherly. "If you do publish, only the most devoted readers will cut past the first pages. Better to wait and revise." Though both men had sworn, like a jury, not to confer, he thought that they had, for they both offered the same objection. *Nothing happens.* Neither mentioned the strengths of the book: historical verisimilitude; the palpable depiction of the saint's torments—he had *cried out in pain* while writing; the precise, lyrical language; its driving rhythms. Had they at least appreciated the hellish amount of research the book entailed? No! That he'd read more than two hundred volumes and taken copious notes did not impress them. And if that were not enough to vouch for the novel's authenticity, like his protagonist, he'd become a recluse. It was he, not Saint Anthony, who had written, "I have come to the desert in order to avoid the troubles of existence." He had lived so exclusively indoors that his neighbors had nicknamed him "the bear of Croisset."

He hadn't intended to be a hermit. Biology and destiny had set in motion a dire sequence of events that changed the climate of his life, reducing the seasons to a perpetual winter. He had to hibernate to survive the tragedies that befell him. The writing, he thought, had saved his sanity.

The run of bad luck began at Christmas of 1846, with what Dr. Flaubert dubbed "the fall from Grace"—Gustave's first nervous attack. He was twenty-five, home from law school on vacation at the reins of a wagon beside his brother. All he remembered before passing out was a blaze of lights and a sudden draining of strength and sensation from his body, as if he had been painlessly incinerated. Achille had barely managed to retrieve the reins in time to avoid a spill.

The family had feared for his life. The word "epilepsy" being more a curse than a diagnosis, the doctors concluded that he suffered from an unknown neurological malady. Over the next few months, despite rest, bloodletting, and the insertion of a seton in the fatty folds of his neck to drain bad vapors from his body, he suffered more seizures. Dr. Flaubert decided Gustave should not risk the stresses of law school for at least a year.

Secretly, he was elated. He could write, which was all he wished to do in the first place and the only thing he'd ever done well. Although "the fall from Grace" was a joke, Gustave knew that his father was disappointed. He had ambitions for his sons: Achille had already risen to eminence in medicine and worked alongside him at the county hospital; he expected Gustave to excel in another profession, preferably the law. *Flaubert père* had no use for scribblers and had paid scant attention to the plays Gustave wrote and performed as a boy. Nor had he shown interest later in the novel he completed at nineteen.

The following December, his father discovered a red lump on his own thigh. Achille recruited an expert and together they operated, but the site became infected, and in March, the great surgeon died.

Gustave's life was beginning to read like the Book of Job.

Two months after his father's death, tragedy befell Caroline, his only sister, his little tomboy. It had been difficult to watch her fall in love and marry a feckless old schoolmate of his. Madame Flaubert, ever the worrier, had insisted that the whole family accompany the newlyweds on their honeymoon to Italy, as if a hovering crowd could prevent her catching a sore throat or chest cold. If only Mother's concern had extended to advice about birth control! For despite the appalling lack of privacy (ten of them traveling together by post chaise through the Midi and on to Genoa by boat), Caroline managed to become pregnant. Two weeks after Flaubert père passed to his Maker, she gave birth to baby Caroline. Within a week, mother Caroline was ailing and, two agonizing months later, died of childbed fever. Her husband fell to pieces; Madame Flaubert took the baby home to be raised by the Flauberts, reduced now to two in residence and Achille, four miles away at the hospital in Rouen.

His dear mother teetered on the verge of collapse. There were tears at every meal and wailing from her rooms when the lamps were extinguished at bedtime. Gustave feared she'd die of grief, even with the infant to love. He offered succor; she accepted. The irony of it! The son who had been a disaster in the making without prospects, who had failed his law school examinations twice, became indispensable. He was flattered to be so desperately needed and proud to save his sweet mother.

Law school was never again mentioned. To keep his sanity while he played the part of loyal son, doting uncle, and aspiring writer, he adopted an eccentric regimen that he stuck to for the next two years. He arose at noon and conducted himself like a family man; but at night, when everyone was sleeping, he labored over his pages, shouting out words as he composed them, crying or laughing as the text dictated.

He was all the more aggrieved by the fourth and final loss, one that felt like a betrayal but was in fact another wedding. His closest friend—his hero—Alfred Le Poittivin, font of all he knew about cynicism, sex, and art, the man who had taken him to his first brothel and suggested Saint Anthony as the subject for the novel, had caved in to family pressures. He took a wife and cut off his former friends. Gustave never saw him again until he lay on his deathbed, the victim of tuberculosis, a scant two years later. Alfred's absence had left a gaping hole in Gustave's life only partially filled by Max and Bouilhet. Gustave often thought that if Alfred had lived, he would have known for sure if the novel were worthy, for Alfred had been peerless in matters of substance and taste. Gustave didn't have the same confidence in Max and Bouilhet.

The odor of Turkish tobacco, stronger than its European counterpart, wafted toward him. Max had emerged from his tent to smoke. "You should write a travel book on Greece to launch your literary career," he said. "You've read the ancient Greeks, you could insert literary landmarks. Or we could collaborate again." Tubes of smoke issued from both nostrils.

Max's timing could not be worse, given Gustave's growing doubts about his literary insight. They *had* written an essay together following their walking tour of Brittany. Precisely four copies existed. He had never thought of it as anything but an exercise in friendship and literary description. To call it a book was preposterous.

"I want to launch my career with a bang," he replied, "with a novel, possibly a play." For the last year and a half, he and Bouilhet had been studying dramatic structure by reading the greatest playwright of all, Shakespeare. How he missed their Sundays together, smoking, eating, sharing manuscripts. "Travel writing is a lesser genre," he added. Would Max take offense? Surely he sensed his sincerity. "I speak for myself, of course, but I must follow my own lights."

Max smiled knowingly. "A lesser genre, perhaps, but a travel book is less risky. If it succeeds, fine. If it doesn't, the critics ignore it." He took a last drag on his cigarette. "And it wouldn't take much work to add to the journal you're already keeping. Just promise you'll consider it." He squashed the cigarette under his boot.

"I shall, Abu Dabu. Not to change the subject, *mon ami,* but I have solved the mystery of why these monuments are so neglected: the ancient Egyptians are as foreign to these Arabs as they are to you and me."

Max nodded. "True. But any fool can see the monuments are extraordinary. Why treat them like rubble when the whole world reveres them? Think of the tourists and money they would attract if they were restored."

Joseph appeared and stood next to Gustave's blanket, glancing diffidently at the ground as he waited for a break in the conversation.

"It's a marvel anything gets accomplished with the confusion of so many nations living cheek by jowl."

"Speaking of confusion . . ." Max nipped into his tent and returned, holding an Ottoman calendar, its squares full of dizzying languages and symbols. Gustave had given up trying to decipher it. All he knew was that the Ottoman day began at sunset, making it nearly impossible to get times straight when meeting with officials of the empire outside major cities. "We will wake at sunrise," Max announced. He consulted the calendar again. "Which is at six thirty-eight." He went back inside.

"What is it, Joseph?" Gustave asked.

"A favor, effendi? A small favor?"

"Certainly. What can I do for you?

They'd hired Joseph based on a letter commending him as a reasonably reliable and honest man—high praise, the writer said, in a profession rife with scoundrels and swindlers. To date he had been a fine dragoman, never truculent, though often reserved. As he approached, Gustave inhaled the stink of aged sweat, sour ass, dirty hair, and other less identifiable bodily odors. He realized he had never seen Joseph bathe or change clothes. In the morning, he passed a rag across his brow, sloshed water in his mouth, and spit. His complete toilette apparently.

"My new esposa is write," he said, shyly pulling a packet of letters from his foul jacket. "She is young and *bellissima,* has not twenty years. She is been with French nuns."

"It's wonderful to receive a letter, isn't it?"

"Ah, when she is write me." Joseph raised his eyes to the sky.

The man reeked so bad that Gustave had to breathe through his mouth. Did he bathe at home with his young and beautiful wife? Surely the nuns had taught her good hygiene.

"Effendi," Joseph began again, "you read them to me? She is write in français."

"Oh, yes, of course. I didn't realize."

He opened the first letter and skimmed it. A demand for money. ("Send it immediately, I tell you.") No salutation or valediction. Complete lack of courtesy and affection. The handwriting was faint, done in pencil. "She says she loves you very much."

"And the other?" He handed it to him.

"Have you shown these to anyone else?"

"No, effendi. These sailors no read. And no privacy."

"Here she is saying she misses you." He touched the page with his finger. "And, again, she loves you."

"You read fast, effendi. There is more?"

Telling the truth, he said, "She wants to buy a new frock."

"I know this." Joseph looked down at his hands.

The other six letters contained more shrill demands for money. She had run up bills with tradesmen. The dressmaker was insisting that she return a garment. The grocer was going to refuse her credit. (He threatens to cut off my balls, she'd written, parroting Joseph's crudeness, or crude herself?) "She sounds lovely," he said. He couldn't wait to tell Max.

"She read," Joseph said, smiling. "I love for that." He frowned. "I no read, effendi. If I read, I no do this work, I join French Legion."

• • •

Stretched on his blanket, Gustave marked time until everyone had bedded down. He enjoyed such perfect privacy in his study at Croisset that he could no longer so much as daydream if he thought someone were observing him.

Beyond the outline of his toes, the campfire crackled and glowed, while overhead, the stars inched through their celestial arcs. He located the Big Dipper, then connected the studs of Orion's belt, which reminded him of Kuchuk Hanem's extravagant jewelry. He liked the rhythm of her name—the little click like a snap of the fingers in the middle of it. KU-chuk HA-nem. Golden creature, instrument of pleasure.

Like other Arabs, she called him *Abu Chanab*—Father Mustache. Why, she asked, did he cover such a fine mouth? Twice she offered to shave it off, taking his face between her warm, oily hands to appraise it. Peering back at her, he had glimpsed her most alluring feature: a small rotten incisor amid an otherwise dazzling smile.

The day they met, she had declared her importance by sending an emissary named Bambeh to the *cange* when they docked in Esneh. Did they wish to see dancing girls? Though she also was an *alma,* Bambeh looked not like a trollop, but a pretty sprig of a girl. She had brought her mistress's pet lamb with her. Hennaed with polka dots and muzzled in black velvet, the animal followed her like a dog. The sight of the two of them had brought tears to his eyes. They *did* wish to see dancing girls, Max told her, but they had plans for the morning. She'd waited two hours while he and Max visited a shop above a school to buy ink and scouted two more monuments. When they returned at noon, they found her perched demurely at Rais Ibrahim's elbow, the crew at her feet, a trail of sheep pellets on the deck.

Attracting stares and cries for baksheesh from Arabs squatting outside mud huts, they followed Bambeh to a courtyard as different from the town that surrounded it as a dream is from waking life. Instead of the dust and mud of Esneh, the courtyard was tinted with confectioners' hues—the pink of desert roses and the brilliant scarlet of two flowering pomegranate trees. Walls painted pale aqua set off the vibrant green of plants in colorful glazed pots.

The first moment he saw Kuchuk Hanem something inside him had melted and not solidified since. The sensation was identical to looking at certain paintings. The plasm of his being streamed invisibly toward the canvas, completing it, as though the painting had been waiting for him since the artist finished it.

Clad in pink silk trousers, she was perfuming her hands. She had just completed her bath, Joseph explained. He caught the odor of rosewater and something like turpentine as she bent to replace a water jug, her bronze arms rippling in the sunlight. Through the filmy purple gauze wrapping her torso, he saw the clear outline of her breasts and felt himself stir.

A statuesque, coffee-colored Syrian, she embodied his fantasy of the East. Her eyes were dark, painted with antimony, her eyebrows black, her nostrils wide and flaring. Her costume was straight from the seraglio. On her head sat a tarboosh ornamented with a gold disk and fake emerald; a blue tassel fanned out over her shoulders like a cockade; and a spray of artificial white flowers was fastened to her hair from ear to ear. And what hair!—as elaborate as the wigs of the ancient Egyptians. Thick, black, and wavy, it was parted in the center into two long, bushy pigtails that were braided together at the nape.

She stepped toward him, accompanied by the faint tinkling of her gold jewelry. Bangles collided on her wrists, while her necklace, a triple rope of beads, whispered like brushed cymbals. Above this sea of sound, her hoop earrings swayed silently. A golden aura enveloped her, as if she had been dipped in that metal or fashioned directly from it, embellished with a goldsmith's granules, globes, and darts to complement the iridescent undulations of her skin.

She greeted them in French. He took her hand and kissed it, noting a fine line of blue writing tattooed on her arm, which he later learned was a verse from the Koran, though not what it said. After perfuming his and Max's hands with attar of roses, she asked if they would like some entertainment. Before he could answer, Max took her arm, and the two vanished down a staircase.

Minutes later, Max shouted, and Gustave followed his voice to the lower level, where Kuchuk lay on a kilim-covered divan. After Max left the room, Gustave entered her for a rapid *coup* more like a greeting than lovemaking.

The niceties followed the sex. She brought out her best glasses and a bottle of rakı. *Lion's Milk,* she called it in Arabic, for its potency and the swirl of white when water was added. He had already experienced its highs and its hangovers, first in Alexandria and again in Cairo.

She and her girls did not resemble the whores or grisettes in Paris, nor the seedy wenches in Kenneh and Cairo. Hers was a prelapsarian paradise, a lecherous Eden devoid of morals and contrition. *Toothsome without being tawdry,* he thought. *Tremulously louche.* She had raised ribaldry and lubricity to high art. Unlike most whores, she was not naughty or coy, but frankly available. Pleasure was the only commandment she obeyed and dancing was sexier than sex itself. A few years earlier, public dancing, like brothels, had been outlawed, forcing the courtesans south from Cairo to lesser cities. The only concession to this were the blindfolds the musicians wore as they sawed on sour violins, beat drums, and rattled tambourines.

Her dance movements were relatively crude: she squeezed her bare breasts together with her jacket and jerked her pelvis back and forth. When the music slowed, she rose up on one foot, then the other, pressing the lifted leg across her shin.

"Sheik Abu Dabu!" Gustave shouted above the music. "I have seen this dance before, on old Greek vases."

Max shook his head. "The male dancers at Cairo were better." They had seen the famous Hasan el-Belbeissi, who was faster, more agile and acrobatic, walking on his hands, tumbling through the air at breakneck speed.

"But not as beautiful," replied Gustave.

Joseph smiled. "We say this on Nile." He pointed to Bambeh, who had replaced Kuchuk Hanem as the soloist. "The beautiful women, they have the ugly feet."

Gustave beheld her misshapen toes and calloused knuckles. His mind raced back to Louise's milk-white, perfectly shaped feet and hands. His hot marble Venus. *Satin slipper, bloody hanky.* At home, one of his prized possessions was the pink satin shoe he had pocketed the second time he bedded her, along with a handkerchief soaked with her menstrual blood. The break with her was still fresh and painful.

Kuchuk's ribaldry surpassed his own. She snatched his tarboosh and put it on. To discourage lice, he and Max had shaved their heads except for occipital knots of hair by which, according to Mahometan belief, they would be whisked to heaven when they died. She polished his pate with her jacket, then shooed everyone upstairs, indicating she wished to copulate with him again.

"Come, my dear," said Gustave, "let me give you a ride." To everyone's amazement, he bent over and she jumped on his back. Then he hobbled off to a small cubicle and took his second turn with her, a brief but intense orgasm.

When they returned to the upstairs courtyard, Kuchuk mounted his back again. "And *I* have seen this before," Max joked, "in a medieval tapestry. So often the Christian tarts ride their customers home when a unicorn is not available."

"We are going to get a cup of coffee," Gustave called back.

With the others following, he stumbled along the alleyway to the café next door, a wooden shack with a roof of sugarcane stalks thrown down helter-skelter. Demitasses of Turkish coffee soon arrived on a copper tray. A few moments later, the muezzin sang out the call to afternoon prayer over the rooftops of the city: *"Allahu Akbar."* Kuchuk glanced through the open window, suddenly aware of the time.

"Beautiful melody," said Max, besotted with rakı. *"Allah il Allah,"* he tweedled, mimicking the muezzin until the whores howled with laughter. It was then that Kuchuk took Gustave's face between her palms and pantomimed shaving off his mustache. *"Abu Chanab,"* she whispered, Father Mustache, planting a kiss on his cheek.

"She say not to cover your pretty mouth," Joseph translated.

He and Max decided they would visit her brothel again that night.

The musicians from the afternoon were already assembled in the courtyard when they returned in full regalia, wearing swords and bearing a bottle of rakı. Oil lamps shedding pools of creamy yellow light burned on tin sconces. The women sat singing together on the divan. A new and older alma with a savage expression and deep-set eyes took him downstairs and made quick work of him. His timing was so derailed by her voluptuous writhing that he stained the divan. When he set to work on her with his mouth, she seemed surprised, but tolerated it silently. Perhaps her magic button had been excised. He loved giving pleasure to a woman as much as he loved receiving it. Because he'd twice fallen in love with women eleven years older than he—Elisa Schlesinger, his first crush, when he was fourteen, and then, of course, Louise—he preferred older prostitutes and was beloved by them in turn. In Egypt, the old whores said they found him more enchanting than Max because of his impressive height and large, cowlike eyes. But he knew they were lying: they were grateful to him for the business.

He downed a glass of rakı, took Kuchuk aside, and, grasping her necklace with his teeth, had sex with her. Her cunt, he wrote later, felt "like rolls of velvet as she made me come." Afterward, showing off her muscularity and grace, she offered him licorice straws from her second mouth.

But Kuchuk Hanem's most remarkable talent was for the Bee, the dance forbidden in all of Egypt. She began by vibrating her torso as quickly as its namesake, shedding her clothing until she was naked. Her body was sinuous, fluid, assuming forms that seemed impossible. Backbends, simple flips, and rapid turns led to undulations that traveled through her flesh like water through a sluice, from her neck to her breasts, belly, and hips, down through her legs until only her feet were shivering to the music. She wore castanets on her fingers and bells on her ankles, accompanying herself vocally with trills and shouts. The chirring, clapping, and tinkling built to a crescendo until she seemed half animal, half angel, moving according to some essential rhythm borrowed from nature in harmony with the whorls of turban shells, the branching lacework of leaves, the khamsin's whirlwind. She was magnetic, paralyzing, her face altering from grave to frantically wanton and grave again.

For an encore, she performed a duet with a cup of coffee placed on the floor. Castanets clacking, she made love to the cup with a series of lascivious movements and ended by clenching it with her teeth and gulping it down. In that one stroke, he felt she had taken him whole into her mouth—or could.

In the past, Gustave had loved all his prostitutes, but never a particular one. His feeling was more for the institution itself, "prostitution" being an old and venerable word, like "university," "Sorbonne," and "Mother Church." But by the time the dancing was over, he was convinced that he was in love with Kuchuk Hanem, and begged to spend the night with her. Though she worried that his presence would attract thieves, in the end she relented. They slept together in a small downstairs room, guarded by her pimps and by Joseph, who had paired up with an Abyssinian whore, forgetting for an evening his young wife. After another *coup,* Kuchuk drifted off, her little hand resting in his, her mound of Venus heating him like a hot water bottle. Delectable snoring issued from her elegant nose and slackened mouth. With her scruffy Papillion dog asleep nearby on his red jacket, they made as happy a family of three as might have lived anywhere on the earth. He gave himself over to reveries of domestic normalcy and oriental perversity.

At 3:00 A.M. he awakened for a final *coup,* rather like the affectionate screwing of an old married couple before breakfast. At dawn she fetched charcoal for the brazier, then returned to bed, warming herself in the heat of his body. The bedclothes that all night had passed for Venetian silk revealed in the daylight the most telling touch: bedbugs, which he amused himself by squashing on the wall. Their nauseating smell combined with Kuchuk's attar of roses created an odor as memorable as her rotten tooth. In his work, he decided, as in life, there must always be a touch of bitterness in the sweet, a hint of calumny in the romance, a jeer in the midst of triumph!

Early the next morning, as agreed, Kuchuk Hanem appeared with her lamb in tow at the *cange* to pose for a portrait. No longer was she clad in diaphanous silks and cottons, much to his disappointment. She wore instead a bizarre combination of European and Ottoman clothes that denoted a prim matronliness—a black cloak, a fichu and cheap cameo at her throat, an embroidered vest and hat in the Armenian style, and European boots. Max took three exposures, all with the spotted lamb: one of her seated under a white umbrella, one standing, and one leaning over the side of the *cange,* so that the waters of the Nile might flow forever above the mantel at Croisset.

In accord with her attire, they had parted decorously. No fervid kisses or tender hugs, no desperate clutching of her ass. He promised to return in a month or two. She stepped gracefully off the boat followed by her sheep like a figure in a nursery rhyme. When she reached the street above the docks, she looked back and wagged her small perfumed hand.

He had detected true longing in that wave, with a soupçon of love and dolor, too. Ever since, he had allowed himself the fantasy that she had found him unusually appealing, and was counting the days until his return—that she was thinking and dreaming of him, reviewing every detail of their lovemaking.

When the photographic papers were developed, Kuchuk had disappeared, leaving only a gray smudge where she and the Nile had briefly intersected in the frame.

4

LA VIE DE FLORENCE ROSSIGNOL

On a clear Monday in February 1850, what Flo saw from her houseboat was nothing less, she thought, than divinely inspired, powered into existence by the love of God.

She'd awakened to the unmistakable jolt of the boat setting sail at dawn. As she watched through the window, the river turned pewter, then silver, like a hand mirror tilting up to catch the ever more brilliant light. After breakfasting with the others, she'd remained on deck, anticipating Abu Simbel.

They had been on the Nile for six weeks and more than nine hundred miles. Going south, the river had been a wide expanse, lined on either side with the fertile croplands that had filled the empire's belly for millennia. Then, at Aswan, the green borders had narrowed and the river with it, fracturing into rapids that boiled over the crags. After the cataracts came the three D's—Dendur, Dakkeh, and Derr, where Charles bought two barrels of dates. Flo had planned to spend the afternoon at a temple, but Derr was the capital of Nubia, and the clamor and poverty of its inhabitants were so dispiriting, she had spent only an hour in town.

Now, as the boat sped upriver, its great crossed sails unfurled in the breeze, sandstone cliffs encroached on both sides, rising up in sheer ocher walls to form a canyon through which the low, twisting river appeared to be fleeing for its life. The river was more tortuous here than in the north, with hairpin turns so sharp that each vista coming into view was an astonishment. Which is how it was that, rounding yet another bend, Flo was staggered by the breathtaking sight on the western bank: cut from the cliff, the faces of enormous stone pharaohs glowed in the morning light. They were the biggest likenesses she had ever seen. If the height of the cliff were three hundred feet, these colossi, she estimated, were easily seventy feet high. Her gaze shifted to the second temple, also carved from the rock and equally imposing, if smaller—the monument to Ramses's queen, Nefertari. Elation buzzed through her body.

Everyone, including the dragoman, Paolo, gathered eagerly as the boat moored alongside a patch of palms. Selina carried her hemp tote, packed with drawing supplies, on her shoulder. She squeezed Flo's hand and stepped onto the gangplank. Flo and Trout followed. Behind them, four brawny Nubians would, if necessary, haul the travelers over the slope of windblown sand that rose, it seemed, a thousand feet up the mountain.

The climb was slow and arduous. *Never look down,* her father had told her when she was a child and they hiked the hills of Kent, near Embley. She focused on the colossi when they were visible, their blank eyes staring impassively into the sun, urging her on. The heat was building, and she was glad she'd worn only her brown Hollands. Unbleached linen was perfect for the climate of Egypt.

Trout struggled alongside, aided by a crewman who pushed her from time to time, his hands hovering just behind the broadest part of her back. Flo hoped to finish the ascent unassisted, but she wouldn't be shy about asking for help. Once she reached the great temple, she could rest. She planned to sit alone in the inner rooms and ponder the Egyptian religion. Unlike most Christians, she hadn't dismissed the Egyptian gods and goddesses as false deities, viewing them, rather, as alternate conceptions of holiness. Surely, the theology of a people who had ruled for four thousand years was worth contemplating.

Trout grunted, and the crewman clamped onto her elbow to steady her. She was dressed for a visit to London, not the Nubian Desert, her cotton twill bodice and skirts already damp with sweat. In front of Flo, following in Paolo's footsteps, Charles and Selina made steady progress. Selina stopped to speak, pointing at something, but the wind tossed aside her words.

At seventeen, Flo had climbed the stairs at Notre Dame—more than four hundred steps, her travel guide had crowed—to the parapeted rooftop and Paris below, dainty as a Persian miniature. Though not as high, this was considerably more difficult. At last she moved from the acutely angled ramp to a patch of level ground. It felt good to stand up straight after so much bending and trudging.

One Ramses was broken, the disjointed head and torso lying on the ground. Higher up, the first colossus was covered to his nostrils in sand. Arabs with shovels appeared to be digging out his visage. But despite neglect and damage, the temple seemed pristine, as if whatever had blasted the figure apart had happened centuries before, and it had been untouched ever since. Certainly no European had disturbed it, since Europe hadn't known of Abu Simbel until the French conquered Egypt. Sailing up the Nile in 1817, Giovanni Belzoni must have gasped as she had when he rounded the bend in the river.

From a closer stance, it was even more incredible that the colossi had once formed part of the undifferentiated mountain they flanked. In a niche above the entrance—at perhaps three times life size—sat another splendid pharaoh wearing the traditional kilt and bearing the orb of the sun on his head. Ramses, she guessed, this one in the guise of his namesake, the sun god Ra.

Leaning against the shin of the headless Ramses (it must have been twenty feet from his sandal to his knee!), she felt small and yet more significant—like a jewel—the opposite of the diminution imposed by Chartres and Westminster Abbey. They had humbled her.

Karnak, two weeks earlier, had been terrifying, the immense columns pressing in, threatening to crush her. She had felt overshadowed in every way. But Abu Simbel filled her with an awe that lifted her up and enlarged her. Paradoxically, the very enormity of the figures was comforting instead of intimidating. *Sublime,* she whispered aloud to no one in particular, gazing up at the serenely composed faces looming above her. Two tourists were creeping down from a niche in the rock alongside the shoulder of the southernmost colossus, and she determined to perch there before exploring the interior.

"Paolo," she said, pointing up to a stone platform, "do you think someone could help me climb up there?"

The guide muttered to one of the crew and shouted back to her. "Brava, Signorella Nightingale. Why not?"

The crewman preceded her, a coil of rope for her to grasp wound around his shoulder. He helped her from foothold to ledge to handhold, and within moments, she was sitting alongside Ramses. Later, she thought, she'd maneuver down to the great ruler's lap, to seek firsthand succor at his glorious breast.

She contemplated the two identical faces receding to her left in perfect alignment. The duplication was soothing. Here is Ramses, and here again, and again. By repeating that serene visage, the ancient sculptors had managed to convey the experience of time itself—of its passage—in a way that spoke not to death and decay but eternity.

Ramses's eyes were far too big, she noticed. Nothing was in strict proportion. Yet these anatomical distortions made the figures more expressive of pure spirit than any other relics she'd seen. It was difficult to imagine that men had built these grand and godly objects. Not beautiful, certainly not realistic in the way of art as she'd always understood it, this was a whole world for which she had no language, only what stirred in her heart.

Above the four Osiridae—statues of Ramses in the guise of Osiris—a relief of yet another Ramses held a statuette in his hand. Was this an offering to or a gift from his divinity? And what did it symbolize? From its central location, she adjudged it important. Another detail to look up in Herr Bunsen's book.

Selina and Charles were picnicking near the next Ramses, sharing a cup of local beer, when Flo climbed down and signaled her intention to enter the temple. Selina waved back, smiling, and lifted her cup in a toast. Flo was so grateful to the Bracebridges. They were more than loving family friends—angels, really. A year ago she had accompanied them to Italy and learned what easygoing companions they were. The first day in Rome she'd returned to the hotel expecting a reprimand for having spent the whole day lying on her back in the Sistine Chapel, but they hadn't even missed her. No, their focus, too, was on books and art and politics—and on one another's ailments—all of which left them delightfully permissive and absentminded.

Because sand had blocked all but about three feet of the temple's doorway, she had to crawl into the magnificence on all fours—properly humbling, she thought. Her guide followed at a discreet distance. As soon as she was snug inside, she'd send him back.

Still on all fours, she found herself atop an interior sand ramp, this one the height of a double flight of stairs and illuminated by sunlight slanting through the impacted entrance. She scooted down on her bottom to the stone floor of a cavern suffused with twilight. Egypt was not only captivating, it was also glorious fun.

Eight Osiridae stood against as many pillars, their arms crossed upon their chests, the crook and flail in either hand to signify dominion over living and departed souls.

The trapped air, dim light, and thick mountain walls created a strange stillness and warmth, as if she had descended into the bowels of the earth. Near her foot, a scarab beetle careered over a tiny hillock of sand. The guide lighted her oil lamp and she continued into a second hall, and then a smaller chamber aglow with trickles of light from an invisible source high in the ceiling. Four more statues of Osiris supported the roof. Lowering herself against one of them, she shooed the guide away. When he hesitated, she shouted "Go back!"

and was startled to hear the chamber echo her words in a diminishing chorus. He retreated to the opposite wall and knelt, head down, to give her the privacy she demanded. Clearly he had instructions not to leave her alone under any circumstances.

She opened her bag, removed her diary, and came across a recent entry: *I had been feeling melancholy when we reached Aswan, but the sheer excitement brought me round. Riding up the rapids was one of the most delightful moments of my life—a moment that lasted four and a half hours!* They'd navigated the cataracts with difficulty, she, Charles, and Trout on board for the thrilling ordeal while Selina continued overland by donkey. *Six times the dahabiyah jutted out of the water like a vessel about to sink and was hauled by the main force of more than a hundred men up the granite rocks. . . . With unerring aim ropes were thrown from the poop to men on the rocks standing in the attitude of the Apollo Belvedere, their keen eyes glistening with eagerness. . . . I expected them to be dashed to pieces at every moment.*

Describing a thing was nearly as exhilarating as the thing itself. She smiled to herself, then uncapped her pen and smoothed a blank page.

> *Now, at Abu Simbel, I feel nothing but comfort, as if in the presence of God. I am as moved by the Egyptian ideas of the afterlife as by our Christian ones. Further, it seems to me that the Egyptian beliefs are not so different in mechanism than the story of Christ's resurrection. Bunsen points out that in the original mythology, only the sun-god Ra journeyed to the afterlife. Each night, when he died in the west, he traveled through the underworld on an infernal river divided into twelve rooms, one for each hour of the night. Emerging each morning at sunrise, he assured the continuation of the world. For the next hundred generations, only the pharaohs joined Ra, sailing to the Field of Reeds. But after a thousand generations (about 200* B.C.*), everyone in the kingdom of Egypt could journey to the golden dawn of eternal life. The*

similarities with Christian belief are striking: the passage through the twelve rooms of the night was, like the crucifixion, the earthly death. Jesus, like the pharaoh, was divine and the first man to attain heaven. If we accept Him, then like the Egyptians who worshipped Ra and Osiris, we receive the gift of eternal life.

She closed her eyes and sat dragging her fingers through the sand. Writing her thoughts had always been calming, a way to weather her deepest storms and sort out her feelings. In fact, after Selina Bracebridge and Mary Clarke, she thought of her diary as her best friend. She called it *Lavie,* which was short for *La Vie de Florence Rossignol,* begun as a French assignment when she was seven. *Lavie* was also the record of her struggles—with Parthe, with Fanny, and with herself.

J'aime Mme. Gale, ma bonne d'enfants, was the first sentence she'd written in it. *I love my nurse, Mrs. Gale.* And then—she recalled this as clearly as if the words had left her pen twenty minutes rather than twenty years ago—"In English her name means a storm, but Mrs. Gale is *"une femme très calme, très placide."* Writing in French made her feel adult and sophisticated, and she attacked it with relish. *Je suis née le 12 mai, en l'année 1820. My mother, whom I love, is called Fanny, and my Father (also very loved) is William Edward Nightingale. Everybody calls him WEN.* She handed the copybook in weekly to the governess, who returned it with corrections in red ink: accents and apostrophes, spelling errors, failure to match case, gender, or number. There were never any comments on the facts or Flo's effusive declarations of affection.

When she wrote about her first serious illness, *Lavie* seemed to come to life, to take on the characteristics of an intimate. Flo had had the whooping cough and had to be isolated, Parthe banished downstairs to prevent contagion. Flo had enjoyed having the bed to herself, being alone. *"J'aime être seule,"* she'd written in her careful French, *"complêtement seule."* On her first trip to London, where she had gone for a wedding, she described the soldiers' band playing at the Court of St. James's Palace and wandering with Fanny through the shining aisles of the best shops. Her dearest relative, WEN's little sister, Aunt Mai, was to be married to Sam, Fanny's baby brother. Flo watched Aunt Mai join hands with Uncle Sam, swear her undying love, and kiss him, too long and too hard, with everyone looking on. *I blushed,* Flo had confided in print. She nearly cried when the young couple drove off in their coach. That, she informed *Lavie,* was marriage. People went away. She was never going to do it, never leave the people she loved.

The people she loved . . . She closed her eyes. Who did not, it turned out, love her as she wished them to. Instead, they had plans for her based not on her talents and desires but on what *they* wanted and what was proper.

The familiar feeling of loneliness, of incipient hopelessness, gripped her—a queasiness in the chest she knew too well. *Lavie* held that story, too—of the first time she had known despair.

It began with unexpected criticism from Fanny soon after she began the diary. Florence was bright, her mother conceded, there was no disputing that; she conquered her academics with ease, and charmed people with engaging conversation. But she was unkind to Parthe. Flo could scarcely believe Fanny thought such a thing! Was it Flo's fault if Parthe were duller, shyer, and less able-bodied? If she was more inclined to doodle on her sketch pad than declaim memorized passages in Father's library? Invariably, docile Parthe cried in frustration while Flo remained dry-eyed. She knew that the gifts and talents with which she'd been blessed (and Parthe, alas, had not) could not be shared by force of will, presuming Flo even had the will to do so. Which she did not.

Not believing that she was a troublemaker, Flo latched on to the flattery instead of the censure in Fanny's critique. She had social graces! She was a brilliant conversationalist with a sunny disposition. Buoyed by this praise, a few days later she had written a letter to her Aunt Anne without clearing it first with Fanny. Her mother flew into a tantrum. "I hope you have got safe to your journey's end," Florence had written. "And I do hope you saw the eclipse of the moon on the day you went. Papa says that you were blind boobies if you did not watch it for a whole hour, as we did."

The next week Fanny began to inquire about an addition to the household staff.

Flo's right foot was numb, she realized. She changed position.

It had taken years for her to grasp what Fanny had intended in hiring Miss Christie, that she had another motive beyond educating her girls: to rein Florence in, to instill in her humility and doubt where there had been too many high spirits, too much confidence, a native arrogance that made her impertinent. But at the time, Flo had been excited at the prospect of a governess. She had imagined long romps through the woods and parklands, and hours spent pasting album pages with pressed flowers and leaves, bird feathers and butterflies. She would ride her pony more than ever under Miss Christie's supervision. Miss Christie would teach her chess, so that eventually she could play with WEN.

Before Miss Christie arrived, Fanny warned the girls not to speak unless spoken to, under any conditions. "That is intended for *you,* Florence," she had added. "I want no outbursts. If you think of something to say, I want you to turn your tongue in your mouth seven times before you speak." Flo had felt her face redden to be singled out for reprimand.

When the girls were called to the sitting room where Miss Christie and Fanny had taken tea, Flo was immediately hopeful. For one thing, Miss Christie looked too young to be a grown-up. Though she had overheard Fanny tell WEN that Miss Christie was almost twenty-one, she could have passed for fourteen. Flo liked her looks, too. She was tall in comparison to Fanny, neatly got up in a navy gabardine bodice and skirt, with blue canvas gloves and a straw hat with a single feather. She nodded at Flo and Parthe, who curtsied as Fanny introduced them. "Good day," Miss Christie said, smiling.

"Good day to you," the girls chimed in unison.

Miss Christie listed the subjects she could teach. She'd begin, she said, with the absolute fundamentals, which, Flo was surprised to learn, had nothing to do with numbers or spelling and everything to do with being quiet, paying strict attention, and doing exactly what Miss Christie bid. She handed her references to Fanny in two sealed envelopes.

Scanning them, Fanny seemed pleased. "Of course the girls will call you Miss Christie, but I hope you don't mind if I shall call you Sarah."

"I'd be honored," said Miss Christie, her cheeks turning pink.

"Thank you for coming. I am quite satisfied that you will fit the bill. You may begin as soon as you can move in. Shall we say on Thursday?" Fanny turned to her daughters. "Girls, do you want to ask Miss Christie anything?"

Parthe shook her head, suddenly shy, while Flo popped off the couch and placed herself directly in front of the new governess. "What's your favorite game?"

Miss Christie paused and glanced at Fanny. Her smile broadened. "Well, I don't *have* a favorite, really. You shall have to teach me yours."

"I would love to!" Flo cried with relish. "There's Grandma's Basket, Giant Steps, Posey in the Pocket—"

"All right, then. There will be time for that," Miss Christie said, reining in her smile somewhat.

Parthe could only squeal more joy, while Flo jumped up and down, as high and as fast as she could, coming perilously close to the cranberry lusters on the side table.

"But first things first," Miss Christie added. "Penmanship—"

"Oh, we already *know* penmanship!" Flo said, though in truth her characters were still round and wobbly.

"Addition and sub—"

"But we've *had* that, *both* of us. Test us, why don't you?"

"Eleven take away four, Flo!" Parthe yelled, peering wildly around the room, "plus twenty take away *eleven*."

"Discipline," Fanny said before Flo could begin to calculate. "First comes discipline."

"We've *had* that already," Flo said, still jumping.

"Have you?" Miss Christie asked.

"I think maybe it's time for another hand," said Fanny. "Yours, Miss Christie." And with that, Fanny accompanied her to the door.

"Hooray!" both girls shouted as they rushed upstairs. "We get Miss Christie, Miss Sarah Christie." For the duration of the afternoon, they ran from room to room trilling the governess's name.

After Miss Christie moved in, Florence wove baskets for her out of long grass, bracelets and rings out of dandelions and the wild violets blooming profusely that spring. Florence wanted Miss Christie to know that she was loved. But alas! Miss Christie didn't *want* love. She wanted obedience.

Days under her tutelage were rigidly scheduled and exceedingly busy. After the maid brushed and coiffed the girls' hair and dressed them in the morning, there was calisthenics, with special attention to legs and arms. Flo had to wear her steel-lined boots all the time. There were prayers morning and evening and, of course, lessons, with an emphasis on rote learning—copying out sentences instructive of both grammar and morality dozens of times to compensate for an error or simply to emblazon them in the mind. The entire regimen left Flo disheartened and frustrated, and despite the consequences, she rebelled. When she left a note saying *I don't like writing these copperplate sentences. It's stupid and I don't wish to do it,* a corrective aphorism was assigned her: *Obedience comes first, understanding later.*

There was much discussion of her sudden outbursts of energy and enthusiasm. She was sparky, Miss Christie said, excessively so. Flo's innate vitality constantly threatened to spill over into a spontaneous shout or jump, a shove in Parthe's direction, or high jinks with the animals, such as encouraging the pony to gallop instead of walk. Inside her, something was always bubbling up—a new idea, another question. Also, she was too curious. Morally speaking, Fanny and Miss Christie agreed, this amounted to an inability to mind her own business. Life, Miss Christie believed, ought to proceed as solemnly as a funeral.

Fanny began to travel more, leaving the girls to Miss Christie's rule for a month or more at a time. Parthe seemed content enough, but Flo missed her mother desperately. Fanny's absences felt like punishments. Had she chosen to stay away until Flo was able to sit still, to fall asleep on time, to listen without interrupting when others spoke? It was no good. Even when Flo succeeded in showing her family a covered cage, a wild animal was still racing around inside it.

After several months, a dizzying monologue began to occupy her mind, a nagging voice that chastised her for every unscripted thought. *Stop it,* she found herself thinking. *Do not think about skipping rope or French fables or drawing the dog.* To lure Fanny home, she sent notes reassuring her mother of her improvement. *I am beginning to yield more, and I am more obliging now than formerly.* When Fanny continued to stay away, Flo slipped into a dark uncertainty. Unable to locate and reform the flaws that so upset everyone, she began to question her very nature. She would have turned herself inside out like a pocket to prove her new purity and bring Fanny home. But she did not know how. And then one July evening at dinner, the voice in her head became something else entirely.

The family had gathered over a fancy meal with meat aspics and pheasant pie to celebrate WEN and Fanny's return to Embley from a long visit to Tapton, in the north. The conversation fluttered around Flo's head like a flock of gulls. It was small talk and she wanted nothing to do with it. She wanted only to be hugged and kissed and petted by her parents. Perhaps then she could be disciplined and serene rather than impulsive and annoying.

She looked at her place setting. To the right and left and above her dishes lay an arsenal of silver—four forks, three spoons, and three knives, not counting the butter knife. Fanny was proud of her table settings, especially when she threw a hunt ball. There was an implement for each foul or fish, every soup, pudding, and torte.

It occurred to Flo that she did not know the respective functions of the different cutlery. All she knew was that her mother no longer loved or wanted her. She had given her away to the implacable Miss

Christie, who was completely resistant to Flo's charms, so much so that Flo had become convinced that she *had* no charms, that there was nothing about her that might please another. Did *anyone* love her? Well, Mrs. Gale, certainly, the old nurse, but she loved everyone equally, whatever their flaws, and at the moment, such a generalized affection was of little comfort.

A chill like pure ice seized her. She dared not pick up a single implement, lest it be the *wrong* one. Her hands remained in her lap, clenched together in a sweaty knot. She wanted to be good—to be perfect—but she understood that she was neither, and far from becoming either. She was a monster, a freak, abnormal as the two-headed chicken that the gamekeeper had brought up to the house last spring, thinking it would amuse the children. It had horrified her.

She felt glued to the dining chair, unable to move. For a while no one noticed that she was not eating, that she was frozen in place. Finally Miss Christie spoke up. "Are you not hungry, my dear Florence?" she asked.

A scorching in her chest, a sudden widening of the eyes: not yet nine years old, Flo felt rage for the first time in her life. She knew that she was not "dear" to Miss Christie, that it was just a polite form of address, but at that moment, it was intolerable.

"I am not," she replied, "dear Miss Christie," the last words tinged with sarcasm. "I am . . . ill."

Flo could almost feel the sensation even now of that utter desolation. But Fanny, she was happy to remember, had not disappointed. She had scraped back her chair, rushed to Flo, and placed her palm on her forehead. "I believe you have a fever, darling. Shall we go up to bed?"

"Oh, yes, Mother. Please." Bed meant that she would be warm and alone and, for at least a few moments, the center of her mother's doting concern.

In the girls' bedroom, Fanny tenderly helped her into her nightgown and sleeping cap before tucking her in, kissing her forehead and both cheeks until Flo's eyes filled with tears of gratitude. WEN appeared at her bedside a few moments later, leaning over her and stroking her hair, his brow furrowed. "Coming down with a chill, are you, my little poppet?" he asked, lingering by the bed with Fanny until Mrs. Gale arrived with rosehip tea and a piece of toast with jam. Flo ate greedily, hoping she would not be chastised for rushing through her food. She wasn't, and her parents' faces hung in the dark room like two lockets on black velvet until she fell asleep.

Soon she couldn't bear to be seen by other children, certain that they'd perceive her monstrosity. She who had been pert and chatty and full of spicy confidence became painfully shy, barely speaking. It was not enough to excel at history, to have perfect French verbs. If anything, it was a liability, turning one into a self-absorbed braggart who flaunted her accomplishments. *Self-promoting,* Fanny called it. To please her mother, Flo decided to become the ideal unselfish daughter, allowing no thoughts in her head that did not put the comfort and benefit of others before her own. She tried especially hard to be solicitous of Parthe, not to outshine her in any way. *Pray let us love one another more than we have done,* she wrote in a note that Parthe still had. *Mama wishes it particularly, it is the will of God, and it will comfort us in our trials through life.*

And then there was that awful daily list Miss Christie and Fanny devised to improve her character. A pale spot still marked where it had been tacked to her bedroom wall:

I PROMISE:

To run before breakfast to the gate and back, or if cold and dark take a long walk before and ½ hour after dinner
To do 20 arms before I dress, and, if ill done, ten more
To draw ½ an hour regularly
Not to lie in bed
To go to bed in proper time
To read the Bible and pray regularly before breakfast & at night

To go to the bathroom regularly after breakfast
To go to Church on Sundays
To read, write and do the Bible
To read any book you put out for me
To read this paper every day

With such a busy schedule, she was able to keep the monster at bay, at least while in the company of others. When she was alone, though, the monster transformed itself into a habit that had plagued her ever since: *dreaming*. It bothered no one else, being invisible to everyone but Flo, for whom it proved an enduring anguish, all the worse for being secret. Her long self-centered reveries were not mere daydreams but epic poems: glory unfolded in her mind's eye, in stanza after stanza, where she featured as a person adored by multitudes for heroic deeds or stunning accomplishments. Florence Nightingale, discoverer of the cure for consumption with attendant audiences with the queen, ceremonies in Parliament, and a stamp in her honor. Or: Florence Nightingale, founder of a school for girls, of a reformatory, author of Blue Books and articles in the *Times*. Diva, doctor, translator of the classics, philosopher, reformer. It was, she knew, an evil pursuit, but no self-imposed edict, no remorse or penance had been sufficient to stop the filthy habit for more than a week or two. Dreaming became the bane of her existence, and nothing short of torture. She could barely keep it under control even now, at age twenty-nine.

A noise startled her from her reverie, a muffled sound that seemed to come from a great distance. A voice calling to her? The guide stirred, lifting his oil lamp and walking to the entry. He cocked his head, then signaled her to follow. She packed up her pen and book.

Climbing out of the entrance, Flo saw a man with a tripod, taking pictures. She hesitated before standing, worried she might ruin his photograph, but he paid her no mind. Charles called out to her and she waved back. It was time to return to the houseboat. She scurried past the photographer without glimpsing his face.

People were scattered about the deck of the dahabiyah, taking the evening air, all except Trout who was already asleep in the stuffy cabin below. Flo shifted in her chair. The dark blue pennant announcing the name of their vessel as the *Parthenope* that Flo had sewn from a petticoat and her only roll of white seam tape waved languidly on the flagpole.

Charles was snoring in the low chair and footstool he favored for naps. Selina, too, had drifted off, Florence saw, the downy globe of one cheek pressed into her shoulder while her hand lay inert over her open book, the fingers grazing the words that had sent her sliding over the edge of attention into a delicious postprandial slumber.

One of the crew stood smoking a water pipe at the bow of the boat. He caught Flo's eye, nodded, and then turned back, white ruffles of smoke about his neck like a jabot.

The wind stirred, lifting the unbound hair at her nape. It was the dry season in Egypt, travel of course being impossible in the summer, when the river flooded, that great upheaval of nourishing mud to which had been attributed ancient Egypt's accomplishments—the pyramids, the gilt sarcophagi, the obelisks and tombs. The air on winter evenings tended to be clear and bracing, though occasionally the desert churned up a wind that prickled with minute particles of sand, and then it was like seeing through scratchy golden gauze. That same dust, suspended in the air, could hue the sunsets in deep reds and purples. Tonight, happily, the air was clear, the sky a mesh of stars under a fingernail moon, perfect subject for a nightscape painting.

She suddenly recalled the photographer outside the temple. Of course, it must have been M. Du Camp! He had said that he planned to record Abu Simbel in detail. That meant his companion, M. Flaubert, was somewhere about, pressing wet paper onto dry stone. He was the quieter of the two, but the more interesting, she suspected.

5

LETTERS

The *cange* lay at anchor immediately to the north of the small rock temple. The sun was just setting, though Gustave did not know the exact hour. He'd abandoned exactitudes. The clockwork universe he'd studied at the royal college had stopped ticking in Egypt, where the complete engagement of the senses jumbled whatever order he might once have grasped. These days he was more plant than man, a thing responding bodily to the life-giving exhalations of the Nile. Rather than clothe himself with Western logic, he preferred to venture forth naked. If it rained, he sucked it up like an elixir into his marrow. When the sun poured down warmth and light, he turned toward it, troposcopic as a sunflower, or away from it, like a parched tortoise. He was all reactive tissue, something his father might once have prodded in a laboratory dish. He allowed no energy for serious thought or long-term planning. Planning—the emblem of the bourgeois herd of which he only occasionally acknowledged himself a dissident member—was anathema. What future awaited him back in France? What kind of books would he write? Would he attempt to publish? He refused to contemplate any of it.

Inside the sleeping cabin, the lamp he held shed a golden annulus within a fainter penumbra of ocher. The textures and hues of the room continued vibrant in the dim light. The red and blue geometrics of the divan covers fashioned from kilim rugs, the Persian carpet on the floor, the froth of mosquito netting pendant from the ceiling—all invited the hand of a painter or a writer. For the sake of this bellyful of colors, he was willing to endure the ubiquitous fleas and biting flies, the pestilential invasions of rats along the tow ropes from the docks.

"Bring the light closer," Max said, hiking up his robe.

Just then, Joseph called down from the upper deck. "A runner is come with post, effendis."

"We will attend to it shortly," Max replied, intent on centering his groin in the brightest part of the light.

Gustave peered at seven blisters on the head and shaft of his friend's noble part. Max retracted his foreskin, the better to expose them.

"The fellow looks angry," Gustave said. "A gift from one of the dancing girls?"

"No doubt. I'll see a proper doctor when we return to Cairo. None in these parts, I'm sure."

Max was right. What passed for medicine in Upper Egypt was superstition verging on perversity. In Kom Ombo, he'd seen barren women exposing their bellies to the urine stream of idiots. Even in Cairo, consumptives routinely kissed the genitals of dervishes in hopes of a cure. "Do they hurt, *mon ami*?"

"I feel them. What about you? Have you checked yourself?"

"Yes. I'm all right."

"I wonder if this little gathering of blisters could be the result of riding in the desert, the sand rubbing me raw."

Gustave shook his head. "I would not think so." He lowered the lamp onto the table. "Sand wouldn't cause discrete sores, would it?"

"The doctor's son speaks and I listen, effendi." Max pulled up his underwear and sat on the divan. The normally lighthearted expression on his face flagged. "My first case of the pox."

"I hope not." Gustave moved the lamp to the top of a small bookcase and sat down opposite Max. "No, I think with the pox you have only one sore." Years before, when he had lost his virginity to a housemaid in Rouen, he thought he had syphilis. Too ashamed to tell his father, he'd conferred instead with the pharmacist, who had dispensed a salve that cleared up his rash in short order. Pox was so common that one could not worry about it and live a normal life. Nevertheless, sometimes he *did* worry about it. He did not wish to lose his mind, following his teeth and hair. In Cairo he had made a side trip without Max to an asylum attached to the mosque of Sultan Kalaoon, thinking to disport himself with lunatics. There, he had come upon a room of syphilitics in every stage of the disease. A dozen stood bent over at the waist, their pelisses hitched up around their bellies the better to show the doctor their bloody, chancred assholes. He'd vowed a lifetime of abstinence on the spot, knowing he wouldn't stick to it.

"I have dipped my pen into too many inkpots," Max said, pouring himself half a tumbler of wine.

They'd finished the good French brandy allotted for the Nile cruise. A dozen more bottles were stored with the rest of their belongings at the villa of Suleiman Pasha in Alexandria. The crew of the *cange,* all Mahometans, didn't admit to consuming alcohol, but had no trouble securing contraband rice wine for the Franks.

Max began to putter with his photographs.

"I'm going up for some air," Gustave told him. "And to get the post."

On a charcoal burner at the bow, Joseph was preparing a hearty dinner of roasted lamb, rice, olives, and fava beans. Given the circumstances, the dragoman's cooking was delectable. And to ensure satiety, they stocked dates, almonds, onions, and bread on board, a combination primed for dyspepsia. Gustave had a strong and ever-enlarging stomach. Before leaving Alexandria, he had to have his best trousers altered to attend a banquet at Suleiman Pasha's. His girth had continued to increase on a diet of Ottoman and Egyptian cuisine. He was particularly fond of meat and cheese pies, called *būrek* in Turkish and *sanbusa* in Arabic, and of baklava, a dessert that appeared on tinned trays in all its declensions with charming names such as "bird's nest," and "maiden's thigh."

Captain Ibrahim was lounging upwind of the brazier, his feet dangling over the bow. Seeing Gustave, he pointed toward his sleeping niche, a recess in the deck where he and the crew slept, as if packed in long boxes. There, tied up in a piece of cloth, Gustave found the post.

A letter from dear Bouilhet, another from *Maman,* and a third he didn't recognize. The consul had probably tossed in the month-old issue of *La Presse.* He'd save it for after dinner, while he smoked.

With his back to the river, he sat in a chair on the port side to read. His mother missed him and sent kisses. Baby Caroline was flourishing, stringing her words into sentences and torturing the cats, which vanished like startled snakes when she toddled into a room. His mother urged him to continue his letters, no matter how brief or haphazard. She closed with bear hugs.

Bouilhet's letter smacked of his usual sass. Gustave read it quickly, chuckling, knowing he'd savor it again in a day or two. Bouilhet had been a scholarship boy at Gustave's preparatory school, but they weren't close until university. The first time he laid eyes on Bouilhet there he had thought he was looking into a mirror or a pane of glass struck by the light to reflect his gaze. Since they were both students, even their clothing was similar. A year after their reunion, Bouilhet had left school for lack of funds, but the friendship had continued. He supported himself by tutoring students in Latin and Greek, leaving him time to work on his epic poem, *Melaenis,* several new stanzas of which he'd copied on a separate sheet.

The third envelope was cream-colored and thick. The paper, slick to the touch, was the kind he liked to use because it allowed his quill to skim along as fast as he could think, and absorbed the ink nicely. High cotton content, no doubt. He was attuned to the few sensual pleasures of his desk: papers, pens, nibs, inks—even pen wipes—provided a particular visual tang, a texture, an odor. He sniffed the envelope. No perfume. The imprint on the sealing wax was illegible.

Carefully, he drew his penknife along the top and withdrew three crisp sheets, evenly folded. The hand was a woman's, orderly and pretty. Not like Louise's, who wrote in a great looping rush. At the height of their affair, she wrote him three times a day, each letter a more volcanic outpouring than the last. He'd kept his departure a secret so he didn't have to bid her farewell. He wanted only silence from her. As to why he was buying her gifts, he hadn't a clue.

This missive was from Miss Nightingale. He examined the envelope again: there was no sign that it had passed through the post office at Alexandria, which would explain how it had reached him so quickly. No doubt, the natives knew where each European party was camped on any given day. The letter had been sped to him via grapevine.

A drawing on the third page caught his eye. He thought it was a sketch of a mummy, but on closer inspection, he noticed that the writer had drawn eyes and a smile on the exposed face of a figure otherwise completely enshrouded. He stroked the smiling face with his forefinger and studied the diagram. Its precision and lighthearted detail indicated a warmth and jocularity he hadn't detected in Miss Nightingale on the road.

He admired the letter's fluency and vivacity. As he read, appetizing whiffs of roast lamb and beans, the clean scent of steamed rice, wafted over him. Whenever he reread the letter years later, he was haunted by a vague memory of hunger—of heightened awareness and the anticipation of pleasure. But now he tempered his enthusiasm. He was wary of Englishwomen, as he seemed especially susceptible to their charms. He had discovered this with Gertrude and Harriet Collier.

He had met the sisters on the beach at Trouville when he was nineteen. They might have remained casual summer acquaintances but for a freakish fire in their cottage. He had spotted the flames and carried Harriet, the invalid sister, to safety in his arms. Afterward, when she suffered from nightmares, Dr. Flaubert insisted on caring for her at home. At Rouen, Gustave and Caroline countered her demons with card games and puppet plays. The trio became fast friends.

When he moved to Paris for law school, he called on the sisters at their house on the Champs-Élysées. At first his visits were chatty family affairs, with Captain and Mrs. Collier in attendance. Because the entire family held writers in the highest regard, he felt especially welcome. They shared his enthusiasm for Hugo, Byron, and Wordsworth, for Chateaubriand and Shakespeare. Both sisters were bluestockings, versed in the classics and contemporary literature. He confided to them that he had written a book called *Novembre,* and read some of it aloud. Chez Collier he felt safe and appreciated.

Both girls were appealing. Gertrude was lively and rambunctious, her cheeks rosy with good health, while Harriet radiated the languishing beauty of the semi-invalid, that incandescent pallor that haunted the pages of his beloved Romantics. Both were devout and decorous, attending church every Sunday and abiding strictly by the rules of chaperonage. The three of them never left the house. This made for a less direct sort of coquetry than he was accustomed to. Flirtations took the form of verbal fencing, particularly for Harriet, whose wit was sufficiently nimble to trade innuendos and double entendres.

Slowly, like a net drifting to the bottom of the sea, his interest settled on her. Her large blue eyes and slightly disheveled clothes were uniquely alluring. She had a spinal disorder and usually lay stretched out in fetching poses on the sofa or chaise longue. Chronic debility lent her an ethereal air. And while he could pinpoint no obvious changes, over the months her demeanor increasingly hinted that she desired him. Was he imagining it, or did her poses and gestures sometimes verge on the overtly suggestive?

He began to daydream obsessively about her—lurid, priapic scenarios in which he rescued and then made passionate love to her. She intruded on his sex life with prostitutes. While a whore was fellating him, he'd picture Harriet on her back, clothed in petticoats and a camisole, her eyes half closed, her legs beginning to fall open. Sometimes, when he visited her, he had to camouflage his arousal by remaining seated with a book in his lap.

These fantasies had no future—which made them more ardent—

because even Harriet, with her reduced prospects for a husband, was afflicted with that peculiar English virtue a *strong sense of duty*. Gertrude sometimes called it "constancy of purpose," speaking in English as though the idea could not be translated because it didn't exist in French. Perhaps it didn't. Nor did he comprehend this duty. He knew it wasn't confined to sex, but wreaked the greatest havoc there. Englishwomen knew nothing about their bodies. Alfred, his closest confidant in things venereal, had once bedded an English maid who did not know what or where the clitoris was. Was it possible in the year 1843 that an educated woman like Harriet Collier was ignorant of her magic button? Alfred claimed his English maid had never masturbated and that after he taught her how, she declared him superfluous.

One day, shortly before he failed his second-year law exams, he found himself alone with Harriet. Gertrude had gone to fetch a book from the library. He was sitting next to her on the sofa, reading aloud, when she took his hand and entwined her fingers with his. A preternatural light in her eyes seemed to draw him into their blueness, pulling him into the vortex of her gaze. She lifted his hand to her pale lips and lightly kissed each fingertip.

Just then, Mrs. Collier paused in the doorway with a smile on her face that chilled him to the bone. When he turned back to Harriet, the expression on *her* face alarmed him even more, for she appeared to be begging for his love, for a respectable future with him in a house like the one in which he suddenly felt like a captive. His stomach flopped over. He must have blanched. He withdrew his hand. When Gertrude returned with her book, he made his excuses and fled, never to return.

Outside in the street, he wanted to scream out of guilt and shame. What courage she must have marshaled to take his hand! And those exquisite, gauzy fingertip kisses! If Mrs. Collier hadn't inadvertently rescued him with that vulgar smile when she thought she'd glimpsed a potential son-in-law, he might have promised Harriet anything. How weak and softhearted he was, how easily seduced! His contempt for marriage, his years of indiscriminate sex had been insufficient defense. *He was still a romantic!* As a corrective, he remained celibate for the next four months.

He didn't know what had happened to Harriet. Gertrude had married and become a patron of the arts. Probably no suitor had claimed Harriet because of her weak constitution and the presumption she couldn't carry an infant to term. What an elegant spinster she would make, clad in dark dresses befitting one no longer prowling for a mate, but set off to one side, like a beautiful vase reduced to holding umbrellas. From time to time he allowed himself to remember her: faintly damp with fever, wearing a fawn silk gown and roses in her hair, she reclined upon a brocade settee or draped herself over an armchair, lank as a set of clothes awaiting their owner to gather them up and put them on.

• • •

My dear Miss Nightingale:

Your letter reached me within two days, carried, I think, on the back of a donkey without benefit of franking but rather because a Mahmoud knew an Essem, who knew an Ismael, who had heard of a Youssef and here it is, in my hand. I hope that mine to you will travel as swiftly.

I owe you a debt of thanks for taking the time to explain the levinge and save me from "the biting hordes." You are right—the standard mosquito netting is insufficient, and I have the welts to prove it!

What a lovely name you have, especially in French: Rossignol. And may I say that I find your French charming, far superior to my jagged shards of English. I hope one day to learn English well enough to read Shakespeare without a dictionary.

We've dropped anchor downriver from Abu Simbel, in a little cove. I wonder if you are nearby and if you have yet seen the mammoth statues of Ramses that flank the great temple. Max is excavating one Ramses for the sake of the official photographs he has been commissioned to make. (As I may have told you, I am documenting the monuments by making archaeological squeezes or molds of the inscriptions, though I am not an archaeologist.) I find it fascinating that the Egyptians and Nubians who live with these splendid monuments have so little feeling for them. They walk past them with no curiosity, as if they were old concert posters on a kiosk.

I regret that I did not meet your traveling companions, but perhaps the opportunity will yet present itself.

I have acquired an Arabic nickname, Abu Chanab, *which means "Father Mustache." Max is called "the Father of Thinness," an apt description. Has your crew told you their nicknames for your party? Ask your dragoman and hope he is not too shy to tell you. Egypt seems a place where one requires an epithet. I shall call you Rossignol, my songbird, until you tell me another.*

We shall be working here for at least another week, so perhaps we shall see you and your party again. I hope so.

I hereby swear that we have done no shooting among crowds, that we have shot only turtledoves for our larder and the odd eagle and lammergeier, the first for the sake of the feathers, the second because the sight of these huge, impatient buzzards strikes panic into my heart. (Max and I lay motionless for a time on the sand as an experiment the other day, and within minutes they began circling overhead.)

We are sailing in a twelve-meter-long cange painted blue (six windows to a side) and flying the tricolors from the stern. Are you sailing under the English flag? How would I know your boat?

From your humble servant,
Father Mustache, to the songbird,
Gustave Flaubert

He stoked his chibouk, lit it, inhaled, and blew a stream of bluish smoke into the night. At home, it was a rare day that he did not smoke thirty bowls, particularly if he were writing. A pure pleasure, like masturbating. He watched the smoke curl upward and dissipate. Indistinguishable voices wafted across the river from the opposite shore, where a bonfire sent flames leaping into the sky. The palm trees behind it, washed in red light, looked like giant branches of sea coral.

He decided to reread the letter, not because he might change it, but because he was pleased with it.

Such an angelic tone! What propriety coming from the doyen of doxies, the connoisseur of cunts, the headmaster of hussies. But, of course, one could not be one's self with women, especially a new acquaintance.

No, it seemed that only with whores could he be true to his nature, indulging the horny beast and following his lusty whims into every crack, hole, and fold of their bodies. As for sharing his intellectual side, his love of the arts and a well-reasoned dismissal of all things bourgeois, only men had proved to be satisfying partners.

Closing the envelope with his letter in it, he applied a glob of red sealing wax. What wife would wish to hear him curse with virtuosity and then discuss *King Lear*? One with the mind of a man and the obscenity of a whore? Such a woman did not exist. Nevertheless, he allowed himself to picture Miss Nightingale's breasts, which would be small and perky, with nipples, he guessed, the color of stewed prunes.

After dinner, Max got out his guidebook and spread a map on the table, a twin of the one he'd given Madame Flaubert. No doubt she studied it longingly each evening, tacked to a wall in her boudoir.

The map appeared antique, the result of the lamplight and its many creases, smears, and fingerprints. Max had opened it so many times to pencil in notes and dates that the folds had the soft, fuzzy pile of velvet. Now he traced the river north from Abu Simbel with his finger, reciting the places they might visit on the second half of their Nile journey: Dendur, to see the Roman temple there, Philae, the jewel of the Nile, Edfu, Esneh again, Luxor, Karnak, and Thebes.

Esneh, where Kuchuk Hanem lived. Gustave sat smoking quietly.

Max's finger came to rest on Kenneh, a small city where the river veered sharply east, then flowed in a gentle arc northwesterly again. His finger began to tap. Instead of following the course of the river, it moved into the Arabian desert. "I wonder," Max began. "Look at this!" He stood up, tipping over his stool. "I say, *Garçon*! Are you listening to me, Short Pants?" He rapped his knuckles on the table. "M. Descambeaux! I am calling on you, you dunce."

"Descambeaux at your service, sir," Gustave replied, suppressing a pang of sadness. Poor Alfred. And poor Caroline. Alfred had invented *Le Garçon,* and Caroline had given the imaginary clown his family name. "I just need to take a shit to clear my head." He squatted and pretended to fart loudly.

"Point your ass in the other direction, please. I am trying to think."

"Thinking? I've heard that's dangerous. The grocer told me it makes your prick shrivel up and fall off. Thinking too much will make you go blind. Spend every spare moment jerking off. You've got to keep yourself well oiled, like a proper gun."

"Oh, *Garçon*"—Max laughed—"have you not a single brain in your head?"

"Just one, like everybody else. And now, I must go shit out a word or two, inspired by the moonlight. I feel a poem coming on, like a cramp."

"What a waste of time you are! But truly, Short Pants, I have a brilliant idea." Max righted the stool and sat back down. He rotated the map toward Gustave. "Have a look. From Kenneh, we could travel east to Koseir."

Gustave followed Max's finger from Kenneh across a blank area to a circle. "What's in Koseir?"

"*Garçon,* you are hopeless. What's in Koseir? Have you never heard of it?"

The dot on the map was tiny; a squashed flea was bigger. "I haven't, O great Sheik Abu Dimple."

"I'll tell you what, *Garçon*—the Red Sea."

It was an electrifying proposition, and Max was correct: Kenneh appeared to be the closest jumping-off point anywhere along the Nile.

While Gustave flipped through Max's guidebook, Max measured the distance between the two points. "How many days would it take to cross the desert there?" he wondered aloud.

Gustave read to him. " 'Travelers returning from India often pass through Koseir.' " He skimmed along, reading to himself. "Ah! Here's something of interest. Instructions about thrashing. 'The *fellah* should be thrashed beforehand, to remind him who is in authority. However, if you mistake a Bedouin for a *fellah,* he might kill you for striking him.' " He closed the book. "We shall have to buy a cudgel."

"What's a *fellah*?" Max asked.

"Don't know."

"Seriously, I shall talk to Captain Ibrahim. It's our one chance for the Red Sea."

Gustave, usually rather phlegmatic, jumped up and spun around. "Yes! I must swim in the Red Sea." And he wanted to be able to *say* he swam in the Red Sea, and most of all, he wanted the *memory* of swimming in the Red Sea, for memory was wealth to him, and he was anxious to fill his coffers. Saint Anthony, he recalled, had spent the last fifty years of his life living on the shore of the Red Sea. Just in case he ever worked on the book again.

He leaned down to peer through the windows of the *cange.* In the sky hung a slender crescent moon, tilted backward. A bright C-shaped haze surrounded it, beyond which multitudinous stars glimmered through wispy clouds. He stuck his head out the window and breathed in the mist rising off the Nile, which was cool and damp, like the air after a soaking rain.

After Max and the crew had retired for the night, Gustave sat alone on deck with a candle. He could hear the crewmen snoring, rustling in their sleep. One lone fellow stood sentry at the stern.

To put things in proper perspective, he liked to read the newspaper backward. As expected, *La Presse* was brimming with irrelevancies—events that had already occurred or about which he could do nothing. He enjoyed the engraved illustrations, the advertisements for opera capes and top hats, remedies for cold sores and backaches. The legal announcements, thick with veiled threats, ruined careers, and domestic melodramas, were like plots for novels with missing pieces.

He was half asleep when he came upon Louise's name in a gossip column on page two. Named the defendant in a civil law suit, she'd taken the stand in self-defense. A gadfly by nature, she seemed to prefer trouble to inattention. Apparently she had stabbed a journalist in his apartment with a kitchen knife she had brought from home for the purpose. He was suing her for damages to his person and his reputation. Oh, too good! The injury had been to her, she had countered in the dock. The journalist had impugned the paternity of her daughter.

Gustave relished the image of Louise defending her honor. Too bad a duel was beyond her! Knowing her as he did, he figured it had been a paring knife and that she'd already found a way to parlay the trial into a poetry commission from the Academy. He was well rid of her. But in case they should meet by chance at a social evening, he saved the article. She'd be pleased that he had read about her (and therefore thought about her) in Egypt. Someday, he thought with glee, she should take up with Max. Obviously they disliked each other because they were so similar—both talented, both careerists and reputation builders with a flair for publicity.

6

MIRAGE

Early the next morning, Gustave had the good fortune to be on the deck of the *cange* when a slave ship was passing. A long, shallow craft, it resembled a huge dugout canoe with masts added at either end. At this cool hour after dawn, the sails were furled and the boat was drifting downriver with the current, toward Cairo. Over its midsection fluttered a tattered canopy rolled up on a metal frame, leaving the boat's cargo in full view. A camel, tethered by its bridle to the mast, stood uncertainly at the stern, its legs widely planted. In front of the camel, seated in rows like oarsmen, a dozen or so Nubian girls huddled together.

The farther upriver Gustave traveled—the farther south—the more primitive the people had become. Alexandria had been cosmopolitan, an Eastern version of Paris, bustling with European, Egyptian, Turkish, African, and Arab denizens. Two hundred and eighty kilometers to the south, in Cairo, the first signs of the vast, untamed interior appeared: burlap bags of gum Arabic, salt, and dates piled up on the docks; covered bazaars where the products of metal, straw, leather, and wood workshops were arrayed; and, of course, the slave markets. Cairo was very much a city, with schools and policemen, soldiers and veiled women billowing through the streets, a steady rush of multifariously intentioned traffic moving in all directions at once. Approaching Abu Simbel, a thousand kilometers farther south, he had sensed another order of change. With every passing kilometer, it seemed he moved back in time. Except for the pyramids at Giza, the monuments of Nubia were the biggest and oldest in Egypt, and they existed in isolation. Nearby were no mud brick houses, no mosques, schools, or gardens—in short, nothing but ancient temples and riverine way stations where a traveler might negotiate for food or flesh. Only stouthearted explorers ventured beyond the second cataracts or dared to leave the security of the riverbank for the unmapped hinterland.

The women in the slave boat did not refuse his gaze; in fact, they seemed emboldened by it. Because he detected no shame in their eyes, he gave himself permission to stare openly, to catalog every detail. The eldest might have been fifteen; the others were barely pubescent. He wondered how they had come to be slaves. Perhaps the girls' families had sold them because they could not afford a dowry for a husband. He was convinced that matrimony was somehow involved in their fate, just as it was for European women. If he had been born a woman, he would have chosen the life of the mistress or the spinster rather than the wife.

It was this kind of thinking that had soured him on his sister's marriage. He had never really accepted the fact that Caroline would one day cease to be the free-spirited painter and reader of books he adored, that she would spend an entire week in Paris hunting for pillowcases and blankets for her trousseau instead of suitable landscapes to sketch. She had always been a delightfully impish child and then a rowdy girl, following her big brother's lead.

Grief tightened his throat. It seemed impossible that she would not dash through the doors and onto the lawn to greet him when he returned to Croisset. How many times had he caught himself pondering gifts for her along the Nile?

Though he had opposed the betrothal, he had said nothing to interfere with her happiness. But on the wedding day, when he saw her in her ivory peau de soie wedding gown, looking more like a pastry than a person, he'd battled the impulse to lift the lace veil from her face, drag her from the church, and return her to her rightful place by his side as they mounted one of their spontaneous theatrical productions or skipped pebbles across the glass skin of the Seine. He had wanted to shake her—shake off her solemnity—and indulge in a session with *Le Garçon*—"Short Pants"—whose mediocre school history Caroline had fabricated. *M. Descambeaux has received from the École du Droit black balls in Torts, Contracts, and Procedures, and two red balls to match his own, one in Comedy and the other in Excuses.* How could Caroline have turned into a matron, depriving him of her good humor and beauty, of the jaunty swish of her skirts along the stone patio? For his *pauvre Caroline,* marriage had been worse than enslavement; it had been a death sentence. His beloved sister had died of a school friend's hard-on, he thought now without rancor. He might as well have infected her with cholera or smallpox.

The price of passion was death; he had always known that.

The sky, a depthless painted-on blue, brightened as the slave boat loomed closer. Several of the women stood to get a better view of the *cange* and him. With the exception of bead necklaces and short grass skirts attached to a string pulled tight around their hips, they were naked. Just the day before, Joseph had cautioned him to avoid the poisonous castor bean plants growing wild along the swampy fringes of the river. Only the Nubians, he said, had found a use for it. Indeed. These slaves had soaked their hair and skin with the oil. In the clear morning light, they gleamed like polished wood.

As the boat veered closer, he locked eyes with a girl whose coiffure resembled a black jester's hat. He had never seen such profuse tresses, except in wigs. Her hair was plaited in fine braids that were bunched together all over her head into points. She lifted one hand and waved shyly at him. He reciprocated. As the boat overtook the *cange,* the women looked back at him, turning their heads over their shoulders in unison, like a flock of birds, and trilling to him with high-pitched voices. The next moment, in one of the many tricks of light Gustave had observed on the Nile, the boat vanished into a blinding explosion of glare where the sun caught fire on the mirrored surface of the river. The avian calls of the Nubian girls hung in the air briefly, and then the river was still again except for the wind and the creaking of the *cange* as it seesawed in the wake of the slave boat. Gustave watched the water until he could no longer distinguish the pattern of the wake from the random figures of the current. A papyrus island, which he had thought firm land, drifted past, with birds chittering among the tall green stalks.

Gustave switched his attention from the river to the meal being assembled nearby. Max had already taken his place at the table and was stirring orange-flavored sugar into his water. "Quick! Eat something," he called out. "We should get an early start today at the rock temples." Was he imagining it, or were they always in a rush to eat and then to leave? He liked to dawdle over his food, but Max hated wasting time. Max was lecherous, but he was no voluptuary, like dear dead Alfred.

Hadji Ismael hurried to arrange Gustave's folding stool beneath him. This one-eyed man never lost sight of his employers, yet didn't move his head excessively, as if his eye could migrate at will to the back of his skull.

Set before Gustave was breakfast: a piece of flat bread and three quail eggs, steamed in their shells. His mouth began to water as he lifted an olive to his lips.

Gustave and a new assistant, Achmet, the youngest crewman, made molds by lamplight that morning in one of the gloomy halls of the great temple, spared the direct sun, but nearly suffocating in the dead air of the cavernous space. It felt to Gustave as if an eternity of repetitive labor had passed since breakfast. He raised his head and peered about in the dim light of the chamber. There were enough bloody inscriptions to keep him busy for a year. At least he was free to choose which ones he copied. The only limitation was that they be contiguous, which assumed that the walls shared something in common with books—that the narrative flowed from left to right or right to left. He had already made squeezes of the inscriptions on the eight columns in the main hall. As for the total number of squeezes, he was completely at the mercy of Max. The longer Max stayed at Abu Simbel taking photographs, the more squeezes he was obliged to produce. There were no diversions nearby to seduce Gustave from his task—no brothels, taverns, or restaurants—nothing but the Nile, and the towering cliffs on either side. Still, his mind was not free while he was required to apply wet paper to unyielding stone.

He looked forward to the time when he had only to supervise Achmet. One of the few literate crew members, Achmet understood that he was preserving the wisdom of his ancient forebears who, until now, had excited no curiosity in him. Gustave had explained that a scholar in France might spend years studying Achmet's squeezes. So, despite the tedium, the man was meticulous, brushing the inscriptions clean as Gustave had demonstrated, wetting the paper, then pressing it into the reliefs with a finer brush. Since taking on the job, Achmet carried himself among the crew with the pride of the anointed, certain that making squeezes was preferable to excavating the head of Ramses or swabbing the decks of the *cange*.

From time to time Gustave clowned and pantomimed for Achmet, who cackled loudly at his japes, clapping his hands over his mouth.

Achmet carefully peeled off two dry squeezes and placed them in their cardboard box. Carting the molds around was like transporting eggs—anything could ruin them. He looked to Gustave for further instruction. Gustave responded with a rolling movement of his hands. *"Continue, mon ami,"* he said. *"Fais un autre."* With that, he picked up one of the lamps and set off toward the entrance to get a breath of air. The cavern stank of burning lamp oil, sweat, the staleness of the ages, and the fine-bore shit of scorpions and beetles.

The next room was bathed in a dusky orange glow. Around two more corners, daylight leaked in. He hoisted himself up the sandy ramp to the entrance, squinting against the stinging onslaught of windblown sand.

Standing in the doorway, he contemplated the scene before him.

Because of the height of the temple, he could not see the river below or its banks, only a glittering streak of blue-silver in the distance, where the Nile snaked away through the cliffs. It looked small and insignificant, like a misplaced piece of a jigsaw puzzle. Closer by, tourists were picnicking and lounging under the stunted acacia trees. There were always tourists camped by the rock temple, but he had no desire to meet any of them and remained in mufti.

Directly before him was the gigantic hill of sand that had swallowed the fourth Ramses up to his nostrils. It was wide as well as steep, always difficult to negotiate. If they did take the caravan to Koseir, he expected they would encounter dunes that would make this one seem a piker.

As he eyed the sand ramp from the top of it, an indistinct vision appeared at the bottom. A mirage, he first thought. But it lacked the illusion of water, the sparkling waves he'd often observed hovering above the desert, especially early in the morning. Was it, perhaps, another sort of mirage? Fata morgana, he recalled, the name of the storied mirage off the Strait of Messina, which had been spotted for hundreds of years, like clockwork. It appeared to passing sailors like a wooded hillside or a ship, the images hanging high on the sky like unfinished paintings.

As he stared, something blue and slender, like a fishing float, bobbed into view. Above it, a scintillant blur the pink of a seashell stretched wide and narrowed again. Then dark dots formed beneath the blue stripe, like clumps of soil hanging from the root of a flower. The entire assemblage moved again. Perhaps it was going sideways; perhaps it was advancing. Long moments passed as the blue stem widened to an oval. And then, as if bursting through a curtain or an invisible membrane, the colored slices merged and a small party climbing the hill led by a woman in blue resolved into sharper focus. He watched the woman's small, foreshortened figure toil uphill. Though she was only halfway along the ramp, he could now see that she wore a pink bonnet. The blue of her dress was the color of a summer day, tender and hopeful. Feeling as if he had witnessed a birth, he slumped down, exhausted and exalted, out of her sight.

He remembered another summer sky, another blue dress. It was July, a few months after Caroline died. He was taking her death mask and a plaster cast of her hand to James Pradier, who had recently made his father's memorial bust. The atelier was immense, one of those airy, high-ceilinged rooms favored by artists, with columns instead of walls, like a ballroom. Close to the windows, alongside a pedestal laden with clay, James stood, dashingly attired in red velvet tights embroidered in gold. Over a white shirt with an extravagant lace jabot he wore a brown canvas apron. His hands were gray with dried clay. He greeted Gustave, pointing to a sofa and one of a pair of overstuffed chairs. In the magical light of the atelier, the chair, with its loosening down stuffing, seemed not shabby, but as if it were sprouting feathery wings.

A woman sat upon a stool with her back to him and James. Blond sausage curls dangled on pale pink shoulders. She was wearing a blue dress. No, blue was not the word. *Azure*. For such a creature with golden tresses, the gown must be azure. Bunches of fabric—smocked sleeves, and a wide gathered skirt—conveyed plenitude, as if the sky had wrapped itself around her for the pure pleasure of *azure*. She sat stock still while Pradier daubed clay from the amorphous lump beside him to the emergent bust on the revolving table.

"Who is your visitor?" the woman asked, her face still hidden.

"No one who would interest you," James answered. "A mere provincial, a young writer from Rouen."

"Oh?" the voice said. "I have heard his footsteps. May I hear his voice?"

"As long as you do not move a centimeter." James nodded at Gustave, giving him permission to speak.

"*Je m'appele* Gustave. Gustave Flaubert."

"Oh, Flaubert. I've heard of you."

"No, you haven't!" James said.

"I certainly have," the voice insisted, rising with irritation. It did not seem attached to the inert figure on the stool.

James turned to Gustave. "Louise will never admit that anyone is unknown to her."

"Perhaps you've mentioned me to her," Gustave said, enjoying the cooling effect of a breeze that blew through the open windows.

"Why would I do that?"

"The death of my father, perhaps?" Gustave conjectured. "He was, after all, a well-known surgeon. Could you have shown her his bust?"

James shook his head and began to throw small pinches onto the head where the hair would go. The clay sat up in tufts like beaten egg whites.

"I shall meet him soon in any case," Louise said. "I must take a break. My neck is aching." She swiveled on her stool and in the next instant was extending an alabaster hand to him. He rose from his chair and, bowing formally, gathered her hand in his and kissed it. "A great pleasure, I'm sure," he mumbled. At twenty-five he could still be flustered by a beautiful woman, and the glimpse of her face, not to mention her shoulders and hair, had undone him. He hoped he was not blushing.

James completed the introductions. "Madame Colet is a poet of some repute." He turned to Louise. "And Gustave is a promising young writer."

"A poet also?" she asked. She moved toward the furniture, sorting out her voluminous skirts behind her, like an exotic bird preening its tail feathers. The neckline of her dress was fashionably low front and back. He tried not to stare.

"I am not a poet, madame. I am a novelist."

Louise arranged herself upon the worn loveseat, taking up most of it. "Have these novels seen the light of day? Who is your publisher?"

After he quit law school, he had revised *Novembre,* but did not intend to publish it yet. He considered it the draft of a novice. Too personal to share with anyone but his closest friends, it aged in a drawer at home, alongside the manuscript of *Smarrh,* the novella he wrote when he was thirteen. He could not mention that to her, either. Nor was it safe to talk about *The Temptation of Saint Anthony,* which he had just begun to research. "I am still a virgin, madame, when it comes to publication. I am revising, awaiting the right opportunity."

She tucked one foot under her petticoats and turned sideways to face him. "That is very wise. Reviewers have memories like elephants, and the first work published must set the standard. Revision is good. Though I myself"—she paused to secure his gaze—"am known for writing rapidly."

James carefully draped a damp canvas cloth over the bust. "Louise cranked out one poem in three days to meet a deadline. Isn't that correct? They say you wrote it in one sitting of fifty-five hours."

"Indeed. I never changed out of my housedress. That was my first prize-winning poem from the Academy. Do you know it, *monsieur*?" she asked Gustave. " 'Le Musée de Versailles'?" She dropped her glance to pick a piece of lint off her bodice, giving him an opportunity—almost inviting him—to stare at it himself. Her rib cage was small and firm, perhaps from boning, a perfect complement to the lavish softness of her breasts, which rose majestically above the neckline and bobbled slightly, like twin puddings, as she moved her arms. The lady, he was pleased to note, was delectably feminine in every regard. The blue satin shoe that peeked from her lacy underskirts might have been a child's slipper. Her face was bright, her eyes oceanic, her features regular, with plump cheeks that lent a petulant pout, even when her face was in repose. He set upon fixing her in his mind until the time when he might request a portrait from her as a keepsake.

"I regret that I do not know the work," Gustave replied. "Could you furnish me with a copy?"

"But of course. It would be my pleasure. Shall I fetch it now? I shall give you a copy of my first book as well, *Fleurs du Midi*—"

"No!" James bellowed. "You are posing for me, are you not?

"It would only take a few moments." Louise explained to Gustave that she lived two blocks away, on rue Fontaine Saint-George. She made sure to mention her husband, the composer Hippolyte, and her daughter, Henriette. This information, Gustave understood, was offered as the bona fides of her availability, not to discourage his interest. As he well knew, everyone in Paris who was anyone took a lover. If he were going to have a sex life despite the risk of triggering a seizure, it would be best on many counts with a respectable married woman rather than a prostitute. He could form a loving and long-term relationship; a pregnancy could be finessed as legitimate progeny.

James compromised. "A few more minutes, Louise, until I finish the hairline, and we'll be done for the day. Perhaps Gustave will accompany you to your flat to save you the return trip."

"It would be my pleasure," he said.

It was clear to them that a flirtation and assignation had been accomplished with the air of complete respectability. Had Louise's husband, Hippolyte, been in the room, Gustave thought with a shiver of delight, there would have been nothing he could have pointed to as improper.

Louise resumed posing. Gustave watched fascinated as James rolled clay between his hands to fashion slender coils. On the bust, they became a crude approximation of the tendrils of hair at her nape.

"Done!" James pronounced, once again covering the bust with a damp cloth. Louise hopped down from the stool and retreated to a dry sink at the far end of the studio to freshen up.

It was then that Gustave handed Caroline's death mask and the cast of her hand to James. Immediately upon seeing the likeness of his sister, his mood plummeted. James stood silently pondering the mask for a long moment. At last, he spoke. The bronze he had used for Dr. Flaubert's bust was a practical and masculine material, ideal for a distinguished man. For Caroline he suggested marble, befitting her delicate beauty. Gustave agreed.

When she rejoined them, Louise was sharply taken aback by the mask, which was unmistakably the face of a dead woman, the eyes closed, the mouth set for eternity. "Oh, my dears," she whispered. "Who?"

"My sister, Caroline. My only sister." Gustave looked down at the floor to control his feelings.

"And so young. How?"

He continued to look down, unable to speak.

"Childbed fever," said James.

Louise stepped nearer and inserted her hand in the crook of Gustave's arm. "I am very sorry, my dear," she whispered, so low the words were barely audible. She touched his hand.

If only he could look up to meet her eyes, to acknowledge her kindness, the physical warmth of her touch. But he was afraid he would burst into tears.

"Come, my new friend, we shall walk and Paris herself will lift your spirits."

Sniffling, Gustave reached one-handed for his handkerchief. His nose was running furiously.

"Let me," she said, removing the cloth from his pocket and touching it lightly to his mouth and nose. "There, *chéri*. That's better, isn't it?"

"Yes."

"Come. The urchins and beggars of Paris are waiting for us."

Still arm in arm, Louise handed Gustave her straw bonnet to hold by its satin ties and they exited through the wide door, clattering down the metal stairs.

Gustave could not believe his luck. Not an hour had passed since he first laid eyes on Louise's curls, and now he was hurrying with this blond Venus to her apartment.

On the street, he fumbled for an instant, unsure as to etiquette. Was the gentleman supposed to be closer to the street in case of horses taking a shit or running amok? Or closer to the houses, to receive the onslaught of emptied chamber pots? He could not for the life of him recall in that moment which was considered more gallant.

Louise's flat occupied the corner of a golden-red brick, pre-Revolutionary house converted to apartments. Though fallen into mild disrepair—there were pieces of slate missing from the roof, gutters slightly askew, windows cracked here and there—the beauty and grandeur of the building's origins overpowered its recent history.

Louise withdrew a key from a lavender velvet wristlet, unlocked the massive door, and gestured him into a fair-sized drawing room.

A pier glass caught their reflections as they entered, she confident, he more tentative. She stationed him on the couch and excused herself.

As the curtains floated up in the breeze, he caught her perfume, a whiff of musk and roses. He began to scan the room for clues to her character. Everything about his goddess was blue. Her eyes, her dress, and now her parlor, He was sitting on a worn blue camelbacked sofa draped with a darker blue silk shawl. Throw rugs in shades of aquamarine were strewn in thoughtful asymmetry along the dark planks of the floor, like garden plantings. The furnishings suggested that Madame Colet was financially pressed, that her chairs and taborets, tables and sconces were finds from flea markets and secondhand shops, with the exception, perhaps, of a finely carved alabaster lamp hanging from the ceiling by three brass chains.

Face and chest freshly powdered, Louise returned bearing a tray with strawberries, a bottle of wine, a pitcher of cream, and bread.

In truth, he had no appetite, at least not for food. But it would be rude to refuse her hospitality, so he accepted the nondescript wine she offered in a cheap glass. He swallowed a mouthful and felt it go directly to his head, where it buzzed and faded, like an annoying insect.

Louise drizzled heavy cream over the sugared strawberries and he watched as white rivulets feathered out into ferny shapes that turned pink as they mingled with the sauce. He smeared a spoonful of the mixture onto his bread. As his teeth sank into the soft white dough, a trickle of jam melted onto his tongue, exploding with sweetness and tartness.

"Delicious," he muttered. "The combination . . ." The flavors surged in his mouth, the crisp crust becoming a moist, tender wad, the fleshy berries yielding to the syrup, all of it clinging to the fat of the cream before it vanished into the cleansing tang of the wine, which flowed tidelike around his mouth. His mouth! He was profoundly grateful for that marvelous organ, which, at this moment, equaled anything he had ever experienced with that other wonder, his prick. Had he ever eaten before? Christ, he thought, the purest culinary bliss I have ever known, the flavor, the savor—

"I am flattered, *monsieur*, that my cooking pleases you."

"And how," he mumbled, his voice drenched with the creamy, sugared fruit. "Is there some secret ingredient perhaps? Honey? Lemon zest?"

"I assure you no."

Soon the tray was empty. She smiled, pleased by his satisfaction.

While she cleared away the dishes, he sat back, content, and peered around the room, noticing its details at leisure. There were knickknacks and sentimental objects scattered about: a miniature vase with straw flowers; an ordinary rock on a table. (Did it represent a love affair, a pleasant afternoon picnicking in the country, an arduous hike in the Alps?) But mostly, there were books. Everywhere. They lined the walls of the salon and the end table shelves. Beneath the coffee table, the floor was stacked with journals and newspapers. Across the desk where it adjoined the wall, bookends kept a regiment of taller books upright. A stack of books leaned in a corner, behind a jade plant. He relaxed into the sofa with a sigh, feeling at home, among his own kind. "My dear Madame Colet," he ventured. "Tell me, what do you like to read?"

A torrent of authors and titles ensued. The conversation, until then a pleasant stream, roared into a deluge as Gustave shouted out names and Louise pulled books down from shelves. Hugo and Aristotle, Vigny, Musset, Byron, Sophocles—beloved Sophocles—and Plato, Montaigne and Rousseau, Chateaubriand. Soon the open books surrounded them like a flock of hungry street pigeons come to partake of the literary feast.

For Gustave, reading was a sacred event. "To me," he explained, "words refine experience, the way a smelter turns ore into steel, giving it the luster and strength of truth that is lacking in its coarse, original form." Quite eloquent, he thought, for a first articulation.

Louise smiled. "Beautifully put. And so true. I could not have said it better."

"And I wonder if you have discovered the master himself." He was testing her, hoping she wouldn't fail. "I am speaking of a writer we have only in translation, and only recently," he hinted.

Louise rushed to her desk, removed a thick portfolio, and plopped down beside him on the couch. Whisking a lace doily to the floor, she placed the folder on the small coffee table, untied its suede closures, and removed a sheaf of paper. Her eyes were blue fireworks. "I've translated *The Tempest*," she announced.

Could it be that his goddess loved Shakespeare as much as he did? So few of his countrymen were conversant with the Bard. For some reason, it had taken the French hundreds of years to discover the greatest writer on earth. "Please," Gustave said. "Would you honor me with a reading?"

Her cheeks flushing, Louise fanned the pages until she found the scene she wanted. "Ah, here is the most captivating speech," she said excitedly. "It is Prospero's. You will undoubtedly recognize it." She paused for a moment, collecting herself like an actress about to declaim, her face growing solemn. When she read, her voice was deeper and more powerful, like a peaceful river that was forced through narrows.

Gustave knew *The Tempest* well. He and Bouilhet had read it out loud together, in French and English, often mystified by the archaic language, but in love with its music and wit. He knew, too, that translation was a difficult art, demanding the precision of a scholar and the vision of a poet. Madame Colet was clearly inspired; she had not lost the passion of the text. But he also knew that Shakespeare rarely wrote in classic Alexandrine couplets. Louise's rhymes were clanging distractions ("Players/layers . . . palace/chalice"), too loud and predictable for the nuanced images. But surely, a negative comment was not the way to her bed. She might even feel insulted. After all, she was a published poet and he—who was he to criticize?

"And our little lives are circled with a snooze," she concluded.

"Brilliant," he lied. He planted a kiss on her knuckles. He couldn't stop staring at her. "You are such an adorable genius, my dear Madame Colet." The last time he had felt so moved, he was fourteen and watching Elisa suckling her infant on the beach. Now he ached to take Louise in his arms.

"You must call me Louise," she said, still using the more formal *vous*.

"My dear Louise." Desire now burned in him like lava rising to the rim of a caldera. He leaned to kiss her cheek. She, too, pressed forward, aligning her face to meet his lips. But at the very moment the fine golden hairs on her upper lip swam into view, he heard a loud click. The door flew open and a child burst into the room, followed by a nurse trying to restrain her. He and Louise snapped apart.

"Maman!" the little girl cried, jumping onto Louise's lap.

Louise made the introductions, but the child was not interested. She wished only to hang from her mother's neck, playing with her earrings as she recounted everything she had seen outdoors, babbling on and on to Louise's delight.

The child was as beautiful as her mother, he observed, further proof that Louise's beauty was not a chance or temporary thing, but an inalterable essence so innate to her being that it could be relied upon to reproduce itself.

Louise cast him a look that conveyed it was time to leave. After peremptory pleasantries all around, he gathered his jacket and hat. Louise suggested that the nurse take Henriette to her room to use the chamber pot while she accompanied her guest to the door.

As they stood prolonging their good-byes, he realized that she had not once mentioned her husband and that the apartment was devoid of male belongings. The esteemed composer must not reside there. "The child's father, does he visit?" he asked.

"We are separated." Louise adjusted the hem of his jacket sleeve to reach his shirt cuff. "It's a complicated arrangement." Later Pradier explained that neither Hippolyte Colet nor Victor Cousin, a previous lover, acknowledged Henriette's paternity.

He kissed her hand, hoping she would not object to the tip of his tongue brushing the skin.

"Tomorrow the nurse will return Henriette to her boarding school," she whispered. "Will you visit again in the afternoon?"

He nodded. The thought of what the next day might bring made him giddy. *"Au revoir."* He turned to go. *"À demain."*

He pushed through the immense old door into the July heat.

• • •

Still slumped in the temple doorway, Gustave regarded his right hand, which lay by his side in a bright patch of light, as separate from him as a specimen in his father's laboratory. The shiny pink scar where his father had scalded him while tending him after his first seizure flamed anew in the desert sun. The burn had pained him for months and left him marked for life with this paternal sign—of deep-seated disapproval? Surely it had been an accident, but one that had acquired symbolic importance. On the scar, sweat formed a glistening slick. He could almost see the moisture evaporate in fetid waves.

The woman in the mirage was clearer now as she trudged purposefully forward. A native guide peripatetically extended an arm to steady her, but she seemed determined to outpace him and avoid his assistance. Behind her, a plumper woman trod more slowly, a native pressing both hands against her back to help her up the steep incline. As Gustave well knew, even where the sand was level, it constantly gave way so that one never had secure footing. The second woman was graceless. Hunkered down, her stout arms extended on either side for balance, she shambled forward like a bear.

Abruptly, she lost her footing and shrieked, continuing to yowl as she skidded onto her back and slid down the slope, finally coming to a stop like an upended tortoise. He sprang to his feet and rushed toward her.

He tacked laterally across the sand for better purchase, leaving zigzagging footprints like the trail of a huge snake. Below him, two guides were attempting to lift the horizontal female, but she was fending them off, kicking and slapping at their hands and shouting shrilly lest, he gathered, they touch her. What, he wondered, would be an acceptable anchor by which they could right this beached whale? The hair, no doubt, but that would be painful and might result in baldness. Surely she would have no objection to a native guide grabbing her by the feet. But to drag her the rest of the way would be more of a sanding than a salvation. What was needed was a magician to levitate her above the dune like one of the whirling, swirling dervishes he'd seen in Cairo.

Her smaller companion accosted him just as he reached the comical scene. It was Miss Nightingale. "Excuse me, sir," she said, squinting into the sun. "Can you help my maid?"

"It would be my honor," Gustave answered in French.

"M. Flaubert?"

"At your service, *mademoiselle*." He pushed back his pom-pommed hood, exposing a sunburned face, shaggy beard, and shaved head.

The squirming figure on the ground paused in her struggles to watch the pair become reacquainted. "Leave off of me!" she screamed as the guide misread her momentary stillness as an invitation to try to hoist her from the ground. Poor fellow, Gustave thought, he thinks the soles of his feet will be blistered if he doesn't get her up in the next few minutes. Bastinadoes all around when news of the debacle reached their captain.

"This is my maid, Trout," Florence began. "Trout, meet Mr. Flau—"

"For the love of God, mum, save the introductions and just get me up. I'm sinking. Is it quicksand I'm in?"

"No, definitely not. Plain sand."

Gustave liked being the hero, but he wasn't certain that he was equal to this feat. He wondered which would be easier to move: deadweight or weight attempting ineffectually to rise? He waved the guides back. "It would help," he told Florence in French, "if she would stop fighting and lie still." Florence translated and Trout quieted, her hand stiffened into a visor on her forehead.

Planting his feet apart on the incline, Gustave bent to the task, placing one arm under Trout's knees and the other under her neck, swashbuckler-like. He lifted with all his strength, but the hot dune immediately shifted under him, spilling him up to his calves in sand. He let go and stood, shaking his head. What was that principle of the lever he had studied in school? The longer the handle, the greater the weight? He remembered an illustration of Archimedes lifting the earth with a pole, but the only lever he had handy were his arms, which weren't getting any longer. He stepped closer. Perhaps the fireman's carry, the maid like a gunnysack over his shoulder?

Miss Nightingale said, "Trout, I think it would work if one person could lift your head and another your feet."

Trout made a sour face. "I don't want these heathens touching me, mum. It ain't proper for an Englishwoman to be handled by such as these."

Gustave resumed his position to try again.

"Let me help," Florence said, bending down.

"No, you are too small."

"I'm very strong,"

"I have no doubt of that, but it would not be enough," Gustave said. "The sand sucks everything down."

They stood pondering while Trout lay in the sun, her face red, sweat forming in droplets on her upper lip and in the rolls of her neck. She wiped her brow with the sleeve of her dress.

"J'ai une idée," Miss Nightingale said. She removed her brown Holland jacket and stuffed it into Gustave's hands, then knelt, bare-armed, beside Trout and whispered into her ear.

"No," Trout objected loudly. "I won't do it!"

Florence stood up. "There is no other way."

Trout's face turned crimson with rage. "I wish I'd never come to this godless desert."

"You are not in England now. You are in Egypt and you are being unnecessarily difficult."

Trout began to bawl; small bubbles inflated and popped at her nostrils.

"As your employer, I must insist." Miss Nightingale retrieved her jacket from Gustave. The native guides shuffled their feet, looking ill at ease and fearful. Relentless sun, indifferent sand. This was, after all, the eastern Sahara. Gustave felt the heat thickening the rough wool of his robes, secreting itself into every fold of fabric and skin, sweat dripping from his armpits, chest, neck, and groin. Through the soles of his boots, his feet were beginning to burn. Trout would soon be Trout *frite* and then they would have to bury or eat her.

Miss Nightingale knelt again, and folding her beige jacket in half, blindfolded Trout, tying the sleeves behind her head. She waved the servants to return to the reluctant lady in distress and gestured for Gustave to take charge. She did not have to say a word. Everyone understood the enterprise. Trout was to be tackled by however many hands as were needed, placed on whatever parts of her body provided traction.

And so the Englishwoman was hefted silently from the dune by six hands and borne like a ceremonial offering toward the temple of Ramses II. Behind Trout's improvised blinders, Gustave thought he detected a muffled sigh of resignation or relief. He followed the pink of Miss Nightingale's bonnet, the tiny masterful hands. She had placed herself alongside the procession, at his shoulder. How delicate she was, deerlike, and yet how practical, resourceful, and forthright. But there was something beyond those familiar English traits in her. He sensed it in her bearing, in the way she had taken charge of the situation—eagerly, like someone with a sense of purpose. It seemed to him that where the French had raised passion to a universal good, the English had substituted purpose, social progress, and sexual prohibition.

The innocent Miss Nightingale (most likely she was a virgin, he theorized) smiled at him, a commendation for a job well executed as the entourage struggled at last into a patch of shade. There they were met by the picnickers he'd observed earlier, a small mob of concerned Europeans oohing and aahing at the sight of an Englishwoman being transported like a pharaoh across the blazing sand.

Among the crowd were Miss Nightingale's companions whom he'd seen before from a distance when he first met her on the road. The man loped forward and arranged a blanket to receive the still-airborne servant. But she wasn't having it and insisted they put her down on her own two feet, whereupon she all but collapsed on the blanket, her skirts deflating around her like laundry in a dead wind.

The natives vanished in a wink, going, he figured, behind the temple or in it for shade. Miss Nightingale hastened to introduce everyone and invited Gustave to join her for sugar water and English biscuits. She really was polite, this little deer, with a heart-shaped faced and lustrous brown hair, some of which had come loose from her pink hat and hung in damp tendrils on her neck and shoulder. Her skin was as pale as cream, with an inner glow, the result of the heat, no doubt. She untied her jacket and shook it out. Her arms were thin, but with well-defined muscles. Unbidden, the image of himself licking them clean of sweat flashed to mind.

When he did not respond to her invitation, she repeated it, but her companion, Charles, had already moved into gear, pumping Gustave's hand. "Biscuits, posh! You must join us for dinner."

Gustave agreed to meet on their houseboat at eight the next evening.

"Along with Mr. Du Camp," Flo added.

"Who?" Charles asked.

Flo reminded her dear friend that she had met two Frenchmen on the road. Didn't he recall? They had had guns.

"I love to shoot," Charles said. "Almost as much as I love to visit Greece. My two favorite pastimes."

Miss Nightingale stepped away, in deference to Mr. Bracebridge, and was conferring with Mrs. Bracebridge, one hand on her bonnet and the other clasping her friend's hand. He watched her moving in her dress, a costume that made her larger than she was from the waist down, and smaller than she was from the waist up. The most fetching fashion for most women, as far as he was concerned, was a bedsheet.

"I must return to work," he said, draining the tumbler of sugar water.

"Mr. Flaubert is an emissary of the French government," Flo explained. The Bracebridges nodded, appropriately impressed if still unclear as to his occupation.

"We are making squeezes of the monuments," he explained. "Inside the temple. I have my man, Achmet, working, but he slacks off if I don't supervise." That was a lie. Achmet worked harder than a man ought, as if in fear for his life. Gustave planned to reward him with a generous baksheesh at journey's end.

"I'm sorry you can't linger," Florence said. She offered him her hand, that dainty and delightful frond of flesh. Ever the cavalier, he bowed and pressed it to his lips. He took the taste of her skin with him as he walked toward the three Ramseses steadily regarding the scene.

7

THE WORLD IS MADE OF WATER

Tonight's meal would have no hand-lettered place cards or menus, not that Selina had not volunteered to make them, but Florence had convinced her that the Frenchmen needed no such formality, as they, too, had been on the Nile eating native fare for months. Menus, groceries, baking, and such were of no earthly interest to Flo. That was her mother's domain, a world of ostentation and waste, where awful "menu French" prevailed, which in England was nothing like the living language but a kind of decorative captioning chefs used to impress their employers. They added *à la française* and *à la reine, glacé,* and *sauté* to the menu like salt and pepper to a brisket. Once Fanny had served "julienne of soup" and Flo had piped up with, "Why not filets of carrots?" in earshot of the assembled guests. Fanny had brooded for a day.

Despite its location in the wilds of Nubia, Abu Simbel suffered no shortage of food vendors catering to the small but steady European trade. Bakers hawked fresh bread; butchers, goats, lambs, and chickens; fishermen, fresh catch. The crew, too, found commodities to their liking—dates and spices, and the henna with which they continually dyed their hands and hair. The captain had procured Nile perch, rice, dried figs, dates, almonds, and fava beans. Paolo would attempt a fruit pudding, using goat's milk and raspberry conserve from home. If that failed, they'd munch biscuits from Fortnam and Mason's slathered with marmalade and Darjeeling tea. In any case, Charles would proffer his best Irish whiskey, a hypnotic strong enough to engulf the memory of any supper in a smoky, intoxicating fog.

Florence spent the afternoon exploring the façade of the great rock temple, writing about and sketching figures and cartouches, all the while knowing M. Flaubert was somewhere nearby. At five-thirty, she and her companions returned to the dahabiyah for the afternoon rest. This was the time for writing letters and journals, for Trout to snooze on the divan and Charles to read the classics. (He had brought, in the original Latin, Strabo, Ptolemy, and Herodotus that he might become better acquainted with the classical view of the late Egyptian dynasties.)

Despite his unconventional clothing, Florence counted M. Flaubert a man of quality. He was tall and hearty, with an expressive face that she took as proof that significant cogitation was ongoing behind his large and lively hazel eyes. Most would call him handsome, though she refused to use that word (along with *beautiful* and *pretty*) because it reduced people to specimens, like the dumb animals at county fairs unknowingly vying for a ribbon. Still, Flaubert would have earned first place, a blue. He had been so helpful. Trout might still be roasting on the sand had he not happened along. He'd been self-possessed and understood her wishes without explanation, captaining the rescue earnestly and without pomp.

Trout, who was sulking in her bunk, had not shown a smidgen of gratitude to Florence, M. Flaubert, or the quaking guides. Once delivered to the fretwork shade of the stumpy trees alongside the rock temple, she had nibbled a few dates, then spent the afternoon feverishly crocheting an infant's layette and drinking small beer. To avoid another spill in the sand, Flo had urged her to allow a crewmen at each elbow for the return walk to the boat. She had flapped down the ramp like a flightless bird.

Flo looked forward to dining with two French adventurers and with no one to glare at her or pinch her leg under the table if she made an immodest remark. She might be herself, Florence Nightingale, idealist and voracious consumer of knowledge, not Miss Nightingale, spinster and object of pity and revulsion, the living monument to Fanny's failure.

There was hardly a ripple that evening, the breeze having moved on, the captain said, to the eastern desert. The Nile resembled a lacquered tray inlaid with nacre stars and a slender moon. One might almost think it solid, the polished stage of a theater with the arch of the heavens as its twinkling proscenium. In the air above the glossy expanse, a current flourished. Swarms of mosquitoes, gnats, midges, and biting flies hung in a particulate mist above the surface, while in pale green and gray patches, moths swam like a school of slow fish dodging bats and nighthawks. The heat had relented enough for the women to wear long sleeves and stockings as protection against the insects.

Trout had decided to take dinner in her cabin. No doubt she felt stranded, socially and geographically, and preferred the role of misunderstood and benighted lady's maid to temporary equal. Not a peep was heard from her that evening.

Because the dinner was the Bracebridges' first social event on the dahabiyah, they decided to dress. They had packed with such occasions in mind—visits with compatriots in Alexandria and Cairo, as well as with new acquaintances made while touring. Charles appeared in a clean white shirt, dinner jacket, and cravat, hair brushed to a shine, whiskers freshly trimmed. Selina, bedecked with cameo earrings and brooch, wore a rose-colored gown covered with a fine alpaca mantle trimmed in rabbit fur.

Florence, who had brought no such finery, was content in a navy silk and wool dress with a white lace collar and matching lace headband to set off the hair curled into a rosette at each ear. A fichu of Sea Island cotton Grandmother Shore had tatted completed her crisp if plain outfit. The year before, at a tiny arcade in Rome, Selina had convinced her to purchase garnet earrings that dangled midway down her neck on gold-filigreed wires. Inserting them in her ears, she'd worried that she looked like a Gypsy. Selina had persuaded her that they suited her complexion, lending a hint of reflected color to her skin, which, on its own, tended toward the paleness of bone china. "No need to be a plain Jane when you have such a lovely face, " Selina had said. "I don't want to look like a baited hook," Flo had replied. Though she enjoyed fine things as much as any young woman, she had adopted plain clothing as a necessary defense against the wrong sort of men. "I would rather look like a vicar's wife," she had explained, accepting the small box of earrings from the merchant, "than a demimondaine." Tonight would mark the third time she had worn them.

At eight sharp, the Frenchmen arrived carrying luggage, M. Du Camp weighted down with two unwieldy sheepskin cases, and M. Flaubert with a portmanteau and a bottle of wine. In full dress, they looked like remnants from Napoleon's army gone native. Ceremonial swords with embossed hilts swung by their sides in ornate scabbards. When they bent at the knee to board the boat, or sat in chairs, they had to coax the swords from behind like a pair of shy dogs. Perhaps they planned a fencing demonstration? They wore tight white pants, like footmen (the better, Flo thought, to show off their legs), and tall leather cavalry boots. In lieu of military jackets, they sported red Turkish vests over voluminous white shirts, the vests Flo had often seen on bare-chested Egyptian men. Only fezzes were missing to completely scramble their attire. Instead, they wore turbans. M. Flaubert's was blood red, fixed at the top with a brooch.

While the captain and Paolo were preparing dinner topside, Charles invited everyone belowdecks. There, he poured five glasses of sherry.

The Bracebridges' cabin was bigger than Flo's, with one large bed in the middle, and a narrow divan on one side. With nowhere proper to sit, everyone stood. Charles gave a brief survey of his belongings, as if, Florence thought, to assure his guests that as "Franks"—Europeans of any nationality—they had a civilization in common to uphold no matter where they found themselves. The trappings Charles so proudly showed off were like so many props in this venture: his globe, Selina's tea caddy, maps and drawing kits, first aid supplies, a telescope, bird and reptile encyclopedias. He read the titles of his books aloud, waiting for recognition on his guests' faces, which was only infrequently forthcoming. If Florence didn't know Charles better, she would have thought he was quizzing them to determine how well educated they were. Charles was good-hearted, but sometimes his enthusiasms rode roughshod over people's patience. He could be a boor.

"My dear," he turned to her, "tell the Frenchmen how many volumes you brought from home."

Before she could answer, he volunteered the information. "Miss Nightingale is modest, but I know to a certainty that there are more than thirty scholarly tomes dealing with Egypt and higher spiritual pursuits."

"Now, Charles," she said, coloring. At the rate Charles was going, she would soon be unrecognizably bookish. Higher spiritual pursuits? Had she ever used those words to him? They sounded like something Selina might have told him.

Just then, Selina changed the subject. "The captain has an ambitious menu. Five courses."

"I believe I can smell our dinner now," Gustave said, sniffing to reinforce his point. She thought he smiled at her.

The odors from the brazier had drifted down, whetting their appetites. They followed their noses back upstairs.

The crew had outdone themselves setting the table: within a collar of purple flowers they'd arranged a branch of dates and sectioned pomegranates, the seeds glittering like rubies. In moments, conversation was flowing as freely as the food and wine.

M. Flaubert had brought along his certificate from the government describing his mission. But it was Du Camp's photographs that captivated everyone. Shedding his white gloves, he passed around his pictures of the monuments at Giza and the mosques of Cairo. Spectacular images of the Sphinx elicited special praise. Florence hadn't yet explored the monuments at Giza, only viewed them from afar, saving them, she explained, for the float downriver. "I glimpsed him from the back of a little ass," she mentioned, studying the picture of the Sphinx. "We rode asses everywhere in Cairo," she added. "They were so small!"

"We rode them, too," Du Camp said. "One's legs hang almost to the ground. They're the Egyptian version of the coach and four."

"It's such a bumpy ride, isn't it? My maid was exhausted. She complained the little beasts would displace her kidneys or cause her lungs to drop to her derriere." (Trout had said "bottom," but the French sounded more polite.) She'd felt ridiculous astride her donkey, a Brobdinagian suddenly transported to Lilliput. "I felt like a giant," she said. "And I hated that my mount was throttled periodically." She was led around like that day after day, touring the mosques and the tombs, her efreet bushwhacking through the crowds, cajoling the donkey forward by clicking, calling, and tugging at the reins, then striking him on the rump. "The poor feeling beast," she lamented. "My weight must have been oppressive. Next time, we shall request horses."

"Horses are hard to come by," Du Camp said, "and impractical in the close city streets." He turned to M. Flaubert, who nodded his agreement. "That's why everyone rides the asses."

"Of course. I hadn't realized that," she said.

M. Flaubert set down his goblet. "If you want to ride a horse," he said, chewing his fish with obvious pleasure, "you must go to the desert."

She liked watching him eat, enjoyed the subtle chewing sounds, the slightly greasy film over his lips, the almost inaudible grunts of delight.

"Why don't you come with us for a ride across the desert?" He smacked the table. "All of you! The little Arabians are miraculous. Do you have a good seat?" he asked Flo.

Florence had always ridden sidesaddle, a terrible way to travel anywhere, with the body positioned at cross-purposes to the forward motion of the animal. At the Hurst, she sometimes rode bareback, like a boy—much to Fanny's horror—gripping for dear life with her thighs, her fingers entwined in the pony's mane. "I've ridden quite a bit," she told him.

"Charles raises Arabian horses," Selina said with pride. Charles nodded, busily removing tiny bones from the head of his fish.

Max said, "You must enlighten us about them, M. Bracebridge."

"Happy to, Max," Charles replied. "If there's one thing I enjoy talking about, it's my lads and lassies."

"And the babies," Selina added.

Flo had heard Charles on the subject many times before. Bloodlines, imports, stud books, racing times. He was passionate about his hobby. But she was surprised to hear Selina so enthusiastic. And she could not remember ever hearing Selina call the foals "babies."

"My stock goes back to the Byerley Turk," Charles began.

Flo doubted either Frenchman knew much about equine pedigrees.

When Charles got no response to the famous name, he took a different tack. "The Bedouins knew a thing or two about horses. Every single Arabian in the world, not to mention every Thoroughbred, traces its origins to the Orient, to the desert."

"Mais oui," Max said. He seemed genuinely curious. "And are they still breeding them?"

"Oh, yes, and we English are forever trying to buy the good ones." Charles folded up his napkin. "They're highly prized. Marvelous animals. Intelligent. Swift. And sweet as honey. I love them as I would my own children."

Selina looked down at her plate for a split second, visibly shaken by Charles's declaration, and then mopped her brow. Flo wondered if in mentioning children, he had violated an unspoken pact between them, one that provided that only Selina, not Charles, could bring up the subject of offspring and thus of her own barrenness. The Frenchmen hadn't noticed anything amiss.

"Initially the sheiks used them as warhorses—only the mares, mind you." Charles added.

As Max and Charles nattered on, Flaubert's eyes grew heavy. Max continued to pose questions—about prices, training methods, cavalry battles. He had, Flo saw, an innate appetite for learning about things whether or not they directly interested him, while M. Flaubert was easily bored.

The sky had turned a deeper shade of black, pushing the stars forward, like a scene in a stereoscope. The Milky Way might have just been sprinkled there by an invisible hand. She whispered as much to Flaubert. He looked up.

"The backbone of the night, we call it. I've never seen it so clearly," he said dreamily.

On the Nile, the horizon often seemed to disappear, leaving a dome of brilliance above and a reflection of speckled silver swimming unanchored below. It was no wonder, Flo thought, that some civilizations (Hindus? Buddhists? She couldn't recall.) believed the universe was an egg, painted on the inside with the blue sky, pinprick stars, and the golden yolk of the sun.

While the crew cleared away the dinner plates, M. Flaubert pulled out her chair and guided her by the elbow to the side of the boat near the cabins, away from the others. He brought along a shot glass full of Irish whiskey.

They leaned over the rail watching the watery moonlight jiggle along the surface. He excused himself and quickly returned, bearing a bottle of wine and a glass, which he handed her. "For you," he said simply.

"Have you read Baron Bunsen's book on the ancient Egyptians?" she asked. "Or studied the hieroglyphic drawings?" Below them, the Nile lapped at the boat like paint jostling inside a bucket. She drank her wine in a bit of a rush. In another moment she'd feel it in her knees.

"I haven't," he confessed. "Not that one. Though I love to read, to do research." He looked sheepish, as if worried he was not making a good impression. "I have read several of the volumes on Egypt written by Napoleon's savants."

"Then perhaps you already know that according to the Egyptian religion, when God created the world it was made of water, including the celestial heavens." She rested her glass on the gunwale. "Isn't that wonderful, to imagine that the stars are made of water, that everything is?"

He frowned. "I embarked on this trip to escape from that . . . studiousness for a while. Often I used to read and write for fourteen hours a day."

"That's remarkable," she said, fighting the feeling she'd been chastened or, worse, ignored. "Are you studying for one of the professions?"

"I was reading law, but I've decided it's not the best course for me. I've given it up." He took a short gulp of whiskey. "Anyway, I suppose that's the effect of the Nile."

"What is?"

"The belief that the world began as water. Without the Nile there would be no Egypt."

"Oh, yes. *Vraiment.*" Florence was relieved that he didn't think the Nile had caused him to give up the law and that he *had* been listening to her. He simply seemed sad and distracted, forlorn. Perhaps something about the law or his inability to pursue it. Despite the sympathy naturally welling up in her, she probed no further, pursuing instead her subject. "And before the Creator made dry land, he made an orb of fire, the sun, but with the spirit of a living being. That, of course, is Ra."

He topped off her glass. "Yes, Ra was his original name, but he had many names, didn't he?" He carefully set the bottle on the deck. "Amun-Ra and also Ra-Horakaty."

"And Aten-Ra," she added. He really *had* read about the Egyptians. She was again relieved, her enthusiasm sparked. "Bunsen says he absorbed the lesser gods and took their names. But that's the scientific view. I prefer the simple story, don't you? Instead of human beings, God creates this sun who is like a man, but more powerful."

"Look at that!" he cried, pointing to the water, where comets flared and extinguished and flared again. They surfaced briefly, an array of pale green and pink efflorescence. "This I have read about—animals that glow at night in the water."

Together they leaned over the side to watch the underwater fireworks. As if the stars were made of water after all, she thought. The creatures—Fish? Snails? Jellyfish?—swam about like underwater birds in loose flocks, sometimes shooting out of the water in a fountain spout.

Standing at ease alongside him, she felt pleasantly small, as if she might take shelter in his substantial presence, his large, shapely limbs and impressive height. Richard Milnes, the "Poetic Parcel," was more refined, with hands just slightly bigger than a woman's and a head that had always reminded her of a Shetland pony, because it was sweet but too massive for his slight body. M. Flaubert radiated palpable warmth, she noted, like the earthy and amicable body heat that collected in a barn at night. This natural warmth, visible in his flushed cheeks, promised safety, too. But she did not trust it, aware as she was of its origin in her own diminutiveness, which she had battled all her life, frequently wanting to scream *I am not a small person.* If they could see into her mind, into her heart, she was gigantic. But except for the years in Europe in the bloom of her womanhood, she went mostly unnoticed by the world, as befit a person of female sex and stature. If only she had been born a man! Even a short man gained admittance to university, Parliament, the army, medical school. If only, if only—

"I wish to be a writer," Flaubert suddenly said. "I have written a book."

She turned to look him full in the face. "But that is marvelous!" she exclaimed, touching his hand in admiration. "Mmm," she said, drinking more wine. "I seriously considered being a writer, too. My family tells me I write the best letters. But in the end, I need to live a more active life. I feared it would be like looking in a mirror day after day, that eventually I should grow quite sick of portraying myself, in whatever guise." She stopped and caught her breath, appalled at having held forth about herself at such length. A breeze encircled them and departed. "Oh, I must beg your pardon. It was rude of me to go on and on, especially as you are the writer, not I."

"It's quite all right, truly. Many people think of becoming writers. They think writing a book is like reading one." He considered his glass of whiskey, then took another drink.

"No, on the contrary, I know it's hard work, that my hand should always be wrapped around the pen, that I should feel chained to my desk—"

"Exactly!" His eyes rested on her face, then he turned away, apparently gazing at the palm islands in the river. "You are exactly right. It's a monotonous life, almost no life at all. But I like that about it, the devotion, the impracticality of it. It's rather like the religious life in the end."

She felt a further need to explain. "Yes, I can see that. But even if I had the talent, it wouldn't be right for me because there is so much I want to *do,* so much that needs to be done in the world. But there is no profession I admire more than writing." Behind her, she heard the others. They were discussing photographic techniques, the revolution of the camera. Charles called it a "first-rate gadget" and poured another jigger of whiskey for himself and Du Camp.

At least the men had remained with the women after dinner. At home, the females moved in a herd to a parlor to discuss trivialities while the men availed themselves of the chamber pots stowed in the buffet for their exclusive use, and retired to the library to smoke and drink brandy while they discussed the state of the world. How she resented that separation! She turned toward her new companion. "What is the subject of your book?"

He placed his shot glass on the deck, removed a pipe from his pocket, and began tamping tobacco into it, glancing up briefly for her permission to smoke. "I dare not say. You'll think me a boor."

"I promise I won't. Cross my heart." She made the motion.

"It's about goodness and temptation, but mostly about goodness." He struck a match and puffed at the pipe until it caught. "Which is why, my friends tell me, it is perfectly dull and should be fed to the flames."

"So, it is a book of philosophy?" She was amazed that he was a philosopher. The physiognomy was wrong—lips too full, eyes too wide, forehead not deep enough, not enough severity in the features. In sum, the face of a pleasure-seeker.

"No, it's a novel about a saint. That is, apparently, one reason it's so boring. It's called *The Temptation of Saint Anthony*."

"I see," she said, somewhat surprised that the young Frenchman should find the topic of saintliness of burning interest.

"But do *you* think it's boring?" She sipped at her wine.

"I've done a good job describing the temptations, but the saint is too stalwart, he's never truly tempted." He exhaled a plume of smoke over the water. "Maybe I should have chosen to write about an ordinary man." He pointed to Max holding forth at the table. "My friend there says the demons and Satan are more alive than Anthony is. Should I ever publish it, it will make a great hypnotic for insomniacs."

She laughed and raised her wineglass to acknowledge the quip. Out of the corner of her eye she saw Selina observing her, a smile on her face. Dear Selina. Charles and Max had moved on to grander subjects: railways and the industrial revolution. "I have no doubt there will be steamers on the Nile . . . railroads in Lower Egypt, and sooner than you think." Charles's voice was booming, stentorian. Du Camp did not contradict him.

She was not entirely in favor of the industrial revolution, having visited the Arkwright Mills in nearby Cromford, the most modern factory in the world, when she was sixteen. The noise of the spinners had been deafening, the air white with lint that caught in her throat and lungs. A supervisor had cuffed two girls in the spinning room as if it were completely natural. Flo knew that her family owned a share in the mills and in the lead mines near the Hurst, too. It was the ceaseless toil of others, of children, that paid for her fine paisley shawls, leather riding boots, and velvet dresses; for Fanny's endless sets of porcelain and WEN's wall of partridge guns. The village children were sickly; they did not learn to read; they had no time for walks in the woods, no money for a pet pony or even a dog. How could such injustice be God's will?

They had said nothing for a while, she realized, turning to gaze at M. Flaubert. Though he was droll, he still seemed sad. The gloom possessed his entire body. He moved little and only slowly. He seemed to require all his energy simply to converse, though the voice itself gave no hint of misery.

Should she do as she had been taught? Fill the silence, prop him up with encouragements, with flattery, with questions whose answers were already known or easily produced? She was not in the mood. And he seemed so sincere. "And are you writing now?" she asked. "Do you have some project under way?" She sipped more wine. It gave her something to do with her hands.

"Other than a personal journal, no. I am simply living, absorbing the colors of the East. And you, *mademoiselle*? Do you keep a journal and will you write a book of your adventures?"

Was he taunting her? His tone was polite, but his brevity almost dismissive. She fanned the pipe smoke from her face. It would be easy to take umbrage and to reply in cutting kind, but something prevented her. His large round eyes looked too vulnerable to endure the slightest cruelty. "No," she announced. "I have been quite unhappy for a long time and I am trying to find my way clear of it." She would leave it at that. If he answered in kind, fine and well. If not, she had gambled only a sentence, a single shocking disclosure. Dangled it, more accurately, like a worm. Was it flirtation if you admitted to a private weakness?

He stared at her face until she blinked and looked away. "You do not jest, I see." Setting his pipe down, he took her hand. The gesture seemed *forward,* and yet completely without guile or affectation, offered with the certainty that she would naturally grasp his motive.

"I have a tragic flaw, you see," she said.

He gazed at her hand. In the moonlight, her flesh was bluish, bloodless.

"And what is that?" he asked.

Now that she had his full attention, it startled and pleased her, the way his warmth had. She reminded herself that she might never see him again, that they were anchored at a four-thousand-year-old temple whose origins were as perplexing as life itself. "I am ambitious," she began. "I want to change the world, make a mark in it. This is not acceptable. I have a mind and wish to use it, which is considered a great failing in a woman." What had Fanny called her desire to palliate the suffering of others? Unthinkable? Impracticable? "My mother says she can never make peace with my ideas, that they are scandalous."

"Your mother must be a conventional woman," Flaubert said. "Perhaps she is frightened for you and wants to protect you."

"Yes, that's part of it." Flo thought back to an early and especially painful rebuff. "But she doesn't approve of me." She looked him square in the face, her tone rising. "She's never approved of me. She didn't even want me to sing when I was a girl."

"What sort of singing?"

"Opera." Flo thought back to the family's European tour. "I was quite young then, only eighteen, but still, she ruined it for me." She explained that she had discovered the power of music in Genoa. She had had a voice tutor. But it was the performances nearly every evening—chamber orchestras and chorales, violin soloists, concerts by top tenors and sopranos—that had awakened her passion. When she attended her first opera, Donizetti's *Lucrezia Borgia,* she was stricken with opera fever. "Music-mad" Fanny had called her, gleefully at first. "After that, I went to the opera three times a week and practiced my scales devoutly."

"You are a soprano?" He smiled; his eyes widened.

"No, I'm nothing because I don't sing anymore." She continued the story. When her music teacher commented upon the drastic improvement of her voice, Fanny reminded her that divas were *famous,* and therefore unworthy of imitation or adulation. "It isn't respectable, apparently."

Still she had dreamed. And dreamed, allowing herself to pretend that hordes of aficionados might stampede through the doors of the parlor to throw themselves at her feet. Her ridiculous name now made perfect sense: Enter the golden-throated, Italian-born Miss Nightingale! Enter the Bird-Throated Gentlewoman Who Could Not *Help* but Be Called to a Career on the Stage! The English Thrush, the diva, holding forth in a lone spotlight center-stage or dying, tormented, closer to the footlights, in a pall of magenta satin and black lace—

"She forbade you to sing?"

"Indirectly, yes. And I had an unusually persistent sore throat for months that winter." As if, Flo had thought at the time, God Himself disapproved and had sent her one infection after another. "The family moved on to Paris, and Fanny refused to hire any more singing masters."

"That is awful," Flaubert said. *"Je suis desolé."*

"Thank you. Now, of course, I have a different ambition—to be of use in the world. Still, my mother says she will never forgive me if I try it."

He gripped her hand firmly, turned her into the shadow cast by the mast of the dahabiyah, and kissed her on the cheek. "You are . . . an Athena," he said. "Brave and above all, clever and uncompromising."

She was totally taken aback. His eyes were softer now, not with sadness or heat, but with sympathy.

"An idealist," he continued. "Or a rebel. No, a revolutionary." He seemed to be working out the details of her nature, half talking to himself.

"A freak," Florence added, "of nature."

"No, no, you will find your way, I am sure of it. I feel it," he declared, "here in my heart"—he pointed to his chest—"and here." He touched his temple.

"I don't mean to sound ungrateful for your compliments, but you hardly know me. Of course, I hope you are right, but what makes you so certain, M. Flaubert?"

"Please, call me Gustave." He beamed at her.

"All right."

"To answer your question: I trust my judgment, my animal instincts." He smiled again. "Call it intuition."

"Oh, *monsieur*—I mean Gustave—if only you were right! I have been so unhappy." A silence had gathered nearby: the threesome at the table had stopped talking. Had they been listening?

Du Camp was packing up his prints, preparing to depart. A wind snapped at the furled sails; the boat creaked in response. Clouds resembling spindrift materialized, streaking the sky with a frothy layer. The world, for all she knew, *was* made of water. Flaubert let her hand drop, planted his pipe in his mouth, retrieved his whiskey and the wine, and escorted her back to the group.

Selina said, "Our friends are going to Philae, too. We shall have to meet again."

"Indubitably," Du Camp chimed in.

"That would be most pleasant," Florence added, her hand still stung with warmth where *monsieur*—no, Gustave!—had grasped it.

He turned to her. "Perhaps you could help me with the squeezes, if that would interest you."

"I'd be delighted," she said. "I'm sure we could adjust our schedule to accommodate a lesson or two." Hearing this, neither Bracebridge objected.

"Shall we plan to meet in Philae?" he asked.

"That would be grand. The Temple of Isis will be full of inscriptions." She could feel a smile stretching across her face for the first time in weeks.

"Très bien," he said, kissing her hand and clicking his heels.

The men said their farewells, gathered up their packages, and started down the gangway.

"But you never showed us what's in your valise!" Florence called out.

"Squeezes! From Luxor." He turned and shrugged his shoulders. "I'll show them to you next time." Max was already ashore. "I completely forgot."

"Alors, au revoir!" she shouted. She waved with both arms, in case he looked back. She realized she was standing on tiptoes.

A moment later, the clouds began to scud past more quickly. From his stool at the foredeck, the captain ordered the crew to secure the sails and anchor in case of a storm. Charles poured himself a last jigger of whiskey and carried it belowdecks, humming as he went. "Good night, dear ladies," he said, blowing kisses.

"I think he had a very good time with Du Camp," Selina confided, dropping an earring into her hand and unfastening the other. "And you?"

"Very nice. Were you bored to death by the talk of machines?"

"Oh, no, my dear, I enjoyed myself sneaking glimpses at you. The conversation looked quite intense." Selina seemed about to burst with joy and curiosity.

Feeling slightly disloyal for withholding the details, Flo simply kissed her good night. "Very lively indeed," she said.

Belowdecks, she stretched out, still dressed, on her divan, head propped on pillows by the window to breathe the fresh, roiling air. Beside her, Trout snored contentedly.

How strange he was, writing the life of a saint, when most writers were more interested in flaws. Their chat, without preliminaries or artifice, had created a hunger in her. She'd spoken her heart and he'd spoken his, both of them with the candor and intensity of the condemned. Because, yes, she felt condemned to live as either a misfit or a failure. Yet, he hadn't been dismayed by anything she said.

She sat up. She'd prolong the evening on paper, unfolding yet another corner of her soul to him in a letter before she went to sleep. As she reached for her desk, the smell of impending rain gusted through the windows.

8

NOT A WOMAN

Max by his side, Gustave was pleasantly tipsy as he trudged home carrying his portmanteau with the half dozen squeezes he'd intended to show his hosts. No surprise, really, that he hadn't. He hardly took pride in them or considered them relevant to his identity. He *had* shown the English party the ridiculous certificate charging him with authoring agricultural reports. The Bracebridges had pored over it admiringly after the meat course. Written the way a puffer fish would write if it could, he had joked, to their delight, it had the single virtue of making him sound like somebody of importance—just not somebody he would actually wish to be.

On the other hand, he had lied to Miss Nightingale when she asked if he were writing anything at present. *L'Encyclopédie du Con* was proving a marvelous exercise—a treatise on the cunt that would ignite glorious mêlées if it ever saw the light of day. He'd allow no treacly lyricism; neither did purely clinical description appeal to him. Being the son of a surgeon, he'd seen every part of the body on the dissecting table at the Hôtel-Dieu—the unlikely valves and pumps within the fist of the heart, the hinges and sockets of the joints, the fine seams of the skull. He knew that sheaths of muscles overlaid the organs like a divinely stitched corset. The body, even dead, had never frightened him.

In his *fantaisie* on the pussy, images bloomed in his mind, casting a wide net of metaphorical association. Kuchuk Hanem's mons Venus took its rightful place alongside the warm tints of Provençal houses; her shaved labia plumped into sharp focus alongside sand dunes, plucked chickens, and jeweled glue pots. How had he begun his paragraph on the imagined twat of his brother's wife? Yes—"a red light that shines on him the way the sun shines on manure." The writing was not a literal record, but the result of imagination fused with invective and sometimes with love. For surely he had been in love with Louise, hadn't he? He thought back to his second meeting with her. She had worn yellow leather gloves with a single button at the wrist that left a coin of flesh where he had pressed his finger, then his lips. They'd removed to his hotel for a sexual triumph that lasted two days and nights. Yes, hers was next. *Wheat fields after a rain, the open mouth of a chick . . .*

The air had cooled as the moon rose in the sky and the wind picked up. Max, toting his unwieldy photo cases, paused to button up his shirt. They picked their way along the shore beneath escarpments that rose up steeply on either riverbank into a wide canyon. They'd moored the boat last in a fleet of dahabiyahs, as far away from their fellow Europeans as possible. Had it not been for Miss Nightingale and her ridiculous maid, he would never have agreed to such a visit. But he could not refuse her. He always found it difficult to be cruel in person (as opposed to in writing). And Max, he knew, welcomed the chance to socialize. His brilliant friend was a gregarious and polished man who enjoyed small talk even if he sometimes approached people the way a dentist eyed a mouthful of rotten teeth.

"I am forced to admit that they were quite pleasant, as pleasant goes," Max remarked as they emerged from beneath a jutting cliff.

"Yes, they were. But then it isn't hard to be nice if one is wealthy. I think they must be loaded." They passed a dahabiyah almost as impressive as Miss Nightingale's where someone was playing the flute. No, it was a duet. Off-key violin arpeggios reached them on the breeze. The sound was haunting.

"My God, Mozart on the Nile." Max groaned.

"I don't think it's Mozart, Du Camp Aga, though I do detect a melody buried in the whining."

"What did you and Miss Nightingale talk about off to yourselves?"

The music droned on, fainter and more sour as they passed its source. A swampy odor—the Nile at low tide—filled his nostrils. He'd become fond of the sulfurous fug, which smelled like fish and sex. Slowing his pace, he answered, "What did you and the Bracebridges discuss?"

"Well, Charles Bracebridge is no slacker. Reads Latin and Greek, has a villa in Athens, loves Byron—"

"Loves Byron?"

"Apparently. They're both great Hellenophiles."

"One point in their favor, then." He made a mental note to ask Bracebridge about the great poet. "That raises them from the ranks of *épiciers* and drudging professionals, don't you think, effendi?"

The *cange* came into view, its upper half pewter in the moonlight, the lower portion dissolved in the black of the river. The sentry called out something in Arabic and Joseph jumped up, tied a blanket around his naked body, and hailed them. With the sentry's help, he hastily deployed the gangplank.

"They are definitely elites," Max said. "But I reserve judgment on the young miss since you monopolized her completely. Quit stalling and tell me what you and she discussed."

Joseph galloped down the gangway and removed Max's cases to the boat.

"Trouble," Gustave said, stopping just short of the *cange.* "We discovered we are both troubled."

"Sounds like you passed confidences." Max playfully blocked his way onto the boat and leered at him.

"We were just making idle chatter."

"She hasn't got much of a figure, has she?" Max moved aside and they boarded the boat. "Does she even have breasts?"

Max's taunting annoyed him. He suddenly felt protective of Miss Nightingale's breasts, whatever their size, whether bee stings (most likely) or lemons. "She isn't like that. I mean, I don't think of her as a woman." He found it difficult to describe her, nor did he want to. "More a kind of presence."

"What does that mean, a *presence*? You make her sound like a ghost."

They unfolded stools and sat down. "I'm not sure." He lit his pipe. "I said it in jest."

"Jest my eye. You spent most of the evening with the little English flower." Max packed his chibouk and lit it.

"Piss off!" Gustave clapped him on the shoulder. "The truth is I was dreaming of Kuchuk Hanem the whole time. And don't forget, you still owe me a photograph of her."

"The great alma, Kuchuk Hanem." Smoking his chibouk, its stem more than a meter long, Max resembled a long-billed bird. "Would she spread her legs, I wonder, for the camera?"

"She might, if we pay or flatter her enough." With the side trip to Koseir, how many more weeks until they returned to Esneh? Three? Five? He would shower her with gifts. Dates. Ribbons. Henna to decorate her hands and feet and pet sheep. One of his quills? She was illiterate, but might find a sexual use for it. "We should make the picture in her house, not on the boat," he cautioned. "In public, she tries to pass herself off as a schoolmarm."

"Good point." Max yawned, then announced he was retiring. He planned to work the next day. Bidding good night, he descended to his cabin, smoke floating up behind him in a wispy wake.

Gustave expelled a few smoke rings, watching them expand and wobble into nothingness.

He was as surprised by what he had said about Miss Nightingale as Max was. Not a woman! Well, she was certainly not a candidate for a muse or mistress, though he could not help but compare her to Louise, who also had a brain and an education but was devoting her life, it seemed, to the martyrdom of love, sacrificing herself on the altar of his unrequital. In the end, he preferred his prostitutes, who gave a convincing impersonation of undying love and harbored no expectations afterward. Nor any literary ambitions. No, he must never give Louise a foothold again. The gifts he had bought her in Egypt, he decided, were obeisance to past trysts, not an invitation for future ones.

Miss Nightingale, by contrast, was not glamorous or, apparently, amorous. *Earnest* suited her best. Her gaze was sharp as a falcon's, and as unsettling. She burned with utter sincerity; commitment to some ideal steadied her gaze. If she knew how to flirt, she hadn't displayed her talent tonight. But she was kind and sympathetic—her consoling touch on his arm had moved—no—melted him.

He drew one more time on the pipe, then tapped it on the side rail, spilling the embers overboard. Just down the beach, light from a native hut illuminated three camels perched on the sand like unwieldy prehistoric birds. They were tethered to an acacia tree, their slender knobby legs folded beneath them, their long necks tucked against their flanks. He listened to the creaking of the masts and rigging, the soft clatter of the wind in the palm fronds, the lulling slosh of the waves. A bud of joy flowered in his chest.

He was drunk and exhausted. Why, he asked himself, had he offered to teach her about making squeezes when he hated it so?

9

THE WEIGHING OF THE HEART

Flo awakened before dawn and lay abed in the pitch darkness, ruminating. The letter she'd written leaned against the candlestick on the top of the bookcase that served as her nightstand.

But now, not another thought about him! She'd not savor the memory of the evening, but put it aside, like a sweet left on view in a dish both to tantalize and reassure. If she saved the pleasure for later, perhaps, before she knew it, the sweet would multiply into a tray of delicacies, mouthful after melting mouthful she could gorge on. If he answered, or came calling.

She unfastened the tapes of her levinge, removed her sleeping cap, and sat up. She lit a candle stub, then thought better of it, candles being so precious, and reached for the oil lamp stowed on a lower shelf. It gave less light but was steadier, and in its wan aura she donned her brown Hollands and a pair of palm slippers. She slipped the letter into her bodice.

She'd wanted to witness the effect of the sunrise on the façade of the great temple of Abu Simbel every day since they'd arrived. Selina and Charles had spoken of joining her, but after a week it was clear that they were unwilling or unable to risk climbing in the dark. According to Bunsen, dawn was extraordinary, and twice a year the light penetrated to the innermost chambers. During the vernal and autumnal equinoxes? She'd look it up this afternoon. The baron's book was a mass of prose knotty as an oak, thick with awkward phrasing rooted in his German. She'd already compiled revisions for the Murray book; perhaps she'd edit Bunsen, too. Now, though, alone and unescorted (the ball and chain was still slumbering), she exited her room and crept across the deck. She'd be back before she was missed.

The crewmen were asleep, and except for the captain and Paolo, who accorded themselves the privilege of a hammock, were snugged in their niches, the foredeck a lumpy expanse of blanketed bodies. Paolo had ordered them to wear trousers under or over their djellabas—indeed, to sleep in them—making it safe for the women to be among them at odd hours. For a few extra piastres, they'd cheerfully complied.

She stepped up the portable stairs and over the gunwale, then down the flimsy gangway with its rope railings and onto the damp shore. There, she extinguished her lamp and stood in the enthralling darkness. The moon had already set and the sky was the depthless black of tarpaper, a few stars pinning it down like nails. A breeze lifted the down on her arms and neck. She scanned the clock of the sky. Could one predict from the stellar alignment the exact moment the sun would swing from one side of the heavens to the other, like the disk of a celestial pendulum?

The sandy incline between the temples was so familiar she knew her way in the dark, the grains cool over her feet. Halfway up, without alarm, she sank to her knees, turned sideways, and tacked to the crest. There she sat upon the rocky earth, waiting for her eyes to adjust to the darkness so that eventually she could just make out the ragged margin between the trees and sky.

The great rock temple of Ramses II was the most imposing sight she'd seen in her twenty-nine years, no small claim for a woman who'd toured most of the European capitals, crossed the Alps and Apennines, and swooned at her own insignificance from the crags and vales of Scotland. It had even replaced the Sistine Chapel, where only a year before she had lain for hours on the floor beside Mariette, drifting upward to join the muscled bliss on Michelangelo's ceiling.

She expected to observe a different grandeur and wisdom in Egypt. Her heart thudding, she faced west, where the colossi loomed invisibly. Slowly, as though limned with pencil on black paper, the outline of their mountain abode emerged from the dark surround. The cliff turned a metallic gray so transitory and ghostly that the statues seemed only now, after three millennia, to succumb with a last glimmer to their eternal stillness. Then the sun cracked open behind her, a ruddled splinter at the horizon. As the light gained radiance, it reversed the first impression of fading glory to one of impending majesty.

Dawn began to burnish the pairs of disproportionate legs, the hands like flounders in the laps. The ancient stone carvers had rendered the lower half of the seated figures crudely, lavishing their skill and passion on the magnificent heads and headdresses, and particularly upon the pharaoh's visage. That face! Repeated everywhere in Egypt, but nowhere more powerfully, it combined serenity with absolute power. Such calmness of soul moved her to exultation. She could look upon that face every day and never tire of it. Even the head that lay choked in the sand did not detract from the awe. Ramses the Great *was* great. He had ruled for more than sixty years of a golden age. What must it have been like when he passed to the Field of Reeds at ninety-six? Four generations had known no other sovereign. They would have mourned his loss like the death of a god.

The sun crept higher in the sky, transfusing the limestone figures with pink light until they flushed, as if rousing from slumber. The nostrils seemed to flare, the lips to part, the eyes to narrow their gaze, surveying from their fastness the landscape at their feet and every living thing within it. With a flash of pain at her throat, Flo's breath caught, as if commandeered by the reviving Osiridae. And then, in the next instant, the moment of their awakening passed and the day lay before her, the stone figures lifeless, archaic monuments. The mountain erupted with the smells of morning—baking earth, the faint steam of evaporating dew, the tang of insect chitin crushed underfoot.

She studied the figure intaglioed into the rock face above the four colossi. Ramses was making an offering to his namesake, the sun god Ra. Not a sacrificial ram, not gold, silver, or armfuls of lotus flowers; instead, he proffered the small figurine *ma'at,* that symbolized justice. The frieze brought tears to her eyes.

At the smaller temple, too, a wall relief had set her weeping with joy, and she'd returned three times to take notes for letters home. *I never understood the Bible,* she'd written, *until I came to Egypt.* Though less impressive, the small temple echoed and affirmed her deepest beliefs. For there, Ramses was crowned by the good and evil principle on either side. What a modern philosophy! Had any theory of the world gone farther into faith and science than this? For she, too, believed that evil was not the simple opposer of good, but its collaborator, the left hand of God, as the good was His right. *Just like her,* the Egyptians believed that evil was the brother, not the foe, of Osiris, the Lord of the Underworld and Eternal Life, though afterward, according to Bunsen, the Egyptians abandoned this idea and scratched out its nose and eyes in the old carvings. But in Ramses's time, good flowed from evil, and out of evil, good. And in the journey to the afterlife, which mimicked the dying and rising sun and was not so different from the hours before the Resurrection, the petitioner's heart was weighed against a feather in the seventh room of the night. If the scales tipped to either side it was devoured. Evil threatened him at every gate and had to be appeased with charms and spells. Some of them were so poetic that she'd memorized them. *O my heart which I had from my mother! O my heart which I had from my mother! Do not stand up as a witness against me!* As she gazed raptly at the temple façade, she felt again a conviction thrumming in her body—that the world was bound together in an intricate, harmonious web governed by natural laws that men could discover slowly and with great effort. That was God's will—the human revelation of divine order.

She kneeled on a rock, still gazing at the faces of Ramses. Were it not for her ideas about evil, her life would have been so much simpler. She could have converted to the church of Rome, working out her destiny within an order, as a nun. But the Catholics preached that evil was easily identified and routed, when in fact it lay tangled with the good, like the clean and dirty blood in the umbilicus. She couldn't subscribe to such an arbitrary notion. Didn't the unborn child need both to survive until he was delivered, and afterward, wasn't he heir to both? Wasn't he marked like Cain? And blessed like Moses?

With the sun fully risen, she made her way down the long ramp, half stepping, half glissading, enjoying the sudden slips and dips like a child. The sun was already strong on her shoulders, though by the time she reached the shore, some twenty minutes later, a breeze had picked up and herringbone clouds had scudded into place like threads on a giant loom, graying the light to a harsh glare. She reached the boat, climbed aboard, and passed the still-somnolent crew. Their hours had been irregular from the start—often they sailed at 4 A.M.—dependent upon the tides and their employers' whims. Only Paolo, puttering with pots and pans about the stern, acknowledged her with a wave of his hand.

"Buon giorno," she called, waving in return. "May I ask you a favor?"

He put aside the utensils and came toward her, inclining his head as he approached.

She withdrew the letter from her dress. "Could you deliver this to M. Flaubert for me?"

"Now, *signorina*?"

"Yes, please." She inspected the letter one last time. It was perfect, the red sealing wax exactly centered on the envelope flap. She handed it to him. He wiped his hands on his trousers before taking it.

"Right away." He bowed his head again, like a butler or valet. *"Subito."* He gave a little salute and hurried down the gangway. She watched him march briskly up the beach, deftly negotiating the mud from last night's rain as he passed by the small fleet of houseboats, bound for the blue *cange* with the tricolor flag.

10

A VISIT TO THE PATRIARCHS

When he awakened, Gustave remembered Max leaving him to sleep alone during the night—in disgust, because he'd been retching.

He felt nauseated now. And tired. Surely it was still early in the morning, though there was no way to know. In its handsome mahogany case with ormolu fittings, the clock on the shelf had read one-thirty ever since he boarded in Cairo. The Egyptians seemed to regard clocks as decorative rather than functional objects. Or perhaps they thought them European good luck charms. In any case, a timepiece was useless in Upper Egypt. His pocket watch had stopped after the first sandstorm. Though Max had carried his in a double case inside a buttoned pocket, sand grains had jammed the mainspring.

He craned his neck for a view of the sun, but the sky was hazy. It looked the way he felt: shitty and glaringly ragged. Too much of Bracebridge's good Irish whiskey after the dinner wine. At home, his mother would have prepared his father's remedy for mornings after: cognac, fresh milk, a raw egg, and a squirt of lemon juice.

The wind, he noted with distaste, had returned after a day and evening of quietude. Waves raced relentlessly shoreward, repeatedly slapping the sand, like the pounding in his head.

He rose from his bed, fighting the urge to vomit, threw off his gown, donned his hooded djellaba, and pulled on his boots. It was then he noticed Achmet skulking in the doorway, a piece of paper in hand. How long had he been standing there? Surely the man had watched while he slept, drool leaking onto his pillow, afraid to wake him. "Effendi," the servant whispered, his eyes cast down. He handed the paper over, bowed, and disappeared.

Gustave recognized the creamy stationery. Miss Nightingale must have stayed up last night writing. Or perhaps she had gotten an early start. He imagined that she preferred sunrises to sunsets, waking brightly and full of energy.

He stuck his head through the doorway and instructed Achmet to bring coffee and bread. Then he slit the missive with his ivory letter-opener, one of the few vanities he'd brought from home.

> *Cher Monsieur,*
>
> *Nous avons tous tellement apprécié votre visite d'hier soir. Je vous prie de remercier Monsieur Du Camp de notre part—votre ami est un photographe vraiment exceptionnel! Il me ferait plaisir de regarder vos compressions archéologiques. Peut-être pourrais-je même vous aider à les faire.*
>
> *Que dire de l'étrange conversation que nous avons eue? De ma part, je l'ai trouvée extraordinaire. C'était comme si on se connaissait depuis des années déjà. . . .*

The letter continued in a more searching tone:

> *Good and evil are two of the subjects that consume me at present, first, in regard to ancient Egyptian beliefs; second, in what I find contradictory and limiting in the Christian interpretations (especially the Roman Catholic, which you yourself no doubt practice). Finally, as one who wishes to do good in the world but has only managed to suffer ineffectually (and also make others suffer on my behalf), I feel confused as to my future course.*

How shall I accomplish good in the world? I hope you do not think me naive.

Perhaps the freedom of being in an exotic land is what impels me to confess this tempest of ideas to you. If so, I hope you are similarly afflicted with candor and curiosity and will wish to spend time with me discussing these things, especially as you have written an entire book on goodness.

As my friend Selina mentioned, we shall stay on here a few more days, then head for the island of Philae, the "jewel of the Nile." I look forward to meeting you there and learning about your squeezes.

Sincerely, your new friend,
Rossignol

P.S. Please give my warmest regards to Max.

He liked her directness, her apparent lack of embarrassment, her tone, so intimate that had she spoken the words instead of writing them, he might have thought them odd. With sparkling honesty, she had suggested they meet for a theological discussion. As far as she knew, he was a man of similar spiritual inclinations. He smiled at the absurd irony.

Or *was* he? Why *had* a degenerate like him written a book about a saint? He thought of himself as a troublemaker interested only in truth, chiefly ugly truths. He had tackled the subject of goodness not on his own account, but Saint Anthony's. Was it possible he harbored a secret wish to do good, like Miss Nightingale, or at least to understand what goodness was? And if he did, how could he reconcile it with his dissipated ways—his studied crassness, his love of perversity and fascination with prostitutes?

He reread her letter, in case something lay hidden between the lines, but her words were crystalline, unsullied by ulterior motives or mixed intentions. So different from Louise's. Miss Nightingale's missives were clarion calls that invited him to question his soul.

He tucked the letter away and went abovedecks. No one about but Captain Ibrahim, lolling on a palm mat. He peeked in the salon, where Max was still sleeping, then returned to his cabin.

Coffee and bread sat on a bright tin tray, courtesy of Achmet, who preferred to move unnoticed to escape remark or criticism. In Egypt, it was best to be invisible except when summoned, and then, to lavish flattery. Only yesterday, when he asked Aouadallah why he was still standing at attention after a day of brutal work, the poor soul had prostrated himself and mumbled a reply. "He say, effendi," Joseph translated, "that it please him enough to be see by you." There would be no revolutions in Egypt anytime soon.

After he finished the meager meal, he had nothing to do and nowhere he wanted to go. He decided to answer Miss Nightingale and send his reply by courier to her before the day was out. He had something specific he wished to discuss with her, something that would not interest Max, a trip—actually, a pilgrimage—he'd made on his own in Cairo. Who better than Miss Nightingale to confide in?—especially as it pertained to the subject at hand.

My dear Rossignol,

Thank you for your kind letter, which arrived with the speed of lightning. I hope this to you fares as well.

I want to tell you about a marvelous discussion I had in Cairo, partly out of pure curiosity, and partly with the idea of revising my book about Saint Anthony. Since it bears on the idea of good and evil, I think it will be of interest to you, too.

While Max (who has little interest in the Christian faith) was busy photographing the necropolis of the Mamelukes, I took our crewman Hasan with me to visit the Coptic patriarchs at their monastery in Cairo. Hasan is fluent in French and Arabic and, most importantly, Coptic, which is the last remnant of the ancient Egyptian language.

I found the patriarch in an open courtyard, seated on a divan built around a copse of trees. Someone had placed handwritten books with many flourishes and illuminations all about him so that he appeared to ride in a gold and white cloud of paper. Four more of his sect clad in long black pelisses manned each corner of the yard.

Hasan introduced me as a Frank traveling the world in search of wisdom and religious truth. Long and flowery salutations followed. "May you prosper forever, my sweet lord, and find happiness in all your days and God grant that you return home safe and happy to your family"—this bestowed on me simply for saying my name!

The bishop greeted me courteously and offered many kindnesses. Out came the little cups of strong sugared coffee, the heavy pastries and gelatinous Turkish Delight—cubes of fruit essence dusted with sugar. A fellow approached from the shadows tricked out with a strange contraption that I initially thought was a bagpipe, for I saw a lumpen shape slung over his shoulder and a metallic mouthpiece in front. He turned out to be carrying hot tea in a goatskin, which he poured from a brass spout by leaning forward. Little glasses were stowed in a separate sack under his arm. After he had served us, he wandered off, chanting, "Chai, chai!"

I posed questions about the Trinity (how three gods could be one); about the Virgin; the Gospels; the Eucharist; and the Resurrection. All the erudition I had acquired for Saint Anthony came flooding back. The four robed figures joined us. They, too, were theologians, in the tradition of catechisticals (the Copts invented the catechistic method), and took stools around the patriarch while I sat cross-legged at his feet on the ground. I took notes while Hasan translated. The bishop was ruminative in his answers, thinking with his head down, as if consulting his great, shapeless beard. When the old fellow tired, one of the spirited younger cohorts took over until everyone was quite exhausted. In all, I spent three hours with the Copts, and hope to go back upon my return to Cairo for another session, maybe to talk to the Armenians as well.

As you must know, the Coptic religion is the oldest of all the Christian sects. They are descended from the ancient Egyptians, but have always been Christian and are highly respected here despite being a tiny minority. While Max and I were first in Cairo last December, we spent many hours tutored in Islam, learning about circumcision, Ramadan (their Easter), the veil, the Prophet, his family, and the dietary laws. We learned more about Islam than I yet know about the Copts.

The Coptic bible is surely closer to what Saint Anthony would have known than the version put forth later by the Roman Catholic Church. He himself was a Coptic Christian and the first monk. He invented the anchorite life.

The most significant theological difference between the Copts and Rome is this: they reject the idea that Jesus was human. This affects their notions of good and evil. They believe that He had only a divine nature, so was not a man at all. If Jesus was not capable of sin, it follows that man is not capable of godliness. This interests me because Saint Anthony was a man who suffered temptation his entire life and was never rid of sin—so not a saint in the way we understand today. He did nothing but live alone in the desert and battle his demons. No healing, no miracles, just the unending struggle to be a human without sin, which is impossible. But if, as the Copts believe, we are born evil and can't achieve goodness, why would he even have tried?

I've been wondering if I may address you as "Rossignol," or "Florence." (I prefer the former.) I heard Mrs. Bracebridge call you "Flo," but perhaps that is reserved for family and the closest of friends; perhaps it would be too intime*. Since we have revealed our failings to each other, might we* se tutoyer*? Would that offend you? We are far from our respective countries in a land where the formalities are largely irrelevant, in my humble opinion.*

Have you noticed that on the Nile almost everyone has but one name? On the cange*, only Rais Ibrahim has a family name, which is Farghali. At first I thought "rais" was his given name and Ibrahim his family name, but "rais" simply means "captain,"* *which you probably know, having your own "rais" on the dahabiyah. Perhaps the Egyptians fancy themselves one big family. I think this lack of a second name serves to keep them in their place and powerless. But enough digression. (For I am in a mood to write tomes to you!)*

Will you let me know that this has arrived, my dear songbird? I should be happy to have your help in making squeezes.

Your friend,
Gustave

11

FRIGHTFUL ROW WITH TROUT

Flo felt lighter than air when she returned to the cabin after her predawn visit to the temple. Trout lay with her face pressed into her pillow. Flo decided not to wake her yet.

Bending to a low cabinet, she retrieved a battered black wooden box. Dear medicine chest, friend since she was seventeen. A carpenter in Wellow had built it to her design. She grasped the brass handle. Affixed on a piano hinge, the lid folded back to make a walled gallery.

Her hands reached toward the contents, fluttering over them like a hummingbird in a sea of blossoms. Arranging her kit was the closest thing to play since childhood. She enjoyed it the way other women took pleasure organizing their jewelry, folding their shawls and pelerines, organizing toiletries on the bureau top. Pride of ownership, the glass and steel in her hands, the orderliness—all were deeply gratifying.

On the top tier in compartments lay salves and implements: tar and camphor ointment, mint liniment, balm of arnica, scissors, golden-eyed straight and curved sailmakers' needles, and last, wrapped in a green velvet square, three surgical needles along with silk thread for sewing up wounds. Satisfied with the inventory, she proceeded to the drawers. Here were metal tubes of smelling salts as well as the boxed set of perfumes she'd bought as souvenirs in Italy the year before, four diminutive glass bottles: orange-blossom from Spain; attar of roses from Smyrna; French lavender; and her favorite, frangipani, from India. She never *wore* perfume. In warm weather it attracted bees, and in winter overpowered the shuttered rooms. Also, she did not wish to advertise herself. But in the bedroom at home, with only Parthe to see, she sniffed it, or daubed it on the hem of her pillowcase, added a drop to the washbasin.

She'd longed to ease suffering for as long as she could remember. At first it was childish play. Then, when she was eleven years old, the sheepdog, Cap, had broken his leg. The shepherd—grizzled old Stennis, was it?—had come to the house to ask for a gun and a single bullet to put the dog away. Flo had interceded. "Let me set the leg," she had begged WEN, tearful. She remembered the burning in her face and neck, how she had felt she might die, too, if they shot the whimpering animal. She'd watched the doctor set broken bones in the village, but she'd only set the cloth limbs of Parthe's dolls. WEN had yielded and Flo had splinted Cap's paw, wrapped it up with clean rags, and covered the whole with an old stocking doused with oil of peppercorns to discourage chewing. She fixed him a bed in the kitchen and brought him milksops and scraps. The dog had recovered.

Since then, her doctoring had grown more sophisticated. In Italy and Egypt she applied leeches to Charles, poultices to both Bracebridges, and cured the servants of stomachaches, headaches, sunstroke, and housemaid's knee. She was familiar with the standard remedies, compelled, as a youngster, to memorize what she overheard when the doctor came around. *James compound: 16 grains for an old woman, 11 for a young woman, 6 for a child.* Homeopathic curatives in tiny glass bulbs stoppered with rubber filled the second drawer of her kit. So little was needed to ameliorate a host of conditions, everything from bad appetite to scurvy. She had the country remedies by heart: Saint John's wort for melancholy, chamomile for nervous agitation, witch hazel for rashes, cider vinegar for bowel distress. They lived in her mind, along with favorite poems and hymns, things that required no effort to memorize because she loved knowing them; they'd become a part of her, and only death would take them from her. What was that Egyptian spell? *I am the woman who lightens darkness and look, it is bright! I have felled the evil spirit, I have—*

A loud thump followed by a shout: Trout lay sprawled on the floor between the two beds, just in front of Flo's feet. Twisted up in her levinge, she thrashed like a butterfly struggling to break out of its cocoon. Flo kneeled at her side. "Are you hurt, Trout?"

"What a question! You have eyes."

A flicker of rage licked at Flo's heart. "Let me help you up." How dare Trout speak to her in such a fashion! She took a deep breath. She would counter with kindness. "You must have fallen in your sleep." She picked gingerly at the tangled net of the levinge. Lately, their roles had reversed.

"I can manage on my own." Trout ripped the netting of the levinge loose from the ceiling, wadded it up, and tossed it to one side.

The violence of the gesture offended Flo. She stood and backed away, fury rising once more in her craw. She fantasized sailing off in the dahabiyah without Trout, leaving the sourpuss asleep over her needlework at the temple. She'd send a punt when they reached Philae, then book passage for Trout to England, meanwhile writing Fanny to dismiss her. But what would Fanny do? Likely berate Flo for ineptitude, maybe take Trout's side. Either way, she'd never let the matter alone. It would join the collection of distortions that passed for Nightingale mythology, already chock full of Flo's worst moments in the bosom of her family reduced to epithets. Homeric ones, now that she thought about it. But nothing beautiful, like *wine-dark sea* or *rosy-fingered dawn*. Not flattering, like *swift-footed Achilles* and *owl-eyed Athena*. No. It was *Flo of the terrible table manners, Flo the queen of melancholy*. And now, *Flo flummoxed by a servant* and *Flo who lost herself on the Nile*. Feeling the ire coloring her neck, she said, "I think it would behoove us to talk about our present situation."

Trout had managed to gather herself together on the edge of the divan. Her face was the red of uncooked mutton; she kneaded her skull absently. "Hmph," she muttered.

"I beg your pardon. Did you speak?"

"What's the use, mum? I wish I'd never come here. If it was up to me, I'd of stayed home where I belong."

Flo heard desperation in Trout's words. Her heart softened a bit. "I didn't know. I'm sorry." She wondered if Fanny had been aware of Trout's reluctance. "Did you tell my mother?"

Trout lowered her gaze. "That's a purely ridiculous question."

"You didn't?"

"Oh, no, mum, I did." Trout stood, turned her back to Flo, and changed into an old shift. "There was no one else, Mariette being indisposed and the other girls inexperienced. Besides, Mrs. Nightingale told me this place was—how did she put it?—a jewel, mum." She sat back down on the bed. "Perfumy and busting with Turkey carpets and velvet drapes. And the creatures, she said, would be straight from the London Zoo. Camels and lions and zebras."

Since Fanny had never set foot in Egypt, it was hard to know if she believed what she had told Trout or was simply inventing enticements. "I'm truly sorry for my mother's inaccuracies," Flo said, hoping that a ready apology would placate Trout and feeling, too, that she should not be held responsible for Fanny's half-truths. "I must say that explains things to a degree." There, she had kept her head and responded kindly. "I didn't know you felt that way."

"You don't know much about me, mum, truth be told."

Flo was at a loss, pulled one moment to sympathy, the next to anger. "But we are here now, and you have a job to do as do I, dear Trout."

Trout rolled up a stocking and plunged her foot into it. "No need to dearie me." She smoothed the stocking on her leg. "You don't even rightly know my name, I'd wager."

Flo was beside herself. She was trying to be accommodating and getting nowhere. They had always called her Trout. The image of a fish no longer entered her mind, though at first it always had—a sleek fish sporting a rainbow and a silky black fin. "Of course I know your name." She reached across the divide between the two divans and patted Trout's hand. "It's Troutwine. How could you think you could be in my employ without—"

"I mean my given name, not my family name."

Flo froze. Who was this impossible person who caused her to feel abashed and ashamed when she had done nothing wrong? Whatever else she was, Trout was not forgiving, she saw that now. She seemed bent on asserting her malcontent and forcing Flo to acknowledge it.

She had never heard anyone, not even other servants, call Trout anything else. The Nightingales did not make a habit of renaming their servants, unlike many of their acquaintances. Fanny considered it demeaning and bad for morale to dub a girl "Mary" or "Jane" simply because it was easier. Perhaps Trout's name was a sore subject with her because in a previous household she'd refused to answer to a fake name, insisting on her real one. Florence was horrified to realize that she had no earthly idea what Trout's name might be. Nor had she seen any of Trout's travel documents. Charles took charge of all that. "What is it, then?" she asked timidly. Tears of frustration welled in her eyes.

"Christa," Trout said, looking up.

"Christa," Flo repeated, leaning against the wall of the dahabiyah. How fitting that her servant bear the feminized name of her Lord, as if the woman were yet another obstacle in her path to discover God's plans for her. She looked into Trout's eyes still puffy from sleep. "May I call you Christa then?"

Trout blew her nose into her handkerchief and tucked a strand of hair behind her ear while she considered. Her dress drooped off one blotchy shoulder. "No, I prefer Trout, mum. Only my family, whatever's left of them, called me Christa."

In the small cabin, Flo felt trapped. Trout would concede nothing for the sake of her feelings. The orderly surface between them had ruptured, and Trout did not wish it repaired. "All right then, Trout, it's time to get up. I'll have my cotton day dress. You may begin with my hair."

Flo took her place on the carpet-covered stool. In a moment,

Trout rose and picked up the hairbrush. Flo felt her fingers moving roughly against her scalp. At first, the brushing was too vigorous, but soon enough, the strokes softened, the touch of the hands lightened. Trout would go no further for the time being. Flo relaxed into the pleasure of her morning coiffure.

At eight o'clock, when Flo went on deck, the Bracebridges had not yet appeared. The crew was engaged in cooking and cleaning the boat when the muezzin's call to prayer rang out from the shore. *Allahu akbar, Allahu akbar!*—God is great, God is great!—the voice plaintive and piercing, an imprecation edged with dolor. The crew stopped what they were about, washed with a bucket of river water, and pulling prayer mats from every crack and crevice, dropped to their hands and knees, facing east. Flo watched the familiar sight of their rumps rising as their heads grazed the floor in the required humility. Up and down they bobbed for several minutes before returning to their chores. What, she wondered, if Englishwomen and -men prayed with their bums to the sky? Women with hooped skirts might be stranded and scandalous, unable to right themselves, rolling in circles like enormous tops.

A crewman crept toward her with an envelope in hand. She thanked him and smiled. He was the man she called Efreet-Youssef, to distinguish him from the other Youssefs among the crew. Why did the Egyptians use the same few names repeatedly? He had been her efreet weeks before in Cairo. In the narrow city streets, he had run in front, holding the halter of the ass on which she rode bouncing up and down as the tiny burro hurtled forward. Otherwise, Paolo had explained, the animal would bolt for his stall or the nearest shade.

Turning the letter over, she felt a pang of disappointment: it was not from Gustave but from Max, a note of thanks for the dinner party. Rather effusive, she thought. Except for the last lines, where he spelled out their itinerary. They'd remain another week at Abu Simbel, photographing and collecting squeezes. Next, as he'd mentioned at dinner, would be Philae. After that, they planned an extra excursion—overland from Kenneh to Koseir on the Red Sea. Then, north again, toward Cairo. He closed with polite regards.

Flo consulted the foldout map in *Murray*. Kenneh lay just north of Karnak and Thebes, where the river jigged to the east, forming an elbow that poked into the eastern Sahara.

How she envied the Frenchmen! They would gallop horses or lope on camels in a caravan, and visit the Red Sea. Who knew what adventures might lie in wait for them in the desert?

With their frail constitutions, the Bracebridges weren't up to an overland trip. It was a wonder they managed any travel. For a good part of every journey, they remained indoors, reading esoteric books, writing letters, and resting—resting hour upon hour. Charles's big, whiskered face beneath the London papers as he dozed on one foreign sofa after another, Selina napping away the afternoons in bed, always in a dress, her hair loose on the pillow like sunrays. And her face, which Flo loved in all its idiosyncrasy, plump and pink, the features clustered too closely together in the center, as if they had stopped growing before the rest of her. The face of a happy child.

Now Selina appeared, slightly dazed, holding and reading a book in one hand as she climbed the steps from her cabin, her skirts swept up in the other hand. As she stepped into a patch of sunshine, she looked up. "Darling Flo," she called in her light soprano. Her face broke into a smile and she closed her book on its scarlet satin page-marker. Charles, she said, was having a tray belowdecks, something about a scrabbling sensation in his chest. They decided to breakfast together.

They ordered eggs and tea while a sailor laid the table, bowing and offering guttural sounds of apology as he whisked between their chairs. The teapot arrived first, aswim with loose pekoe leaves. Efreet-Youssef offered a cinnamon stick, but the women politely refused it. He returned to the brazier on the bow.

"I've been wanting to talk to you," Flo said.

"And I, you," said Selina. Selina was never without her fan, and now she wagged it slowly, like a dog's tail in greeting. "If we don't talk, whatever we've done or seen doesn't seem quite complete. I always need my Florence addendum." Selina raised one eyebrow, anticipating. "Is it about last night, the Frenchman?"

"I do want to talk about that. But no"—Flo smiled shyly—"I've been wanting to ask you why it is you decided to travel without a maid. You had one in Rome. You don't mind the question, do you?"

"Why would I mind? I have no secrets from you, and in any case, there's no secret involved. I didn't bring a maid because I have Charles and you, and I am more comfortable in close quarters doing things for myself. Our lodgings in Rome were spacious, but here . . ." Selina hugged herself tightly.

"Who fixes your hair, then? Charles?" Flo's chair scrooped as she dragged it into the shade of the reed awning.

Efreet-Youssef served the eggs, a bowl of olives, and a plate of cheese, then retreated backward, bowing, the same way Florence had left the queen's presence when presented at court. Despite his desire to be invisible, Flo could smell an oily aroma whenever Efreet-Youssef approached. Hair pomade, she supposed. He was clean. After he scrubbed the pots and dishes with sand, he rubbed it on himself before jumping into the river.

"Charles do my hair? That would be a sorry sight!" Selina tapped at her boiled egg. They always ordered three-minute eggs, but as the crew didn't have a timepiece, they never came right. "I do my own coif, can't you tell?" Selina turned her head from side to side. "A simple chignon, nothing more ambitious. Why do you ask?" Selina cinched up her mouth around a spoonful of eggs.

"I'm having problems with Trout." Three weeks earlier, Flo had recounted Trout's hypochondriasis to Selina and they'd joked about it. Later, when Trout took ill with a pounding headache as they sailed south from Derr, Flo had doctored her and the tension between them had dissipated for a time. Trout had thanked Flo for her ministrations. Flo explained now what had happened that morning, how humiliated she had been when challenged about her servant's name. "She resents me, I'm afraid, and nothing I do reaches her, nothing pleases her."

"Goodness!" Selina said. "I've never had a servant challenge me, though one reads about it in Mr. Dickens and in the papers. There have been cases of forged characters, theft—"

"Trout had excellent characters, one of them from the husband of a woman she cared for while the poor thing was dying." Flo sighed. "I think she despises me."

"Nonsense. You are one of the kindest people on the face of the earth. I'm sure it will pass. And remember: she is a servant. The point is whether you are satisfied with her, not she you." Selina frowned. "You haven't touched your food."

"I'm not hungry."

Selina blotted her lips with a square of cotton damask. "Try some anyway. Perhaps appetite will follow."

Flo obeyed, spooning egg onto a crust, sipping at her tea. "What would you do?"

"Continue as usual. Ignore the ups and downs."

"She hates it here. Did I say that already?" Flo slumped back in her chair.

"Would you like me to speak to her?"

Flo didn't have to think twice. "No, then she'll think I'm weak of will. No, I'll speak to her." But Flo knew she wouldn't, as she had no inkling of what to say. She'd simply wait. The situation might improve on its own. If not, she'd reason her way through to a solution and when she hit upon the answer, inform Trout as kindly as possible.

"Don't let it upset you. Trout will come around to remembering her place." Selina gulped some tea and set her cup down, ringing, on the saucer. "May I change the subject?"

Flo nodded, her face brightening.

Selina plied her with questions about the dinner party and the Frenchman. Flo admitted gladly that she was intrigued by M. Flaubert and felt a strange kinship with him. She did not mention that she had written to him. The omission would spare Selina, who would fret if he did not reply.

"Did you ask if he knew Mary Clarke?"

It hadn't occurred to Flo to ask Gustave if he knew her. "He doesn't live in Paris," she explained. "He's from Rouen." She handed her dirty dish to the servant. "Dear Clarkey," Flo said with a sigh, the warmth of recollected affection radiating throughout her chest. Both she and Selina had the highest opinion of Mary and considered her the ultimate authority in matters of taste. Flo's reverence for Mary's wisdom in affairs of the heart was unmitigated, zealous. For here was a courageous woman with an entirely original way of living, a woman who had suffered the loss three years earlier of her great amour, Claude Fauriel, and *did not let it ruin her life*.

Flo laughed suddenly. "Did I ever tell you what happened when I came home after first meeting her? I must have."

Selina hesitated, thinking. "I'm not sure."

"About my plans for Embley Park?" She pictured the Gothic manse with its steep gables and rows of mullioned windows. WEN had built it for Fanny in Hampshire, conveniently close to the London social scene.

Selina leaned forward. "No, I don't think so."

Flo smiled, remembering herself at age nineteen. "It was quite outrageous now I recall it. No wonder Fanny was beside herself."

"Oh, do tell now." Selina's fan had stopped moving.

Flo explained that the first thought that crossed her mind when she returned home from Paris after meeting Mary was to convert Embley into a boardinghouse for intellectuals and musicians. Men and women, living communally, would maintain stimulating friendships as equals, enjoying solitude in their rooms, and fellowship at meals and in the evenings. No one would marry, except to have children. "I wished to live as Clarkey did, don't you see, in a scintillating salon."

"I'm sure that Clarkey would find Mr. Flaubert suitable for her salon," Selina said. "So tall, such a warm and welcoming manner. I had the sense he was an independent spirit. And isn't M. Du Camp a delight with the camera?"

Though Flo loved modern inventions and all things scientific, she hadn't paid much heed to the pictures. She was drawn more to Gustave's brown-green eyes, which bulged slightly in their sockets like marbles. "I am more interested in the squeezes," she said, thinking his heavy eyelids gave Gustave a drowsy and somewhat dissolute expression. "M. Flaubert"—she smiled at Selina as she folded up her napkin—"actually, we are on a first-name basis."

"You *do* like him, don't you?" Selina smiled and blinked.

Flo felt her cheeks redden. "He seems good-natured, and he is intelligent. I hardly know him, but I *do,* I like him." She drank some tea. What had drawn her to him most was his artistic refinement coupled with his frankness. "He's been unhappy, too," she said quietly, "like me."

"He" had referred to Richard Milnes for so long that his face suddenly popped into her mind. She'd loved Richard's company—just not enough to marry him. They had talked and talked, a constant chatter like lovebirds, but never about sadness. She'd never felt the impulse simply to gaze at his face the way she had wanted to gaze at Gustave's. No one knew how much it had pained her to refuse Richard, or that she'd made a vow to herself afterward in *Lavie: Now no more love, no more marriage. Only work, whatever it may be.*

"I see," Selina said. "Unhappiness." She wiped her hands with her napkin. "There would be plenty to talk about if one were honest." Selina smiled at her, opened her book to the satin marker, and began to read.

Flo remembered vividly the first time she met Mary. She was eighteen, and nearing the end of the two-year-long Grand Tour with her family during which, to Fanny's delight and surprise, Flo had attracted the attention of eligible males from eighteen to eighty throughout Europe. The Nightingales had been in Paris about a week when Fanny left her calling card and a letter of introduction at the Clarkes'. The next morning she had received by first post a charming note on green linen paper inviting the Nightingales to a soiree that evening. "And when I read that word 'soiree,' I imagined we should have a *very* good time," Fanny said, picking her way toward the coach in front of their apartment as they set off for the party. "The young Miss Clarke is quite the *salonnière*. Seems she has taken over Madame Récamier's circle with her blessing."

"Who?" Parthe asked.

"The most famous hostess in Paris," Flo said crisply.

"Well, I don't care," Parthe cheerfully announced, pulling her skirts closer to make room for her sister on the leather seat. Up in the driver's box, the coachman shouted, and with a crack of his whip, the cab lurched forward.

At four-thirty, darkness was descending upon the city, accumulating in alleys and passageways like indigo dispersing in a dye vat. Lamplighters had begun their slow inroads, attending first to the bridges, while in the imposing *hôtels particuliers* along the boulevards, yellow oblongs of candlelit rooms hung in the darkening air like perfectly taut strings of paper lanterns.

After Italy, Flo had felt fed up and bored. What she missed most was music, especially since Fanny had canceled her singing lessons. In Paris there was only one weekly opera performance. Luckily, Flo had annotated all the librettos from Genoa, including observations on the costumes and singers, which enabled her to occupy herself reliving the performances. Parthe had imitated her sister, matching her swoon for swoon, sigh for sigh at concerts. But it was Flo whom Fanny chastised, Flo whom Fanny worried about. Why, she had asked only the day before, must Flo continue to take things to extremes? Flo did not care to answer. She had thrown back her head and stomped from the room.

"Here we are," Fanny said, pulling Flo from her daydream. The liveried footman alighted from his niche, opened the door, and spread a rug upon the ground. Fanny exited first, taking care over the narrow wooden step.

The ladies Clarke occupied the third and fourth floors of an imposing house on the rue du Bac, from which sounds of merriment drifted down to the front stoop. The three Nightingale women smiled at each other in anticipation. They had barely knocked on the door when a maid appeared and led them, skirts clutched in their fists, up three flights of marble stairs. At the landing, the maid opened the door to number 7, then padded away without a word.

They gathered at the threshold like three hens staring into a new coop, caught between pecks and clucks. The sounds of mirth had subsided, and they waited. When no one appeared, Fanny withdrew an ivory fan, snapped it open, and stepped into the room. They removed their coats, laying them across a wooden bench, and ventured farther into the foyer. The air was warm, scented with spiced apples and ripe cheese.

Hesitantly, they stepped into the adjoining room, a small salon sparely furnished with sofas, drapes, and easy chairs in various shades of pink velvet. Overall, the room gave the impression of a soft hand extended in welcome. In the corner sat an elderly woman in a gray satin gown with spectacles and a white mobcap. Engrossed in her book, she'd clearly not heard them. Not one to stand on ceremony, Florence approached her. *"Bon soir,"* she said.

Just then, three children raced across the room, a blindfolded woman lunging after them. The children skittered out of the way, then flew, shrieking, into the hallway, sideswiping Fanny and Parthe as if they were pieces of furniture. The woman's hands seized Flo's blue silk skirt. *"Maman, c'est toi?"* she called out. *"Oh, pardon!"* She untied the towel around her eyes.

Florence laughed. "*Non, pardonnez*-moi!"

At which the senior Mrs. Clarke looked up from her book.

Into the gaping silence that naturally follows chaos, everyone spoke at once, then fell silent, and then laughed.

The woman with the blindfold was the daughter, Miss Mary Clarke. Florence was amazed that this slight woman dressed in a casual wrapper should be the great *salonnière*. Her reddish hair, not conventionally dressed by any measure, lay in soft, loose curls around her face, more like the fuzzy aura of a sheepdog than Parisian coiffure. She was short, with soft hazel eyes and pale, lightly freckled skin.

With almost no bosom and tiny hands, she appeared elfin. This was a children's party, she explained, one she gave every Saturday evening for the offspring of friends and neighbors. Children, too, needed a regular social life, she believed, to be fully civilized.

Flo was constantly surprised in the hours that followed. Surprised that they had been invited to a children's party, since they had no children in their entourage. (Would Fanny feel insulted?) Surprised by the casual food and its service—butter cake, popcorn, cream puffs, and bonbons laid out à la russe on a wine-tasting table. Surprised, too, by the children. First, that they were permitted the run of the two-story flat. Throughout the evening, they galloped rambunctiously upstairs, and several times swooped back through the adults, rowdy as geese. Second, that they were not dressed like children, but rather as miniature adults—the boys in long trousers and frock coats, the girls in tea gowns like their mothers'.

In fact, every room chez Clarke contained some surprise or other. In the kitchen, two famous men were fussing with a tea kettle. Miss Clarke introduced them as her best friends in the world. They were the Orientalist Julius Mohl, and Claude Fauriel, a scholar of Provençal poetry, which he recited from memory whenever Miss Clarke wished. Flo had never known an unmarried woman whose best friends were men. Miss Clarke was by now in her thirties and seemed to have dispensed with chaperones altogether. By comparison, Flo existed in a cloister.

Finally, there was the perpetual surprise of "Clarkey" herself, a woman without a shred of pretension, and surely the most extraordinary person Flo had ever encountered. It was impossible not to love her. She did nothing to conceal her emotions, was kind to everyone, and encouraged memorable friendships among those who frequented her salon. Indeed, her enthusiasm and easygoing nature were contagious. Having spent the early part of her life figuring out how to live, she told Florence, she was now completely unfettered by social convention. Yet, her reputation remained impeccable.

While the children and the two distinguished scholars resumed the game of Blindman's Buff, Mary consulted with the cook and introduced the Nightingales to three scowling fur puffs sitting on the windowsills. Her Persian cats. Miss Clarke was, in fact, besotted with cats of every description. Over the years that followed, kittens would travel back and forth between Embley Park and Paris, some more cooperatively than others.

"She is the perfect candidate for a friend," Fanny said on the way home that first evening. "We'll have to see her whenever we go to Paris, and *she* can visit us when she comes to see her sister at Cold Overton!"

Flo had never heard her mother so enthusiastic about another woman. Though by Fanny's standards Miss Clarke was a maverick, her salon attracted the best minds of Europe: Tocqueville, Victor Hugo, Stendhal, Madame de Staël. No doubt, Fanny hoped to find husbands for her daughters there.

Flo had spent most of that winter at Clarkey's, equally charmed by Messrs. Mohl and Fauriel, who, having discovered the depth of her education, undertook lively exchanges with her. Being at Mary's was like being back in Father's library, a place where Flo did not have to demur, where she could express her opinions and display her intellect rather than hide it.

It was Clarkey's idea of *amitié amoureuse*—chaste love—that made her friendships with men possible, she explained to Flo that year. There was no earthly reason, Clarkey argued, why men and women could not be loving friends rather than succumb to marriage, with its insuperable desolations and duties. Clarkey was not opposed to marriage so much as beyond it. She was madly in love with Claude Fauriel, with whom she'd spent every evening for the past eleven years. Still, she did not intend to marry him or anyone else. She encouraged Flo to pursue her interests and, like Mary, avoid the matrimonial bed. It felt to Flo as if a strong-willed woman from the George Sand novels she relished had come to life and befriended her.

• • •

Just before Flo left for the day's excursion, Joseph brought her a second letter. She was in a rush, but went below and read it quickly, delighted by the speed of Gustave's reply, and by his warmth, which seemed to transfer directly from the paper. His observations about the Copts were provocative and new, especially their view of Jesus as purely a god, not a man. Since the Copts were the direct descendants of the ancient Egyptians, she wondered if the idea of a divine man derived from the worship of pharaohs like Ramses the Great.

She tucked the letter inside her diary. Not surprisingly, Selina did not inquire about details when Flo reported that he had written and all was well.

Flo drifted the rest of the day, revisiting the temples while Selina sketched them from different vantages. Selina excelled with a pencil and watercolors, capturing the essence of things with a few assured strokes, conveying bulk and gravity as surely as if her paper bulged with sand and granite where her marks divided the dun surface. Flo had no talent for art.

But she *did* have talents, she reminded herself, just not ordinary ones. Her big ideas and flair for organization were unseemly, especially coming from a woman—which was why the future loomed not like a sunny path but a brick wall. What *could* she do with her life? Continue teaching the boys at the Ragged School when she returned home? Or would Fanny deny her that, too? Once, she had brought to Embley three boys with grimy hands and knickers—sniveling boys with chopped hair and nostrils rimmed in black who shrieked and stampeded up the stairs to her room, where she read to them. Fanny had reacted as though intruders had absconded with the silver plate and Limoges. Later, she'd sent the upstairs maid to scrub the woodwork and furniture, as if poverty were a contagious disease. How could her younger daughter, she demanded at dinner, bring rabble into their home? Home being the sanctum sanctorum to Fanny, more venerated than a cathedral. WEN had laughed off the shouting, as if they were in a cartoon out of *Punch.* He refused to take sides, saying he could not abide displays of temper. He hated it when the servants had to fix their eyes on the floorboards. He had retreated to the library, after which Parthe promptly swooned in the parlor, claiming a headache. Fanny's furor had lasted for two full days, doubled, she claimed, by her daughters, the one inexplicably delicate, the other incorrigibly stubborn.

They sailed for Philae midweek, catching a fair wind. Flo relaxed. She sat on deck and watched the verdant border on either side reappear as narrow fields of corn and barley waving in sinuous patterns. The Nubian Desert carpeted the high cliffs with sand on either side, the river threading between them like a winding column of mercury. After the halting upriver sail, the boat skimmed the water, pulled powerfully along by the current's twisting green ropes. Against the rocky banks, the river flung airborne sprays of lace, while the damp sails drying in the sunny air smelled fresh and bright as a laundry line. Sometimes the wind and current were so strong, the crew had to furl them.

The second day, spotting sand spilling from the heights in golden waterfalls, they weighed anchor so that she and Selina—Trout wasn't interested—could feel the dry droplets sift through their fingers. They climbed up the cliff on a goat path. The unceasing wind had swept the desert plateau into a thicker version of the river, its currents frozen in great furrows and dips, a swirled sea of figured ridges stretching to the horizon.

When they set sail from Abu Simbel, the Frenchmen were still moored at the small temple. There were no farewells and no more chance encounters, no more letters or notes. She had decided it was best—more dignified and less chancy—not to write again, to wait for the reunion in Philae. Besides, she liked his letter about the patriarchs so much that she could not imagine he would ever write her a better one. She set aside her hope, locked into a compartment in her mind. She did not reread his letter after the day it arrived, when she had read it four times. Though its existence was a small comfort, she was cautious not to daydream about him. She did not want to risk disappointment. Besides, what would she dream? Surely not of marriage or a tryst. All she knew was that she wanted to be standing alongside him again, chatting and joking.

She distracted herself with the extensive library she'd brought to Egypt, her beloved dead languages—Latin, Greek, and now Hebrew, which she was teaching herself so she could read the Old Testament in the original. Dead languages were comforting: because they never altered, you could master them completely. Since they were no longer spoken, they were not part of the social fabric that so chafed her, not part of the insincerity, hypocrisy, and deceit with which living languages teemed. A thousand years of obsolescence had purified them as surely as if they had been cooked down to their essence over a slow flame. The words meant exactly what the dictionaries said and nothing more, nothing newer, nothing sub rosa. They were orderly, neatly contained in vocabulary lists she could tick off, in verb conjugations, tenses, and moods to memorize, declensions of nouns to recite that made a singsongy poetry. And there was no shortage of texts. A cornucopia waited in her cabin: Hesiod and Ovid; Sophocles; Pliny the Elder; Tacitus; and Sappho, poor Sappho, torn to shreds. And Epictetus and Claudian; Livy; Pindar. All of them fixed forever, unamendable as yesterday.

And though she knew it was evil, she was again in thrall to her awful *dreaming*—to fantasies of her own storied greatness—which she despised and felt obliged to confess to her diary. Though a vapid solution, dreaming countered her despair. Oh, the French was superior: *desespoir,* the sound more beautiful, more expressive of the feeling, the final syllable—des-es-*poir*—mimicking the sound of her life's breath leaking out, attenuating into the void . . .

Except to answer direct questions, Trout had retreated into a cordial standoff based in silence. Having brought enough wool to clothe a flock of sheared sheep, she crocheted constantly, her hook stabbing into the skeins with the avidity of a hungry bird. Growing arms and a collar, a bed jacket accumulated in her lap; a baby blanket was also in the offing or perhaps it was a coverlet for her room at home. In the evening, she read her Bible.

The rift opened a deep old wound in Flo, which began to fester, setting her mind on a familiar path of disgust—with the upper classes, of which she was a guilt-ridden if alien member, and with herself for her inability to transcend her privilege, and her unwillingness to renounce it. She did not know which was worse: being thwarted by her family or the guilt of knowing what a burden she was to them. She always had to protect them from her own unhappiness.

If her desire to care for the sick were monstrous, then *she* was monstrous. There was no middle ground. Those who cooked the fowl or grew the corn? Do not look at them. They are not like us. Which is why she spent so much of her free time going back and forth to Wellow along the muddy path from Embley, reminding herself that they were *exactly* like her. In Wellow, when old Mrs. Crane suffered, she would rub her limbs by the hour and the old woman spoke to her as if to a daughter. But there was no muddy path between her and Trout. She hardly had a language in which to communicate with her. It was laughable to think she could help the world's unfortunates when she could not deal with a lone maidservant.

And so it was that as they neared the island of Philae on the fourth day, a black mood enveloped Flo, so dark and bottomless that even dreaming provided no respite. She wanted only to sleep.

12

LAMENTATION AT PHILAE

On a bright morning in late March, the *cange* drifted, sails furled, toward Philae. Gustave had glimpsed the island, an outcropping of red and black granite no bigger than the place des Vosges, when they had sailed past it, going upriver, but they hadn't stopped. Joseph had insisted that the proper approach was from the south, as the priests of Isis and Osiris had intended their suppliants to behold it.

When it seemed they had gone too far north, the captain thundered a command and the crew rowed furiously across the current toward the southern tip. There Gustave set eyes on the ancient quay with its grand submerged staircase. The crew moored the boat. He watched as the rope smeared the green slurry of algae on the north face of the stone piling.

Wearing his slippers on his hands, he sloshed up underwater steps the color of splotched limes. Midway, there entered his mind the vivid image of Cleopatra disembarking in splendor, her gold-trimmed, Tyrian purple robes deflating like the fins and tails of an ornamental carp as they dragged through the graduated shallows. Surely there would have been pomp and circumstance when the queen paid homage to the gods. For a musical flourish, he clapped the slippers together.

Ashore, he wrung out his djellaba, which was sopping wet from the waist down. The approach to the temple of Isis was either across open ground or through two long colonnades; he chose the easternmost colonnade. Max, being more nimble, soon outpaced him on the western side, while Joseph, bare-chested under his red vest and wearing his usual Turkish trousers, paused to light a pipe at the top of the stairs.

Walking in the slashed shade of the columns, Gustave heard the cataracts downriver at Aswan. The miles between softened the roar to calming ambient refreshment, like a hotel fountain. Philae, he wrote in his head: the orchestra section of the Nile's concert hall, best seats to hear the liquid tympany of the rapids, but still distant enough that one could think and converse.

The island was enchanting. Gusts rattled the palm trees sprouting from the rocks at odd angles. Light filtering through the forests of columns wove a luminous tapestry that hung in the air, turning and changing by the moment like a rotating pane of glass. He could not have dreamed up a more quintessentially Oriental paradise. Only dancing girls and music were missing—preferably harps and flutes to ricochet among the ruins. An occasional birdcall and the subdued ground dither of lizards and insects broke the silence. "No one lives here!" he shouted into the golden air.

Trailing pipe smoke, Joseph hurried toward him, a rare sight. Usually he moved at the pace set by the slow clock of the pyramids and the colossi, to whom a millennium was but a forward tick, the imagined blink of a stone eye.

Max stood fingering the hieroglyphs on one of the pylons of the temple to Isis. He threw his arm around Gustave's shoulder. "Yes, O Sheik Mustache. Amazing to see a holy place so totally abandoned." Somewhat out of breath, Joseph added, "They say the last priest he die in anno 500. The peoples stay away, afraid for ghosts."

Gustave leaned against a fallen pillar and scanned the view. He was standing in a painted postcard, the sky hand-tinted cerulean for added grandeur. Philae was almost too beautiful to be real. A profusion of chapels and temples—sacred, Joseph had said, to Egyptians,

Greeks, Romans, and early Christians alike—conveyed a wealth of choices, like so many stuffed chairs invitingly angled in a room. Everywhere columns of varied vintages drew his eyes upward, testaments to orderliness and stability. Of all Egyptian sites, Philae was the most human in scale, as casual and unimposing as a rambling country estate lapsed into dereliction.

Max stepped back from the pylon and framed it with his thumbs and forefingers. "A perfect time of day for photographs," he announced. "I'm going back for my equipment. Perhaps you'll pose for me, *Garçon,* at one of the temples?"

Gustave pivoted, pointed his rump in Max's direction, and pretended to fart. Max ignored him, loping back to the boat with Joseph following. The Father of Thinness moved with the deftness of one who had grown up negotiating rocky scapes instead of Parisian pavement, as if he had hooves instead of feet. He'd have made an excellent goatherd.

Gustave struck out for the interior, following a promenade of lotus-topped pillars, the gritty earth crunching beneath his leather carpet slippers. In moments he found a trove of columns with bas-reliefs still polychromed in the jewel tones the Egyptians favored: gold and turquoise, green, orange, marine blues, and red—red for blood and evil, he recalled. Antiquity and beauty had not deterred graffiti artists in the past thousand years. Signatures in Greek and Latin and what he took to be demotic, the common man's hieroglyphics, provided chilling proof that a Constantine, Junonius, and Theodora had once lived and graved a small eternity in the sandstone. He, on the contrary, had no desire to leave tailings of himself in the Orient, but rather to take tokens of it home. *A monkey, six meters of Dacca cloth . . . maybe a mummy . . . a red vest. . . .*

Though surely the painted pillars had once had a roof, Gustave preferred them as they were, with ceilings made of weather. He liked the turn of phrase. The gods were in charge of rolling out a sky to match the human drama below. At the moment, distinct puffs like dumplings floated in blue soup.

He noted again the watery silence—cloistral, somber, imbued with a ritual purposefulness, though the ritual had been lost in the sweep of time. He knew that as the Egyptian religion moved south from Abydos to Thebes to Karnak, it became more specialized, and that the temples at Philae were dedicated to the worship of Isis and her mate, Osiris, the god of the underworld and afterlife. Whatever the lost ceremonies were, they had inspired a gorgeous setting—façades carved in intricate relief, rocks exquisitely hewn and fitted—a model of perfection for the perfect eternity to follow.

Just then, something cream-colored protruding from the nearest wall caught his eye. It reminded him of the straw pigeon nests that stuck out from the upper stories of homes in Cairo. Closer up, he saw it was a scroll of paper jammed between two blocks. He pulled it loose and unrolled it. *Dear God,* it read in a familiar and handsome hand, *take me to you. I do not wish to live. Your faithful servant.* Stunned, he wiped his brow and stuffed the paper into the pouch of his robe.

Around the corner he spied another note, rolled tight as a cigarette, and forced into an intaglio of Ra in his bark. His heart began to pound. *I am no use to You or myself. I do not think I am a human being but a deviation from Nature.* Despite the English, he understood the gist: desperation.

Rossignol's handwriting was neat and diminutive, marked somehow by *inwardness,* by containment, claiming scant space on the slip of paper as if not to offend, or as if she might be graded on her copperplate in a note pleading for a quick, painless, and passive death. Such politesse was, he hoped, the mark of a pious soul afraid to take her own life, or perhaps convinced she would go to hell if she did.

Miss Nightingale had departed Abu Simbel on her blue-bannered craft a week before he had. *Parthenope,* that was the name on the pennant. Her sister's awful moniker. Like naming a woman "Veritas" or "Fido."

He had never heard of leaving notes to God in temple walls, but away from good, gray England, it might be an acceptable substitute for a church prayer box.

He heard a whimper followed by a sob. Folding himself in half, he bent through the low doorway to investigate. Inside, he was able to stand. The floor was hard-packed earth dappled with sunlight.

He heard a gasp edged with high squeaks, like the harmonics of a violin bow, and recognized the terrible restraint of someone determined to avert all-out caterwauling. She mumbled a few words between the stifled sobs.

With a hand on either side, he groped his way through the glutinous dark of a stone passageway and down a short flight of stairs until the wall on one side ended in what he presumed was the entrance to a room. Cushioning his head with his hand, he stooped into a duskier realm with pinholes of light leaking through the roof. The air was so stale and arid it stung his lungs, like the heavy, pungent atmosphere of a disused root cellar. He sensed more than saw a figure huddled on the floor. *"Bonjour?"* he called. "*Est-ce-qu'il-y-a quelqu'un?* Rossignol?" He stepped forward.

"Go away!"

"*C'est moi,* Gustave. Please, let me come in." He took a step and stretched his hand into the muzzy, desiccated air.

"No." The shape squirmed into the corner, revealing the outline of an arch, like a saint's niche within a cathedral. He recognized the pretty curve of her bonnet brim.

"Please, Rossignol."

"Don't come any closer."

"All right." He retracted his hand. "I shall stay where I am." He peered into the room without success for her face. "Do you mind if I visit a while?" It would take a few more minutes for his eyes to adjust to the dismal light.

"What? What are you saying?" She seemed befuddled by the mundanity of his question.

"I'm just going to take a seat now." He was overcome with a rare compassion, the same tenderness he had felt for Caroline, and also, oddly, for Louise's little pink slippers—a hollowness in his chest that radiated out, turning his hands and feet rubbery. He had to keep a calm head, for it occurred to him that the notes might be more than requests to be whisked heavenward. Perhaps she had brought the means of her liberation. A knife. Or poison. Dahabiyahs were notoriously vermin infested, with poison casually stocked alongside coffee and chickpeas. He decided he would not leave her. Eventually Max and Joseph would search him out; then the three of them could chivvy her into returning with them, or, if necessary, gently overwhelm her. He had merely to keep her engaged and talking. Above all, he must show no alarm, despite the rapid throbbing in his neck. He must cultivate an offhand attitude when in reality he wanted to rescue her, hurling himself forward like the lifeguards at Trouville to breast the waves, his heart about to burst, every muscle burning with the effort. Instead, his limbs tingled with unspent urgency.

"What are you writing, Rossignol?" He could distinguish her more clearly now, scratching on a pad of paper, a lady's aide-mémoire that dangled from a cord around her neck. A cord. A noose!

"Nothing much," she managed, her voice unsteady.

He had crossed his legs Indian-style, but now he stretched them out in front and leaned back against the stone. "If I were guessing," he said mildly, "I'd say you were praying."

She turned and looked squarely at him, her face blank with astonishment. "How did you know?" Curiosity seemed to calm her; she sounded more normal.

"I found some notes outside the temple." He gestured toward the corridor behind them.

"You didn't take them, did you?" Her voice tightened with concern. He could see her features clearly now.

"I read them. Would you like me to replace them where I found them?" He felt the pebbled earth pressing through the damp wool homespun of his robe. His buttocks were starting to itch.

"Oh, yes," she said solemnly. "I would appreciate that. I chose the placement with great care."

"Let's do it together," he proposed. "I have them in my pocket." He patted the pouch where he'd lodged them, imagined mounding his body around hers in a soft fortress. Was the poor girl mad? Was he? In fact he thought he was, but she was mad in a different way, too much sincerity and care for other people, while his madness had to do with detesting almost everyone.

"Just give them to me." Her voice was still shaking. "I can do it on my own." She began to collect herself, her skirts shushing along the rock and sand. Rising to a squat, she braced herself with one hand on the wall.

"I shall help you with them outside and then escort you to your boat." What more could he say that would not call attention to the seriousness of his concern?

"All right." She straightened up with difficulty, wedged the newest note in a crevice, and moved closer, standing above him. He didn't budge. Into the freighted silence between them, she at last lowered herself onto the floor alongside him, primly covering her knees with her dress. He thought of reaching out to pat her arm, but she was wary as a wild animal and might interpret the slightest motion as a threat and vanish into the gloom, there driven to some drastic act.

She stared at him unabashedly. He watched the wisp of a smile solidify into a blithesome grin. The instant he offered a smile in return, she metamorphosed into a different person: her shoulders lowered; her neck softened from a post into a slender curve; her arms settled against her torso, relaxed as wings. She seemed to be sane again. He was pleased that he had managed to soothe her with his cleverness and rationality.

She covered her mouth with her hand to stifle a giggle, but the hand flew up, as though yanked on a string, and she exploded with laughter. Unlike her sobbing, she did nothing to fight the impulse, producing guffaws and snickers limited only by the necessity to draw breath.

He shivered in the oven of the chamber. Was she laughing at him? Surely she *was* mad. What would she do next, especially if she *had* brought a knife or poison? Didn't the insane cackle at the most unlikely moments—while setting buildings afire, diving from rooftops, stabbing their husbands with pitchforks?

"Oh, Gustave," she said with a sigh, "I am sorry to have worried you, for you *are* worried, I see it in your face." She leaned closer, inspecting him.

Her eyes glimmered, wet with tears of hilarity. Although she was small with a flat chest, she was distinctly feminine, her torso rising like the stem of a water lily from the circular pad of her skirt. "I have been through this before, this . . . hopelessness. I shall recover." She picked up one of his hands balled into fists in his lap. "I never thought anyone would find my letters. They were intended only for God." She pried open his fingers and sandwiched his hand between hers. Her face turned serious again, the veins at her temples suddenly prominent, blue pentimenti of the keening woman he had found moments before.

Was she going to cry? He hated it when women cried. His mother cried daily, not that she lacked a reason to be in perpetual mourning, but he could not abide it. Each of Mme. Flaubert's tears pierced his heart like a sliver of glass. Louise's tears had been largely histrionic, intended to melt his resolve, to provoke pity followed by guilt. In the end he had become immune to them.

"Gustave, *dis-moi que tu me pardonnes.* Forgive me especially for frightening you," she added. She held his hand in hers. Rather surprising for an Englishwoman, but in her case not coquetry, simply the sign of an openhearted and trusting nature.

"Of course," he heard himself say, "I forgive you. But only if you swear you are not so despondent as the notes suggest. No, disregard that." He erased the words with his free hand from the air. He *knew* she was desperate, and that suicide might beckon again even if her crisis had passed for now. He started over. "Promise me that if you *are* so melancholy, you will take me as your confidant here, away from home."

She nodded. "I am not, and I shall."

Had they just been married? The order and brevity of her words sounded like vows. He withdrew his hand, then thought better of it, and took both of hers. From his mouth (his best feature, everyone said, and his favorite body part after his prick) poured words that bypassed his brain. "My dear Rossignol, I sensed I would be your friend from the moment we met. Fate has brought us together in Egypt for a purpose." He stood outside himself, marveling at the florid declaration.

"Oh," she said, glancing down demurely, "if only that were true. But even if it were, we shall soon be parted." She ignored the tears spilling down her cheeks, as if they were someone else's, or droplets of rain. He was happy to ignore them, too. "In any case, you may not find me a worthy friend," she continued. "I am, I'm told, too intense. Too serious. Too ambitious. Oh, and too talkative and I have an impossibly deep, passional nature that *will* find its outlet. I have loved music too much and friends too much and my family insufficiently—"

"*Arrête,* Rossignol!" A tender pity surged in him. Beneath the cleverness, candor, and humor, she was shattered by self-doubt. "You must defend yourself first from yourself, for the world will be all too eager to find fault with you." The rock upon which he sat might have been proclaiming, oracle-like, for all he felt connected to his words, though he intended them sincerely and, to tell the truth, found them moving and sage.

She shifted her weight, copying his position, her feet extended in front, her back against the wall, next to his. She sighed. "As a woman, I am unnatural." She measured her bony hand against his meatier one. "Everyone says so. I wish to be of use, but to my family I am only a burden, which I loathe. Since I cannot change my sex, I would be better off dea—"

"Don't say it! Or if you must, consider it only philosophically." Their hands were still palm to palm. He locked his fingers around hers and squeezed them, shaking her hand with conviction for both of them.

"All right," she relented. "Let's consider it philosophically. Which of us shall be Socrates and which the questioner?" She turned toward him and removed her bonnet, which had flattened her hair into two shining wings plastered to her head. Between them, the white of her scalp was startling. A bead of sweat slid down her forehead. He regretted that he did not have a handkerchief to offer her, only the fetid hem of his robe.

He rarely confided in women. Certainly not his dear mother, who, given more information, fretted more, fluttering around baby Caroline's nursery in paroxysms of dread and grief with her arms upraised and her hair in a tangle. She'd always been a worrier with a gloomy disposition, and who could blame her? Long before the recent tragedies, she'd borne inordinate losses. When she was nine days old, her mother had died, and her father when she was five years old. In the eight years between Gustave and Achille, three babies had died in her arms. Tragedy had shaped her into a woman who suffered in anticipation as much as from outcomes. No, he told her only ebullient news. As for women of his class, they were untrustworthy gossips who viewed him as a potential investment, like a bank bond. Louise had used his confidences to taunt him.

"I have a question, then," he told Florence. "Shall I give up, too, as you wish to? I've already told you that I am a failed novelist—"

"What a noble undertaking, the pursuit of art," she interrupted. "How I admire you."

He wanted to disabuse her of the naive veneration he heard in her voice. "The truth is that I am fit for nothing else, least of all ordinary life. I wish to write, but that will require all my resources, my will and bodily strength, my time and affections, and yet I may fail again."

To his annoyance, she still looked starry-eyed, as if in the presence of Rousseau, Molière, or even a lesser light like Lamartine. "I hate conventionality," he added, determined to give her a taste of his soured reality. "People are sheep. Sheep-mayors and sheep-grocers. In the esteemed Academy, immortal sheep! I shall never marry, never have children. I hate all that. I refuse to become the standard-bearer of all that I despise for the sake of offspring."

She stared at him, mouth slightly agape.

He hadn't planned to tell quite so much, but in all likelihood, they'd never meet outside Egypt. Of course, they could continue a friendship by mail. She seemed to enjoy writing letters and was at ease on the page. But the prospect was unappealing. Rossignol was much more interesting in the flesh, more mercurial, more chemically alive, like a fire. By comparison, her letters emitted only sparks. Anyway, he mused, it was impossible for a man and a woman truly to be friends the way he and Bouilhet were friends. The way he had been a friend with Alfred, the way, mostly, he and Max were friends. Women were more like household accoutrements—walking, talking furnishings with especially alluring appendages and apertures. Except for whores, who had no interest in conversation, other than bantering about price. It was better that way. Prostitutes kept alive his ideal of an honest love unfettered by gingerbread morality. As for Miss Nightingale, she was, apparently, another sort of being—female and an intellectual (unlike Louise, who was more enamored of her own career than of ideas). Plus, Miss Nightingale had a touch of severity that was aesthetically pleasing. He had never met anyone like her. Nevertheless, he was sure that if he told her the truth of himself, she'd be appalled. And there was nothing worse, nothing more enraging, nothing that caused his gut to churn more than the expression of disapproval on a woman's face. It made him feel like a bad smell. He was especially susceptible to his mother's outrage, even when it was unjustified.

"I, too, shall never marry," Florence said, breaking his reverie. She seemed proud of it, her chin tilted up, her expression defiant. He'd never heard a woman say that. "But *continue,* Gustave. I didn't mean to interrupt, only to second your notion."

Leaving out his seizures (known only to his family, Bouilhet, and Max), he recited all his recent desolations: failing law school, the tragic year when Alfred, his father, and sister had been flattened one after another, like stick puppets at a saint's fair. She listened attentively, with murmurs of sympathy. "When I was a younger man, I took refuge in the Romantics," he explained. "I thought I'd found my life's work and a way to rise above the petty world—like Byron, Wordsworth."

"Yes, great poets. And Byron, so heroic, a martyr to Greek freedom."

He and Alfred had dressed like the dashing Byron for a time. After Gustave dispensed with the cape and scarf, he retained the stance of the man, who was as notorious for his scandals, debt, and sexual appetite as for his verse.

"Later I came to reject the writers who held an optimistic view of humanity. How," he asked her, "could Rousseau think the common man noble? How could anyone? For the common man is uncouth. Boring. He is married to tradition, distrustful of new ideas, of art itself!" He could feel the blood of his convictions coursing through his neck and head. Even in the twilit room, his face must be red as a boil. "Only Rabelais and Byron wrote in a spirit of malice, only they dared laugh at the human race."

"It is true," she said, unperturbed. "The common man is dirty. He cannot read and therefore barely thinks. But how can he rise above his station without education and the right to determine his destiny? That is why I felt so much sympathy with the Italian reformers," she added. "I knew some of them in France and Switzerland, the great social and political thinkers in exile there."

Amazing! While he was laboring all night until dawn in his study on *Saint Anthony,* she had been discussing the fate of the Italian states with visionaries. Perhaps *he* was the naive one. Of course, he *had* been in Paris for the revolution of 1848, though not by design. He had ventured out once from Max's flat to observe from the ramparts but had never participated. The truth was that without the guidance of his friends, he had few opinions about politics. Mostly, he had to admit, he was simply *against* things. He aspired to misanthropy, though he had trouble pulling it off face-to-face. There was always the danger, too, that he would end his days as a sullen windbag. He had to take the measure of himself. He had to succeed. The failure of *Saint Anthony* had nearly broken him.

How much time had passed—half an hour? An hour? The light inside the temple seemed brighter than before, the silence denser, more liturgical.

"Luckily, you have had advantages," she said. "You are not a common man and never could be. And most important, you have a calling, which your first failure has not altered."

"Yes," he muttered. "But it has made me cynical."

"Then that is another thing we share," she announced, looking almost excited. "I have grown cynical myself."

"About what, Rossignol? The music?"

"No, not that. I've grown cynical about people, my own class of people. They are so smug, so comfortable sitting in judgment."

"The bourgeois herd."

"Two years ago at church, I . . . well . . . sort of lost my temper and made my opinions known."

He pricked up his ears. "Oh?"

"The vicar had the gall to say it was extraordinary that Jesus arose from the working classes, as if only the rich had a brain or sentiment."

"And not at all in the spirit of the man Himself." He loved the thought of her dressing down a cleric.

"I wanted to shout, *We are all Pontius Pilate here,* but instead, as I went through the receiving line, I told him it would have been more extraordinary if Jesus had arisen from *this* class of people. Whereupon he pinched my elbow and steered me outside and asked why I hated my own kind." She shook her head with resignation.

"Perhaps your vicar has never actually read the Bible?" he joked.

She did not respond at first, staring grimly at the floor. "I was so angry, but then I thought, 'Look at me. I have been educated primarily to *enjoy* my life, to play the pianoforte, to speak French, to attend lectures and recitals. Who am I to judge him? I am no better—"

"You are, you are much, much better!" He touched her cheek.

"But all my luxuries and leisure depend upon the drudgery of people who are barely acknowledged as human beings." Sighing, she looked into his eyes.

"No, you are better. You are nothing like those people."

"Perhaps you are right. At least I notice the inequity." She smiled a little. "At least I do not say what the wealthy always say of the poor: 'Let them suffer here below becau—"

"'Because Heaven will be their recompense. They are not like us.' Blah-blah-blah-blah."

"Exactly!"

They looked at each other beyond the few seconds allowed in the presence of other people, who were always monitoring the length and propriety of a glance. He was aware of the soft skin of her cradling hand. But instead of an awakening in his groin, he felt his bottom itching. In her presence, he couldn't just reach around and scratch his ass. Pity. Had he ever felt that free in front of Caroline? He couldn't recall.

"You have laid bare your heart," she whispered. "Will you keep a secret of mine that only one other human being knows?"

"*Mais oui.* On my life!" He thought back to the day he and Alfred had commingled their blood with finger pricks as boys. Secrets thrilled him.

She yawned and hiccuped, her manners apparently suspended during extreme spiritual distress. Might she next burp or pass wind in his presence? The thought excited him, like the voyeur's fantasy that the woman he has been secretly watching continues to undress, knowing she is being watched.

"Promise you will not laugh or think me crazy if I tell you." Her voice was firm and serious.

Could he promise that? He thought he must, whatever he might actually believe. "Again, on my life."

She scooped up sand from the floor and let it sift through her fingers, gathering her thoughts. "I, too, have a calling."

At last, he thought, the mysterious source of her despondency and of her fierce commitment would be revealed.

"My calling is from God." She closed her eyes, rapturous, then opened them, looking stunned. "I mean to say that when I was seventeen, God spoke to me."

"I see," Gustave whispered respectfully. He added a weight to the scale in his mind on the side of her craziness. In France, many people conversed with God, most of them wretched peasants desperate to distinguish themselves from the flock, to leave off being sheep. He was crestfallen to think that brilliant Rossignol was similarly deluded: Joan of Arc redux. He cleared his throat. "Are there many mystics in England?" He might have been asking about the weather.

"Mystics?" It was clear from the tone of her voice that she had never applied the word to herself. "No, I've never heard of any. Is that what I am, then, a mystic?" Her voice was shaky, tinged with fear. Or was it anger?

"I don't know," Gustave floundered. "That is what we call them in France, the people who speak to God."

"But I didn't speak to God!" She lurched forward, her back ramrod straight. "He spoke to *me*. He called me to His service. I had no say in it. I was merely the vessel—"

"I'm so sorry. I hope I haven't offended you—"

"Offended me? No, but clearly you think me mad."

Anger, then. She made to move away from him, but he held on to her arm. A rivulet of sweat streaked between his shoulder blades. The room had disappeared from awareness for a time. Now it was stifling again.

"I don't think you are mad," he lied. "I am sometimes rude or tactless without meaning to be." A pressure was building behind his eyes, a headache coming on. Or was he about to have a seizure? He'd never been able to identify the warning signs before he vanished into the black maze of nonexistence. To prevent or at least anticipate future episodes, he tried to remember afterward what he had been doing or feeling. But only afterward, when it felt like he'd died and revived, after a chunk of his life had been severed with an ax. "But please, tell me how and when it happened to you, Rossignol." If he did have a seizure, would she know what to do?

"Gustave? Are you quite all right?" Her head was inclined toward him, an expression of care on her face so intense it seemed that her whole life force were focused on him in a single beam of attention.

"I am fine." The pain was receding. He breathed more easily. "I have been thinking that we should swear to have no secrets today, no shame between us." Did he dare divulge the secret of his illness? He wanted to, but not quite yet. "I myself have done things I would be ashamed to tell you—"

"But I am not *ashamed*!" She pulled her arm free and scooted away on the floor, horrified, though she did not leave. A wave of gratitude washed over him—gratitude to Philae and its ancient architects. Where but in such a sacred and exotic quarter could this chimerical conversation continue?

"You must forgive . . . my ineptitude." His words issued from his throat like thread catching on a spool. "I was only saying *I* have secrets, I have things I am ashamed of." The words kept coming, colored this way, then that, like the endless silk scarf of a magician. "Ashamed of my behavior on occasion with women. I have, in short, sinned. But you! You are blessed. You are blessed that God chose you." He felt utterly lost. How had one remark altered her mood so sharply? His words lay at his feet, a tangle of knots, a hatful of failed tricks.

"You understand nothing of this event," she said sharply. "I am not blessed. He called me to His service, but that was twelve years ago and I still do not know what I am to do." She kicked at the floor, raising a flurry of dust motes that settled erratically, like bits of gold leaf.

It took every drop of his self-control not to laugh: a woman considering suicide because her god was fickle or had a poor memory? He took several deep breaths to vanquish the hoot that hovered in his throat like a sneeze in the nose. He could feel a smile forming in his face, a disembodied grin in the sepulchral gloom. He bit his lip until his eyes teared.

She began to keen, to sob. She covered her face with her hands, as if to block the anguish from issuing forth. He had never seen such a display, not of grief, but of grief denied, of grief beat back with a hammer, of great blockades erected and then broached. He was unable to look away, like an onlooker at a fire. He had paid to watch women masturbate, but that was not nearly as intimate as watching this young Englishwoman try to subdue the beast of her raw feeling.

She looked up, her nose dripping. "It is not a blessing, but a curse." Her voice was thin as a wire.

He crawled across the space between them and rested his head against her shoulder. Philae held them in its silted-up silence. Barely touching her for fear she'd collapse under the weight of an embrace or move away again, he encircled her with his arms. "I am waiting for the muse to visit me," he managed to whisper, "just as you are waiting for God to speak to you again." Were they not both self-made pariahs? He felt himself in complete sympathy with her, as if they *had* mingled their blood in the purity and innocence of childhood.

She wiped her face on her sleeve and, still within the crook of his arm, raised her head and in a small voice asked, "What sins have you committed with women?"

He thought for a moment, considering his options. Did not the location alone cast the whole enterprise in a unique and liberating light? He was inside a derelict temple in Egypt where, for all he knew, orgies had been conducted with sacred whores, and hearts excised and weighed on golden scales. He decided not to consider custom or pride, which could only lead to lies and silence. "Because I cannot betray my calling by marrying," he began, "I no longer court proper women."

Florence listened while he explained how disillusioned he had been that Louise, a fellow artist, had tricked him into believing that she yearned for something other than a bourgeois existence when in fact she wanted a husband *and* a lover, and that was not revolutionary in the least. "That marked the beginning of my life as a cynic," he explained.

He had been cruel to Louise. But now, miles and months removed, his fury had been replaced by wistfulness, by the memory of her tongue darting between his lips like a hungry bird, the salty tang of golden thatch under her arms. "In the main," he continued to Florence, "I have found another outlet for my passions in the brothels of Paris." In the spirit of full disclosure he added, "And Egypt."

She did not move, her head still nuzzled against his chest. He felt her bony rib cage rising and falling. "Brothels?"

"Oui. J'ai frequenté des bordels presque depuis mon enfance."

Her voice altered, resembling a schoolgirl's neutrally reciting the population of Spain, the successor to Henry VIII. No, it was the sexual peccadilloes of members of Parliament. "It's bruited about that lords in England do the same. Not that I would know. Or condone it." She looked up at him. "I am sure it is degrading to all concerned."

"Of course," he lied. Clearly, Florence knew nothing about brothels. How could she, being English, rich, pious, and protected? Had he ever felt degraded? He did not think so. Had he ever degraded the women? Without doubt. He had once fucked an old woman while wearing a hat and smoking a cigar as two friends cheered him on, then passed her around like a bottle of cognac.

"I suppose it is better than deceiving a girl by promising to marry her to gain an advantage," she added.

In other circumstances, he might have found it amusing to think of sex as an "advantage" rather than his rightful due. The only time, as far as he was concerned, that sex was not an advantage was when it led to marriage. Then he feared it. But he wouldn't say that. He could never say that. Because once he began to think so coldheartedly, so truthfully, love in the brothel became impossible, the brothel itself distasteful, actually a pathetic substitute. No, he could not give up his whores.

"I shall die a virgin, I suppose," she said, brushing away a channel of sand in the pleat of her skirt, "though I came close to marrying once." She told him about refusing Richard. "I reasoned that if I married, I would be a prisoner of my household, unable to do whatever it is God wishes of me. My family didn't understand how much it pained me to disappoint them. And myself, for I have a deeply passional nature."

"So you said earlier."

"Not just carnal passion."

"I understand. There is the mind. Ah, and the yearning spirit." She would die, he thought, without ever discovering the bazaar of flavors, sights, and sensations that was the body. A shame, all those nerve endings wasted. He remembered the corpses in his father's dissecting room, he and Caroline watching the autopsies from the apartment across the way, happy to be horrified.

"As I said, I am excessive in my likes and dislikes—my likes especially." She was matter-of-fact again, her hands folded in her lap. "And with such a passionate nature, everyone believes that I am at greater risk than usual when I travel. I have a chaperone everywhere and at all times in England. Abroad, they say I am what is called in hunting parlance an easy target."

"After a certain age, my sister, too, required a chaperone." It was the age of breasts and blood, he thought but did not say. "When she was young, I schooled her to be a tomboy and a free spirit. She was a painter and actress. Then she grew up and married." He had been angry with Caroline for yielding to convention, for joining the ranks of the enemy, only recently realizing that she had no choice unless she wished to become one of the sexless spinsters he joked about to her. Sometimes when they were together with her new husband, she would look at him as if to say *It's not so bad. I've paid the price. Why can't you?* Or perhaps he had only imagined that message in her glance. As a bride she seemed unquestionably happy, nearly gloating, not the Caroline he knew and loved. But why should he grow up to be like her? Why should any man wish to become a silo—a stolid, stationary provider for every hungry mouth?

She continued, "Everything must be planned with chaperoning in mind. You and Max follow your fancies, free to move about. You can be invisible—men among men—while wherever I go, I am a bauble trying to hang in the air as invisibly as a spider's thread."

He shifted to one haunch to relieve the itching. Stung with sweat, it had intensified. "Oh, but that is not quite correct, Rossignol. Max and I are not always safe. It just seems so to you. Of course," he conceded, "we *are* safer than you would be."

"Without the Bracebridges, I should be mad by now. They took me to Italy last year to prevent a civil war at home." She had been feuding with her family, she explained, for ten years, ever since they returned from their Grand Tour and Fanny undertook to marry her off. She enumerated a few of the battles: the opposition to mathematics as being manly, Fanny forbidding her to volunteer at hospitals and orphanages, both parents' distaste for her work at the Ragged School, their horror at the amount of time she spent with the poor villagers.

"I am meant to sit quietly, look pretty, and entertain at the piano—in short, to be useless in a world where so much needs to be done."

"Yes," he said, "I see that now." He did understand. He recognized the dull world she described. However, his unhappiness was of a different stripe, for he refused to aspire to the usefulness within it that she so desired. Could she grasp his nature after all? he wondered.

"According to Father, every man in the world has his mind on seduction and conquest, and will revert to it at the first opportunity, like a traveler to his native language. Then he becomes a ravening monster. The way Father talks, it is only their suits and cravats that separate men from beasts."

"He's trying to frighten you to protect you. It isn't true." Actually, it was. He was certainly guilty of making the lives of unescorted women miserable, taunting them on the street, catcalling when drunk and sometimes when sober.

"I must be out in the world to accomplish anything, but how will I do it if the world is so dangerous that I can't take a walk alone?"

"Dear girl," he said, petting her hair, "here's an idea. Why don't you come with Max and me to Koseir. It's on the Red—"

"Sea. Yes, I know where it is. I looked it up on the map when Max wrote me about it."

Max hadn't told him that he'd written to her. The lout! Did he have his rascally eye on what he called "English pudding"? He'd set him straight: Miss Nightingale was not to be prey, but comrade. "The Bracebridges could come along or wait for you in Kenneh."

She sat up briskly, eyes glittering. "Is that a genuine invitation?"

"It is." He swept the air gallantly with his hand and bowed his head. "It would be my great pleasure to remove you from your scheduled itinerary. Imagine"—he stretched an arm toward the opposite wall, using it as a canvas—"the sun turning the sea to a golden laver that stretches to the horizon. Immersing yourself in the ancient waters where all those Egyptians drowned with their horses and chariots." But the more he painted the scene, the more disheartened she became. "What is wrong, Rossignol?"

"I shall still need a chaperone. The Bracebridges are in poor health and would never allow me to go with the two of you. The chaperone must be a male relative or older woman or married couple. Those are the rules, even in the Orient, even in the emptiness of the Sahara."

"You can take your servant, *La Truite.* It might do her good."

"Trout?" she repeated dubiously. Her face, moments before glowing like an alabaster lamp, clouded over. "I don't think she'll agree to it."

"Leave it to me." He dreaded the thought of flirting with the churlish hen, but then he had slept with whores older than Trout. "Oh, but I cannot!" He smacked his thigh. "She doesn't speak French!"

"She hates me," said Flo. "It would turn her against the idea if I translated for you. She'd smell a plot."

"But Max can get by. I shall set him the task." Even in broken English, Max was adept at melting hearts with the saga of his life as an orphan. (He never mentioned his wealth and that his parents died when he was nearly grown.) "Max could photograph the old biddy. So few people have seen a photograph, let alone owned one. Surely she could be bought with a portrait of herself on the rump of a camel. He could say he needs her as a model on the caravan."

Florence clapped her hands. "If only it could be done."

How good it was to see her animated. He felt himself expand with pleasure, too. Not only had he cheered her up; he'd also found a way to put some distance between himself and Max. Max would be less inclined to ask for his assistance if Miss Nightingale came along. She would be Gustave's project for the desert trip.

"Let's find Max," he said, offering his hand as she stood.

They brushed off their clothes and located the entrance, then crept up the stairs. Bending through the doorway as one, they stepped onto a slab of light on the threshold. Flo extended her palm. "Oh, my letters, please."

He'd nearly forgotten them. "Will you put them back?"

"No. I left one inside the chamber of Osiris. That is enough."

Reluctant to return them—he cherished his mementos of women—he dug one of the two from his pocket. "I seem to have only this," he said, placing it in her palm. She tucked it in her bodice. *A mummy . . . dates from Derr . . . Rossignol's secret scroll . . .*

They tramped arm in arm over the rubble in silence. As they neared the temple to Isis, Max hailed them excitedly. *"Venez ici!"* he shouted, waving to them. "Look what I've found." Hadji Ismael lounged nearby, braiding a palm frond, his one eye focused elsewhere. Joseph was nowhere to be seen.

Max indicated a stele behind the pylons. When they did not react, he pointed to a French inscription incised near the ground: *En l'année 1799, Napoleon à conquis les Mamelukes dans la Bataille des Pyramides.*

"Do you think our great emperor wrote his name everywhere, like Ramses?" Gustave asked. "Why is there no mention of his sweetheart, Josephine?" He winked at Flo, who began to laugh. In a moment, they were both howling. He assured Max they were not laughing at him. The truth was they were laughing because they needed to after the intense encounter in the temple. Anything might have triggered it.

"Laugh all you want," Max said, kicking at the ground. "I have photographed this historical marker for my book." Behind his bluster was clearly dismay.

"I suppose we shall need a squeeze of this," Gustave said.

"As a matter of fact, yes."

"You did promise to teach me how to make a squeeze, M. Flaubert," Flo said nonchalantly. "Might it be this one?"

So he was M. Flaubert again. "This one is awfully low," he said. "It will be difficult, with a lot of bending and groveling in dirt. A higher engraving would be easier."

Max tapped Flo on the shoulder and pointed to the back of Gustave's robes. Two ovals of solidly caked sand formed a tawny imprint of his buttocks. Gustave hung his head in mock shame. "All right," he conceded, "we shall make a squeeze of this. We shall call it 'What the Great French Left Behind.'" He wiggled his fanny. Flo and Max howled.

"Agreed." Max shook his hand and bowed to Flo.

"Tomorrow?" Flo asked.

"I shall send a letter to your dahabiyah, setting the time. And now"—he extended his elbow to her—"shouldn't you be returning?" He patted her hand as she linked it with his. Max looked to him for a clue, but Gustave gave no hint of the events that had played out while Max was taking photographs. "I will see you back on the *cange,*" he said, keeping his face impassive.

Staying within the perimeter wall of granite and sandstone, they trudged along, arm in arm, toward the dahabiyah.

"What do you think of the temple to Osiris?" Flo asked. Judging by her tone, it was clearly a place deeply laden with meaning for her. She pointed to it in the near distance.

"I'm not quite sure." He had been so distracted by her desperate notes when he wandered by that he had paid no attention once inside. "Let's go down to the beach here," he said. Forming a stirrup with his hands, he gave her a boost over the low wall.

"This is not the way I came," Flo said, scrambling over the top. "I never climbed the wall."

"But you came alone today." He hadn't thought about it in those terms until that moment. "You had no chaperone."

"That's true. But it's an uninhabited island. And I was only gone a short while."

He wagged a finger at her. "Still, you've broken the rules as you explained them to me."

"I suppose so."

It genuinely pleased him that she had shown some gumption, that she had the potential, like Caroline, to be a miscreant. What other rules might she be willing to break?

From the shore, the encircling river fractured and multiplied the light like the beveled edge of a looking glass. He felt deeply content, as when he and Caroline wandered the riverbank at home with no destination.

They reached Trajan's bed, an open-sided tomb that resembled a greenhouse, with vigorous weeds growing up through the floor. In the cove below, they spied the dahabiyah. Selina and Charles were sitting under the reed panel, drinking tea and reading.

Selina raised her arm in welcome. "You've come back, my dear. And with an old friend."

He saw that Miss Nightingale was blushing and smiling, happy to see her dear friend. Or was she, possibly, happy to be seen in his company? For an unpleasant moment he wondered if the Bracebridges had a role in finding a match for Flo. He banished the thought.

As she set foot on the gangplank, Flo waved good-bye. He waved, then turned around, his back burning with her gaze.

They had been in the temple of Osiris? He made a mental note to return. It was one of the most important monuments on Philae. He'd noticed nothing but Miss Nightingale.

13

MAHATTA

The next day, as promised, a letter from Gustave arrived before breakfast. His plans had changed. They were relocating the *cange* to the eastern side of Philae to camp there later in the week. In the meantime, he and Max would trek overland past the cataracts to Aswan to replenish their stores. He would return in a few days and write again.

Flo was disappointed. She wondered why the crew could not shop for him and suspected other reasons were at play. (Brothels immediately came to mind.) Also, he made no more mention of making squeezes together. Had he formed no attachment to her, no special affection after their talk yesterday? Did he not at least pity her? Perhaps he did, and that was the problem.

She pushed these questions from her mind and decided to resume work on the long letter she had started to Parthe. Another diversion presented itself later in the morning when Charles announced that he and Selina had been invited to dinner at Mahatta, a village on the eastern bank of the river, a short ride by boat from Philae. Flo could come along if she wished.

She *did* wish. If she stayed busy, she might keep at bay her desolate thoughts as well as new fantasies of Gustave—brief flashes intense as lightning. (Gustave leaning forward to wipe dust from her brow; the two of them rambling hand in hand; removing a smudge from his earlobe after licking her finger . . .) The word *lover* glittered in her mind, like a stage marquee. Richard had never been a candidate for anything but wedlock. In retrospect, she found his frivolity and his determination never to feel dejection, except as it could be conveyed in rhyme, limiting.

That was unkind. Surely he'd felt miserable the day she refused him, a bright afternoon the previous October sharply etched in her mind. They'd been chatting in the parlor at Embley. Curled up in a corner of the sofa, Richard was paging through a sheaf of poems, preparing to read to her. She loved the way he lolled and lounged against the furnishings. He was no taller than she, and she theorized that he adopted these postures partly to prevent easy comparison. Whatever the motive, the way he dispensed with the strict horizontals and verticals of his surroundings was catlike and comforting.

He stood and walked to the fireplace, leaning on the mantel, one foot braced against the wall.

She often listened with pleasure to his poetry as well as drafts of his biography of Keats. He read without histrionics, his voice smooth and intimate, completely different from the voice he used in Parliament, which was quavering and too effusive for the setting. She'd heard him speak there several times, dismayed once to observe an opponent parodying his florid diction.

"This one is called 'Familiar Love,'" he announced.

She sat on the sofa in front of him, attentive if somewhat alarmed by the title. A proposal had been in the air for weeks. Had he come to demand an answer at last? He was thirty-nine and she was twenty-nine. She'd known him for seven years.

"Familiar Love," he repeated, clearing his throat.

We read together, reading the same book
Our heads bent forward in a half embrace . . .

Her mind wandered, taking stock again of how she felt, preparing what she might say (nothing came to mind!) if he asked. By any logical measure, her equivocation was irrational, for from the beginning they had a natural affinity for each other. She'd been considering him for years, because his asking seemed inevitably keyed to the rhythm of life, like bird migration or the falling of leaves.

Their backgrounds couldn't have been more similar unless they were siblings. Both came from privilege, the Milnes having made their fortune in the wool trade in the previous century. Like her, he was one of two children. Both came from Dissenter Unitarian families and had been educated at home, she because women were not permitted to attend the public schools and because the academies for girls weren't intellectually rigorous enough to meet WEN's standards; and Richard because he was a frail child, prone to lung ailments. They'd both sojourned during their youth in Italy with their families.

Her parents had made it clear that they found Richard an ideal match for either sister, with charm enough to impress Parthe, and a wit that passed muster with Flo. He was a pleasant-looking man, with an open gaze, fair brown hair, and a broad forehead. He had published several volumes of verse and was an important figure in Mayfair. The lively breakfasts he threw at 26 Pall Mall when Parliament was in session attracted everyone of note—politicians, scientists, artists, writers, and socialites.

Had he ever seriously considered Parthe? At first, Fanny had set both daughters on display like auction items in the cunningly appointed public rooms at Embley: propped up like costumed dolls upon the horsehair sofa, their skirts arranged just so, their feet clad in glove-leather slippers; or ranged around the dining table along with the silver epergnes overflowing with flowers and fruit. Parthenope needed no persuasion to enter the fray. She ached for a life spent in the service of a husband and children. She was perfectly happy en famille, while Florence was utterly downcast to the point of madness at home. Had her family been Mahometans, Florence thought grimly now, they could have offered a bargain—two wives for the price of one.

"We had experience of a blissful state," Richard read. She remembered the line; it was stiff and airless, not like Richard at all. She forced her attention back to the poem. He'd be expecting her to comment on it.

Richard's voice rose with pride as he continued.

The beauty of the Spirit-Bride,
Who guided the rapt Florentine . . .

Oh, the Spirit-Bride! She couldn't bear it. Yet, she thought she loved Richard. She couldn't imagine a more empathetic soul; he was more like her than any man she had met. Only WEN had treated her with such equality and gaiety.

She loved to hear him describe his years at Cambridge, where he was a member of the exclusive Apostles society, though he'd never taken his exams, his nerves being inflamed. He had let her read the journal he kept during the three years he spent in Europe after university. In Italy he'd read poetry and soaked up the Mediterranean until it had tinged his soul with sunlight. He often spoke with Flo of his plan to make prolonged visits there, and when she returned from her trip to Italy with the Bracebridges, he'd been her keenest listener.

Once, he'd taken her (chaperoned by WEN) to Cambridge. The library was splendid, with its black-and-white checkered floor, its busts of great thinkers, and portrait medallions on the walls. Oriel windows spilled morning sun on row after row of bookshelves. A strange thought had occurred to her there, which she had whispered to him: "If I began reading now," she lamented, "I would not live long enough to read all these books." Richard had wiped away a tear from her cheek and guided her back outside.

He arranged for tea that afternoon in the dormitory of a friend who kept a tame bear cub. For Flo, the main attraction had been the room itself. What she would have given for a place she didn't have to share, a room that was a shrine to learning, with walnut bookshelves surrounding a sturdy old desk on whose scarred top a ream of white foolscap lay like a pool of cream.

She'd tried to mesmerize the cub, but it waved its paws at her. Richard had intervened, tenderly returning the animal to its cage, where, after a few moments, she succeeded and the bear lay down, purring like a cat. What other man would have trusted her with the creature, or come to her aid more gallantly without making her feel foolish? Since that visit, the dorm room at New College had appeared, altered, in her dreams, furnished with a globe, a fur throw (the bear, she wondered, made docile?), and three young men listening raptly to her.

Yes, she admired him. Surely that was part of love.

She sensed from the slight rise and crackle of Richard's voice that the poem was ending:

To braid Life's thorns into a regal crown,
We passed into the outer world, to prove
The strength miraculous of united Love.

Still clutching the sheaf of paper, he lunged toward the sofa and dropped down on one knee, a worried expression on his face. "Marry me, Florence?"

"I do love you, Richard," she said, taking his hand and pressing it to her cheek.

"So you say." He was staring at the Aubusson carpet on the floor. "Repeatedly."

"If I cannot agree, it is not a judgment on you, my dear friend," she told him. "Please trust me and try to understand."

"You can't spare my feelings, even if you want to," he replied, his voice low, more hiss than whisper. "If you refuse me, so be it." He sat back on his haunches, letting his hand slip from her grasp. He looked like a child who had been slapped.

"I am not certain it is *you* I am refusing." As soon as she said it, a contradictory image came to mind: Richard's monogram embroidered on every towel, tablecloth, pillowcase, shirt, and bathrobe, the graceful M's like so many waves rushing toward her in a storm of Milnes-ness. Her own initials would vanish except on lawn handkerchiefs with which she might dab away a tear on difficult days, days when the M's dictated every moment, even if Richard did not plan it to be so.

"Not *me*?" His face had gone a deep crimson.

It was a ridiculous thing to have said. She stumbled on. "I couldn't bear to lose our friendship."

"But you don't care for me enough to marry me. I don't understand." He rested his head on his knees. Was he weeping?

Had she any doubts before of her monstrosity, there could be none in that instant. "I am not sure I shall ever marry. I think I should be lost as a wife. To any man."

"No winters in Rome for you, then?" He rose and retrieved the glass of wine he'd set on the mantel and drained it, his back to her.

If only she could have spared him this pain. Perhaps more candor would soften the wound. "Darling Richard," she said, "please wait here a moment. I must show you something." She rushed up to the bedroom to retrieve her diary. When she returned, she thrust it into his hands, a book no other eyes had seen. "I beg you, Richard, read this. You have been generous to share your journal with me."

As in the poem he'd just recited, they bent their heads over Flo's neat handwriting and read together silently:

> I have an intellectual nature which requires satisfaction, and that would find it in Richard. I have a passional nature which requires satisfaction, and that would find it in him. I have an active moral nature which requires satisfaction, and that would *not* find it in his life. . . . I could not satisfy this nature by making society and arranging domestic things. . . . To be nailed to a continuation and exaggeration of my present life would be intolerable. Voluntarily to put it out of my power ever to be able to seize the chance of forming for myself a true and rich life would seem to me like suicide.

Richard gasped and took a step back from her. "I am your *suicide*?" he shouted. He turned and walked from the room, glaring at her from the hallway. That his sadness had flared into fury, Flo thought, was probably better for him because it left him with the satisfactions of indignation, while despair held no satisfactions at all.

Every day that had passed since, she'd missed his company. And though they'd never done more than peck on the lips or place a hand on the other's arm, she sensed he, too, had a passionate nature, a molten core just waiting to be ignited by the right partner. Now she'd never know the pleasure of that unbridled warmth.

After her refusal, Richard stopped coming to visit, his absence as palpable as his presence had been. In company together, he avoided her, gliding casually to the other side of the room, dining, by conspiracy with his hosts, out of earshot at the other end of the table, dancing at the opposite side of the ballroom. And always refusing her glance, as if she were invisible. It made her weep to think how much he must loathe her for rejecting him.

That afternoon, she continued writing to Parthe about Philae. There was no one she liked writing to more than Parthe, for the two of them shared so much that it was easy, almost like writing in her diary. Like the earlier letter about Abu Simbel, this one threatened to stretch into a religious tract. She'd spent many hours in the chamber of Osiris, whose life shared much with Old and New Testament stories. Osiris's jealous brother, Set, had chopped him into thirteen pieces and scattered them in the Nile. But Isis, Osiris's wife, aided by crocodiles, found all the pieces but one—her husband's penis. So she fashioned him a penis of gold that allowed him to father their son, Horus. Afterward, Osiris descended to the infernal river of the underworld. There, in the seventh room of the night, he judged the worthiness of souls to pass to the Field of Reeds, the Egyptian heaven. Hieroglyphs in the chamber depicted Osiris's severed body parts in caskets and containers of all shapes—here a foot, there an arm, his entire trunk and legs in a shallow drawer. A Nilometer that measured the height of the river bore his severed head. In another panel, he lay fully assembled on a cow-legged bed. Was it not resurrection, piece by bodily piece? As for the penis—a word Flo had never spoken that made her color to see it on the page—perhaps it stood for nature's regenerative powers. Or male resolve. She'd never seen an adult human penis. Those of the donkeys she rode were embarrassing when they emerged, the length of their bellies, red and slick. It was distressing to imagine WEN naked, and impossible to picture how the organ produced her and Parthe. Better to focus on the face and hands of a man; that was her policy.

She decided to omit the golden penis from her letter.

John Frederick Lewis was a friend of the Bracebridges who had lived and painted in Egypt for nearly a decade, most of it in Cairo. Now he and Mrs. Lewis (he had recently married) had set up housekeeping on the Upper Nile, in Mahatta. "Mr. Lewis is a world traveler," Selina had told her that morning. "He has hardly lived in England since coming of age."

"How I envy him that," said Flo. She fancied traveling to India and the Holy Land, but without a husband, future tours were unlikely. The Bracebridges were not as adventuresome or energetic as she was. The Egypt trip would probably be the most daring and the last of her life.

At three o'clock, Selina knocked on the cabin door and entered. She looked refreshed, having just napped. "Are you getting ready, my dear?" she asked. With a nod, Selina acknowledged Trout, sitting on her divan, a wool stocking stretched over a darning egg in one hand, and a threaded needle in the other.

"Mum," Trout said, barely lifting her eyes from the work.

"I can be ready in a trice," said Flo, capping her inkwell and wiping her pen.

Selina edged closer and took stock of her friend. "You must wear more clothing."

"Oh?"

"Once the sun sets, the temperature could drop to freezing."

"Really? Freezing?"

"That is what Paolo said. Hoarfrost is common this time of year."

Paolo was an excellent dragoman, precise and pragmatic. He never exaggerated to inflate his own importance. "I shall bring a cape then." Flo set aside her travel desk and reached for the garment.

"Charles said we must wear *all* our clothes." Selina had an impish gleam in her eye. "At the same time."

"No!"

"I told him you and I should look like snowballs. Snowballs in the desert." Selina giggled. She was such a jolly soul.

Laughing, Flo pictured the crew rolling them along the shore, coating them like sweet rolls in sand instead of sugar. She patted the divan for Selina to sit next to her. "I'm going to check with *Murray.*" She retrieved the book from the cabinet between her bed and Trout's, blowing away the fine veil of grit on the cover. Selina put her arm around Flo's neck, straightening her lace collar.

"It says the thermometer can vary between one hundred twenty in the day and thirty at night. But I believe that's in the Sahara—"

"Those were Paolo's words. He says the weather will be chilly tonight and we shall be exposed to it. Apparently the Lewises are living in a tent."

"I didn't know." Flo imagined a soldier's pup tent, low and insubstantial, made of scratchy Scottish wool the color of dirty drawers.

"Yes, so wear something under your dress and two pairs of stockings. And bring a blanket. Some of the amenities are lacking. They asked that we bring along chairs and carpets."

"The conditions sound primitive."

"Charles is worried about dyspepsia. He fears he will have to eat while reclining if there is a shortage of chairs. But he's eager to see

Mr. Lewis and meet his bride." Selina twisted her wedding band back and forth, a habit she frequently resorted to when discussing Charles. "I think it will be less like dinner than a hiking trip."

It might be a lark. Flo loved it when things turned unpredictable.

"I can't wait to see Mr. Lewis's paintings and drawings," Selina continued. "Did I tell you he lived in Spain after his Grand Tour? He published a folio of his Spanish drawings. Marvelous. We have it at home." Selina rose from the divan and fluffed out her dress.

Trout said, "May I stay here then, mum? I won't be needed, sounds like."

Flo and Selina raised eyebrows. "Your services will not be required," Flo said.

"Thank you, mum. I want to finish these socks. The sand eats holes through them worse than the mice back home."

"You will remain on board with the captain and crew," Flo added. "They will serve you whatever they cook for dinner." Let it be a local dish, she thought. Croquettes of Nile mud. Quail's feet. Beak of eagle in mashed lentils.

"Yes, mum."

Selina turned to Flo. "We shall leave in half an hour. Come up when you are ready. Charles will send the men down for the carpets." She kissed Flo on the cheek. "Bundle up, my dear."

"I shall."

Though Flo didn't have woolen petticoats, high boots, or a muffler, she prepared as best she could. She wore her brown Hollands under the navy wool dress, and her black hooded cloak. In a hatbox, she packed two shawls (one wool, one lace), gloves, and a scarf. She readied a blanket, folding it and placing it at the foot of her bed with her parcels.

The stone walls of Philae cast long shadows like trenches onto the shore by the time they rounded the northern tip of the island in the late afternoon. From the dahabiyah, they boarded a small felucca with a single furled lateen sail. Four men took up oars, one with a carpet rolled around his neck like the thick ecclesiastic collar of an exotic sect. The crew placed three folding chairs in the boat bottom and upon them cushions on which the three Europeans knelt or sat. The craft sat low in the water, laden with its cargo of household goods and clothing.

As Flo had learned on their trip up to Nubia, the cataracts of the Nile weren't waterfalls in the strict sense, but a series of rapids, the result of an upheaval that had split the cliffs alongside, raining down treacherous boulders and slabs of granite that formed broken chains, some jutting straight out of the water, most submerged, detectable only from currents eddying and foaming around them.

As they paddled along between the rocky defiles—the last fragments of the cataracts downstream—Flo observed the sky and shore. Clouds like lambs' tails dissipated into feathers; the sakias on land creaked as a camel or ox circled around, bringing up bucketfuls of water for irrigation. Nightfall in Egypt was often rapid, the sun a fireball so quickly extinguished at the horizon that she expected to hear it sizzle as it dipped into the river. At other times, orange and purple streamers hung in the sky long after the sun had disappeared. Tonight the dying light changed to a soft, opaline blush, the color of ascensions to heaven and the shriven eyelids of saints. The Nile parted around the boat's prow like shirred pink silk.

In half an hour, Mahatta came into view, nestled in a cove shaped like a sickle. The crew leaped from the boat and dragged it across the shingle. Disembarking, Flo felt graceless and stiff in her swaddling of clothes. After about a quarter mile, the first habitations appeared, reed and mud huts of traders wayfaring before the tumultuous ride down the cataracts. Farther along, they encountered the stone and brick dwellings of the cataract sheiks, who lived in big, boisterous clans. Flo had met them while they negotiated with Charles to drag the *Parthenope* up the rapids.

Florence liked what she saw and heard as they entered Mahatta—civilization, Nubian-style, with its hallmark sounds and scents—the thuds and groans of pack animals settling in for the night, the guttural chatter of merchants gathered by open-air fires, cooking spiced lamb or baking bread in clay ovens. She'd always warmed to the bustle of human beings at day's end. At Embley, the muffled racket of pots, the chirp and hum of servants' voices before and after supper were calming, palliative. In fact, she preferred them to the decorous volleys at the dining table. In this way, Mahatta reminded her of home. Most important, it was a *living* city. She'd spent the past three weeks among the remains of the long dead, whose culinary clatter and disagreements about seasonings hadn't been preserved in their scrupulous engravings.

After passing an orderly kitchen garden, they came upon a tent the size of a Hampshire cottage. Its flaps were tautly fastened to the ground, a miniature turret crowning each corner. Though torches illuminated the scene, there was no apparent entrance, and no sentry to announce their arrival.

They stood about, unsure what to do. Efreet-Youssef, always the most accommodating crewman, crawled under the tent face-first on his belly, inching forward like a worm until he disappeared. Flo could hear him announce, "Effendi, Bracebridge Bey! Bracebridge Bey!"

Lifting a flap of the tent and securing it with a red swag, Mr. Lewis strode forth, looking pleased, and welcomed his guests.

Flo could not help staring, so taken was she by Lewis's demeanor and attire, for the man had gone completely native. He had adopted the costume of an Ottoman vizier—or was it a viceroy?—blue *gubbeh,* white caftan, red turban, and a ragged white beard. Mrs. Lewis, a plain young woman clad in an English frock, stood quietly off to one side, rather like a second wife, Flo thought. She wondered why the wife wore such drabbery while her husband was tricked out like a peacock. For safety? To remind Mr. Lewis that, despite his clothing, he was not an Oriental, but an Englishman playing dressup? Selina, standing alongside, pinched Flo's arm. *Can you believe it?*

Mr. Lewis handed his guests into the tent, where a woman removed Flo's blanket from her shoulders and folded it assiduously upon a wooden stool. She wore trousers and a veil, both of pink muslin so transparent that it appeared less like cloth than concentrated infusions of dawn light. Her posture was as studied and impeccable as a dancer's. Whenever this Rosy Dawn (as Flo decided to dub her) moved, her bracelets, necklaces, and fringes sewn with coins jingled. The effect was hypnotic, the sound of faeries and stardust.

The meal was standard English fare, though how the Lewises managed it, Flo could not imagine and decided not to ask. She did not wish to appear overly impressed.

Mr. Lewis was pleasant and intelligent; Mrs. Lewis remained something of an enigma. Oh, she was recognizable as an Englishwoman of good breeding (from Hampton, Middlesex, it turned out), but why was she here on the arm of a man more than twice her age? Had her parents shipped her out with the intent of making a match? Why else would she have traveled to Cairo at age eighteen? Had the two met beforehand? Unlikely. Mr. Lewis had not been home for decades. Had she brought a dowry that allowed Mr. Lewis to continue living abroad (and rather luxuriously), or had it been a case of love? At moments like this, Flo felt like a child too young to play a game with complicated rules, and also like a spinster so old that she'd forgotten the arcana of marriage. Clearly, she should be grateful that Fanny and WEN had not packed her off to some forsaken corner of the world! Oh, they wouldn't have dared. Finally, she tried to imagine what Gustave would make of their hosts. Would he think Mrs. Lewis a craven seeker after security? Or a young woman who'd fallen under the spell of an older man? Flo knew the truth lay outside these pat melodramas, neither of which approached how Mrs. Lewis must *feel* so far from home, living in a tent on the Nile! And that is what Flo most wished to know: Mrs. Lewis's *heart*.

Servants laid the borrowed carpets upon the packed earthen floor and seated the three English in chairs. (No dyspepsia for Charles after all.) The dining table was a round brass platter balanced on collapsible wooden legs, with barely enough room for plates and cutlery. Rosy Dawn passed trays and poured wine from a tall ewer.

After the food was served, Flo asked, "What convinced you to move house from Cairo to Mahatta?" The sound of her own chewing (a piece of mutton) naturally muffled the sounds around her, but after she had swallowed, she immediately sensed from the continuing silence that everyone else knew the answer to this question. Also, that it might have been rude to ask it.

Charles started to answer, but Mr. Lewis held up his hand, patriarch-like, indicating he would entertain the query, no matter how touchy or tasteless. His robes hung down from his wrist in biblical blue and white scallops. "My dear Miss Nightingale, how kind of you to ask." He placed his fork on the table. A lengthy reply? Loss of appetite? Everyone stopped eating.

Across the table, Flo saw that the color had drained from Mrs. Lewis's face. Selina, sitting next to Flo, fidgeted.

Mr. Lewis sighed as he blotted his purplish lips within the fleece of his beard. "Our neighbor in Cairo, Rifat Pasha, wished to buy our property to expand his garden."

"He wanted to plant trees," Mrs. Lewis added in a monotone. "Almond trees."

"Almond trees!" Charles repeated with enthusiasm. "Lovely, *lovely.* Lovely blossoms. Lovely aroma." He fell silent, his voice petering out. He looked at Flo helplessly. Had he also not heard the story or forgotten it?

Mrs. Lewis sniffled, withdrew a handkerchief from her sleeve, and dabbed at her nose.

Selina said, "Perhaps I should have told Miss Nightingale about your mishap."

Flo felt her cheeks turning pink. Mrs. Lewis nodded and continued to hold the handkerchief in place, as though a nosebleed were pending.

"When we refused to sell," Mr. Lewis resumed, "our neighbor finished his demitasse of Turkish coffee, went home, and sent his slave to burn our house down that afternoon. That is the method of purchase in Egypt. My dear bride lost everything she had shipped out from England."

"How awful for you and Mrs. Lewis," Flo said. "I am sorry to inject the memory of it into our meal. I didn't know." She couldn't help thinking that Mr. Lewis's regal garments carried no clout in Cairo. It seemed plausible that his neighbor considered Mr. Lewis an arrogant interloper or an imposter. Perhaps Mr. Lewis should have offered compensation—baksheesh of a kind—in lieu of a sale. After ten years in Egypt, could he be ignorant of the customs? Or did he know, and object to them on principle?

"A terrible loss of property," continued Mr. Lewis. "My wife's piano, plate and crystal, her furniture." He shook his head. "Family items she had hoped to pass on to the next generation."

Mrs. Lewis blew her nose as proof of the depth of her loss. Rosy Dawn approached and handed her a fresh damask napkin, then returned to her shadowy corner. Charles, seated next to Mrs. Lewis, patted her hand.

"At least no one was harmed," Mr. Lewis said. He beckoned to Rosy Dawn to refill his wineglass. "Except the slave responsible for the fire. Several people witnessed him setting the blaze. Rifat Pasha administered a severe bastinado for his lack of stealth." Mr. Lewis laughed and helped himself to a potato.

"So we heard," Mrs. Lewis said, smiling. Evidently she appreciated her husband's humor in the midst of her sadness. Flo didn't know why, but she was taking a dislike to the woman, though in the next instant she wondered if this judgment might simply be the result of her own general bad mood Abruptly she wished she were dining with Gustave and Max. The impact of this realization made her sigh aloud.

Looking freshly alarmed, Charles turned back to Mr. Lewis. "What about your work, the watercolors and sketches?"

"Miraculously, nothing was lost."

Furtively, Flo studied Rosy Dawn—the purple silk sash, the blue jacket that ended just beneath her bosom with a fringe of gold coins that left her midriff visible through the pink gauze. She wore her hair in lustrous black ringlets that reached her shoulders. A painter would have had to use every pigment in his box to capture the shadings on her silks, which were as iridescent as scarab wings. When the woman raised her gaze from the floor, Flo saw that her eyes were a luminous and flickering green. At that moment, the woman returned Flo's glance with a look so searing that Flo felt rebuked. The sensation was identical to how she'd felt when she and Trout had argued. She felt again the sting of Trout's words: *You don't know much about me, mum, truth be told.*

A servant appeared carrying a wooden platter of sweets. Another carried a kettle of tea brewed at the brazier outside. "Bird's nest pastries," Mrs. Lewis said. "And Turkish delight. It's a *Turkish* delicacy made of—"

"We know," Flo said, taking one of each, not wanting to appear gluttonous, though she could have easily consumed half a dozen. She watched Selina place a pale green gelatinous square dusted with sugar into her mouth. She chewed it slowly, her eyelids closing as she savored it.

After dinner, they viewed Mr. Lewis's watercolors and sketchbooks. He had made thousands of drawings. "I have enough material here for a lifetime of painting," he said, turning the leaves of his portfolios while his guests oohed appreciatively. He said he planned to return with Mrs. Lewis to England the next year and start a family. Charles congratulated him, shaking his hand and clapping him on the back, saying that he had captured in his work all that was foreign and flamboyant in Cairo just as he had captured Spain's hauteur and dash. Mrs. Lewis glowed with pride.

Flo, who loved art but did not always approve of it—the Italians were too fond of the naked breast, in her opinion, and the Dutch too gloomy—was at first enamored of Mr. Lewis's renderings, seduced by their beauty. They were scrumptious Eastern delicacies meant to be consumed by the eyes instead of the mouth. He was masterful with a brush, and his hues had a depth she'd never before seen except in oil paintings. One composition showed a street bazaar; in another, schoolboys gathered around a low, tiled table under the tutelage of colorfully garbed imams. Harem portraits featured languid women in lavishly decorated rooms with carved wooden shutters (from which, Flo mused, Rosy Dawn might have stepped). In all the work, a honeyed light poured down, picking out the brilliant white coils of turbans and the ruby stripes of pajama trousers with a fierce purity and sensuality. But there was something troubling, too, and the longer she looked at the pictures, the less she liked them. She couldn't say why. Certainly, Lewis had captured the faces of the Orientals, from the hawk-nosed Greek sailors to the satin ebony cheeks of the Nubians. The colors were truer, if possible, than in life. The tactile billow of the textiles, the undulant curves of the camels, the brick and wooden textures were all magnificent. And then she saw what it was, or rather what was lacking. There was not a speck of dirt or disarray anywhere. Not a hint of stink. Everything had been glamorized, like a still life with flawless fruit and a smudgeless glass set upon a pristine tablecloth. If there was a beggar or cripple, his robes were not as tattered and threadbare as in life, his skin eruptions entirely omitted. Streets and alleyways lacked steaming piles of animal manure and sewage standing in open culverts. No pulpy filth smeared the ground of the markets; no spavined mules limped through the bazaars; no mangy dogs begged for scraps. Mr. Lewis had captured the splendor of Eastern fairy tales, of Aladdin's lamp and flying carpets, but not of the Egypt she had seen. The world he had created was too beautiful, completely devoid of suffering and evil. And therefore—and worst of all—not in need of redemption.

At eight forty-five, Flo, Selina, and Charles packed up to return to Philae. The temperature had dropped, and cold penetrated every joint and exposed inch of skin. They covered themselves with blankets while walking, but it was colder on the water. Charles draped each of the women and himself with a kilim rug to cut the wind. The wool was heavy and itchy, with a smell like stale tobacco. A slow rain of dirt sifted down from it onto Flo's clothing.

Luckily, despite going upstream, they caught a countercurrent and were back at Philae in ten minutes. Nevertheless, 9 P.M. was well past their usual bedtime, and Flo went straight to her cabin. Trout was sleeping under a quilted coverlet without her levinge. Flo wondered whether to follow suit. *Murray* warned severely about fleas, which cold did not discourage so much as impel to a warm body. It recommended sinking a dahabiyah after hiring it, which also took care of rats, but the *Parthenope* had not been doused. Nevertheless, she decided to take her chances, and for the first time curled into bed without the device.

There were numberless islands above the cataracts, some no bigger than a tabletop, others, like Elephantine, large and mountainous. Selina and Flo, once again in the felucca, were bound for medium-size Bidji, just offshore of Mahatta, where Mr. Lewis sometimes worked for greater privacy. Selina, enthused at the prospect of drawing the temple ruins on Bidji, had brought her sketchbook. "Everyone has done the Sphinx," she told Flo as they neared the island.

Flo remembered Selina's delicate pencil sketch of it at the start of the trip.

"But how many have sketched Bidji? Perhaps I shall be the second, after Mr. Lewis, of course."

Mrs. Lewis, looking more festive and relaxed than the evening before, greeted them at a rickety wooden dock. She wore a white cotton dress with a yellow apron over it, like a governess. The crew helped the passengers ashore, then set off for the other side of the island. Mrs. Lewis called after them in Arabic.

"What did you say, Mrs. Lewis?" Flo asked, impressed at her hostess's fluency in the language.

"Please, call me Marian. I said they should return in four hours."

"I do hope they have the same notion of the hour as we do, Marian," Selina said. She carried her drawing supplies close to her body like a banker his accounts.

"Time is more approximate in Nubia," Mrs. Lewis said gaily. "The important thing is that they will return well before dark."

Marian Lewis, Flo noted, was very sure of herself. She had the confidence and manner of a beautiful woman, though she was as ordinary as Parthe, who had the manner of a frightened rabbit. It was irritating to see a woman behave as if she were beautiful without actually *being* beautiful. Flo wondered how Mrs. Lewis managed it. Early on, someone must have convinced her of it, based, Flo reasoned, not on fact but on feeling. Her family might have constantly told her how gorgeous she was, not out of a desire to lie, but blinded by the purest love. Flo had met mothers like this, so enamored of their children that they considered others' offspring negligible. Fanny was not such a mother, prone as she was to harping on the tiniest flaws. With Fanny as a mother, Flo did not even know if she were beautiful.

A child of about four ran from a nearby hut to greet Mrs. Lewis. She pushed up the hem of the Englishwoman's dress and embraced her stockinged legs. "Zehnab!" Mrs. Lewis cried, petting her on the head. The child wore nothing but a bead necklace around her neck and another around her waist. She jumped up and down, clutching Mrs. Lewis's skirts, raising them up in small handfuls, like flowers. The child's woolly hair radiated from her head like a ring around the moon.

The little girl kissed Flo's hand as Mrs. Lewis introduced her. Flo was so taken with her that she immediately began to wonder what she might give her as a present. She hadn't thought to bring trinkets. Would Selina be willing to part with a couple of pencils or pieces or chalk? She whispered the question, and Selina nodded enthusiastically.

"And here is more of the family," said Mrs. Lewis.

An old man clad in a sheer white robe approached with two girls in tow, an adolescent and a younger child. Flo felt she'd been delivered to a pagan heaven and here was its St. Peter, accompanied by two angels. With open faces and kindly expressions, they appeared to exist in a state of contentment that Flo had never known or could no longer remember—the paradise that was her childhood, before Miss Christie? The trio beamed at her. They were clean and polished-looking, from their neatly oiled and coiffed hair to the dazzling red of the elder's tunic. Mrs. Lewis explained that one big family inhabited Bidji and that he was its patriarch. Flo wished she could speak to him directly. Was there any bigger obstacle in the world than language? She saw Selina curtsy and followed suit.

The old man was Zehnab's great-great-grandfather. The older girl, Fatima, was Zehnab's mother and a widow at sixteen. The last girl, Azrah, was Zehnab's aunt. She was ten and had just been married.

After a deep salaam, the old man left the girls with the women.

"It's a short swim from Bidji to Mahatta," Mrs. Lewis said. "Azrah swims over to visit us several times a week. Sometimes she brings little Zehnab."

Azrah, the new bride, was anxious to show off her house, a typical Nubian mud dome consisting of two rooms, one furnished with a clay divan and water jar, the second one reserved for chickens. Azrah was happy with her life, Mrs. Lewis declared, and especially proud of two pillows angled neatly on the divan. Though Flo could not stand up in the squat dwelling, she appreciated its cleanliness and practicality.

Mrs. Lewis had prepared a picnic to eat under the trees. She asked Fatima to fetch it, and soon the six of them were lounging on an Indian paisley bedcover, munching on pistachio nuts, durra bread, durra cakes, olives, and white cheese. Nothing English, unlike the evening before. While the food was being passed, Selina dug into her tote, pulled out three pencils, and placed them in Flo's pocket.

Mrs. Lewis was an adept translator, and the Nubian children—the wife, widow, and bride—had many questions for her. Azrah was fascinated by Mrs. Lewis's gold wedding band, which she removed and passed among the three girls to try on. Flo wondered how Mr. Lewis would react if he saw the ring so casually handled.

Selina began to sketch Zehnab while the older girls asked to hear the story of Mrs. Lewis's wedding. Mrs. Lewis was happy to oblige. Since grooms paid a bride price in Egypt, they wanted to know how much Mr. Lewis had given for her.

"Thirty shillings," she said, laughing. She translated the conversation for the women.

Fatima said that was very little and seemed disconcerted by Mrs. Lewis's bargain price. She asked how often Mr. Lewis beat her.

"Never," chuckled Mrs. Lewis.

Surprised by that answer, Fatima and Azrah conferred briefly before the next question. "What is wrong with him that he does not beat you?" Azrah asked. She looked agitated.

"It is because he loves me," Mrs. Lewis replied. "In England, men do not beat their wives." She fussed with her mousy hair, pushing it back from her forehead.

Again, the older girls conferred, withdrawing to a corner of the picnic cloth while Zehnab continued to pose for Selina, frequently peeking at herself taking shape on the sketch pad. Selina seemed delighted by the little girl.

"Is the thirty shillings part true?" Flo asked.

"Oh, yes," Mrs. Lewis answered, more cheerful than ever. "The *cadi* who married us demanded a price be paid, so my dear husband gave thirty shillings for the poor plate."

"It must have been a strange but happy day," Flo said.

"Unusual, to be sure." Mrs. Lewis seemed lost in a momentary reverie of the event. "But wonderful, too. That is the day Mr. Lewis bought me my Berber slave. Oh, but you saw her, last night at dinner."

Flo could not believe it! That there should still be slaves in Egypt was criminal. But that Marian Lewis should delight in owning one was nothing short of loathsome and evil. She recalled the hostile glare of Rosy Dawn when she caught Flo staring at her, and felt deeply ashamed. "You must love Mr. Lewis very much," Flo mumbled. "Such an extravagant wedding gift." Selina, like Flo an abolitionist, took one of Zehnab's hands and held it, avoiding Mrs. Lewis's eyes.

"Have you thought about arranging to educate little Zehnab?" Flo asked. "She seems so bright and energetic. You could send her to the nuns in Cairo."

"Whatever for?" Mrs. Lewis replied.

Wasn't it obvious? Flo thought of Felicetta Sensi, the little urchin she'd placed a year ago in the convent school at Trinità dei Monti, proud to have removed her from the harsh, perverting streets of Rome. Since then, she'd been paying for the child's education with her dress allowance. "For her betterment and the betterment of her whole family." Flo stared unblinking into Marian Lewis's face. Was it really going to be necessary to explain the idea of progress to her?

"That would be a waste of time. The child is perfectly happy here as she is."

The older girls rejoined the group, still watching Mrs. Lewis piteously.

Flo decided it was useless to express her outrage.

"Could you translate something, Marian?" Selina asked, handing Zehnab the portrait she'd made.

"Of course."

"Tell the girls that we like them very much." Selina tore off several sheets of paper and signaled to Flo to produce the pencils. "These are gifts for them."

As Mrs. Lewis translated, the girls eagerly accepted their presents, chattering and tugging on Flo and Selina. "They want to embrace you," Mrs. Lewis said, "to thank you."

"That would be lovely," said Flo. The five hugged and bussed. Selina clung to the little girls with tears in her eyes as Mrs. Lewis watched impassively.

Fatima returned to the subject of Mrs. Lewis's nuptials with what seemed to be an expression of concern. Would Mr. Lewis be sending her home since he did not think enough of her to beat her?

Mrs. Lewis laughed, then laughed again as she translated for Selina and Flo. Englishmen, she explained, did not send their wives home. They remained married to one woman forever.

The Nubians shrugged and abandoned the topic, still pitying Marian Lewis, Flo thought, who was the last person in the world to recognize pity when it was directed at her.

• • •

"I gather you disapproved of her," Selina said on the boat ride home. She swatted at a wayward insect swept up in a current of air. The men had unfurled the sail, and the boat was moving at a clip, combing the water into patches of green corduroy. "As did I. That she should brag about owning a fellow human being!" Selina frowned and shook her head.

"Awful," Flo said. "I think she's a brat."

"Do you?" Selina yawned.

"Yes. She has too high an opinion of herself, and quite apart from what others think of her."

Selina didn't seem to be as enraged about Marian Lewis as she was. In another moment, she nodded off, her cheeks a tawny pink in the fading light.

Sweet Selina, compassionate Selina. Remarkably, when it came to people like Marian Lewis, who were spoiled rotten and oblivious to their own flaws, she kept an open mind, while Flo detested Mrs. Lewis's complacency. No doubt, privately Marian Lewis set herself above the likes of Selina and Flo, Selina because of her age and faded beauty, Flo because she was a spinster seven years older than she. Most frustrating, it was impossible to impress Mrs. Lewis, as she wasn't interested in anything she didn't already know.

Something beyond mere disapproval irked Flo. Why was she *so* enraged? The anger was akin to the way she sometimes felt toward Fanny. With Fanny, the intensity of feeling made sense: Fanny had the power not only to block her ambitions, but also to withhold her love. Marian Lewis's greatest offense was that she was sickeningly content, immune to what people like Flo thought of her. Also, she had accomplished something Flo had not: she had found her place in life and was reveling in it.

It disgusted Flo finally to realize that what she felt was pure jealousy, and of someone she did not admire!

The next morning, the post arrived shortly after breakfast. Flo had two letters, one from Fanny. Nothing yet from Gustave, but it was only Wednesday, and she calculated that he was still in Aswan, perhaps performing obscene acts. She found herself hungering for his unique company. He didn't shy away from topics many people considered impolite. She no longer gave a fig for polite conversation. She much preferred to be unconventional.

Fanny's letter was full of cheerful reportage and advice. Flo decided to put off answering it until she had completed the Philae letter. She wanted to explore further the parallels between Osiris and Christ. Had Osiris not died for his people, too? In the seventh room, he was a fearsome presence, though she was convinced that, like Jesus, his terrible death had made him a compassionate and loving god.

She recognized the handwriting on the second letter. "It's from Clarkey," she cried out to Selina.

"I can't wait to hear the latest from Paris," Selina trilled.

Mary Clarke's letters were generous and stylish and, most of all, *funny.* She had a knack for inventing words that sounded half French and half English, but made perfect sense. She "trigged up" her apartment when it was dirty, and now so did Flo and Selina. The entire Clarkey circle had adopted the term.

The stationery was a somber tan instead of Mary's usual peach. Flo flipped it over and saw that she must have borrowed it; Julius Mohl's name appeared on the back flap.

February 11, 1850

Chère Pup,

I received your letter, posted from Cairo, with the wondrous description of your boat ride up the canal on your way to the Nile. Now I picture you, Selina, and Charles scampering up the great pyramid, scratching your initials on the ceiling of a secret passage known only to pharaohs. I know you are having a splendid time and will write me your adventures in detail.

I've been sitting on a secret for three long months because I wanted to be able to change my mind up until the last minute.

Personally, I don't give a snap for surprises, so before I tell you my news, I hope you'll accept my apology for waiting too long to share it with you. I believe you shall be happy for me. For I am happy, despite my indecision beforehand.

Julius Mohl and I were married three months ago. (Espoused "before men and angles," as Smollett said—I think in Humphrey Clinker.*) I was so unsure of this decision that when we published the banns, I paid a poster boy to plaster over them immediately. Other than Herr Mohl and me, no one knew of the engagement.*

Married life suits me. Julius has moved into my apartment and installed his gigantique library. I write this surrounded by Ninevah and Ur in all their glorious dust and gold.

As you know, I planned never to marry, and this conviction strengthened after Claude died, for he was the love of my life—at least so I believed at the time. Julius and I comforted each other for the great friend we had lost. This shared grief brought him closer to my attention and me to his. And though Julius is seven years my junior, I believe we are well matched. As a woman nearing fifty, I dare not call myself a "new" bride; I think of myself as a bride who has at last been brought out of mothballs.

We had no official celebrations. Instead, two days later, Julius and I traveled to Berlin, where we spent three weeks with delightful and elite company. Herr Mohl, the celebrated Orientalist, had spent so many years in Paris that none of his colleagues recognized him on sight!

As you know, for years I favored ardent friendships over romances, for I was not willing to trade a roomful of loving friends for one partner who might become possessive and boring and keep me from the social life so essential to my happiness. In short, the salon continues in full force, Julius being my assistant and constant companion. The only difference is that he no longer goes home at the end of the evening. (Before I forget to tell you, upon our return we had the pleasure of an evening with your friend Richard Monckton Milnes, who is an avid admirer of French literature.

He takes a scholarly interest in the Marquis de Sade, Julius told me after he left.)

Florence, dear, though this interlude in Egypt is only a hiatus in the family wars, I believe that once your ambitions take firmer shape, you shall fulfill them. Ultimately, I know you shall make your way in a world that is often hostile to women like us who break the standard mold.

The next time you visit, though everyone will address me as Madame Mohl, I shall still be your Clarkey (what's in a name, a rose would smell as sweet, etc.), and eager as always to hear your latest thoughts and plans.

Your loving,
Mary

Flo's temples were pounding; her face was on fire. Because they always shared their letters from Clarkey, she handed it without a word to Selina, but did not watch her read it. Being married, and happily so, Selina would doubtless be pleased.

Flo, however, felt devastated, betrayed. It could not be! She did not *want* it to be! But she couldn't say so, even to Selina. It was unkind and rude, small-minded and selfish. It would sound mentally unbalanced. It wasn't as if Mary had sworn to Flo to remain celibate. Yet Mary had violated her deepest precept. How could she? What had changed? If it were a union of convenience, Flo found it all the more abhorrent.

She could not imagine answering Mary's letter. Ever. For Mary was no longer Mary, but a stranger. Anyway, what could she say? *I feel wretched about your marriage. How could you?* She didn't wish to hurt Mary, though Mary had unknowingly cut her to the quick.

Selina finished reading. "Hurrah for Clarkey!" She waved the letter aloft. "Wonderful news! Aren't you thrilled for her?"

Flo sped through everything she might say that would not give her away, but could only manage, "I am surprised. Aren't you?" She could not force an iota of joy into her voice, further proof that deep down she *was* a wretched person, unable to be happy for a friend. She felt sick to her stomach, light-headed. "I'm a bit woozy," she said, touching her hair.

"Is there anything I can do?"

"I think I'll have a lie down." She stood and hurried belowdecks without waiting for Selina's response. Even with her closest confidante Flo was too ashamed to admit how she felt.

She lay facing the row of windows, eyes closed. A sense of dread overpowered her and she trembled. Mary had been her ally; now she was alone. And still she did not regret refusing Richard. She would do it again.

Despite her rational resolve, a feeling of terror began to overwhelm her. Lacking Clarkey's resources, how could she achieve anything without Fanny and WEN's consent? What would she do for money and where would she go and what would become of her shadowy sister, Parthe, who yearned always to be by her side, unable to take a forward step on her own? Poor Parthe! Poor Flo, with her sister stuck to her like dock weed to a lamb.

The sun was high in the sky when Flo opened her eyes. Soon it would be time for lunch. Selina or Charles would mention Mary's marriage, the thought of which terrified her most for what it predicted of her own future. She would have to feign a headache.

A welcome breeze passed into the cabin through the open windows. Where did breezes come from and where did they go? The Greeks thought the winds slept in caves and in bags carried by the gods. If only she could disappear as the wind did, without fanfare or ceremony or people asking why. She was utterly alone with an ambition that was fierce and truly monstrous, for it could not be satisfied without changing the entire world.

14

TOOTHACHE

At first, Flo ignored Trout's guttural sounds. It was just past dawn. So often now, she suspected Trout of testing her. "What is the matter, for heaven's sake?" she finally asked, lacing up her boots. It seemed she might be dressing herself unaided today.

"Toothache." Trout's voice was muffled by the pillow, which, Flo saw as she leaned closer, was wet with drool and flecked with blood. "A bad one."

"Do you have all your teeth?" Flo realized as she asked it how rude and irrelevant the question was. She knew very well that Trout had front and side teeth. Fanny would not have hired a maid with a gapped smile or a mouth like burned-out ruins.

"Yes, mum. My teeth are good. So said the dentist." Trout's words were gluey and ill-formed, as if she had dumplings in her mouth. Obviously, talking was uncomfortable.

Flo was surprised. "You have visited a dentist?"

"Yes, at Hanover Square. You, mum?"

"Of course." Flo had had two wisdom teeth pulled.

"A nice gentleman," Trout recollected. "I asked was he willing to fix the teeth of a servant." Trout paused and swallowed carefully.

" 'Don't you worry,' he said. 'I can fix your tooth in no time.' Then he said he guessed I weighed about eleven stone and gave me a tonic."

"Eleven stone you weigh?" The number was higher than Flo would have expected.

"Eleven stone and three."

This seemed to be a point of pride.

"I think I'm half man, my arms are so strong." Trout turned slowly, keeping pressure on her jaw with one hand. "Thirteen and three-quarter inches, I've been told, at the bicep."

Flo wondered at Trout's use of *bicep,* and who would have measured her muscle, and why.

"The dentist stopped my tooth with that stuff."

"Gutta-percha?"

"That's it. Oh, ouch!" Trout's hand flew to her right cheek and she burrowed her face into the pillow.

"Shooting pains?"

Trout nodded. "What am I to do? I cannot think as they have dentists in these parts."

Florence bent over, pausing for assent before she gently pressed her hand on Trout's forehead. The skin was cool and damp. Trout's body gave way under her touch, like a brick wall suddenly crumbling into a heap.

"Thank you," Trout whispered. "You are kind." She adjusted her position in the bed.

"I'm sorry you are not feeling well."

"I'm sorry I'm a bother to you. Egypt is doing me in."

"It's all right. It's not your fault." At last, Flo thought, Trout had decided to trust her. Flo felt so much better being kind than being strict with her.

Though Flo had never suffered a toothache, she'd watched WEN and Fanny and Grandmother Shore endure them. She was certain Trout's was genuine and that she hadn't called it forth by dint of her hypochondriacal nerves. "Will you let me help you?" she asked.

"Yes, mum. I'd be grateful. I can do nothing with this pain gnawing at me."

"I shall try my best to cure you, then," Flo said. Her mind was churning, for when it came to ague and catarrhs, wens, rashes, and simple fractures, she had experience. But of teeth, she knew nothing except what to do for any swelling or inflammation.

"Are you hungry?" she asked. "Could you take some sopped bread or soup?"

"It don't seem right you serving me."

"We cannot choose our illnesses." Flo stepped away from Trout's bed. "No more than we can choose our station in life. I shall be back shortly."

Flo felt a sudden infusion of purposefulness, a welcome sensation. She went on deck and asked Charles for some whiskey, which he readily poured into a teacup. She instructed Paolo to prepare tepid broth with bread.

Back in the cabin, Trout lay flat on her back, her eyelids drooping, and the right side of her face puffy. Flo poured out a jigger of "medicine" (Trout eschewed spirits), which Trout downed in one swallow. Tea would be good, too, Flo thought, the accompaniment at any sickbed. She went back upstairs and ordered a pot.

Trout was dozing when she returned. She decided not to awaken her. She opened her medical chest and removed cotton wool, swabs, bandage gauze, and a few vials. She began a log in her journal book: *Trout,* 7 A.M.: *Swollen jaw, painful tooth. No apparent fever. Patient fully cognizant.*

Efreet-Youssef poked his head into the cabin. He went barefoot on board the dahabiyah, and except for the pleasant slap of his feet when he worked on deck raising or lowering sails, she never heard him move about. "Madami," he whispered, shyly looking down as she turned to him. He held out his hand with a letter in it. Nodding in gratitude, she took it. He disappeared as silently as if he had levitated upstairs. Flo glanced at Trout: still sleeping. She sat on the divan and ripped open the envelope.

My dear Rossignol,

We returned to Philae three days late from Aswan, where we succeeded in securing supplies and diverting ourselves. Not knowing what would be available farther downstream, we also purchased (against Joseph's objections) a few provisions for the trip to Koseir.

The guidebook says it is a four-day walk from Kenneh to the Red Sea, but our mounts, not we, will be doing the walking. We will not, as I expected, be riding horses, but camels. (Can one sit a trotting dromedary? Do they trot? Do they gallop?) Apparently the road is poor, and water can be a problem, with dried-up and contaminated wells. (We saw a well near Edfu with the carcass of a decomposing goat draped across its mouth. The stench would have given an archbishop second thoughts about the existence of God.)

I have thought often of you in the past week, hoping that you are feeling happier and even enjoying yourself—and banishing any extreme thoughts.

I wonder if you are as preoccupied with fantasies of the Red Sea as I am—writing in the clouds, my mother used to call my daydreaming. Max, on the other hand, is sharpening his nibs and pencils. Everything is fodder for his literary ambitions, which differ from mine. I do not think he lives in the present at all, but in some frantic future packed with ink bottles and reams of paper whereon he rehashes and thus brings to due importance the events which pass for ordinary life to the rest of us poor sods not inclined to publish the existence of every stray cat of a thought that crosses our minds. I shall have to cut out his tongue if he suggests one more time that I write a travel book, as if my life, too, were a poor rag to be soaked in the fluid of adventure, then squeezed out drop by drop onto the page as words. Bollocks! I want to feel the desert sun drumming the back of my neck, count the armies of stars arrayed in the night sky. I want the hot Saharan air to parch my nose and lungs so that I may know the pleasure of quenching an immeasurable thirst. Sometimes I think Max undertakes things only so he can write about them afterward.

Twice I have promised to teach you to make a squeeze. It is now 6:30 A.M. and we are camped in tents among the palms on the eastern side of Philae. I shall come by at ten to make good on my word. I know this is very short notice and if you are otherwise occupied, we shall make a future date.

Wear your pretty pink bonnet.

Your friend,
Gve. Flaubert

P.S. Bring drinking water if you can manage it.

Flo read the letter twice, then tucked it in her desk. She decided she would go. And though there wasn't time for a reply, she couldn't resist looking in *Murray,* if only for a moment. She scanned the index: "old Koseir" and then there, on page 398, "Koseir":

ROUTE 27

Kenneh to Koseir, by the Russafa Road.

	Miles
Kenneh to Beer Amber	11¾
Wells of El Egáyta	21¾
Well of Hammamát	24½
Well called Moie-t (or Sayál-t) Hagee Soolayman	33
Beer el Ingleez	15
Ambagee	5¼
Koseir	6
Total miles:	**117½**

The names of the landmarks sent a tingle radiating from her nape to the top of her head and looping back down her spine. Beer Amber! Beer el Ingleez! The names of the wells that would sustain their very lives! The mileage was daunting. Five times the distance from Embley to London, among Bedouins and Ababdeh, the tribe named after the local desert. She floated in exotic precincts: herself astride a camel, rocking forward on the lumbering beast . . . herd animals wearing an orchestra of brass bells. There might be gazelles . . . there might be lions—

Trout moaned. Flo shut the book. She had still to deal with the toothache. Strings attached to door handles? Pliers? Or simple sedatives and hot soaks? Dentistry was not a true medical art but an offshoot of the barbershop. The chairs were identical. When the cottagers at Wellow were down with toothache, the usual remedy was extraction, but she was not prepared to remove Trout's tooth—yet. Nor did she know the technique. Besides, the thought was abhorrent, for if there was something more worrisome than Trout with a toothache, it was Trout with a gaping, bloody wound so close to the brain, with the attendant risk of morbid infection. Could a person die from a toothache? How would she get to Koseir without Trout?

Charles and Selina arrived. From the stairs, Charles called out, "Good job, Flo. Excellent work," and asked if he could be of assistance. She sent him away. Selina stayed to help and offer encouragement.

By nine, she'd finished the preliminaries. Trout, obedient, almost sweet, had taken nourishment. She was behaving bravely. She had rinsed her mouth with warm water. Flo had wrapped a forefinger in gauze saturated with whiskey and gently massaged the painful area in hopes of numbing it, which was only partially successful. Selina had brought a clean pillowslip. While she was changing the pillow, Flo stopped stock still as if she'd spotted a snake. Tucked beneath Trout's pillow like an amulet was the iron key that had gone missing from her chatelaine. What did it unlock? Or signify? Perhaps it was just an odd talisman.

She packed the tooth in cotton wool soaked in whiskey. "No talking now for a bit," she cautioned her patient. "Let it rest." Trout nodded obediently, a few tears coursing down her sweaty cheeks. Selina mopped Trout's forehead with a damp cloth.

The soup and bread sops did not mix well with the whiskey. No sooner had Flo tied up Trout's jaw prettily, with a gauze bow under the chin, than Trout tore it off and vomited into a bowl Flo proffered just in time. "Oh, mum, I'm so ashamed," Trout said.

"Do not think of it," Flo said. "Illness has its own timetables, like the railroad. We simply don't know what they are. We shall try food again later."

The whiskey was having an effect. In a few moments, Trout dropped off. "Gilbert," she whined in her sleep, "when shall I see you?"

"Who is Gilbert?" asked Selina.

"I don't know. She has a married sister in Ryton. Maybe it's her husband. Or perhaps she has a brother, too." Flo wiped her hands on a towel. "What shall I do, Selina? Gustave will be here any moment."

"You shall go with him," Selina said firmly. "Trout's toothache can wait a few hours."

"Could you stay with her?" She knew Selina would agree, but felt obliged to ask.

Selina nodded and clasped her hand. "Do you need Charles to chaperone?"

"No, I feel perfectly safe with Monsieur Flaubert. I am sure he will protect me if necessary."

Selina didn't comment.

"He is a gentleman."

The two regarded the servant in her narrow bed. Trout was a tall woman, and one bare foot stuck out from under the blanket like a chunk of granite. Flo jotted a note in her log: *Patient drowsy.* She felt Trout's forehead. *Still no sign of fever.* She tugged the cover over the offending foot.

"Ultimately, she is as much my charge as I am hers." Flo sat on her bed with a sigh, weaving her fingers together. "Perhaps I should stay."

"Don't worry. She will be fine until you return. If the pain worsens, I could dose her with a bit of laudanum." Selina put her arm around Flo. "I shall talk to Charles right now." Charles had charge of the opium balls and laudanum. Selina stood to leave.

"Could you . . . help me with my clothes and coiffure before you go?" At age twenty-nine, Flo had never dressed herself, nor thought of doing so, as was proper for a lady of rank whose clothing required a second set of hands.

"Yes, of course. I should have thought of it myself."

After Flo changed into her brown cotton dress, Selina did up the long expanse of small covered buttons on the back.

"My hair," Flo said. "Nothing fancy. There's no time. I just want it to be neat, under control."

She sat on the bed while Selina brushed her hair.

"Don't trouble yourself too much," Flo said, "I'll be wearing my bonnet." She reached behind to touch the lank brown hair fanned across her shoulders.

"I'll do my best." Selina parted the hair down the middle, then gathered most of it into a bun. "You have such lovely hair, Flo."

"Thank you, dear Selina." Flo began to braid the strands of hair by her ear while Selina braided their counterpart at the other ear. "It *is* just a toothache. And I do so want to learn to make a squeeze." And I do so want an adventure with Gustave, she thought.

Selina pinned the side braids into the chignon. "And it's a lovely way to spend the morning." She replaced the comb and brush in the fittings of Flo's vanity case. "I find M. Flaubert a gentleman of interest, don't you?" she added.

Any girl over age fourteen knew the phrase "a gentleman of interest," but it was unusual to hear it from Selina, who never played Cupid. It designated a marriage prospect—not only for Flo, but also for all womankind as surely as if Gustave's name were inscribed in a transcontinental social roster. "Actually," Flo said, "he behaves like a brother toward me." She hoped she was not blushing. Though she loved Selina, Flo hated how public an event affection inevitably became. Marrying in a church while scrutinized by dozens of people struck her as a barbaric custom. At least Clarkey had had the good taste to have a private wedding, thus sparing her friends the tribal spectacle.

"Ach du . . . liebe dich," Trout whimpered in her sleep.

Selina said, "She will be sleeping like an infant when you return."

Twisting around suddenly, her eyes still closed, Trout said, "Miss Florence, you must go meet your gentleman. He might be the face in the fire."

Face in a fire? Flo reached for her log: 9:45 *Delirium.* She looked at Selina as she tore the page from her journal book. "Do note any changes, would you, Selina? It's so easy to forget. A written record is best."

Selina picked up the paper and held it to her breast. "I shall."

"I wonder if the tooth is loose," Flo mused, pausing as she turned to leave the cabin. "It didn't seem so."

In a faint and cracking voice, Trout warbled, *"Der Mond is aufgegangen, die gold'nen Sternleinn prangen."*

"Did you know she spoke German?" asked Selina.

But Flo's mind was elsewhere. She had heard a pleasant baritone voice abovedeck and, plucking her bonnet from its hook, took the stairs two at a time, leaving Selina standing in the cabin with her question unanswered. In Flo's haste and distraction, she forgot to arrange to take along water.

"Bonjour," she called out a moment later, coming on deck.

Charles had already concocted a glass of lemon water for Gustave, and the two men sat at the table under the reed awning, conversing in French. After tramping across Philae to reach the dahabiyah, Gustave's pelisse was full of burrs and sand. His face shone with perspiration.

"Bonjour." He stood, and offered her a chair. He had pushed back the hood of his robe, revealing a clean-shaven face. And what a handsome face it was without the beard (and despite the bald head)—youthful and fresh, the skin flushed from the heat, his cheeks the color of peaches, with high spots of pink and deeper rose.

"You've shaved off your beard," she observed, smiling.

"Tea?" Charles asked her. "I've already brewed a pot."

"Yes, please."

"Have you breakfasted, I hope?" Gustave asked her.

"Oh, yes," she lied. Actually, with all the hullabaloo, she'd forgotten to eat. She spied one of his crewmen on the shore, a muscular, dark-skinned fellow. He sat cross-legged in the sand, intently picking his nose. Alongside him lay several bundles and a yoke with two buckets.

"I understand from Mr. Bracebridge that your maid is ill with a toothache." Gustave gulped the flavored water, finishing half of it.

"Yes, but let us not talk about it. I have done nothing else for the past three hours." Charles shot her a surprised glance, his eyes briefly widening, his brow furrowed in mild disapproval or surprise. There were times she wished she could bite her lip rather than blurt out what was on her mind.

Gustave seemed unperturbed by her directness. He lifted his glass and turned it in the striped shade of the reed awning. Splinters of sunlight swarmed there, like fireflies in a jar. "As you wish, Rossignol."

Hearing the nickname, Charles looked up, his features sharpening. It occurred to Flo that her nickname suggested a greater intimacy between her and Gustave than Charles would have been aware of. The truth was, she liked it when he called her "Rossignol." The word had the physicality of a touch, as if he had taken her hand or tapped her shoulder. Also, no one else had ever thought to call her by a nickname. Was that because she appeared too serious, too stern?

The three sat sipping at their beverages, Charles observing them, Flo noticed, as intently as a man expecting rain with his hand out the window. Gustave was apparently oblivious to the alarm he had raised. Finally, as if satisfied that nothing more would be revealed to him, Charles spoke: "And where will you make these squeezes? You will be staying on the island, will you not?"

Good grief, Flo thought, did he expect her to run off with Gustave? "I would not worry you by going far afield," she replied.

"I'll look after your charge," Gustave assured him. "We shall be at the Temple of Isis with my man, not fifteen minutes' walk from here."

"Good, good," Charles said, tamping his pipe with tobacco. "I shall be interested to see the results of your expedition." He struck a match and inhaled, sucking furiously.

"Oh, Charles," Flo said, once again not quite in control of her emotions, "you make it sound as if we are going to Timbuktu. We shall be back by luncheon. Not to worry."

Charles rose and planted a kiss on top of her head, then offered his hand to Gustave. "I shall see you later, then."

Gustave half rose from his seat. *"Oui, monsieur."*

Flo raised her hand in farewell.

After Charles was out of earshot, Gustave said, "I think he suspects us of something."

"That is what I thought, too." She finished her tea. "He's being protective of me, that's all."

"But it will be a shame to disappoint him."

The making of squeezes turned out to be simple and repetitious, rather like hanging wallpaper.

It was ironic, Gustave pointed out, that the archaeologist's record of carved stone should be so flimsy and inimical to permanence. The massive pylons of the Temple to Isis would become thin, translucent sheets with the texture of old newspaper.

"So a stone and its squeeze," Flo said, "are as unlike a pair of objects as a candle and a flame."

"True. I've been thinking of a death mask and the living human, but I like your analogy better."

They began with the pylon on the eastern side of the temple. Aouadallah placed the implements wrapped in a linen roll on the rocky earth. With a small knife, he slit the string on a bundle of folio-size paper. "Five hundred sheets," Gustave said, fanning the edge of the pile with his thumb. "A ream. Can you guess how many reams we brought on our trip?"

"Twenty?"

"More than two hundred."

Flo was silent.

"Max arrived at this number, I believe, by multiplying his ambition by his insanity."

She laughed. What a splendid time she was going to have on the desert trip listening to the Frenchmen cleverly bait each other.

"There are three steps in the manufacture of squeezes," he explained. "The first is to remove debris from the reliefs." He picked up one of several brushes and began to sweep the stone surface. She watched as he inserted the bristles into each incised line. He handed her an identical brush and indicated where she should begin.

Kneeling at the base of the pylon, Flo sensed the magnitude of the job. On close inspection, the stone was thick with the grit and grime of the ages. "Do you think we are the first to clean these stones since they were carved?" she asked. "That would be at least a millennium." She loved the idea; it endowed her hands with the wise golden light of history.

He stopped his brushing to beam at her. "I see you have a penchant for the dramatic, Rossignol."

Her cheeks were suddenly warm. *Rossignol* was the tolling of a bell that she wished for and waited to answer. She had felt the same eagerness in the library at home as a child. A hidden door in the shelves led to a secret room that WEN allowed her to enter when she performed recitations especially well or answered a difficult question. How fervidly she had craved her father's approval, his pride in her intellect. "The dramatic? Is it dramatic to imagine that the last hand that touched this surface belonged to an ancient artisan?"

"I am certain the priests of the temple kept the place presentable. So perhaps it has been half a millennium. Would that please you as well?" He changed brushes, selecting a narrow one with stiffer bristles. She watched as he loosened dirt caught in the kilt of an Egyptian soldier. Or did only royalty wear the white linen skirts? "We must be careful," he said, grunting between strokes, "when using the harder brush. It abrades the stone. Just flick it back and forth, like so."

They continued to broom the surface for half an hour. Aouadallah, clad in only a loincloth and turban, joined them, working at a faster pace than either of them. Flo marveled at the rich hue of his skin, identical to the walnut chiffonier in her bedroom at Lea Hurst.

The sound of the whisking was pleasant, like a servant methodically sweeping a walkway.

The sun crept higher. Flo reached an area where the carving was obliterated, hacked out like the name of a friend fallen from favor. She touched his sleeve.

"Change of regime, I bet," he said.

"Yes." The redactors, she knew, had been impassioned, executing their erasures violently. They especially detested Pharaoh Akhenaten, who had decreed that the Egyptians worship only the sun god Aten. Everywhere his name was carved, they'd axed it out, a death sentence on a man already deceased.

Aouadallah retrieved a goatskin from his pack. "Wine, effendi?"

"Yes. *Merci.*" Taking the skin, he dispatched Aouadallah to the riverbank. They would need water for the next step in the process.

She watched him raise the goatskin above his head and, without spilling a drop, squeeze it until a red stream arced gracefully into his open mouth. She'd never manage that on the first try. She was no Saracen, no Bedouin, but a woman from Hampshire. The thought deflated her. She sighed as he repeated the performance.

"I shall help you," he said, reading her thoughts. How much he communicated with his eyes!—the pleasure he'd take in teaching her, his certainty she'd succeed, the deep satisfaction of cool wine in a dry throat.

"All right."

"I shall shoot the wine directly into your mouth."

Was that a leer on his face?

"Do you still feel safe?" He pointed with one hand to the dark square of Aouadallah's burnished back retreating down the hillside and lifted the goatskin with the other.

Why should she not feel safe? Safe if he squeezed the wine into her mouth (which proposal seemed mildly obscene)? If he were teasing, making fun of her, she didn't care for it one bit. Just then, a globule of sweat fell from her nose onto her bodice. She withdrew a lace handkerchief from her sleeve and blotted it, turning away from him.

What time was it? The sun was still aslant—11 A.M.? Nearly time to return, though they'd hardly begun. "I have no idea what you are talking about," she snapped.

"I meant only that our chaperone has left us."

She said nothing, still unsure of his meaning.

"I thought perhaps you hadn't noticed we were alone," he continued. "And then I thought it might amuse you to realize it." His tone lent no closure to the words, which hung light as a bird in the air, as if he were prepared to continue flying explanations until she accepted one. "Have I offended you?" He looked crestfallen.

Had she once again overreacted? She worried that her brief flashes of temper were harbingers of imminent bitterness and pettiness—the fruits of a stifled and vague ambition. "I am not offended. I was merely confused. And"—she decided to follow his example of candor—"a bit frightened. I thought you were joking at my expense."

He stared at her and she stared back, two birds that had just landed on the same branch. "I know that feeling," he said at last, "of not knowing another's intention and thinking it—"

"Thinking it," she interrupted, "a weakness in yourself?" This, too, was bolder than she'd intended.

"Exactly." He looked pleased, as if in light of the edginess of the subject, he admired her ability to identify it. He wiped his wet forehead with the sleeve of his robe. "We should stop cleaning now. Here comes the water."

Bowed under a yoke with two buckets of river water, Aouadallah trudged toward them. He was breathing hard as he set the yoke down. The water looked like lime aspic.

From a knapsack, Gustave withdrew a sponge and submerged it. "This is the messy part!" he shouted with glee. Working rapidly with the sopping sponge, he wet down the stone, flinging small jeweled arcs and scattered beads of water. Flo followed suit with the enthusiasm of a child. In their wake, Aouadallah pasted sheets of paper onto the wet surface. Using a stiffer wire brush, Gustave pushed the paper into the reliefs until it adhered. Together, the three established a smooth, mechanical movement, working until they'd papered the lower third of the wall. "That's good," said Gustave.

Wiping her brow, she stepped back to regard the result.

In the thin sliver of shade cast by the temple wall, Aouadallah dropped to the ground and lit a short-stemmed pipe. "Now we simply wait," Gustave said. "This is the boring part."

"The work is so physical," Flo said. She felt clammy circles of sweat spreading out from her armpits. She hadn't noticed the heat before, enjoying herself thoroughly. She'd always liked manual labor. Fanny considered it drudgery. Ironing, mucking out stalls, and grooming the ponies, all done on the sly.

"I think your dress may be ruined." He touched a patch of the garment that had dried to a lighter shade than the rest.

"I don't care." She removed her bonnet and fanned herself. "When do we take them down?"

"As soon as they are dry. Not long." He dipped a sponge in the bucket and mopped his neck with it, then shook back his hood to dribble water on his head. Flo felt much hotter watching him refresh himself. He stopped, dipped the sponge again, wrung it out, and leaned toward her. "May I?"

Before she could answer, he began carefully patting her face, the way a medical man would bathe a febrile patient. She remembered the story of his sister, Caroline. Had he sat by her bed when she was feverish? Was he reenacting the kindnesses he had lavished on her while she was dying? The thought was disquieting, and she pushed it from her mind. "Oh," she said, "that feels quite wonderful."

"Yes." He continued to apply the sponge to her cheeks and temples, careful to avoid her sleeves. "I would make a terrible woman," he said, "if only because of the clothing you must endure, though no one admires a well-cut frock more than I."

She had closed her eyes, but opened them as he led her by the arm to a spot where they sat in a small wedge of dappled shade cast by a locust tree growing out of the temple floor.

"I have often tried to imagine what it must be like."

"What what is like?" She was happy to listen to whatever he had to say as long as the sponging continued.

"Being a woman. Wearing all those petticoats and whalebone corsets. Shawls that catch on doorknobs and in wheel spokes. And tiaras."

"Tiaras?"

"You know what I mean—the gewgaws, the paraphernalia."

She did; still, she wished to draw him out. "But is not a man equally constrained in a vest and trousers, cravat, coat, and hat?" Water trickled down between her breasts. "None of us lives nearly so simply as the Nubians," she added.

"True."

"But I do understand," she continued. "It's a question of degree. How much whalebone? How many petticoats and hoops? I, for example, will not wear a hooped skirt."

"Exactly! But a man's clothing is more practical and less confining."

"Yet you yourself have complained about the lack of freedom in middle-class life." She touched the coarse cloth of his djellaba. "And here, you dress in robes."

"I suppose we are both prisoners of our privilege."

"Yes." She felt suddenly anxious. This was the stopping point in her own contemplations, the place beyond which she could venture no further because her life was at odds with her beliefs, the place where self-doubt crept in to ruin her moral clarity. For the very privilege that so confined her had also spared her from bondage and hopelessness of a different sort.

"I should like to spend a month as a man," she said, her face as frank as the sun.

"I can understand that."

It was pleasant to talk with no boundaries and in the middle of an ancient temple with a whiff of Aouadallah's pipe tobacco on the air, which she equated with serious male topics of discussion. She felt completely unconstrained, a child at play. "Are they dry yet? What if the wind comes up?"

Gustave rose and tested an edge of paper. "About another twenty minutes, I think, though leaving them longer doesn't hurt." He folded his arms beneath his head and lay on the ground.

"Good," said Flo. She thought fleetingly of Trout—surely it was past noon—and decided that she could be late. She'd stay until they took the squeezes down.

The sun was overhead, withdrawing any remaining shade, beating down directly on them.

Aouadallah had dozed off, his pipe beside him on the ground, his worry beads slipped from his fingers.

Gustave stood up again. "Can you picture me all tricked out in laces and fichus and millinery with beaded flowers? Or, conversely, beneath a veil?" He twisted his hood around so that the black pompoms dangled below his eyes.

She laughed until she was out of breath as he dramatized his femininity, shaking his hips, stringing a few Arabic words together into a song. " Habibi!" he croaked in a falsetto. "Darling, Allah, Karnak, Asiyoot, Edfu." When he had reduced her to hiccups and tears, he tested the paper again. "Done," he declared. His voice was naturally loud, she realized.

They peeled the squeezes loose from the wall, lifting them like bandages from a wound. "Max says blotter paper would have been better, but it takes too long to dry and costs too much."

The squeezes were thin and translucent as a baby's fingernails. She held one up to the sun and saw how beautifully it had captured the hieroglyphs. Not a detail had been lost. Though the work was boring, the results were superb. He numbered each sheet, noting its date and location on a sketch of the temple.

"They are so lovely," she said. "With all those delicate curves and lines, they remind me of hats."

"Yes, like felt hats for ladies. The molded shapes are subtle. The creases and folds make the style." He seemed pleased by their joint powers of expression.

With Aouadallah, they stacked them on a simple tin tray. They had made more than forty.

"Or they could be French pastries," Flo added. "They look good enough to eat." She had missed breakfast. Soon everything would call food to mind.

"*Turkish* pastries," he said. "We had them in Cairo, made of perhaps fifty thin layers of dough, with honey and nuts between."

By now she was salivating. Her stomach growled. Had he heard it?

He gathered up the brushes but left the buckets for the next round. "Am I not a slave to Max?" he asked. "He expects me to make squeezes at every monument. That means thousands if he has his way. Thousands of hats."

"You must reason with him." They set off toward the dahabiyah, back down the hill toward the river.

"It is difficult. He is as insistent as a sore toe."

"I like that," she said. She could imagine more conversations in which the goal was to capture things in words, things almost too ephemeral and delicate for expression. It would be like writing poems in the air. "Now I must go and tend to my maid."

"Do a good job. We will need her for Koseir. Make her feel indebted to you, Rossignol. Spare nothing."

"I would treat her well in any case," Flo said, immediately regretting the self-righteous tone. She stopped and touched his hand. "But I shall follow your advice. I shall lavish on her greater sweetness and care than ever."

Back on the dahabiyah, she felt gay and relaxed for the first time in a long while—eager, indeed, to show Selina and Charles her ruined brown dress.

15

KENNEH

The infamous Street of Scholars in Kenneh was not the site of a school or mosque, but where the almas plied their trade. Sadly, Gustave had no appetite for whores by the time he reached it. The return visit to Kuchuk Hanem a week before had resulted in heartbreak and disillusion. Love belonged in the brothel, but there, too, it could inflict pain. For seven weeks he had indulged the fantasy that Kuchuk Hanem took special interest in him and was eagerly anticipating his return. Her lovemaking on the second visit was desultory, mechanical. She didn't feel well, she explained to Joseph. Even after Max brought out the camera, she couldn't shake her malaise, agreeing to pose in her sexy silk trousers and jacket only when Gustave offered a bonus. It saddened him to learn that she'd sold her pet polka-dotted lamb to the butcher. She posed instead with a kitten, a blur of fur that whirled from her grasp like a dust devil. The two resulting photographs—he captioned them "Bored" and "Impatient"—depressed him even more. He told Max to keep the portraits.

"I agree they won't do for the mantel, but don't you want them for your desk drawer?" Max asked that morning as they docked at Kenneh. "Look"—he pointed to her breasts—"you can see her nipples in this one."

"I don't care. I don't want them."

Max made kissing sounds. "My poor boy, has she broken your heart?" He smacked his lips again while holding up the pair of calotypes.

They bore no resemblance to the woman whose memory Gustave had been savoring. Gone was the delicious naughtiness of the whore who had jumped on his back and then curled up beside him, holding his hand while she slept. Had she even remembered him? He might as well have wooed his right hand.

He hated this vestige of the romantic in himself, the vulnerability of it. Were his dreamier, mooning self ever to escape the confines of the whorehouse, he'd be sunk.

Gustave and Max encountered a man in white robes soon after going ashore. He was Père Issa, the French consular agent in Kenneh. He buttonholed them as they passed in front of his house, happy to encounter a pair of genuine Frenchmen.

They decamped to a café where they explained their missions to him.

"So, you are tourists, I take it?" he asked, smiling.

Gustave was relieved not to have to continue the impersonation of a bureaucrat. "Yes. We are here to experience the riches of the Orient."

Max explained that they wished to take a caravan trip to the Red Sea and asked if Père Issa might help. The consul responded enthusiastically, offering to aid in securing camels and guides. Furthermore, he had a brother in Koseir who would welcome their company.

"We wish to take an English lady, a friend, with us," Gustave told him.

"Is that so?" The consul drained his cup of Turkish coffee. "How can I be of assistance?"

Half an hour later, lounging on a divan in a brothel, Gustave opened his manuscript and reread the sentence at the top of the page:

A woman's cunt is as distinctive as her face, the lips below as unique as those above.

While Max of the still-pimpled prick took his pleasure upstairs, Gustave paid two almas to pose instead of servicing him. New entries for *L'Encyclopédie du Con.*

Yussefa's mons venus is more merkin than mound. A springy thicket of curls rises up like an evergreen forest in the midst of a desert. . . . Fatima, smooth as sea glass, shaves or waxes her entire body. Her pubis, oiled and plump, is a hillock cleft by labia edged with a frill of looser skin the same color as the dark circles beneath her eyes. Gazing at her face, one cannot help but recall those ribbons of purplish flesh bedecking the sweet gift package in the declivity below.

At his signal, one alma refreshed her pose, the gold coins dangling from her jacket pleasantly clicking. The women were naked from the waist down.

Kenneh was small enough that word of their arrival had spread quickly. In Egypt, windows and sometimes doors remained open in fair weather, with much of life conducted within public earshot.

It was all so different from home, where narrow vestibules and locked doors led to the place of greatest seclusion and seat of family power, the bedroom, as if every *citoyen* were expected to harbor secrets. Living out of doors, like the Egyptians, a lie carried no farther than the human voice.

The models lay side by side on their backs with their knees raised up.

Vertical grins, vertical grins! Like the professional girls of France, whores here are happy to display their bottoms. What could be more enticing than to watch from behind a woman bending over until that second little mouth appears in a pout. Below the crack of the derriere, the assholes, too, are charming, the entire assem-

blage like an exclamation point, as if their behinds are perpetually elated or surprised.

It was heartening to write something obscene and unpremeditated. On the other hand, it gave rise to a vexing old question: Why did he write exclusively of saints and whores, as if there were nothing of interest between the two extremes? Max had remonstrated with him for this. Write about regular provincials, he'd urged, going so far as to suggest the case of a woman named Delamare who had shocked the hamlet of Ry with her adultery and suicide. But he could not stomach the thought of writing about ordinary people, people whom in reality he would despise. To inhabit the cheery smugness of the grocer or pharmacist, the clerk or banker's wife with their endless platitudes?—unthinkable. Nor did he wish to write about himself.

Rossignol came to mind. Would she be a suitable subject? Unlike rebellious men who took up dissipation, high-minded women like Rossignol turned to religion for solace. O for the days of temple whores and pagan bacchanals! What had befallen the practice of sacred copulation? Now there was a way for the English lark to converse with God! Actually, if he believed in God, Gustave, too, could have warmed to the religious life. He had experienced a diminished version of its appeal in writing the life of a saint who spent a monomaniacal half century in the desert.

He jotted down words alongside his crude sketches, notes for later, when he would create flesh, bone, color, perfume—desire itself—by means of other little marks on paper through the miracle of language. To be lost in it, to comb through its vast nomenclatures for botany, for cloud formations and machine parts, its heaps of ornaments and junk—how he missed it!

He put down his pencil and glanced outside. The window framed a bright collage of the street. As he beheld it, he began to compose it in his mind: sunlight teeming with dust motes, moving swatches of color, and voices circulating like currents of incoherent verse. For him it was always thus—the world and then, simultaneously, his rendering of it, as organically attached as a shadow. Was that not enough to occupy the rest of his life? To fashion from roiling chaos his own sacrifice to lay upon the altar not of God, but of Art? Or were they the same? Could he return to Croisset and resume life within his hermitage without regard to the failure of *The Temptation*?

He resumed sketching. Perhaps after he'd completed a second or third book, he'd return to it. Now he must press forward with a new project. Between the insufferable *bêtise* of bourgeois life and rank, undifferentiated failure, lay only one option: the pursuit of art as a sacred calling. To capture the quicksilver iridescence of a pigeon's breast while all around you men admired bird droppings on each other's heads like the latest fashion in hats. The sheer nobility of the enterprise filled him with premature pride. What appealed to him was not just the escape Art provided from the ordinary world of commerce and family, from shoveling the shit of mediocrity from pile to identical pile, but also its difficulty, the purity of intention, the tricky simplicity of it. Better a sublime writing flop than law or industry, with their endless iterations and vulgarities, their superfluous *stuff*. For when he wrote well, there was nothing like it. Time stood still and he disappeared into its transfixing calm.

He took a deep breath. Perhaps he could return to the writing life. What else was there?

The whores began to dress. He closed his notebook and bid them farewell, blowing loud kisses off his fingertips. *"Adieu, monsieur,"* they chimed. As the door slammed behind them, a sudden gust billowed the red curtains at the window like skirts kicked up by a dancer. He heard Max stepping briskly across the floor overhead.

But what would his subject be? What had been left unsaid by the greats? By Balzac, Rabelais, Hugo, Corneille, and Stendahl? And if he didn't write about sainthood or depravity, what could he tackle? The question took up residence in his belly like an ill-digested meal. And there it remained.

16

A CABINET OF RELICS

Trout's toothache followed an erratic course over the next two days. She improved, then worsened, sometimes better in the morning, sometimes in the evening. The swelling, too, increased and shrank unpredictably. But she slept through the nights, and awoke rested.

Flo didn't mind caring for her patient, though without her medical texts, she had to improvise. Twice a day she applied whiskey-infused cotton wool to the inflamed area and immobilized Trout's jaw. She continued the warm broths and added a vinegar and chamomile wash six times a day, boiling the concoction first.

With Trout indisposed, Selina replaced her as lady's maid, helping Flo to dress and coif. Trout watched with dismay, but abided by Flo's strict order for complete bed rest. The only exception was the chamber pot, which Trout would not so much as allow Flo or Selina to touch.

On the third morning, after an hour-long application of the cotton wool, pus and blood erupted from the area around the tooth. Trout was appalled, Flo relieved. Within hours, the gums were less tender and the swelling had decreased. "One more day in bed," Flo told her that afternoon. "That is the best medicine."

For all Trout's complaining, Flo was surprised to note, she clearly did not enjoy being ill and the object of so much attention. She was a compliant patient, following Flo's regimens to the dot, but seemed faintly humiliated to require help from others. After the pain subsided, Flo made her promise not to chew on that side of her mouth until she could consult a dentist on the Continent or back home. "Even if you are tempted," Flo insisted, as Trout, thinner and pastier, prepared to take the stairs for her first breakfast on deck in four days. "You mustn't forget." Trout agreed.

After she recovered, Trout's demeanor changed, though Flo could not say exactly how or why. At first she thought Trout had sweetened (perhaps in gratitude?). But the change was subtler than that. Trout seemed no happier, merely a tad less sullen and more cooperative. Perhaps the change was simply the kittenish softness of persons who have been ill and not yet fully regained their strength. What energy Trout had she seemed to waste in restlessness, pacing back and forth on the deck, her crocheting slung around her neck or stashed in her pocket. She spoke little and sat apart, writing in her brown notebook, silently watching the river's green ribbons spool past. She must be lonely, Flo thought, though neither woman made an effort to alleviate that fact. They hardly spoke.

Four days later, on a bright Tuesday in April, they drifted into Keneh. After lunch, Flo went ashore with Efreet-Youssef, along the wide curve of sand that served as the harbor, eager to find Gustave's *cange.*

The overall impression of the town was of buildings thrown up overnight to make a dazzling first impression. Close to the river, mud brick houses with lopsided balconies leaned over the dusty thoroughfares, creating doglegged passageways that hovered uncertainly above the streets. Most were whitewashed or painted in bright colors—turquoise famously warded off the evil eye. Farther inland, she glimpsed grimmer wooden shacks, and streets converging into alleys or footpaths irregular and narrow as animal tracks. A gentle disrepair marked every structure, suggesting that neither better materials nor greater precision would count for much against the onslaught of the heat and the sand and the inundation.

She soon found the *cange,* its tricolor bunting deflated in the still air. She waved to the sailors swabbing the deck. They waved back, calling out greetings in Arabic to her and Youssef. Joseph came running, obviously dragged from a nap by a crewman. Bowing, he explained that the two gentlemen had gone into town for supplies. He did not know when they would return.

Supplies again. And, suspiciously, without Joseph's assistance. She tore a sheet of paper from her aide-mémoire:

My dear Gustave:

We arrived in Kenneh today at noon. Can you come to the Parthenope *tomorrow night? Would 7:30, directly after dinner, be convenient? I hope you are prepared to convince the customers. I am counting on it!*

Yours in haste,
Rossignol

She folded the note in half and handed it to Joseph.

She decided to wander around the colorful quarters of the harbor before returning to the houseboat. As when she rode a donkey, Youssef trotted in semicircles around her, persistent as a housefly, a man determined to be in two places at once. In the midst of his flurry, she could walk unhampered by tradesmen and beggars. They passed all manner of shops—a local pottery; a dark, narrow booth beneath a palm-leaf canopy vending oil, olives, and dried herbs; a bakery; a saddlery.

As she made her way through the glare and dust, she noted a warm sensation in her belly and, with alarm, felt it spread into her face and limbs—the beginning of an attack of nerves. These episodes inevitably caught her off guard, as if her body knew something her brain had not yet realized. Today's anxiety, she guessed, was a measure of how eagerly she was anticipating the trip to Koseir, and how much she dreaded its going by the wayside.

Her hands and knees beginning to shake, she tried to quicken her step lest the nervousness escalate. Her head felt light, as if it might detach from her body and float off, like a soap bubble. She stopped to collect herself, looking for something to lean upon. There was nothing but Youssef. In Egypt, everyone sat upon the ground. She bent forward into her own shade, clutching his arm.

"Madami, madami," he whispered, looking terrified.

It was hellish to have a mind divorced from her will, a mind that in a frantic instant leaped from ember to consuming flame, from a singular concern to every worry at once. She had never told anyone about this affliction (or was it merely another character flaw?)—it would sound insane. At home, she took refuge in the bedroom and locked Parthe out. In Egypt, however, there was nowhere to hide to regain composure. Suddenly it felt to her that not just Koseir was at stake, but also the rest of her life. When the trip ended in five months, she'd be trapped again in the bosom of her suffocating family.

Her face was burning now, her head abuzz. The battle would resume, with endless arguments over her appetite for government reports, her desire to learn statistics, her unseemly projects. Every single thing she wished to do made Parthe sick and Fanny scream and slam doors and throw cushions to the floor. Even WEN would desert her—good, mild WEN!—because she *was* monstrous. It was hopeless, utterly hopeless. She had no future at all.

Oh, but there *was* one light on the horizon—Kaiserswerth, near Cologne, which she planned to visit on the way home. For years, Baron Bunsen had kept her abreast of this institute of deaconesses, the only Protestant equivalent to a convent. Two years ago, he'd arranged a weeklong sojourn for her. Fanny had given her grudging permission. As far as she knew, Flo's visit was merely a side trip from a family jaunt to Carlsbad, where WEN would consult an eye specialist. When, at the last moment, Fanny canceled both trips, Flo became despondent, saying she wished to die, but careful not to reveal to her mother the source of her distress in case another chance for Kaiserswerth arose in the future. And now it had, though she'd not allowed herself to fantasize about it in any detail in case her hopes were shattered again.

Youssef looked frozen in place, afraid to move. For she had touched him—which was strictly taboo under Mahometan law—and he, in return, was touching her. If anything befell her, he would pay the penalty, perhaps with his life. She looked up, offering a thin little smile that did nothing to reassure him. Sweat accumulated in the furrows of his brow. His face had gone ashen.

"I am all right," she said. She straightened up and left off gripping him. Certainly he would not wish to be seen with her holding his arm!

"Madami?"

"We shall go now." She adjusted her bonnet, and tugged both cuffs over her wrists. She felt wretched.

"You are safe with me, madami."

"Yes. *Merci beaucoup.*" The very sky felt oppressive, a pitiless blue, devoid of a single puff. Daylight on the Nile was as startling as the flare of a match, and as revealing.

He extended his forearm to her as if they were going into a formal dinner. She gladly took it. Thus they promenaded slowly down the beach. Please God, she thought, let Charles and Selina not be abovedecks to see how rattled I am. She slowed her pace, nearly creeping, her feet so heavy her shoes might have been filled with sand. Despite this caution, the panic was unabated.

Trembling, she continued stiffly down the beach.

When she was younger, she'd tried simply to bury her disappointments. Then, too, she had suffered physically—the same breathless panic, weeping so strenuous that it left her exhausted and speechless. In her twenties, it occurred to her it might be better to *cling* to her losses, to cherish them like relics. Wasn't that the purpose of history? To remember triumphs and defeats? And if she didn't have any triumphs, shouldn't she catalog the losses? When Fanny canceled the first Kaiserswerth trip, a new tactic had occurred to her: deceit. At twenty-eight, she'd taken up outright lying. It was so simple—she would tell Fanny about Kaiserswerth, but only *after* she had done it. She'd conspired with the Bracebridges before they left for Egypt. Charles and Selina wouldn't flaunt defying Fanny, but Fanny would be far away in England while they toured Europe. "We shan't be lying," Selina had told Charles at Flo's prompting, "so much as not paying attention to Flo's daily doings." Since then, Flo had pondered Kaiserswerth the way one ponders a sliver of light under a door one dares not open—yet.

The voices of children had replaced the low mutter of tradesmen. She turned to see youngsters naked in the river noisily splashing, hacking at the water with their elbows so that it broke apart in great liquid slabs. At her side, still supporting her arm, she felt Youssef's presence, the bodily solace of it. He stared ahead with a cool formality, his movements graceful, his robes fluttering in a steady ripple just above the sand. The surf crashed, then crashed again. They passed tea and water vendors.

Back in the days when the sisters discussed such private matters—before Flo turned Richard down, thus dashing Parthe's hopes of floating through life like a feather on her bonnet—Parthe had tried to lift her from her funks. Out of love, for if there was one certainty in Flo's life it was that Parthe loved her without limit, a love so overwhelming that it mystified Flo. It was dutiful, to be sure, an unchanging affection based on blood. But it never wavered, even when Flo behaved badly, ungratefully. Did Parthe depend on Flo as a cure for her own loneliness? Was it jealousy turned inside out? Parthe herself was unable to elaborate on the subject, and no one held her accountable for her actions. Flo loved Parthe and at the same time considered her completely exasperating. One might as well be vexed at a puppy.

They were walking more smoothly now. A light breeze swept the shore. Flo glanced back at the chain of footprints on the sand; it hardly seemed possible she had placed her feet there. Her legs felt remote, disconnected. Beside her, Youssef breathed calmly. She turned to him and smiled. He cast his eyes down, too modest, she thought, to acknowledge her gratitude. He stopped and gently withdrew his forearm from her hand, removed a clay jar from his pack, and offered her a drink of water. She had the sudden urge to embrace him, to clasp him to her breast. He might allow her to hold him, rigidly, not knowing what else to do, while she wept freely, luxuriantly, without the need or expectation of understanding.

She took the jar from his hand and drank. The water was cool, and smelled like the garden at home in early morning, the scent of dew on soil. He watched, pleased, as she swallowed.

He pointed down the beach toward the dahabiyah, as if to warn of its proximity. She nodded. "*Merci.* You are a good man." He smiled shyly and offered his arm again. She took it, at ease in their newfound sympathy.

The houseboat was seesawing gently in the shallow water. Aside from the captain lounging near the brazier, paring his nails, it seemed deserted. In the middle of the afternoon everyone was asleep or resting.

She curtsied her thanks to Youssef and quietly went belowdecks, still wishing to cry and exhausted from not allowing herself to. Her throat ached as if she had swallowed an apple whole. Trout was asleep, her needlework in a pile on the floor beside her bed.

Lowering herself on the divan, she stared at her small hands.

Twice in the past two years she believed she'd found a way to pursue God's calling—two crippling disappointments in her cabinet of relics, both set in motion by kind men trying to help.

The first was Dr. Fowler, a family friend who ran the Salisbury Infirmary. They had become confidants, discussing the latest medical treatments, from bandages and surgical procedures to homeopathy. While they ambled through the park among the giant rhododendrons, she explained how one could convert Embley into a hospital. She'd thought of everything, from how to dispose of the sewage to installing dumbwaiters to reduce the time orderlies spent on the stairs delivering meals.

Miraculously, Dr. Fowler found nothing repellent in her ideas, and invited her to work alongside him, tending patients, writing their letters, managing supplies. For the first time in her life, she had a plan with a sponsor. But after three screaming debacles in as many days, Fanny crushed it. Flo's aspirations, she said, were *so unappetizing* as to constitute a blemish on the family's name. Only slatterns and opium smokers, tipplers and laudanum addicts hung about hospitals. She banished Dr. Fowler from the house. Flo went to bed for a week.

Dr. Samuel Howe, world famous for his work in America with the blind and deaf, set the second crisis in motion. After several afternoons of talking, he suggested that she, too, devote herself to the handicapped. Of course, he lamented, no formal curriculum existed for such work. He recommended nursing. No, that was not his word. What was it? Caretaking? A *caretaking* career? She could not recall.

She had plunged into the subject up to her neck, reading government blue books on the education of the deaf and blind in Europe and Canada. And then—she could still remember the shiver of excitement as she wrote the letter—she arranged to visit a boys' academy for the deaf while in Rome with Selina and Charles. She had barely slept the night before her appointment. But when she arrived, clear-eyed and articulate, immaculately garbed in a modish lavender bodice and skirt, the headmaster denied her entrance. He had thought Florence was a man's name. Undeterred, the next day she returned with Charles, who conspired to pass her off as his personal secretary. Or had he said "assistant"? Or was it "attendant"? Charles had pulled himself up to his full height, spewing his best flourishes in Italian to no avail. The headmaster, a self-righteous Benedictine, proudly informed them that no woman had ever set foot in the institution. Her presence, he observed in a tone suggesting she had offered to perform the dance of the seven veils, would have a deleterious effect on the boys. Devastated, she had returned to the hotel and retired for the rest of the day. That evening, she gave the purple dress to Mariette. She would no longer be a public embellishment. She wished to work, not brighten a dim room.

When she returned from Italy, she found Parthe, whose health had always been delicate, a confirmed invalid. This was the height of what the blood mob dubbed "the Parthe situation," of which Flo was believed to be the root cause. The doctor declared it a case of hysteria and predicted that Parthe would never thrive without her sister's steady companionship. Fanny immediately ordered Flo to devote the next six months to Parthe. What had she written in *Lavie*? "I feel myself perishing when I go to bed. I wish it were my grave." She obeyed Fanny, staying home with Parthe even though she found her sister's debilitation a frightening harbinger of her own future. Parthe worsened anyway, suffering a complete collapse within three months. When the Bracebridges intervened with the invitation to Egypt, Fanny had reluctantly agreed. Though the Bracebridges were rather reclusive, they knew important people. In Italy they had introduced Flo to the Herberts, a couple powerful in government circles. People had talked about Sidney Herbert being a prospect for prime minister from the time he reached his majority. Fanny probably considered Egypt a potential matchmaking excursion. In any case, all her attention was focused on Parthe.

The aromas of food preparation tinged the air, the piquancy of raw chopped onions, the charred odor of the brazier heating up.

As Flo prepared herself for dinner, she spotted a letter at the foot of her bed, and on top of it, artfully arranged, a twig with two supple green leaves—a gift, no doubt, from Youssef, who could enter and leave a room without displacing a molecule.

5 p.m., Tuesday

My dear Rossignol,

We have found an ally, a Christian gentleman who will help present our brief for the Koseir trip. Do not fret. Max and I and our new friend will be persuasive. All you will have to do is smile and keep Trout topside.

Yours until tomorrow at 7:30,
Gve.

What impressed her most about Gustave was his liveliness. And now he would put it to use to help her sway Selina and Charles and, most especially, Trout!

But what if Trout exerted her will? What rights did a servant have? At home, she was free to quit. Oddly, when Fanny hired her, Trout had set two conditions of employment, neither of which suggested that she would be put off by the hardships of travel. The first was her preference for the filthiest, most arduous jobs—blacking the grates, scrubbing the flags on the stoop, polishing boots. While other maids took a bashful pride in their feminine limitations, Trout had the unself-conscious bearing of a draft animal as she moved trunks and furniture about the house. The second condition was a special curfew. Without providing a reason, she had asked permission to come home at ten instead of nine in the evening.

The real question, Flo knew, was this: how deep was Trout's loyalty? Flo thought she had ingratiated herself to a degree during the toothache ordeal, but the threat remained that even if Charles and Selina agreed to the caravan, Trout might not.

17

PÈRE ISSA

Flo hated the thought of conspiring against the Bracebridges, especially as they were willing to conspire *with* her for the upcoming Kaiserswerth visit. Nevertheless, she pondered her strategy all day. Though loving, permissive, and endearingly absentminded, Charles and Selina bore in loco parentis the responsibility for her safety. This was no mere formality: they would require assurances about the trip that she, Gustave, and Max would have to provide. The discussion must be unfettered, logical as a clock. Her only chance for success was to dull with the semblance of rationality an enterprise that in truth glittered like a jeweled dagger with the perils of the unknown.

Selina in particular knew the strength of Flo's determination, though she had never tested it. After dinner, she surprised Flo by expressing her reservations. Trout had gone to retrieve her needlework, and Charles to fetch his brandy, leaving the two women alone on deck as they waited for the Frenchmen.

"I cannot help worrying that there will be many opportunities for mishaps," Selina said, unfastening the catch on the mosaic bar pin she'd bought in Rome the year before. "It's crooked," she explained, stabbing the pin afresh into one side of her collar.

Flo was about to reply when Selina hurried on. "Oh, I trust M. Flaubert implicitly. It is the wilderness that concerns me."

"But you read the guidebook, didn't you?" Flo had pressed it into Selina's hands that morning.

"Yes, Sweet, I did—"

"Then you know that our own military use the route our caravan will take. As do diplomats and missionaries."

"Certainly, Flo. I read it all." Selina worked the pin back and forth at her throat, attempting to level it.

"I'm only saying that if missionaries use it, surely the route is safe." Flo folded her hands and wove her fingers together until they whitened. She feared no eventualities except being denied permission to go or, to a lesser degree, offending her dear friends.

"There!" Selina announced. "Is it straight now?"

Flo appraised the long, narrow brooch. Pliny's doves, encircled in black, held between them a blue garland of flowers. "It is."

Selina poured herself a glass of orange-flavored sugar water. "Something to drink, dear?"

Flo shook her head.

"As I understand it," Selina went on, "it is not the *preferred* passage. Too rugged, I believe." She sat down at the table. "And I saw no mention of families taking it out to India." Avoiding Flo's eye, she stared at the liquid in her glass.

Surely this was a bad sign. For the first time Selina was clearly discomfited by Flo's intensity. They had never argued, never adamantly taken sides about anything. Selina had never been flint or fuel for Flo's fire but always the snuffer, the damper, the cool ration of water.

"Yes, but the caravan route is shorter and quicker," Flo said. Was that actually true? What was short was the description of it in *Murray*—just a page, not counting the list of landmarks. In fact, Murray, wishing to sell guidebooks, rarely sounded a note of alarm. A traveler would be hard-pressed to find mention of death or danger, save for ubiquitous warnings about the importance of respecting the honor and independence of Bedouins. As for the terrain, it was always "majestic." Treacherous ravines and steep defiles became "echoing choirs for travelers who would give voice to their desert delight."

Selina fussed with the damask tablecloth, tugging it over the corners of the wobbly table. "Flo, dear, I have no wish to argue. You know I have only your welfare at heart."

An infuriating tear made its way down Flo's cheek. "I'm *counting* on this trip, Selina, really I am." Dabbing at her nose with a monogrammed linen handkerchief withdrawn from her sleeve, she lowered herself into one of the chairs. "It may be arduous, but I am equal to it. I'm *sure* I am."

Charles had emerged from his cabin by now and stood at the stern, chatting with Paolo. Flo could hear the two reminiscing again about Greece. Twice Paolo had been Charles's cicerone in Greece, so that, though Paolo was, in fact, from Malta, to Charles, he *was* Greece. Surely, Charles missed his club in London—the smoky, tweedy, liquor-tinged press of other Hellenophiles who worshipped at the altar of the Golden Age. Indeed, some (though not Charles) had joined the battle for Greek independence as young men.

Selina took Flo's hand. "I just want you to be safe."

"Is Charles so worried, too?"

Selina lowered her voice to a near-whisper. "I'm not certain. I haven't raised the issue with him. I didn't want to draw his attention to it."

Flo sometimes forgot how clever Selina was, her jackdaw intellect cloaked in a fabric of pleasantries, smiles, and melodic speech. She and Charles loved each other more than any couple Flo knew, but that didn't stop Selina from leading Charles around to her point of view like a bull with a nose ring. *Brava,* Selina!

"In any case, I doubt he's given it much thought since you first mentioned it." Selina tried to straighten the well-used tablecloth with the heel of her hand, Sisyphus clearing dust from the path of his rock.

"Perhaps he's more concerned about the company I'm keeping. My honor and all that." She regretted it instantly. Why could she not keep a civil tongue?

Selina shook her head, looking pained. "That's hardly fair, Flo, and you know it." She let go of Flo's hand, leaned back in her chair. "Charles adores you. And he trusts your judgment as much as I do."

"I'm sorry, Selina. I'm just *so* eager for this trip." It was true: she didn't doubt Charles's loving regard. But it was infuriating to have her fate rest even in his benevolent hands. "You know how much I cherish you both." Selina looked away from her. Was she reluctant to convey bad news? "Has he said anything at all about the trip?"

A breeze stirred, lifting the hair off Selina's forehead.

"I believe he'll want to know what your plans are. You know Charles—he thinks in terms of schedules and tactics." Selina paused, her face full of pleasure. "My quartermaster. Wonderful trait in a husband, to be so practical."

Indeed. Where would they be without Charles's zest for organizing? It was Charles who insisted on lugging supplies from home. Without his foresight and insistence, they would have had no jams, no milled soaps and hairdressings, no laudanum, lye, oatmeal, or cocoa. Without gregarious, calendar-crazed Charles, there would have been no afternoon teas with consular agents, no lunches with delegates, no picnics with slave-mongering wives of watercolorists on remote islands. Left to Flo, they would not have met a single Englishman during the two-thousand-mile journey on the Nile. And would such isolation really have been wise or advisable? Not all the meetings had been boring; not every English tourist was an insensitive dolt.

How easy it was to complain about a thing when one had no shortage of it. Fanny was right: sometimes Flo *was* a selfish brat no better than Marian Lewis. Worse—a brat on the outside; on the inside, a monster. And forever at war with herself.

"Don't fret, Sweet," said Selina. "Let us see how things unfold. Just let people speak their minds. Have faith, dear Flo."

If only Selina knew! Flo had faith enough for a dozen women, one for each year since God had so decisively if mysteriously put her under His thumb. How could she tell Selina that she not only wanted what *she* wanted, but also what God wanted *for her*.

Selina cupped Flo's chin. "You shall be happy, I know it. We both wish it more than anything."

There was movement on the beach, four men ambling toward the houseboat. In the uncanny pink light of dusk, their footprints were steeped in violet shadows and the Nile stilled to a vast deposit of jade. No such hue ever bathed the lawns or beaches of England.

Joseph led the way, followed by a stranger wearing a dazzling white *gubbeh* and tarboosh. Gustave and Max, for their parts, were dressed, ridiculously, *à la Nizam*—like Egyptian infantrymen—in baggy pants with tall boots, wide belts, and scarlet jackets.

The mere sight of their costumes lightened Flo's mood. It struck her then that she was not simply drawn to Gustave; she was also drawn to *herself* as she might be in his company, to the freedom he elicited in her, his wildness perhaps unleashing its equivalent in her. She, too, might dress outrageously, pull pranks, tell jokes. He more than tolerated her moodiness; he *embraced* it. Little wonder that she burned to go to Koseir! Not so much for the place or the adventure as for a different self, a Florence driven not by selfishness or monstrosity, but by the simple prospect of joy.

Charles hailed the quartet and, with Paolo, handed them aboard. Introductions followed, cemented with handshakes, curtsies, the brushing of lips on hands. Max, Charles, and the stranger laid on courtesies and compliments in a thick impasto, tossing out verbal flourishes like bandalores in a game of "around the world." Flo envisioned herself and Gustave parodying them later. They would bow to each other and knock heads, melt to the floor laughing, pleased with their private whimsy.

The stranger, Père Issa, was a Christian from Bethlehem who served as the French consular agent in Kenneh. A tall, immaculate man of indeterminate race with olive skin and green eyes, he wore a gold hoop in his ear, like a storybook pirate. Flo was struck by his long, slender fingers and glossy, almond-shaped nails. Overall, he cut the elegant figure of a man who had just emerged clean and pleasantly scented from a Turkish bath. Yet, for all this splendor, he was the farthest thing from an English gentleman she could imagine. The word *exotic* jumped to mind. *Alluringly foreign.*

But what was that at the end of the pinky finger of his right (but not his left) hand? A tapered fingernail grown beyond all utility flitted about him like a winged insect as he gesticulated. A weapon? Decoration? Mark of rank? She scrupulously avoided staring, but there it was, again and again, nearly two inches long. Following her covert gaze to the weird appendage, Gustave nodded, ever so slightly. *Yes, I see it, too.*

Selina welcomed everyone to the table, and Efreet-Youssef, always at the ready, pulled out chairs for each guest in turn, then blended into a nearby shadow. Charles poured two fingers of brandy from his crystal decanter for the men, while Selina and Flo took sugared water. Appearing on deck, Trout waved away the offer of a beverage before installing herself decisively in a chair several paces behind Selina, where she proceeded to count out crochet stitches.

"Ah, my dear Madame Trout, allow me to introduce to you Père Issa, our distinguished guest," Gustave said, his voice a rich tapestry of regard, the words plumped in gold. Paolo translated perfectly.

Forty-two doubles and turn work, Flo heard her mutter. Would Trout stop crocheting? Finally, she rose with a little sigh and set her bundle on the chair. "How do you do, Mr. Issa."

"Enchanté." Following the French custom, the consul reached for her hand, which was not offered. Trout retreated a step. "I beg your pardon, sir. I do not parlay-voo."

Rebuffed but still smiling, Père Issa bowed to Trout, then returned to his hosts.

Trout coiled yarn around her index finger and resumed her place behind Selina.

"We are gathered to discuss the excursion I spoke of last week," Flo told her maid. She had mentioned Koseir in passing, only to stress that Trout would be going, for when given the option, Trout preferred to remain on the boat. There had been so many side trips to tombs, temples, bazaars, and ruins that Trout had stopped asking for details, and Flo had ceased providing them.

"Yes, mum," Trout said, eyes on her yarn, wrists ticking forward and back. Loop up, wrap around, loop back, pull through. Another plank in the barricade nailed in place.

"It will be a stimulating journey, Madame Trout," said Gustave, laying on solicitude with a trowel. "I hope you will enjoy yourself in our company."

Paolo deftly translated. She thought to correct him and Gustave—Trout, after all, was a *mademoiselle*—but decided against it. A title of any sort gave Trout added gravitas, raised her social standing. Surely this pleased her.

"Thank you, sir. That's most kind of you." Trout said this loudly and slowly, as though to ensure his understanding. She had no inkling, thought Flo. Would it be better to keep her in the dark until the last moment, thereby adding the burden of guilt if she thought of refusing? Gustave seemed to have a strategy.

After talk about the weather, the river, and a brief recounting of the descent of the cataracts (by general accord a lark as compared with the ascent), Max unfolded a map onto the tabletop. He pointed to Kenneh and then to a brown dot on the Red Sea's western shore. Koseir. Trout, still counting stitches, paid no mind. Charles and Selina were rapt.

"Well, just a knuckle away, really," Charles said approvingly, swirling his brandy before plunging his nose into the glass.

"The crew will be specialists, of course, who've made the crossing tens of times," said Max. "Hundreds, I daresay."

"And Père Issa's brother is, by chance, the French consular agent in Koseir," Gustave added. His face gleamed in the tender pink light. Later, he might fatten (for he seemed inclined to fleshiness) and lose his hair. But now, perhaps out of gratitude for his presence, Flo imagined pressing her lips against his. (Was that all there was to a kiss? In which case, why did people keep at it for more than a second?) His lips would be soft and yielding, she expected, like flower petals, dry and warm as the center of fresh-baked bread.

"How fortunate," said Selina.

"Dandy," Charles agreed.

"My brother, Elias, he has a villa by the sea," Père Issa explained, motioning with both hands. His palms, Flo noticed, were several shades lighter than the rest of him, like the chalked hands in the posters for the Ethiopian Serenaders, a minstrel show that played London every year. "He will be honored to entertain you as his guests."

"Well, isn't that grand?" Selina clapped her hands. "Isn't it, Charles?"

"Indeed." Charles turned to Flo in English. "After crossing the desert, a good bed will, I'm sure, be most welcome."

At this mention of beds and lackings thereof, Trout looked up and began listening.

"You have made the trip yourself, Père Issa?" Selina inquired.

"Many times."

Charles set his snifter on the table and removed a leather pouch from his frock coat. "What I want to know, *monsieur*, is how remote, how out of the *way* the road is." He fiddled with his tobacco and pipe. "For instance, have you encountered other caravans on your trips? Are there highwaymen? Bandits?"

"Many pilgrims cross at this time of year." Père Issa licked the rim of his glass delicately, like a cat. "And no, no bandits. It is quite safe. Protected by the Bedouins."

Safe compared to an omnibus? Flo wondered, or to a trek through the Australian outback? She knew the desert was forsaken, lacking in life-sustaining food or water, and thus a test of will and endurance. Brigands had never entered her mind.

"Excellent." Charles leaned back in his chair and drew on his pipe. Looking equally content, Selina gave his arm a knowing squeeze.

Was that it, then? Had it been decided? Flo trembled at the thought. Had Charles agreed, just that easily?

"What's this about, mum?" Trout asked in a hushed tone that Flo had come to detest, a tone that tugged at Flo's sleeve without exactly asserting itself.

"We were just speaking about the villa of Père Elias, M. Issa's brother," Flo said carefully, forcing a smile. Levity was called for—mirth—a touch of fancy. "M. Issa says it hangs on a cliff high above the sea, with cooling winds. And it's white as sugar." Now she was in the swing of it. "With feather beds in every room. He says we'll be treated like royalty."

Trout's stilled crochet hook protruded between her fingers like the beak of a baby bird. "And the desert?"

Behind Trout's head, the sky had turned a molten orange; while along the shore, the palms had darkened into fringed, black paper cutouts. The air was empty, eerily silent. There were so many birds along the Nile that when they roosted at night, the quiet was sudden and almost disturbing, like that afternoon she thought she'd gone deaf, before hearing the Voice. "We'll traverse it, of course," Flo answered.

"What desert would that be, mum?" For an instant, Trout's eyes flashed red, like a dog's, reflecting the sun as it smoldered at the horizon.

"The same desert you've already romped through, dear Trout. The eastern Sahara, which some call the Nubian—"

"But where are we going? What's at the other *side* of the desert?" Resentment was etched all over Trout's face—in her furrowed brow, her skeptical gaze and pinched mouth.

"La Mer Rouge!" Gustave cried, leaping from his chair and lowering himself on one knee before Trout.

"The Red Sea?" Trout ignored the man kneeling before her and strode over to the map, trailing her yarn. She had no idea where she was, had she? Flo dreaded the moment of her recognition. For though Trout had felt free to complain profusely about all manner of irritation, up until now she had followed Flo blindly. Flo wondered if Trout knew she had the power to refuse, to wreck everything. Would she dare?

"Here is the destination," Selina said, tapping Koseir, "and here is where we are at present. And all of *this*"—she swept her hand from the narrow funnel at Suez to the Gulf of Aden—"is the Red Sea. The Red Sea of Moses and the Hebrews!"

"Heaven protect us!" said Trout. "It's the other side of the world."

"Il est à l'autre extrémité du monde," Paolo repeated for the Frenchmen.

"Non, mais non," Gustave wailed. "It is en *Égypte.*"

"Is it then?" Trout ran her tongue over her lips, which were dry and cracked.

"Mais oui, madame." Gustave approached once more, lifted Trout's hand, and gently moved it from Kenneh to the coast. *"C'est notre voyage. Il sera merveilleux."*

Trout looked dubious. "Where will we sleep, mum?"

"In tents," Flo said. "We shall be quite comfortable. We shall have our own cook. And travel by camel in a caravan."

Incredulous, Trout turned to Selina. "You don't mind riding one of those beasts, mum?"

"No, I don't. Though I shan't be going. Mr. Bracebridge and I are staying in Kenneh."

Please don't say why, Flo's eyes begged. Don't say the trip is difficult or your health isn't up to it. *Oh, please.*

"We need to take care of some business."

"That's right," Charles said.

Flo wanted to kiss him. A co-conspirator! How had she not understood how much he loved her? She wished she could take flight, not like a bird, but unpredictably, zigzagging around the boat like a punctured balloon. *Fffft! Fwat!* Charles *had* agreed without the question ever being put.

Just then, Père Issa hailed Rais Ibrahim coming aboard with four live chickens. The consul excused himself and joined the captain on the bow. They were apparently old friends.

Trout drooped over the table like a general over the scheme of a lost battle. She studied the map legend, measuring distances with her finger joints. "It's a hundred mile, seems." Her voice verged on indignance. "More than a hundred. How long will it take?"

"Quatre jours," said Max. "Four days."

Trout looked ready to cry. Good! Better for her to dissolve than ignite. Let her be miserable, just so long as she did not refuse. Would she risk rebellion in front of all these people? *A public disgrace.* Would not humiliation override her fear? Trout shut her eyes. Silently praying? Counting to ten?

Selina signaled Youssef for more sugar water. Charles smoked his pipe and muttered to Paolo. It was an intermission of sorts, Flo thought. The play wasn't over.

Eyes still closed, Trout began to sway where she stood, in wider and wider arcs. Max jumped up and escorted her back to her chair, his hand extended like that of a maître d'. She obeyed him. Oh, if only Trout could fall just a little in love with Max, if only she could allow herself that folly, though maiden ladies of a certain age—Trout's age—did not exactly fall in love. Indeed, it was difficult to imagine Trout with any man except an employer. Bring me my slippers, Trout. Yes, sir. My eggs. Yes, sir. No endearments or entanglements, just the emotionless propriety of service. For who could love Trout? She was not cuddlesome or amusing, nor the least bit feminine. Barrel-chested and tall, with outsized hands, she had about her something of the warrior. Amazon Trout. She was not afraid of men, Fanny had said, even clutches of them drinking and gambling. Fanny had once seen Trout walking past such ruffians into a pub. But even ugly women were not safe alone in the streets, Fanny had stressed. Trout had simply been lucky. Men were brutes.

"Madame Trout," Max said, "I hope that you will agree to be my model in the desert."

Flo grinned as Paulo issued the invitation in English.

"Your model?" she repeated uncertainly.

"You will establish *scale* in my photographs, my dear lady. You will be among the first human beings to be photographed in the eastern Sahara—perhaps the *very* first. An innovator, a pioneer."

"Will I?" A droplet of sweat slid down Trout's temple, catching the last gleam of light. No, she would not cry.

"Have you ever sat for a photograph?" Max asked.

A pointless question, Flo thought—the Nightingales themselves had yet to be photographed. The camera was a newfangled machine, with unreliable results. But Max was pointedly making a fuss over Trout; surely his flattery could nudge her past the point of refusal.

"Yes, sir, I have," Trout said, and proceeded to brush the front of her dress with her two hands, as though tidying up to pose for a likeness. A pretentious gesture. Flo fought the impulse to laugh.

"Remarkable," said Charles. "Congratulations, Trout. You are at the forefront of science and art."

"Is that so, Mr. Bracebridge?"

Barely able to discern the outlines of Trout's face, Flo could no longer restrain herself. "How is it that you have been photographed, Trout?"

"Oh, I have a friend, mum, Gilbert, who's made my picture four times now. Once as myself, and three historical scenes."

Gustave raised his glass. "To the future of art," he cried. "And to Madame Trout, the photographers' Muse!" Paolo translated.

"I don't mind if I do, sir," Trout said, at length. "Pose for you, I mean. But I will be wanting some photographs for myself, then." Trout wound her loose yarn back onto the ball. Flo hadn't known Trout to bargain so brazenly. But Max agreed, and offered to show Trout the next day the pictures the others had seen at Abu Simbel, when she was belowdecks.

Just then, Efreet-Youssef appeared from the shadows and placed an oil lamp on the table.

"You will bathe in the Red Sea!" Gustave pantomimed swimming with his arms.

"Not I, sir," Trout said "No. I won't be bathing in any foreign waters."

Now that an accommodation seemed, miraculously, to have been reached, Florence was barely listening. Let Trout sweat, posing on the beach of the Red Sea, furiously fanning herself as Max hunched under the black hood of the camera. Let her stand atop a dune, or ride sidesaddle on a camel. Let her go on posturing sophistication, with trips to the dentist and a photographer friend who placed her in *tableaux vivants*. Flo was no longer bothered by any of it. She was going to Koseir!

Gustave produced three slim packages. "I have taken the liberty of buying the ladies gifts," he said, and handed over the paper bundles, each one fastened with twine to which a cinnamon stick had been tied.

Flo and Selina immediately lifted theirs to inhale the sweet, pungent odor of that hard curl of spice. Trout, wasting no time, forced the string over the package, ripped the paper apart, and promptly shrieked, hurling the gift to the floor.

"What *is* it?" Flo asked, rising to her feet.

"A dead animal, mum." Trout covered her face with her hands. "A strange sort of . . . cat mummy!" She shuddered at the idea.

Charles, ever chivalrous, tore Selina's parcel from her hands.

"Non, non, non!" Gustave cried. *"Quel est le problème? Vous n'aimez pas mon cadeau?"*

Gustave had gone bright red, the shade he turned with any strong emotion, Flo had noticed. Some people reddened, others blanched. She herself was inclined to a paler pink, still evidence of a throbbing vitality. Most women prized a pale complexion as more ethereal and less carnal.

Charles removed the article from its wrapping and set it upon the table. He stared wonderingly at it, picked it up it by one end like something foul, and held it aloft with two fingers.

"Hair!" cried Flo.

"Les cheveux d'une femme Egyptienne," Gustave explained. *"Elles sont très belles, n'est-ce pas?"*

"You see, it's only a woman's hair," Flo told Trout soothingly. She unwrapped her own thick black braid, though the surprise had been ruined.

Still grimacing, Trout prodded hers with one foot, as if to ensure it wasn't alive. "I was thinking maybe a dead rat. I heard as the natives eat vermin here. Maybe a rat for dinner, I thought."

Drawn by the commotion, Père Issa rejoined the group.

"May I offer you or the captain another drink?" Charles asked, a glint in his eye. "Some brandy for your rat entrée, eh?" He tossed the mane into the air and emitted a tuba-size guffaw.

Selina grabbed his elbow, but he ignored her.

"Rodent flambé, anyone?"

"Charles, please!" Selina cried in vain. "You are embarrassing Trout."

Gustave, meantime, was doing what Flo imagined a *gentilhomme* would always do for a woman under duress: he had taken Trout's arm and was whispering apologies, first in French and then in his broken English, offering himself up as buffoon, if necessary, to regain her good graces. "Pardon me, sweet lady," Flo overheard. "I am much desolated to scare you with hairs." At this, Trout chuckled, which he matched with a giggle and Charles amplified to a horselaugh until they were all howling. And how wonderful it was to laugh! Charles and Gustave had a gift for it; Flo, alas, did not. But, then, hadn't Fanny taught her to stifle the impulse and cover her mouth? No belly laughs permitted, only tittering behind a fan or gloved hand.

Flo linked arms with her maid. "Hair is *very* expensive, you know. You could have a fine wig made, Trout. We all could, in Paris. What a lovely gift, Gustave. *Merci beaucoup.*"

"Indeed," Selina nodded. "A great luxury. Thank you."

"Gustave always finds the best presents," said Max. "I was with him when he bought the hair. The women wept and carried on while they were shorn. You see, the husbands forced them, for the money."

"Oh, goodness," Selina said, her voice sober again. "I wish I didn't know that."

The sky was by now completely dark. Noting the late hour, Père Issa prepared to depart. "Tomorrow, *mes amis,* I shall help you hire the caravan and crew. And I shall send word to my brother advising him of your arrival next week." With that, he bowed, his robes languidly moving against his body, like a gentle tide. *"Bonsoir à tous."*

Flo watched Père Issa's white *gubbeh* float down the gangplank. Back on shore, he hurried into the crowd on the cay, his turban like a French knot pulled taut on its thread until it shrank into a swirled nub. In a moment he was indistinguishable from anyone else on shore.

Trout excused herself and went below. Then, in a ploy that Flo suspected was designed to leave her alone with Gustave, Selina fetched Charles's telescope and proposed that Max look at the moon.

"Aren't you going to ask me how I happened upon Père Issa?" Gustave moved his chair closer. They sat at the table, the map between them.

"Bien sûr."

"He found *us*, actually. He was eager to meet two authentic Frenchmen. What great good luck, isn't it?"

"Does he really have a brother in Koseir?"

"Of course, my dear. I am not a liar. I merely emphasize."

"And does his brother have a house?"

"He does, indeed. And quite a grand one, according to you."

"You understood my English?"

"I grasped the gist of it, or, I suppose, the intention."

"I see."

Her eyes were drawn to the lamp. Paradoxically, its small, wavering flame made the darkness around it more pronounced.

She had reached a strange pass, having run out of what to say—she, the brilliant conversationalist whose head positively raced with too many ideas. She stared at the lamp, willing a genie to pipe forth from it in scarves of smoke. She stretched her fingers, folded them together, then pulled them apart to scratch her arm, her nails embarrassingly loud over the woven fabric.

At last she remembered the consul's hand. "I saw you noticed Père Issa's nail?" She wiggled her little finger in the lamplight.

"Unusual, *n'est-ce pas,* Rossignol?"

"Yes."

"I've seen it before in the East. Haven't you?"

Mostly, Charles had done the talking with the few Oriental men they'd met, and, determined not to offend them, she'd always stared at her feet, or into a neutral space to the side of them, while cultivating a vacant expression. The surreptitious glances she took at the cataract "bigs," half naked in the river as they hoisted the *Parthenope* up and down the rapids, hardly counted, so far away were they, and clothed in froth. "No," she said. "I haven't."

"It is a local custom, like the turban. Or like worry beads."

"It must also be a mark of wealth," Flo said. "For with such a nail, one could not possibly do a jot of manual work." She was pleased with her logic.

"No, nothing like that, though it *does* have a use." He set his empty snifter on the table and, inserting two fingers in the collar of his shirt, cranked his head from side to side. "I'm sorry, I don't mean to be mysterious. I shall explain it to you when we are alone."

Flo looked around. Max, Charles, and Selina were out of earshot. Paolo and Joseph were smoking the captain's narghile at the bow. "But we are alone *now*."

He lifted her hand into his lap. Setting up a rhythm, he stroked the side of her thumb and then of each finger, moving from digit to digit. "Then we must be more alone," he said at last.

He was barely touching her, but she felt the contact before it happened, each hair pricking up from its follicle in anticipation.

"*Truly* alone."

She found herself unable to speak—unable, in fact, to do anything save feel each finger as it was touched, all of her senses collected there, imprisoned in that single spot. *Falling in love?* No, not love, precisely, but *falling*, yes. And just where she would land was unclear and, in this moment, irrelevant.

Max returned to the table, downed the last of his brandy, and rolled up the map. Catching Gustave's eye, and not caring, apparently, if she overheard, he grunted something about leaving, then returned to the Bracebridges.

"I shall come to see you the day after tomorrow," Gustave said. "If there is anything you need for the trip, we shall buy it together in Kenneh." He released her hand. "Then, at dawn the following day, we depart!"

"Thank you."

"De rien."

"And for Trout, too."

"Ah, well. She did not require so much persuasion."

"She did not, did she?" Why had he stopped? The desolation of her abandoned hand was unbearable. She reached for his hand and placed it between hers, which he allowed without acknowledging. "But I think there is more mystery to Trout than that," she said. She *was* able to speak, though sentience remained centered in her hand. How strange to feel split in two, the Flo who was speaking and the Flo who was only a hand.

Not daring to mimic him, to touch his fingers, she simply held his hand until it grew heavy in hers, inanimate as a stone. Nor did she know how to free it, return it to him. It was all so awkward. He was waiting, she knew, for her to revive it, but shyness and inexperience stopped her. His hand could have been a dead fish.

Max, who seemed always to be in charge, slapped his friend on the back, impatient to go. Gustave retrieved his hand. In another moment, the three men were tromping down the gangplank, the light from Joseph's lamp flickering over their well-liquored faces as they clambered ashore.

Turning back to the *Parthenope,* Gustave began to wave, his arm tick-tocking overhead like an upside-down pendulum as he sang *au revoir* alternated with *bonsoir* until his voice grew faint. This was for her, she was certain; he must have sensed how intently she was watching him.

In this simple act, she recognized that another connection had been forged between them. The evening had been entirely proper. Yet, the secret weight of their conspiracy had pressed them closer. They had resorted to tactics just short of lying. Surely, had they robbed a bank or committed some equally egregious crime together, it would have felt little different—no less forbidden, and no less astonishing.

18

CARAVAN

Once a week, the Kenneh market occupied a dusty street at the northern tip of the harbor, itself no more than a sloping beach. Narrow booths lined either side of the winding thoroughfare. When the merchants were not sweeping sand from their stalls, they sat out front hawking their goods, or took refuge within from the heat and wind, bent over their accounts or chatting with customers.

One could not shop quickly. Ceremonies had to be observed. In the Orient, a substantial sale required the leisure to establish goodwill and to offset the innately degrading effects of cold cash. Tea and sweets lubricated the extensive dickering process. With Joseph's help, they spent an hour purchasing staples: *kamr-ed-din*—apricot paste—along with a crock of olives, freshly butchered chickens, several dozen eggs, and a slaughtered lamb. They still needed lamps and lamp oil, goatskins and saddlebags. The caravan crew supplied nothing but camels and desert expertise.

It was hard for Gustave to talk to Miss Nightingale as they squeezed through crowds that surged through the street like a riptide or, conversely, stood in scattered formations immovable as lampposts. Miss Nightingale was often busy translating for Trout or distracted by Max's peripatetic presence. Walking faster than seemed humanly possibly, Max scouted the shops ahead and rushed back to report. He couldn't resist fingering the merchandise, while Gustave was more restrained and deliberate, not wishing to convey too much interest to keep the price low. For despite his native costume, he knew that he could never really pass for an Oriental. Besides being in the company of two European women, small incongruities gave him away. His nails and robes were too clean; his skin, though tanned, too pink. He was fleshier and taller than most Egyptians.

They stopped at a chandler's stall. "It's very bright in the market, isn't it?" Miss Nightingale remarked, shading her eyes with her hand.

"And also very dark," Gustave countered. He pointed to the back of the booth where the face of the beturbaned owner swam up like a reflection at the bottom of a well.

"Let's go in," she said, pulling Trout by the arm linked in hers. Clearly, the maid had been enlisted as chaperone.

Inside, the shop was stuffy and close. While he, Miss Nightingale, and Trout lingered over rows and rows of the clay lamps ubiquitous in the Orient, Joseph negotiated for candles at the back of the shop, where the owner kept them to guard against pilferage.

They proceeded to a saddlery to buy goatskins and camel bags. Gustave delighted in the profusion of kilim pouches in vivid patterns of madder, brown, blue, ivory, and black. "Let's take our time," he suggested.

"Yes," Miss Nightingale replied, "I hate to rush. These are all so handsome."

Even Trout took an interest in the selection. An hour later, pleased with their purchases and full of more sweets, they followed Joseph up a hill. The open-air shop at the crest was strung with clotheslines fluttering with scarves and homespun robes of every description. Sunlight and wind playing through the textiles created the atmosphere of a carnival.

"You must to cover the head," Joseph told the women, patting his skull.

"Oh, I have a shawl," Miss Nightingale replied. "I'll be fine."

In his butchered French, Joseph explained that she and her friend must wear kaffiyehs. Nothing else would do in the desert.

She examined a kaffiyeh whipping on the line. "I am sure my English cloth is just as good, if not better."

Joseph whispered and Gustave passed it along. "He says he will not be responsible if you do not wear proper headgear."

Looking amused, Miss Nightingale translated this warning for Trout. "But he has no idea what English cloth is like."

"I am sure you are right, Rossignol, but it is just as easy to buy a kaffiyeh." He picked out a red-and-white one trimmed with yellow silk. "Very pretty, isn't it?

"Yes, but—"

"Let it be a gift from me, Rossignol," he insisted. He quickly selected a second, plainer one with black-and-white stripes. "And this is for you, Trout." He pressed it into her hand over her objections, eliciting a polite smile. She folded it under her arm.

"Trout has a very practical straw hat she can wear," Miss Nightingale said. "But these will make lovely souvenirs. Thank you, Gustave."

"Well, I shall wear the Arab headgear," he said pointedly, unfolding the one he'd chosen for himself and draping it around his head. "There. I am ready for the khamsins."

"Surely you have heard of the Arkwright Mills, Gustave."

"The what?" he asked. Trout pricked up her ears at the familiar English words.

"The Arkwright Mills. The most famous in the world. They weave the finest cotton cloth."

"Is that so?" He passed a handful of piastres to Joseph to pay for the scarves.

"Quite so. You see, the mill is a new industrial design. The looms are gigantic and run day and night. I've seen them myself—"

"I had no idea." She seemed quite enthusiastic, even a tad mulish on the subject.

"Oh, yes, indeed." She turned to her maid. "Isn't that right, Trout?

And they use only the strongest cotton, grown on the sea islands of Georgia and South Carolina."

He feigned interest while eyeing a chunky amber necklace. Prayer beads. He picked up the strand. The amber was warm and oily in his hand. Perfect to finger in his pocket or for his desk. *A red vest, six meters of Dacca cloth, a monkey, a mummy. . . .* the mummy! Joseph had told him there was a shop in Kenneh specializing in Egyptian antiquities. But where was it?

She was still enthusing about the cloth. The mills weren't far from her home. She had visited them with her father. Did he know that the girls who worked at the mill lived together in dormitories? He did not.

"Pardon me for interrupting," he told Miss Nightingale, "but we must leave. There's one more thing I want to buy—a mummy."

"Oh." She fidgeted with a sleeve. "A mummy, you say?"

"But first, let's try this on for size." He carefully arranged the kaffiyeh around her face, demonstrating how she might fasten it to cover all but her eyes. It was charming on her; the yellow silk had been an inspired choice. "It looks beautiful, doesn't it, Trout? Biblical."

"Really?" She stroked the cloth covering her hair. "What do you say, Trout?"

"I wouldn't know, mum. You do look more Egyptian."

"It's very flattering," he insisted, taking her arm as they strolled from the shop. Perhaps that would be the end of the talking jag about the mills. He hoped so.

The antiquities shop was close to the harbor; they had passed it on their way to the butcher's. Inside, cheaply executed reproductions abounded—clay heads of pharaohs, models of the pyramids and the Sphinx. When Gustave inquired about a genuine mummy, the merchant smiled and bowed effusively, promising an answer by the time the *monsieur* returned from Koseir.

Miss Nightingale wore the kaffiyeh for the rest of the excursion. But she remained silent, clasping fast to his arm each time he offered it.

. . .

The next morning, she appeared wearing a green eyeshade suspended from her bonnet. She had brought it out to Egypt at the urging of Herr Professor Baron Bunsen, about whom, by 7 A.M., he did not wish to hear one more word. This contraption lent her the remote but insidious expression of a card sharp. She seemed nervous. And apparently, when she was nervous, she chattered. With relish, she had already recited a compendium of facts about each of the wells en route, the climate, and the living conditions of the Ababdeh (mud hovels too squat to stand up in; poor diet).

"And scattered among this fastness of sand," she declared as the crewmen were loading up the camels, "are remains of ancient cities and Roman garrisons."

Her chatter about the mill had been odd, but now, as the caravan prepared to depart, she turned into an automaton—not a charming mechanical bird that chirped in a gilded cage at the turn of a key, or a little clown who spun about on tiptoes. There was nothing charming about the change that had come over her.

"I didn't know the empire extended this far east," Gustave replied. He wanted only to mount his camel and gallop away. But he saw that she fervently wished to be taken seriously, to be treated as his equal, to be of help in any capacity. To this end, she had brought her levinge with the promise of demonstrating it. She also seemed to have decided to pour into him every drop she knew about the eastern desert. He already felt like a big cranky baby in need of burping. Nothing he had said thus far and no studied silence on his part had stanched her endless flood of data.

"Oh, indeed. They guarded the wealth that passed from India across the Red Sea and thence to Rome. I read it in the baron's book."

Oh, God. He'd explode if she continued on this path.

So much for his tentative hope that they shared a deep connection beneath the obvious divisions of nationality and sex, that she might prove to be a confidante, like Bouilhet, or like Louise, but without the sexual entanglement. No, she was not his twin, but his *opposite.* He would take his greatest pleasure in the memory of what he saw; she in anticipating it. He wished to be surprised; she wanted to know in detail what to expect before it arrived. The idea of crossing the desert alongside a talking textbook filled him with dread.

He kept wishing for Max, always helpful in deflecting the garrulous and setting the nervous at ease, to appear on the scene, but he was busy with Hadji Ismael, apparently rebundling the camera equipment to pass through the eye of a needle. Nor could Gustave hold Miss Nightingale's hand in that moment without embarrassing her, though touch might have done the trick as the virginal Rossignol had never recoiled from his contact.

"Peppercorns, silks and cinnamon, emeralds and rubies," she continued.

Dacca cloth, dates from Derr, a red vest, maybe a mummy, Miss Nightingale's note to God, he countered mentally. She was clearly in an agitated state, incapable of actual conversation. Still, he had to shut her up. "I don't care about any of that," he said. "I shall be happy simply to swim in the Red Sea." He turned away.

What he had said wasn't strictly true. The journey through the desert did interest him—not what had been built or abandoned, but the desert's vast *néant*—the nothingness of it.

She fell silent, as if upbraided. They departed a few minutes later, the awkwardness between them now thick in the air.

Gustave maintained a veneer of courtesy and solicitude, but kept his distance from her the rest of the day without drawing attention to the fact. He sensed that her capricious behavior was not under her control and that her intentions were likely innocent enough—merely to be of use to him, somehow to repay him for the favor of bringing her along. Still, he had to avoid her: should she inflict another didactic eruption on him, he might behave rudely indeed. Better to politely disengage. For these reasons he spent the brief free moments after supper the first evening continuing a missive to Bouilhet he'd begun several days before.

15 April 1850

My dear right testicle,

The caravan has begun!

Our party consists of ten camels and ten people—we four "Franks," Joseph, and five Arab camel drivers, silent characters in dirty white woolen robes who speak no French and communicate through Joseph, who hired them yesterday from a larger, grimier throng of applicants at Père Issa's house. For his part, the dragoman seems pleased to be in a position of greater authority.

Tough-skinned and tough-minded, the camel drivers are a different breed from the Nile crew—gaunter and more leathery, with hands and faces like the crackled fell of roast lamb. They wear colorful kaffiyehs and turbans and sleep in their clothes. They conduct themselves with more reserve and dignity than the river crew, as if the desert had leached every trace of nonchalance and frivolity from them. Too little water, too much heat and wind, Joseph explained, have taught them to expend as little energy as possible.

We started from a wadi east of Kenneh, watering the camels immediately before departing. They will not drink again for days. As Joseph translated, the headman, a grizzled, bearded Mohammed, shouted out two cautions:

1. We must never, ever, wander out of sight. Our lives depend on complying with this rule. If a man falls into the Nile, he is heard and seen before it swallows him. In the desert, he vanishes silently, before he ever realizes he is lost behind a drift like every other drift.

2. Water must be consumed sparingly.

No maps of the routes through the eastern desert exist save those in the minds of the Bedouin and the camel drivers. Also, there are no proper roads, only depressions in sand on the rocky outcrops where hoofprints of camels, horses, or flocks occasionally survive the onslaught of the wind long enough to mark the way.

Miss Nightingale's servant, Trout, speaks only when addressed. Both women ride sidesaddle, no easy feat on a humped quadruped. I cringe to think of the discomfort on their joints and the danger of being so high from the ground without firm purchase. Perched in the colorful weavings and braided leather of double-pommeled saddles, they could be dolls precariously posed on a high shelf.

We stopped for lunch at the village of Lakeita and bought two watermelons. Joseph served boiled eggs, which we ate with apricot paste and bread. The Nile water we collected at the wadi was pure and sweet, better than any wine, Max said. In the quiet of early afternoon, we passed through a steep gorge as hot as a furnace. I was determined to observe every detail—the subtle shadings of yellow, dun, and brown, the mountains serried like blue stacks of books in the distance—but what filled the center of my vision for the next four hours were Miss Nightingale and her maid jiggling above the skinny asses of their camels.

In late afternoon, we passed our first caravan in a narrow defile. Père Issa said we'd encounter pilgrims, Koseir being the port from which they sail to Jedda, then travel overland to Mecca for the hajj. Our first fellow traveler was a man who carried his two wives in baskets suspended from either side of his camel. The wind gusted, ruffling sand around the camel's legs so that it seemed to fly forward through clouds. Every one of these beasts is bedecked with colorful tack—halters, bridles, saddles, and cinches woven with beads, tassels, and coins. Perhaps this decoration identifies them to their owners. Surely it is a mark of value and pride.

Whatever intelligence camels possess is not reflected in their faces. Their expression is of a man encountering a rank odor. Their tongues are long, thick paddles spotted with green from their forage. If provoked, they can spit great distances.

And now, mon ami, *I find my head drawn to the packed sand under the kilim that is my mattress.*

• • •

The schedule each day was rigid: rise between three and four, travel until noon, lunch, rest during the hottest part of the day, resume riding until sundown, then sup before sleeping. No time for diversions or side trips.

Although Gustave did not intend to avoid Miss Nightingale further, the next day passed without substantial conversation other than a quick greeting at lunch, after which everyone passed out in the heat. Other than when they were dining or resting, the journey was as solitary for the travelers as if they were in separate railroad cars. He urged his camel forward to join hers, but the beast refused. In fact, the camels rarely tolerated walking abreast, preferring to plod single file. And like prisoners called to the guillotine, not one was in a hurry.

As the light paled to dull pewter in late afternoon, the camels became vigilant. Lifting their heads, they sniffed the air suspiciously. A distant fire? Abruptly, one of them shat and then they all stopped to shit, as if a group stink would protect them. After this cooperation, they turned wary and distrustful of each other. They have transformed themselves into the quintessential French family, he thought, disappointed he could not share the joke with anyone. The camels jittered forward, then balked.

The caravan crew were prepared for this skittishness: they began to serenade the beasts, ending with shrill, falsetto ululations that resembled a battle cry. Why among the seventy trunks of supplies had he not brought earplugs?

"Camels like musica!" Joseph shouted over the din.

The camels responded by twitching their tails and flicking their ears, quickening the pace to a rolling trot that set the riders bouncing hard in their saddles. Gustave tried to read their mood from their bodies as with the cats at home, but dromedaries proved inscrutable. Long-lashed, half-closed eyes gave them the woozy mien of opium smokers.

Just as the caravan resumed walking in formation again, Trout shrieked. Joseph's mount had bolted and galloped within a hair's breadth of hers. Gustave watched his red jacket fly off to the side and heard his terrified cries. So fleet was Joseph's camel that it appeared to skim the ground, and after fifty meters, blended into the landscape and vanished, exactly as the headman, Mohammed, had foretold, leaving Joseph's ghostly voice trailing behind. In another moment, that, too, disappeared, as if he had never been among them, as if he had vaporized.

Miss Nightingale clamped her hand to her mouth in horror. Gustave and she stared at each other, hardly blinking. While two camel drivers chased after Joseph, the others encircled the Franks. Mohammed inserted ropes through the animals' nostrils and urged the riders to hold them taut.

"Dear God," implored Miss Nightingale. "Poor Joseph. What shall we do?"

Trout was crying, her face beet-red, her mount furious, stomping in place and bellowing.

"We shall wait for him," said Gustave.

"Pray God the men will find him. They must know the area," she replied.

"But it will soon be dark," Max pointed out, calmly lighting his pipe.

Gustave felt like striking him or, at the very least, elbowing him hard in the ribs, but he was stuck atop his camel and couldn't dismount without risking a broken leg. Tomorrow he'd learn to command his camel to knee. "Then we shall sleep here and look for him in the morning." He glared at Max to convey that he should say nothing else to alarm the women.

Instantly, Max changed his tune. "I suppose the camel knows where the wells are and will eventually take Joseph to one." Clearly he made this up to placate Gustave. How did the bugger remain so equable? Gustave worried that all the excitement would trigger a seizure. And how would they communicate with Mohammed and his crew?

Miss Nightingale spoke repeatedly to Trout, who did not respond or look relieved.

The dromedaries lowed and grunted as if calling after their comrade. Had God made a more unwieldy animal? Or a more uncomfortable mount? Now that Gustave had stopped moving, he realized his ass was sore and his nuts felt busted.

At last, the guides helped them dismount and tied the camels to stakes in the sand. Lying together, they looked like a flock of overgrown ostriches.

They all walked toward the campfire already sending up smoke.

"I have read that camels always return to their caravans," Gustave told Miss Nightingale, wishing to calm her, "that a runaway camel is no real cause for alarm."

"Oh, that is good to know. Very good." She sighed and delicately wiped her mouth on a handkerchief withdrawn from her sleeve. Max tried to catch his eye, but Gustave refused him. It was hard enough to lie without Max staring at him.

They sat in a circle and in utter silence watched the headman cook the first of the chickens in a dome-bottomed pan over open flames. Gustave had never smelled anything more delicious. The key to exquisite food, he decided, was not the chef's recipe but the diner's hunger.

They ate without talking, as if it would be disloyal to Joseph to enjoy the meal too much. The crew pitched the tents. Their steadiness, whatever its source, and Joseph's waiting tent felt like reassurances that he was safe.

After dinner, Max unloaded his camera to photograph the moon, which had hung in the sky full and bright since the afternoon. He knew better than to ask Gustave to participate. As for Miss Nightingale, she waved him off politely and reminded him that Trout was his model. Gustave couldn't wait to see the result: the desert at night with a lone and lost-looking English maid. Max instructed her not to stiffen up or pose, that it would be a candid shot. Gustave found the term amusing, since the camera was always candid; it was incapable of lying.

Outside her tent, Miss Nightingale sat wrapped in shawls and blankets. The desert air was chilly.

"Are you not using your levinge tonight?" he asked.

"I was going to, but it seems there are no insects out here. And to be truthful, I am too tired to fiddle with it."

"Yes, always be truthful with me," he told her, "and I shall be with you. Perhaps you can use it when we reach Koseir. I'm certain there will be plenty of bugs on the coast." The sand was still warm beneath the surface, and he scooped it over his legs by the handful.

She laughed. "I never thought I'd look forward to biting flies. But I do want you to see the contraption, for the rest of your trip. In Constantinople I expect the insects will be ferocious—flies, ticks, mosquitoes, sand gnats probably—"

"Would you like some sand?" He interrupted her to forestall a fact-filled disquisition on bugs. "It's as good as a bed warmer."

"Oh. Yes, I shall try a little." She extended her hand, palm up, and he filled it. The first stars were out, the sky a regal purple with pink and orange banners.

"Mm," she hummed. "That is pleasant."

"How is our fish doing?"

"Travel is completely wasted on Trout." She sighed and studied the ground as if consigning her thoughts there, possibly envisioning her maid there, too.

"I hope I was not rude yesterday," he said. What was it about men and women who didn't know each other well? he wondered. Though romance was not his object, there was awkwardness simply because he was a man and she was a woman. Each time they met, they had to reestablish their footing, treading carefully, putting on their best faces. The brothel was easier, Caroline was easier, his dear mother, even, was easier. The pussyfooting about reminded him of taking exams at school. So exhausting, so much precision required!

"Rude?"

"When I cut you off talking about the baron's book."

"Oh, yes."

An expression settled on her face that he had come to recognize. Her eyes seemed to lighten and her face to slacken, as if an inner vision were replacing whatever artifice or intention had held it taut. She inclined her head quizzically, and a smile gradually formed. When her lips parted and the teeth showed, she would have formulated a thought and was likely to say anything.

"You only startled me. You see, sometimes I talk too much." She said this without any self-consciousness, trepidation, or shame, the way another woman might say, "I like apples."

He was relieved; he had passed the exam and now they were back in the cave on Philae. "I thought you were ill at ease."

"I don't know if I was. It just happens. And once I start, I can't abide silence, nor can I be derailed, except by a shock. I understood from your reply that I must stop." She spilled the last few grains of warm sand from her hand. "Do you think it strange?"

"No." He dribbled more warm sand on her hand and wrist. He had the urge to bury her in it as if they were children playing on the beach on a hot August day, baking together in the sun. "Not strange. It is . . . feminine. A feminine trait."

"Oh?"

He explained that when he didn't understand a woman he assumed it was because her experience was different from his. She listened dutifully. Only a few glimmers of twilight remained at the horizon. On the plain beyond the camp, he could see the outlines of Trout and Max, Trout with her hand on her straw hat.

In the light of the oil lamp, Miss Nightingale's face glowed. A sudden tenderness came over him. She was lovely and also pitiful. He knew she must be rich and yet she suffered—clearly she suffered—because she had nothing to do in the world. He felt their connection come alive again like a foot gone numb prickling awake.

"That is sweet," she pronounced. "But in my experience, women are not so different from men as they are made out to be. Still, they are expected to act differently, to want different things, and most important, not to want too much."

"Mon ami," he whispered. "I understand." At that moment, he realized what he and the intense, birdlike Englishwoman had in common: ambition; hers to accomplish something in the world, his to accomplish something in *spite* of that world. "I know you wish to do good—"

"I do. Desperately."

"But the world is a much nastier place than you imagine." Her purpose was so virtuous, her motives so pure and unreasonable. It would be easy to worry about her, to wish to rescue her, though obviously she did not wish to be rescued by him or anyone.

"I am sure you are right. You have seen more of the world than I."

Their conversation always followed this pattern—dark silences punctuated by profoundly bright and intimate jabs, like shining knives laying them painlessly open to each other.

A small commotion was under way beyond the encampment. Trout and Max were waving and shouting. He stood to get a better view.

"I hear something," Rossignol said.

The sound of an animal running—pounding at top speed—catapulted through the empty air. And then, just as rapidly as he had vanished, Joseph materialized, galloping hard on his camel and weeping with joy.

16 April 1850

Two gory complications today: the salted lamb carcass was reeking by noon and we discarded it. The moment it hit the sand, vultures descended upon it, rending it in bloody chunks. The feeding was so brutal Miss Nightingale averted her gaze. Later in the afternoon, one of the pack camels broke a leg. Mohammed slit its throat and gave it to an Abadi tribesman.

We have now ridden through a khamsin, which appeared at the horizon as a plume of dark brown with rusty margins that swept back and forth like a broom. The name derives from the Arabic for "fifty," because the storm sometimes lasts as many days, long enough to drive man and beast insane. Khamsin sand is a horizontal as well as a vertical force. It pours like salt, ascends in billows, and slashes sideways like rain, wrapping the traveler in its stinging net. In the eyes, it cuts like splinters of glass. It can move or make mountains. One camel driver told Joseph that he saw an entire caravan buried in less than an hour.

Max is sick. He ate something at the Ababdeh village and has been puking and shitting ever since. He has a fever and speaks to no one. The rest of us are hale and hearty.

Despite bad food and water, my mind has been a beehive, producing ideas to fill the emptiness of the desert. Three schemes for a book are buzzing in my head, all stories of insatiable love, whether earthly or mystical, and all, no doubt, the unconscious plotting of that stubborn romantic who lives, much beleaguered, in my heart (and who had such a pitiful second visit to Kuchuk Hanem).

The first, "A Night with Don Juan," worries me—wouldn't it still entail writing about whores? And if he fucks everyone, where is the suspense, where the makings of a plot? The second, still lacking a title, is the mythological legend of the Egyptian woman, Anubis, who wished to screw a god. Same problems as the first idea. Finally, I am considering writing about a rural Flemish girl, a young mystic who dies a virgin. (I don't know what she dies of, but she will have to expire if she won't fuck!) No whore here, but a heroine who succumbs to spiritual masturbation after practicing the manual kind. Is there anyone I would not offend no matter how delicately I approach her obsessions?

While I agonize over my writing, my mother hatches plans for me. In her last letter, she again mentioned her wish that I find a little job. To remain respectable, she thinks I must do something visible that other people can verify. Appearances impress her inordinately. I wrote back immediately, pointing out that the pittance I could earn would be inconsequential and that it is a delusion to believe that one can work a day job and still write in the evening. Finally, I sealed my fate, I hope, by hinting that a job would keep me from spending time with her. When I get home, I shall explain the great undertaking I am about to begin—as soon as I know what it is myself.

Gustave had little inclination to converse after spending eleven hours a day on a camel. First, fatigue settled in like lead weights. The landscape was exhausting—unremittingly splendid or unceasingly boring. Either way it deadened the mind.

Max, normally gregarious and loquacious, was in a stupor from drinking rakı. Since water was in short supply, he sipped it straight, hoping to settle his guts or numb them into submission. Gustave had lost track of the number of times Max dismounted to shit or puke. The women stared off in the other direction for modesty's sake. Their camels couldn't abide each other and began to spit if they came too close.

After three days in the desert, Gustave hungered for a color other than brown. Especially green. There was nothing green. The desert was a gigantic theater hung with numberless scrims in shades of tan, ecru, ivory, beige, and mauve. When the wind blew, he passed through them as if through scratchy tulle. Though he had never enjoyed the taste of plain water, he'd never again take it for granted, nor for that matter small beer, the cheapest blended cabernet, coffee, or tea. Nor the transforming power of sugar, though not even sugar had made the water at Hagee Soolayman palatable that day. Execrable taste and odor! Rotten eggs with a smear of fresh dog shit.

They ate the last two chickens for dinner and afterward Max and Trout went to bed. Everyone was exhausted, having ridden an extra two hours by moonlight before the meal.

Gustave and Miss Nightingale stretched out on blankets in the open air. Her logorrhea seemed to have subsided completely. They lounged in a comfortable, even velvety silence together. How pleasant it was simply to enjoy each other's presence.

Gustave stared up at the sky. The darkness seemed to absorb him the way air drank in moisture. "The desert at night is so mysterious," he said. "It's like walking across a room in which the ceiling disappears. Suddenly, instead of plaster rosettes overhead there are stars."

"Mm," she agreed, leaning forward slightly.

"Then a little farther, the walls dissolve. Now you do not know what obstacles lie in your path. You might be treading the edge of the earth, about to walk into the ocean, or off a cliff. Every molecule has lost its reflective shine, its very identity, to the darkness."

"I do like your rhapsodies," she said.

Could she see his face in the darkness? He could barely discern hers. He was avid to continue. "Daylight is different here, too, because you see everything without interruption and for a great distance; on the other hand, there is only nothingness to see. Night: a sponge that sucks you up inside it. Daytime: a bright nothingness that spits you out."

Rossignol continued the thread. "This explains perfectly what I have been feeling—claustrophobia at night, and in the daylight, a sort of paralyzing humility."

"Yes."

"Mm."

They both lay back, content to return to the rich silence.

The third night, my dear friend:

If Plato buried his proverbial table in the eastern desert, it would quickly be eaten away by the sun and scouring gusts, proving what he said about reality—that ultimately, it consists not of things but of abstractions—ideas about things, i.e., the idea of a table buried in sand. My dear Bouilhet: reality is mental! Any other explanation is wishful thinking. Reality is therefore unreliable, something perceived through thought and dedication, or, if you are a writer, by judicious decanting into words. Today as I scanned the huge surround in vain for a trace of greenery, it struck me that if reality is not substance—the thing described—then it must be the way it is described—which means style! Style is everything. When I realized this, a spasm passed through me ten times stronger than any orgasm. I must focus on my style; everything else is negotiable. (Though I still need an ostensible subject other than whores and saints.) This insight was the gift and the lesson of the desert's style, which consists not of sand or mountains, but the light, which creates mirages and other optical fascinations. If I were Max, I'd photograph the emptiness of the desert instead of all the man-made attempts to subdue or outlast it, for to ride in the desert is to experience firsthand the shifting and shifty nature of what we call reality or truth.

These realizations so thrilled me, that as my camel dipped down for me to alight, I lost my footing and tumbled to the ground. (A camel is like a boat: when one dismounts, the earth feels strange, the legs even stranger.) Good old Max rushed over, worried I was in the throes of an attack.

These past three days, thrown together in close quarters, I have learned that despite my dismissal of most people in theory, once I've spent time with someone, my sympathy seeps out against my will like mother's milk at her infant's cries. My curiosity also makes it difficult to remain aloof. In short, I have taken an interest in Trout. Her stoicism moves me. Also, the unpredictability of her questions and answers, some of which are naive and some worldly. She and I have conversed in short bursts with Miss Nightingale or Max translating. Miss Nightingale seems grateful for the attention to her maid, as it lightens her burden of being the woman's only human connection.

Like most working people, Trout knows nothing of politics and revolution and yet I don't think I am mistaken when I say that revolutions are always undertaken in the name of people like Trout. Her family lives in straitened circumstances, working on farms or, worse, as colliers.

Tomorrow we reach Koseir. Writing the name raises my pulse. This is the farthest east we shall travel, at least in Egypt.

I hope the gods continue to send poems and plays your way. Read some Shakespeare aloud for me. And now, my oil lamp sputters, my eyes close. Adieu, *dear friend.*

Je t'embrasse.
G. Bourgeoisophobus

19

KOSEIR

Gustave was excitable and nervous on the last day of the caravan. It was his habit, he explained, to grow increasingly impatient the closer he came to his goal. He hounded Joseph with questions: How many kilometers until Koseir? How many more hours? At midday, when the wind shifted, he sniffed the air, clapped his hands, and howled like a wolf, convinced he smelled the Red Sea. Dismounting his camel, he charged over the next rise. Flo sniffed the air, too—not a hint of coolness or salt. Moments later he returned, crestfallen. For the next two hours he alternated between clownish prattle and strained silences during which she thought he might spontaneously combust from the heat of his anticipation.

Oddly, she was in complete sympathy with his shenanigans, for he behaved exactly as she would have if Fanny and Miss Christie had not dampened her spirit. The only difference between herself and Gustave was that he expressed his ardor. Adorably. Inspiringly. If only she might act so free, so true to her nature! Furthermore, since he didn't bother to hide his foolishness, she was inclined to trust it, and thereby trust *him*. How could she not trust a man who had confided that he patronized brothels?

In the afternoon, when the road dipped and flattened into a pattern of ridges like a seabed, he howled again and galloped off. In his wake, salt air arrived on a gust, and Koseir nudged the horizon in a dazzling white clump like a toy city. This time he returned content to parade with the rest of them as the road narrowed into the dusty main street of the town. They passed merchant stalls and cafés where men smoked narghiles and played backgammon at small wooden tables. At the last row of houses before the sea, the Arabs deposited them in the street, arranged the camels in a train, and bid farewell, calling loudly to each other as if to celebrate the end of a long enforced silence. Gustave stood silently in the road, looking dazed.

Her feet swollen and half numb after so many hours in the saddle, Flo felt light as thistle down. Each step she took was an unpredictable experience—as if a puppeteer were controlling her limbs from above, she explained to Trout. "And how do you feel?" she asked.

"Like I'm made of India rubber, mum." Trout ventured small, wobbly steps, like a tightrope walker. "I can't get purchase. It feels like I'm still riding the beast."

Flo laughed.

Just then, Père Elias greeted them in the street. Flo could not help gawking: he was the exact double of Père Issa, down to his beard and braided leather sandals. And his hands? Yes, the same peculiar nail flourished on his pinkie. Gustave had promised to explain it but never had. She must ask him again.

"My brother did not tell you we were twins?" Père Elias inquired of his startled guests. "Our mother dressed us alike in every detail. She was determined to make us undistinguishable so Father would not know which one to beat." He laughed. "I like to think that though we live apart, we still dress alike, not so difficult in the Orient because one doesn't wear much." He lifted the hem of his pelisse to illustrate his point.

"And you have the identical occupation," Max said as they followed him inside. "Both French consuls."

"I think you'll find we're very much alike." He ushered them into his villa and ordered his houseboy to make coffee.

They sorted out the sleeping arrangements, and a servant took the bags and parcels to their rooms. Joseph retired to the veranda, where a hammock awaited him. Flo followed the consul into the salon.

She and Trout sat upon one divan, Gustave and Père Elias on another. Max, hypervigilant about breakage, toted the photographic equipment himself. She heard him repeatedly struggling up the stairs.

An exchange between the men proceeded in rapid French. Père Elias inquired about friends and kinsmen in Kenneh, but after a fusillade of names, it turned out they knew no one in common but his twin. Flo kept her gaze elsewhere, preferring to study her surroundings rather than join the conversation.

Divans with pillows in the Ottoman style lined the sitting room, while fringed carpets in shades of red, cream, salmon, and blue overlapped on the stone floor. Against the stark white walls, the effect was beautiful, like an indoor garden. Brass trays and bowls, placed about for decoration, glowed like patches of sunlight in a shady glen. She made a mental note to buy brassware gifts.

Trout was drifting toward oblivion, her head lolling to one side, her eyelids fluttering shut. As Flo watched her, she felt a stab of envy, the emotion she most detested in herself. Why did a lowly servant enjoy peace of mind while she was deprived of it? Other than simple chores, Trout didn't have to lift a finger, relying on the others for every need. She didn't have to communicate with anyone but Flo, whose concentration was excruciatingly punctured by overheard smatterings of conversations and the babble of vendors and beggars. Cocooned in a noisy silence, Trout, on the other hand, could relax into a state of carefree helplessness.

The problem, Flo knew, was that she liked to be in charge, and even when she wasn't, she followed events as if she were. It wasn't that she didn't trust people to do their jobs; she simply knew she could do them better. But being responsible was as often a torment to her as a joy. She paid for whatever confidence and power it bestowed with exhausting, unrelenting vigilance. Lately, observing Trout, she had begun to wonder what it would be like to entrust herself to another's care, body and soul. Wasn't that what she had tasted the first evening with Gustave on the houseboat when she felt herself shrink until she was pleasantly small? And in the cave at Philae, too, while he sprawled next to her, radiating warmth? Surely that liquefying sensation of ease had something to do with wishing to yield herself to another.

Trout snorted. Her eyes flew open, then shut. The men chuckled, nodded at Flo, and resumed talking.

Max returned and took a seat between the two pairs. "What have I missed?" he asked her. A droplet of sweat coursed down his cheek and was sucked up by his collar. "What have they been talking about?"

"You shall have to ask Gustave," Flo replied.

"You didn't hear them?"

It was rare for Max to press. Usually he was the epitome of coolness, a French version of the Poetic Parcel now that she thought about it, though Richard had redeeming qualities Max probably lacked—interest in the poor, for one. "I'm afraid I was resting."

"Ah," Max said. "You must be tired." He reached forward and patted her arm. "But Trout is sawing lumber for the gods!"

Flo's heart pounded as jealousy stabbed and stabbed. It was so unjust and ridiculous that she envied Trout. Trout, who went everywhere alone—to the dentist, to the pub, on the train to Ryton. Were Flo to suffer a toothache, at least two people would accompany her to the dentist—Fanny, out of solicitude, and Parthe because she could not tolerate Flo's going anywhere without her. "I'm sure you have no idea how I feel, Max."

He leaned back. He fiddled with the top button of his shirt. "I hope I have not given offense in some way."

She sighed, close to tears. "Forgive me, I *am* tired." Which was a lie. Fueled by frustration, she could have sprinted into the street and screamed. Or, like Gustave, howled.

"Is anything amiss?" Gustave asked.

Was there a universally disquieting tone in human speech, she wondered, for the other two turned to her and Max as if an alarm had been raised.

"I was just teasing Miss Nightingale about her maid." Max pointed to the sleeper, whose fitful snoring now sounded like the buzzing of a fly trapped at a window.

"You must all be fatigued from the journey," Père Elias observed. "Would you care to retire to your rooms? We shall not dine until after dark."

"Though I, for one, am about to drop," Gustave said, "I want to walk on the beach. The Red Sea! Perhaps I could take a plunge—"

"The water is still cold at this time of year," said Père Elias. "But the tide is out and if you go north, toward Old Koseir, you will find seashells just inside the cove."

"Then I shall wet my toes. Who wants to come along?"

"I do." Flo's hand shot up like one of the boys in her Ragged School classroom. Fanny was right: too much enthusiasm. She was sure she was flushing.

"I'll stay here," said Max, patting his dyspeptic belly.

"Hakim, my houseboy, will go with you, if you desire." Père Elias indicated the boy serving them thimblefuls of coffee in small white cups.

At the threshold of manhood, with a tall, long-limbed body, the boy still had the dewiness and brightness of a child. Flo had never seen such luxuriant eyelashes, pointy clumps of them, like shiny feathers. His skin was flawless as a newborn's except for his upper lip and jaw, where the first down had sprouted in sparse patches. Rather like Parthe's, she realized with dismay. Did a woman dare shave her face?

"We will be fine alone," Gustave said. He polished off his coffee in one swallow.

"I need my bonnet," Flo said. "I shall meet you in a moment." She gently shook the maid, who came to consciousness reluctantly.

Trout had no interest in seeing the water. "I shall stay, mum, and unpack your things for the night."

"That is kind." As Trout awakened, Flo noticed her anger subsiding, as if it were the idea of Trout more than the actual person that annoyed her. "But then you must rest. It's plain you are sleepy."

Trout rubbed her eyes with both fists, like a baby. "That I am."

• • •

As they descended the slope from Père Elias's garden to the shore, the sky turned a lambent green. Flo stopped to retie her hat, stalling as she watched the bilious color scud above the whitecaps in streaks and fumes. On the second day in the desert, the sky had turned the same putrid shade before the wind picked up, wailing like a banshee and charging the air with grit.

"Shall we go then, Rossignol?" Gustave asked.

"I think a storm is coming. Perhaps another khamsin."

"I wouldn't worry." He pointed down the beach. "It's clear to the north, where we're headed."

They had taken refuge under whatever they could grab while the camels hunkered down, their backs to the wind, and sand heaped up around them. Flo had watched through a tear in the scratchy blanket until abruptly, as if someone had closed a chute in the sky, the khamsin ceased. Then just as they stood up, there had been another flash of green followed by hail the size of English peas. And the sound! Like a war. An assault by a thousand drummers, each pounding a different rhythm—

"Let's walk toward the clear, *chèrie,* and find those shells."

The green patch was scuttling southward, propelling itself like an octopus. The sun blinked on. "I've been collecting shells since I was a little girl." She followed him to the edge of the water.

After he removed his boots, tied the laces together, and slung one shoe over his shoulder, he rolled his trousers and stepped into the surf. "This is bliss!" he shouted. "We have arrived in Paradise." A groan issued from deep in his throat as he waded in.

It was thrilling to watch him relish each new sensation, to see his thick, strong feet with their long toes, the tournure of his calves, and the light brown hair on them, which she had a sudden desire to pet.

They continued walking, a wide swath between them—he in the surf, she on the damp packed sand of the tidal zone.

"These little waves nip like kittens," he said. "Cold teeth, though."

Immediately the spume solidified to fur; she felt the needle-sharp milk teeth.

"Will you join me?"

"I can't."

"Why, dear Rossignol?"

She did not expect the question. "I simply can't—that's all."

He dashed some spray toward her with the heel of his hand. "Afraid of the cold? It is not so bad." He submerged his hand in the water, extended it toward her, dripping. "Here, feel."

She grasped his frigid fingers and quickly released them, then dried her hand on the other sleeve. "I don't want to get my dress wet," she explained. "If I take off my shoes, the hem of my dress will drag in the water. I can't roll it up as you have your pant legs."

"Quelle domage."

"Yes."

Pivoting, he addressed the sky like an audience. "I am here," he announced. "I am walking in the Red Sea. *The Red Sea!"* he trumpeted. Two fishermen mending nets turned to stare. He scooped up a handful of water and licked it. "Salty! Saltier than salt cod or tapenade."

Beyond him, a dull red fishing boat was nearing the beach, its dingy lateen sails loosely furled. Two men plied primitive oars, poles with a circular piece of wood lashed at one end.

Shivering, Gustave walked out of the surf, dried his feet with his shirttails, then replaced his boots. They continued north. He began to hum, occasionally singing words to a tune she didn't know. She felt happy. They did not have to talk. She did not have to answer questions. The breeze was bracing, while the sun, hovering to the west above the town, warmed her left shoulder and the back of her neck.

They reached the natural jetty of the cove, a rocky scarp where children jumped, shrieking, into the chilly water. The beach was broad and fully exposed, with mounds of shells bleaching in the sun at the high tide line. Closer to the surf, bubbling holes where crabs and mollusks lived appeared at each recession of the waves.

Flo hurried up the dune. "Look!" she cried. "I've never seen so many shells in one spot." She dropped to her knees and immediately found half of a blue-black pen shell flashing iridescent rainbows of nacre. "Oh, I wish we had thought to bring a basket or camel bag. We have nothing to put them in."

Gustave silently unbuttoned his shirt and arranged it into a makeshift sack. She tried not to stare, but other than natives, she had rarely seen bare-chested men—only field hands at the Hurst in summer, and then from afar. Gustave's chest was rosy, like his cheeks, with a perfect fan of hair between his breasts that narrowed to a furry chevron at his midline and disappeared beneath his trousers. His clavicle was as cleanly chiseled as a statue's, the shoulders pleasantly rounded. Like fruit, she thought, feeling the idea in her mouth. And nothing at all like Richard, who was shorter and who, when not lolling on the furniture or floor, moved in fits and starts, like a small dog.

"Such riches, Rossignol," he said, kneeling beside her. He had tied the shirtsleeves into a soft handle for the bag, which he placed between them before scooping up two clattering handfuls from the trove.

The shells might have been a stash of anything rare or delectable: jewels, gold coins, bonbons, puppies. Flo felt something in herself creak open and give way, like the door to a secret room. It seemed that she left her body or it left her. The two of them played with the mindless absorption of children.

She'd never seen such a varied and colorful shell assortment. Some looked fresh from the ocean depths or wherever they lived. Did anyone even know? There were turrets and turbans, heavy cones with runelike markings, volutes with fine spires lined in orange and rose. One bivalve had widening purple and gold rays like the sky in a Bible illustration.

Movements at the periphery caught her eye—small crabs scuttling sideways, brandishing single pincers. She tapped his arm and pointed them out.

"I would not like to sit on one of those. They look ferocious." Whipped about by the breeze, his voice came and went at her like a train whistle.

"Do you suppose they are all right-handed?" she asked.

"I don't know. Would nature design them otherwise?" He placed an elongated, fluted clamshell in her lap.

"That one looks like a bird's wing."

"Or an angel's."

"We are alone," she suddenly said.

"Yes." He continued to sort his pile.

"Really alone."

He looked about the beach. There were children and fishermen, a few strollers playing keep away with the surf. "Not to worry—we have some company."

"I mean we can talk now. Remember?"

His expression remained blank. She would have to prod him. "You said we must be more alone to discuss Père Issa." She wriggled her little finger under his nose, at last eliciting a flash of recognition.

"I'd forgotten."

She brushed sand from her lap and placed another shell in the makeshift bag. "His brother has an identical fingernail."

"Does he? I hadn't noticed." He squinted as he lifted a specimen to the light. "Look at this one, so delicate, as translucent as"—he paused and stared at her—"as your earlobe with the sun shining through it."

Reflexively, she touched her ear, then took the shell, which was ivory with pink undertones. "Isn't it miraculous—the way spiders spin silk, and shells make this lovely bone china?" She tossed it in the sack.

"And some have portholes and make pearls." He laid an abalone shell on her lap.

"I wish I could make something out of that one. A brooch. Or a necklace."

"Be careful not to cut yourself. The edges are sharp."

"I shall."

She felt wonderful. There was nothing she had to do, nothing to figure out, no reason to be watchful. She could sleep on the beach, if she wished, like Trout. No, it was better to stay awake and feel this logy, indefinite joy. Though now that they were talking, she noticed, time had resumed, for the sand had turned a deeper shade of gold, with tiny flecks—mica?—glinting like electrum.

"All right. I shall explain the nail."

"Good. You promised, so you must." She folded her hands in her lap like a child waiting for her bedtime story.

"Where to begin?" He sighed. "You know that human habits vary around the world—for example, where we are now."

"Of course."

"And it is not a matter simply of dress, language, and currency. Customs regarding matrimony and courtship are different, too."

Was there some reason he was going back to the story of the Flood? She wanted to hurry him along, but decided not to for the moment.

"And physical customs are also different. Sexual practices, if I may be absolutely blunt."

"You may." The door that had creaked open now swung back a tiny but perceptible notch. She pulled herself to a more upright position, her hands flat upon her knees, which were buried in sand under the damp, heavy folds of her dress, bits of which surrounded her like blue flotsam.

"Ideas of pleasure are different, I am told, and I have read and somewhat experienced. . . ." His voice trailed off, as if he had gone down the wrong path. In a second, he resumed. "In the East, pleasure is more highly regarded—"

"Is that why a Mohametan may take as many as four wives?" she interjected brightly. "To increase his pleasure?" She was glad of her candor. Proud of it. She would not be shocked by anything he said. "Or is it to produce more children?"

"I don't know."

"We had animals at the Hurst—that's our summer home in the north—cows and horses. Lots of cats—"

He stared at her, visibly perplexed.

"I saw them whelp and nurse," she explained. "And mate."

"Oh," he said, smiling. "I don't doubt you know the facts of life."

"Yes." She was relieved to have that out of the way. She didn't want him to think her completely naive.

He threw a handful of rejects to the side and pulled the sack closer. "But, of course, human beings don't engage in sex merely to procreate. Sex is an expression of love. Of mutual enjoyment."

She'd always pictured Fanny lying stiff as a board under WEN. Every woman. It was something the man did to the woman. She watched the surf arrive tatted with bubbly froth. "Naturally," she agreed. "Why else would husband and wife kiss? The lower animals don't."

"Kissing. *Exactement.* The nail is like that. Not that it's used on the lips." His eyes darted about for a split second. They undeniably darted. Closer by than before, two crabs challenged each other. The crabs were losing their shyness, she thought, ignoring the two of them as if they were permanent fixtures on the beach, like trees.

"In the East, a woman's pleasure is also highly regarded. The nail is grown to further that regard."

How did a nail help a woman's regard? She could not parse the sentence. No, the woman was not regarded, her pleasure was. She remained silent, hoping he would expand upon the point, but concisely. If he could conclude his disquisition in one short sentence, it would be preferable to this gradual seeping revelation. "Further" suggested distance, and she was certain he was speaking of something requiring closeness, something he couldn't demonstrate.

"Another lovely one." He placed a reddish-brown shell that resembled a turkey's wing in her hand.

"'Further'? I mean, please explain 'further.'"

"Dear Rossignol." His voice dropped and his eyes grew soft. "I shall say it plain. The nail is used to stroke that part of a woman's body that is the center of her pleasure. I've been told married men take pride in that nail. So do their wives. When you think about it, the nail is a public declaration of mutual devotion. A *carte d'amitié.*"

"A valentine?"

"*Oui.*"

The center of her pleasure. She was blushing, but she didn't care. Her curiosity, always the source of her boldness, trumped any discomfort. She hesitated over a huge orange scallop. "I don't quite understand," she said softly. She emphasized the word "quite," suggesting her lack of clarity was a matter of refinement, not substance—of inches, not miles.

"My father, by the way, was a surgeon, so I learned about the human body firsthand as a young boy. We lived in a wing of the hospital."

This was no help, either.

"You mother must have explained it to you," he said. It was a question.

"Yes." She saw that his cheeks had turned the color of rouge pots. Her own felt feverish. A match touched to either one of us would ignite, she thought.

"I believe the name for this part of the woman's body is the same in both languages—"

"Stop!" She nearly grazed his mouth with her hand. "There is no need to say it. I'm sure I know to what you refer."

She might retch if he named a part of herself she didn't recognize. Her brain switched on—she actually felt it engage inside her skull like a mouse scurrying in a wall—as she tried to recollect everything she'd read and heard of female anatomy. What had Fanny said? There had been advice about menstrual rags, though Fanny hadn't used those words, prompted by a collie bitch in heat trailing blood across the rug and hearth. Fanny had called it "a woman's time of the month." Parthe had been in the room, too. After breakfast. Fanny was embarrassed and avoided looking at the girls. It was an agony to watch her mother squirm, so Flo had focused on the lime trees just leafing out chartreuse in the orchard.

As she replayed that morning in her mind, she watched the waves curling shoreward, breaking into white freshets. Parthe had sat open-mouthed as a baby bird having food shoved down its craw. And then Fanny had said those dreadful words. *You will bleed every month*. Parthe was twelve, Flo eleven, leggy little girls still playing with dolls. *So you can have babies.* Fanny had repeated herself about *days of blood* and *rinsing out the rags in cold water so the stain doesn't set.* At first Parthe hadn't moved or made a sound. But then she smiled and nodded. Proud, pleased with herself. Not so Flo, who was silent, horrified, her whole body cold. Later, she was sure, they had laughed at her behind her back. Fanny had told all the aunts what Flo had said when she finally spoke. Which was, "Well, *I'm* not going to do it. I don't *want* any children, so I shan't have to." Fanny had regarded her like a cat with a half-dead mouse, with pure power and gratification. "It isn't up to you. It happens to every woman." Then Fanny had guffawed and Parthe had mimicked her, their faces twisting up in horrid grins.

But what had any of that to do with Père Issa's nail?

Gustave was staring at the sand. At a loss for words? Wondering at her strangeness? Regretting the entire conversation?

"Uterus," she said. "It's the uterus, isn't it?"

He took her hand as a big wave far out crashed silently at the limit of her vision. The sea droned on, its boring lesson. "Ah, Rossignol. I am so glad we met. We shall be the greatest of friends." Was he going to shake her hand to congratulate her for a correct answer? "I've never known anyone quite like you," he said.

Her feet were numb from sitting on them so long, and she felt woozy. A sickening heat proleptic of dizziness spread through her face and chest. Her monster was rousing itself, like a Cyclops in a cave. There was something unspeakably wrong with her, and everyone sensed it. He held her gaze, then looked away.

Like a criminal in the dock, she could barely utter the words. Guilty. Guilty, guilty, guilty! I confess I know nothing. I confess my vanity of mind. "Is that it?"

He was still holding her hand, which felt to her detached and dead. He shook his head almost imperceptibly. "It's not exactly the word I had in mind."

He was being polite, she knew, when, in fact, he pitied her. His kindness revolted her, or rather she found herself revolting to be the object of it. She was so humiliated she had to put her head down to avoid fainting. She heard herself whimper.

"Rossignol? Are you all right?"

She couldn't answer.

"I've upset you, I see, when all I wished was to give you a candid answer. When one travels, one learns strange things," he said more lightly. "One sees strange things. Rossignol?"

"Yes," she whispered.

"Are you ill?"

"I don't know." Her voice seemed to waft away.

He placed his hand flat upon her back. It was heavy and warm. "Perhaps you've never heard of this organ."

She exhaled and inhaled and felt the ground beneath her once more. Sand had worked its way into her stockings, and each time she moved it grated the flesh. "I don't know." If only she could skip the next few moments of her life, but they would pass in perfect agony, one second dragging after another like a bag of rocks as her childish ignorance was revealed. Her stomach felt like sour custard.

"In France, women are taught such things, but in England. Well, I've heard rumors that they aren't."

If only she knew what he was talking about! Was it one thing or many?

His hand moved in circles on her back, as WEN's used to do when she fell and scraped her elbows and knees. It soothed her into a sort of trance. If she kept her eyes closed to aid the illusion, she could believe he was stroking her hair, her arm, the soles of her feet.

"I'm sorry your mother or sisters or aunts didn't educate you."

She felt stupid beyond measure. Where was her reason, her logic? Where but deep in the well of her shame? And yet, when he soothed her, she cared a bit less. "There are women who cannot bear children," she tried. "Likewise, perhaps not everyone has this . . . thing."

"No, everyone has it." The warm circles stopped. "At least at birth. Though there are places in the world, some not far from here, where they cut this organ out to deprive the woman of her pleasure."

"Oh, no. Oh, that's, oh, no." She felt ill. As if her ears were stuffed with cotton wool, sounds were indistinct, the sea reduced to a faint murmur. She took a breath, then two more.

"Never mind about that." His voice deepened. "I am an idiot to mention it—"

"Perhaps *mine* has been cut out." The thought breached her last defenses. She broke down weeping big plinking tears like an overwrought toddler.

"No, no. Definitely no! You are innocent, Rossignol. That's all." He patted her back rapidly. "I am sure you are complete. Only barbarians deprive their women of pleasure."

Pleasure. She understood the word but was certain she'd never known the pleasure he spoke of. She had never felt any particular sensation there, only painless bleeding, the occasional itch. Perhaps she would never feel the happiness women were supposed to feel. She lifted her head and looked at him. *"Mais peut-être—"*

"No, I will not hear any 'buts.' You have been done a disservice, simply that. Everyone knows the English are terrible prudes."

"I didn't know we are prudes." She furrowed her brow. "But I have often heard it said that the French are the opposite. Loose. Too amorous. Immoral," she added, hoping it wouldn't offend him.

"Bollocks! The French are worldlier. I heard of another Englishwoman your age who knew nothing of her own body, so you are not alone." He put his arm around her and squeezed her in an avuncular hug. "Promise me you will forget all this."

She considered the idea and rejected it out of hand. "No. I wish to know about it, if I can bear the added embarrassment." Actually, she didn't think she could be further embarrassed. She'd never felt so unsure of herself, so ignorant, so *reduced* in stature in another's eyes. Yet, at the same time, safe.

"You must never be embarrassed with me. Will you try?" The arm upon her shoulders went suddenly limp. He lowered it to his side. "I said those same words to my darling Caroline, who died so young."

"Oh, your poor sister. I am sorry." They had returned to familiar ground, to the world of the loved and lost where she felt more herself, more normal.

"I wonder if I'll ever get used to the idea."

"Surely, with time."

"I expect to see her running to greet me when I get home. I keep imagining it. And then"—he choked up—"I stop myself and grieve all over again."

Parthe would race to greet Flo when she returned, and Flo would be elated to see her, for despite their differences, she loved her sister.

Gustave's face was wet. He let out a low moan, then lay his head on her lap, crossing his arms awkwardly at the chest, as if he didn't know where to put them or didn't wish to impose the bulk of himself on her.

He was so genuine, she thought, patting his wide, sunburned, and surprisingly hairy back. "There, there," she murmured. "It's good to cry, isn't it?"

"Yes," he blubbered into her dress. "Yes."

He was so quixotic! Listening to him sniffle and snob, she marveled at the openness of his emotion and felt honored by his trust. He pulled a handkerchief with difficulty from his back pocket and blew his nose in three short bursts. Then he was quiet. They sat breathing together, each in a world of private contemplation. She watched the waves rushing toward her. One might think of them as hopeless, their furious repetitive energy spent and spent and spent. Or one could find them cheerful, full of merry abandon. They were a mirror, she decided, of their observer.

Precisely because she was reduced to meekness and shame, she wanted to ask more about the pleasure center, but surely, after his outpouring of grief, it would seem selfish. There would be other occasions. Maybe they could talk in the evenings on the return trip; perhaps he'd be less occupied with other things. In some ways he was like a sibling to her, an intimate completely different from Parthe, who was tentative and fearful, waiting to follow Flo's example, while Gustave was an explorer and guide who presented her with curiosities and oddments from the larger world.

He sat up and moved closer, cupped her ear with both hands, and whispered a single word into it. As she'd feared, it was a word she'd never heard or read. She couldn't bear to repeat it in the silence that followed. But being polite and kind, he said it again—louder, slower, clearer—as if inscribing it on her brain.

Oh, Fanny, she thought, what have you done to me?

That evening, Flo sat in her nightgown on the edge of the bed and watched the flimsy white curtains at the windows billowing like the waves they framed in the moonlight. With the lightest touch, the breeze tugged at everything in the room.

She was a mystery to herself. In her monthly bath, she was a slick object that sank in the zinc tub except for ten nursery-rhyme toes. She'd never seen her whole body naked in a mirror, and her backside not at all.

After removing her slippers, she turned down the bedcover, stretched out flat, and pulled it to her chin. She extinguished the oil lamp and lay listening to the sea's pulse, the regular whoosh and pause.

It was a luxury to be alone in the dark. To be alone. At home, Parthe was always in the room. Seventeen bedrooms and still they shared. At her cousins', too, it was unsociable—egotistical, by Fanny's lights—to sleep in a room by oneself. One mustn't do anything that was too important to be interrupted, not even sleep. One must be ready to offer companionship and comfort to others around the clock. From this single restriction she might go mad. But since the caravan began she'd had her privacy, and tonight Trout was sleeping downstairs, in the servants' quarters. Max and Gustave shared the chamber next to hers, but the walls were thick as a tomb's.

Gustave's contention that the English were prudes seemed plausible enough. But there was the evidence of Mary Clarke, a Scots woman who, for all her propriety, had chosen to live in Paris, where she kept company with two men night after night for a dozen years without marrying either man. Why hadn't Clarkey told her about the pleasure place? If anyone knew, she did.

Perhaps customs were different on the whole of the Continent. When doctors in Italy and France attended on WEN and Charles, both men had undressed. But when Great-Grandmother Shore lay dying, the doctor literally didn't *see* her. Modesty could not be dispensed with, even at the risk of death! He had merely examined her head, hands, feet, and a few inches of what was politely called the décolleté. Everything else was a guess.

Flo. *Flo.* When she thought of herself, the image in the tilting looking glass of the mahogany dresser came to mind—the top half of a creature corseted and laced into an unchanging shape. Rather like a vase when you got right down to it, the arms being handles, the head a single blossom, like a peony. How did she look from an angle? Was her profile strong? When Parthe sketched her reading on the settee, she was shocked to see the length of her own nose.

She might as well live in a rented costume. The drawings in her medical books were no help either, with their stylized ovals, circles, and wands for the innards, and their doll-blank exteriors. The spark of life was planted in a place too deep for her to see or touch. No one could. Her torso and legs? A small Antarctica, where she didn't trespass. Why had it never occurred to her that she could lock herself in a room and place a hand mirror between her legs?

The thought made her shiver.

An owl pierced the quiet, its downward-sliding *whu!* so sharp it blotted out the crashing surf. It took a moment to collect herself, to sink back into the lumpen mattress and close her eyes.

She began with her breasts, small by any measure, tracing lightly, raising gooseflesh, the nipples quickly shriveling into points as if with cold. But it felt wrong to touch them. Were they not God's design, intended for an infant's nourishment?

She curled her hand into a fist and placed it by her side.

Yet, perversely, there they were *all* the time, as if at any moment she might be called upon to strip off her camisole and feed a regiment. Some men found them stunning, stirring. Naughty. Richard had several times managed to fondle hers, pretending it accidental, but coloring furiously.

Her fingertips barely alighting, she pulled on them, gathering a funnel shape. She felt a tug deep inside, in a place she'd never felt anything and couldn't identify. A radiating twinge like a flame inside her flared and dimmed.

The desert sand had lent itself to astounding textures, tawny curves and scoops so like flesh one could hardly believe they were just mounds of dirt. The dunes' shapeliness pleased the eye the way the hollow of her belly and the jutting swells and slopes of her hips pleased her roving hand. There were massive drifts like the thighs and shoulders, breasts and buttocks of a giant race that slept beneath the sand, that *were* the sand, figures defined by clefts and ramparts of unmitigated, velvety black. For five days she had marked time by their expanding and subsiding shadows, watching them ripen from palest gold through deep persimmon to ebony. Gustave had pointed out plaques where camel urine had dried to a varnished gloss. Elsewhere, the sand gleamed in creamy tufts, like frosting. Tier after tier of caramelized sugar. If you looked long enough, you felt sick, as if you'd eaten a gouty meal.

All this accidental sculpture at the wind's decree, she thought, pulling up a knee and turning onto her side, resting there.

Beneath the coverlet, the air was close, humid with sweat and bodily exhalations. In the desert, her sense of perspective had vanished until a distant pit could be the dimple of an elbow or a mile-long crevasse. The soft down of her thighs, the softer skin inside them. Move my hand away. Don't.

Don't! She felt so guilty. Was her body not hers? Apparently it was not. In the darkness, she resolved not to care.

She was too shy to sleep naked, and wore a nightgown and drawers on the hottest nights. The slaves, the destitute hajjis, the Ababdeh in their mud huts—all seemed less naked, less ashamed, than she was in her nightgown. Their skin seemed a more natural covering than hers, which was the pallid, sickly shade of animals you found when you turned over a rock.

She must get a French medical text. A text would be proof beyond the nudes so beloved by the French, who thought it perfectly acceptable to *draw from life,* which she'd always suspected was a ruse for men to ogle naked girls. A *fine art tradition,* Clarkey had said at the Louvre when Flo turned away from Ingres's painting of a naked Turkish concubine sprawled on one haunch, defiantly gazing over her shoulder at the gallerygoers.

She tried to imagine a long nail drawn across the different folds and bulges. Or a finger. If only she knew where to touch—how to touch—so that the unpredictable trickles of pleasure—they felt like music swelling within her—would continue.

It was very hot in the room. Suddenly she wanted nothing but to sleep.

Tomorrow she would unpack the hand mirror—she couldn't possibly use the one she had borrowed for her coiffure from Charles. Tomorrow she'd look.

The next morning she awakened before sunrise and worked on a letter to her mob based on notes she'd scribbled in *Lavie* each night. Fanny and Parthe would be incredulous—aghast—at her descriptions of the journey's hardships and splendors. (Hopefully, Fanny would not hold it against the Bracebridges, whose reputation for mildness verging on laxity was well known.) And while Flo hadn't intended to scheme, as she wrote she realized that once the family learned she'd caravanned through the desert, Kaiserswerth would seem tame to them in comparison. They might even welcome the news.

The past five days had been more stimulating than five *years* in England. Life had flown at her in such a welter of color and pity and threat, she'd been unable to absorb it all—the indescribable palette of earth and sky, the sandstorm, the death rattle of a dying camel. Now she took her time to catalog the details, to chew things over lest she forget them.

Never before had she seen human beings so debased, whether the buck-naked Ababdeh children, or the skeletal Ethiopes with pendulous breasts that reached their waists but were no thicker than a tea towel. Most appalling were the pilgrims who wandered for months or years en route to Mecca with nothing but a begging bowl, all the while marrying, dying, giving birth. Yet, in all this blaring cornucopia of sensation, the conversation with Gustave the previous afternoon loomed foremost in her mind. Assuming she could ever articulate her thoughts about it, there was no one—not even Mary Clarke *Mohl*—to whom she could confide the sensations on the beach. Between herself and Gustave an electric current like Mr. Faraday's had jolted on and off, now emitting pretty glimmers, now hot sparks, now a skywide aurora borealis. All of which lay beyond her powers to probe and understand.

Except for one simple but enormous realization that had surfaced like cream in a jug of milk when she opened her eyes that morning: Gustave seemed to have forgotten that she was a woman! Or chosen to disregard the fact. Oh, there were the customary displays of chivalry, as on the third day when he and Max tramped on foot to guide her and Trout on camels through a steep pass. If the desert had had doors, surely he would have opened every one for her. But when they were alone, he no longer made allowance for her sex. And she had felt this difference as a bodily excitement just short of terror—a quivering in her belly and limbs—as if someone had set her down in front of footlights without telling her the play, or what role she must act.

Was this not what she had always wished and railed for and dreamed of? To be treated no differently than a man? And yet she found herself in foreign territory, ignorant of the language and customs, unsure how to react. Should she have taken offense when he spoke so frankly of carnal matters? Did she dare show enthusiasm for things she barely comprehended? Certainly she didn't know how a lady would have responded. She did not know how a gentleman would have responded either, "gentleman" being a pretty word for a stranger with secrets. In her opinion, a gentleman was like nothing so much as the man in the moon. He revealed always and only the same distant half of himself to her, while his male friends were privy to all of him at gatherings after dinner in WEN's paneled library. Sometimes, after everyone had gone home, she stood alone in this room which, despite regular airing, reeked of pipe smoke fixed with the antiseptic bite of brandy—pungent traces of the male of the species, like the footprints of a rare animal never observed in the wild.

It was too much to think about all at once. She set aside her paper and pen, crossed to the window, and peered out. The sea provided instant comfort, enfolding her with hypnotic insistence as the waves unwound onto the beach, dragging with them the solacing sight and sound of gulls wheeling overhead, herons hunting along the strand with deliberate, stately steps.

It's a misnomer, she suddenly thought. The water was a sparkling aquamarine, as clear in the shallows as a polished jewel. Had it ever been red? Chevalier Bunsen proposed the name resulted from a clerical error, "reed" having been shortened by mistake over the centuries to "red." So: the Reed Sea.

Her head swam, her temples pulsed. From the multitude of rollers in the distance she settled on a particular foment of whitecaps peeling toward the shore and watched until it dissipated in the sand. And there, beyond the boats, another string of white curls. Then another.

20

THE DYING SUN

Trout had stopped complaining, but Flo knew she wasn't feeling well. At least the toothache hadn't returned, though neuralgia and eyestrain were obvious the next morning at breakfast, which they took on the terrace at eight-thirty, later than usual. Flo, too, was spent after four parching days in the desert.

Max and Gustave had decamped at dawn for Old Koseir and environs, where Max planned to photograph whatever ruins he found. She took a moment to adjust to the news, surprised that she'd had no warning of it. They might have left a note. Gustave, especially. Of course, if it were up to him, he'd likely have remained at the villa, but Max, or rather his camera, was always in charge. Père Elias didn't know when they'd return. That evening? The next day?

Père Elias's French was excellent; he confessed that his job as consular agent in so remote an outpost made few demands on his time and talents. A generous and solicitous host, he fancied himself a Frenchman based on a visit to Paris and Marseilles twenty years earlier. On second inspection, Flo noticed European touches in the house: a diptych of pastel street scenes of the Marais, a modest library of French classics, and a Louis XVI chair with ormolu mounts on the legs.

After breakfast, he offered to show the women his ground-floor quarters at the back of the house, where, he said, something special awaited them. They followed him down a narrow hallway to his bedroom, which faced east, with large windows to funnel the sea breezes. It was furnished simply, with a bed under netting, a nightstand, and an armoire. It could have been a hotel room but for his slippers on the rug. She could hear the surf as they followed him outside to a spacious walled pavilion with no roof. In the center, like an object in a sculpture garden, sat an empty pink porcelain bathtub on a bed of crushed shells.

Flo circled the gleaming fixture. Bronze dolphins cavorted at the front, one for hot and one for cold. The bronze feet were webbed like a pelican's. It was spotless. If not the only bathtub in Koseir, surely it was the most lavish. Lavish in the Italian mode. Overdone. *De trop*. It was as impractical as a piece of art, too, as there were no pipes or plumbing of any sort attached to it other than a length of coarse rope tied to a rubber stopper upended in the drain. Another harmless affectation, like the gilt chair. "How do you fill it, then?" she asked. The boy Hakim must tote bucket after bucket from a well, an unreasonable scheme.

"From the sea, of course. A saltwater bath is salutary."

"Wouldn't it be simpler to bathe in the sea?"

Père Elias seemed eager to answer her questions. "There is a *hammam* not far from here, a classic, tiled beauty built by the Ottomans half a century ago. That is where I bathe."

He ran his fingers along the slick surface of the curled edge. "But there is no privacy there. Here, I can eat while I am soaking, or invite the musicians to play. I spend many hours in this tub. My wife, Najmah, may God bless her soul, used to say it was my second wife."

"Are you not a Christian?"

"Yes. It was a joke, *bien sûr.*"

Trout asked her, "How does he heat the water, mum?"

In the summer, he explained, it wasn't necessary. In the spring and autumn, the water was left to warm in the sun, the tub covered between baths. On cold days, water was heated over a fire. He pointed to a cauldron in a sand pit near the outer door.

The women followed his arm, nodding.

He combed his long, white beard with his fingers, pulling it to a point. "I spend whole days in this tub, working, writing letters. I do my best thinking here. I like to sleep in the tub, just so." Hiking up his robe, he stepped over the rim and lay down, wrapping an arm around each side, his body loosely arranged. "The tub is French. The style of it."

"Of course," said Flo.

Frowning, Trout turned to her. "I have a fear of water bringing disease, don't you, mum? Fevers, the typhoid, boils. Why take a chance?"

"But this is salt water, Trout, not fresh. It will be like bathing in the sea." Trout had a valid point, though. Water did harbor disease. There was the example, always before her since childhood, of the poisoned stream at Lea, in which she and Parthe were cautioned never to set foot or finger. Yet, people rarely fell ill from bathing in the sea or in springs. There were water cures all over Europe, not to mention the Malvern spa in Worcestershire, where the whole family often took the healing mineral waters. Perhaps the constant motion of springs kept the water safe. Still, she thought the Ottomans had hit upon something with their *hammams*. In Cairo, she'd felt especially clean and calm after her Turkish baths.

"If you say so, mum," Trout said.

Flo determined to try the tub.

"You may spend all day in it if you wish," he said, beaming. "And you, Mademoiselle Trout?"

"Oui," Trout ventured.

Her first word of French.

"I have good, thick Turkish towels, ladies. And now let me make the preparations." He led them back through the bedroom. At the hallway, turning, he caused a momentary pileup. *"Je suis très content."*

She and Trout spent the morning as friends might in a mild experiment. They didn't speak much. Trout didn't like conversation. Modesty ruled out the food and musicians, but Flo brought a book and Trout her needlework. Flo went first, because she was the lady, and to set an example. While she soaked, Trout crocheted.

The water made her skin sting—the salt, she supposed. She lay back, her neck on a wadded-up towel for a pillow, and took her book in hand. It was pleasant to read and drift off. But now and then her mind wandered to Gustave and Max. What were they actually doing? *Murray* said next to nothing about Old Koseir. With a jolt, it occurred to her to wonder why they hadn't invited her to come. Riding a horse to an ancient port was less perilous than crossing the eastern desert. And surely Gustave knew she would have liked to see another antiquity. Probably Max had vetoed the idea. Satisfied, she slid down until she was covered up to her nose, then dropped her book onto the bed of crushed shells. But then, shouldn't Gustave have insisted on it? No, she was building castles in the air. *Stop it. Stop right now.*

She relinquished the tub to Trout, convincing her first not simply to wash, but also to loll. While Trout napped for half an hour submerged to her neck, Flo took up her book determinedly.

The towels were the size of bedsheets, which was a godsend, as Flo was so shy she didn't like to undress even in front of Parthe. She and Trout devised a system to avoid the embarrassment of their nakedness. Looking demurely away, one held the towel high as a curtain while the other got in and out of the tub. For the first time since her toothache, Trout seemed at ease, laughing at her pale toes puckered like small cabbages.

In the afternoon, Trout asked if they might collect shells for friends back home. They could watch the sunset as well. Though Koseir faced east, there was a spot at the cove, Père Elias said, where the shoreline jutted west and a slice of sun was visible at this time of year. The view wasn't as spectacular as a western sunset, he warned, but it was striking nonetheless. He insisted on accompanying them and brought Hakim to carry the gilt chair. Flo couldn't convince him she had no need of such a luxury.

"Unless I have a guest, I don't often bother to go there," Père Elias said as they set off.

Until the strand narrowed, they walked four abreast on the same path that she and Gustave had taken. Then she paired off with the consul, and Trout with Hakim. The wind picked up, gusting in starts and fits. The tide was coming in fast, flinging longer and longer sheets of glossy jade edged with spume onto the beach.

Behind her, Trout scuffed along, one hand holding her black straw bonnet in place. Hakim matched her pace, gripping the chair in one fist like a strange ceremonial shield.

"Your servant is a lovely boy, so polite. Have you trained him yourself?" she asked the consul.

"Hakim? Yes. He's an Abadi, you know. His people live in the caves outside Koseir."

She'd read about the cave dwellers in *Murray*. "The troglodytes?"

"I've never heard that name. But from here to the Nile valley, they are all Ababdeh and all blood relations."

"I didn't know."

"*Mais oui*. There are many clans and sheiks, but whether they fish the sea or keep goats, drive camels, or live in caves, they are all Ababdeh. And they are all Bedouins."

It was confusing because she knew that not all Bedouins were Ababdeh. She determined to read up on them back in Kenneh.

As the tide devoured more of the beach, they moved their path inland, shuffling through the flyaway sand of low, lumpy dunes until they reached the cove.

Though the shells was less spectacular than on Flo's first visit, Trout was delighted at the array. She knelt in the sand and rummaged, refusing the chair. Hakim planted it next to Flo instead. Thinking it rude to refuse, she sat on the cushioned seat, a yellow-and-green petit point of bees and leaves.

The Ababdeh tribesmen she'd seen in the desert were lean and tall, with thick, pomaded hair. The staffs they carried gave them an air of dignity and ferocity. "Hakim doesn't look like an Ababdeh."

"He is gentle, but has the cleverness of his people. The sheiks are a hot-blooded bunch hard put to maintain peace." Père Elias squatted in the sand beside her. "Did you know they are the only people in Egypt who don't pay tribute to the viceroy?" She could see his freckled scalp where the hair had thinned. "The children are notorious beggars."

"They were all so thin," Flo recalled. "They looked hungry."

"They live on nothing but goats' milk and durra cakes. Fish if they are near the sea. In a bad year, many of them die. That is their life."

The children she'd seen had bony baskets for ribs and skin stretched taut over their skulls, which gave even the toddlers a ghoulish look, especially in the light of the campfire. Hakim, by comparison, was fleshy and well fed.

The visible edge of the sun had enlarged in the minutes since they arrived. A bulge of pink, it hovered above the dunes, separated by a narrow band of blue. She focused her attention on the sky and sea. From now until sundown, they would change hue and aspect dozens of times, each phase more flitting than the last, like a vastly speeded-up magic lantern show. At home, in the forced sociability of the parlor, she often retreated to the fireplace, to the flames dipping and fluttering, sparks glittering up the chimney. Anything was preferable to needlework or listening to WEN read the newspaper aloud. Hakim stood watching in that same way, as if sending his mind elsewhere.

The tide continued its assault; they picked up and moved farther up the beach. Behind them, the shore lay beneath a pane of green glass.

"Trout, please sit for a while," Flo said from her chair. "I am happy to stand."

"No, mum. In the chair I should be too far from the ground." She continued to cull from the debris.

Driven by the wind, the sky had lowered and shifted forward, an army on the attack, with clouds elongating into pink and orange troops sweeping shoreward.

"How did he come to live with you? I thought the Ababdeh shunned cities."

"*Vraiment.* I found him. He came to town looking for work as a camel driver. He'd run away from his father, who is a sheik. It was his time to marry."

"He seems so young to take a wife, even for a primitive." She wondered if Hakim sensed they were speaking about him.

"The Ababdeh men marry when they have their first down."

Was there anywhere in Egypt that children were not married off in a routine commercial transaction? "Why won't he take a wife?"

A flock of ibises tilted through the pink air and disappeared to the west. Harried by the wind, the landscape was rushing into its next incarnation, like a theater with its stage sets being hurriedly deployed.

"Hakim is afraid of women," the consul whispered. "Especially young girls. He doesn't mind the old ones."

Flo couldn't imagine any man afraid of a woman.

"His mother had picked a bride. Hakim says he will never wed. So, you see, he's a misfit."

She had sensed his suffering. She stared briefly at him, knowing he wouldn't flinch. He stood utterly still and straight in his long white tunic. In the rosy light, his eyes glowed a honeyed brown with bright points in the centers like candle flames. Could like souls recognize each other across continents and languages?

"My wife had just died and I felt sorry for him. I tried to help the family reconcile, but he refuses. Now they shun him. His mother has threatened to starve herself to death."

"So, in a way, you've adopted him?"

The consul nodded. "He's a good boy. Quick. He'll be an excellent cook when I am finished with him."

The sky altered again. It seemed impossible, but overhead the clouds had formed a checkered pattern of blue and orange like a giant game board. The sun had dropped behind the dunes, deepening the colors by the second.

"Trout!" she called. "The sky!"

Hakim helped the maid to her feet. She curtsied to him and looked up. "That is something, mum. Quite a show."

Flo was too thrilled to stay seated. "Come sit down and watch with us."

"I don't mind if I do." Trout eased herself into the chair. "Oh, it's grand. I shall never see another like it. Nor never could back home."

21

OLD KOSEIR

Once the ancient port of Aennum, Old Koseir lay eight kilometers north of Koseir. Max planned to photograph the ruins. On the way, he talked as if buried monuments lay readily protruding from the sand, waiting for him to trip over them.

"We have arrived!" he announced after nearly two hours on the dusty road.

"How can you tell?" Gustave joked, for there were no inhabitants, and other than random rubble, only derelict Arab houses and huts. The port was not evident.

True to his character, Max was not discouraged. Instead of photographing, he decided to excavate the site. Gustave was happy not to make squeezes. The day would be a simple outing.

He climbed down from his horse. Clouds had scudded in on a breeze, turning the sky to a gray pot lid. He had brought Horace's *Odes,* a bilingual edition to polish his Latin. While Max scouted the area, he piled sand beneath his blanket for a pillow and, with a goatskin of wine by his side, reclined.

Forlorn, windswept, bleak: Old Koseir suited his mood. The excitement and fatigue of crossing the eastern Sahara combined with his time on the beach with Miss Nightingale had left him altogether perplexed.

On the first night of the caravan, he had felt disloyal retreating to his tent to write Bouilhet. But beneath her logorrhea, that erudite confection, there had been a voice that cried out—indeed, that clawed at him—saying, *listen, look at me, dote on me,* be *with me!* Mercifully, she had returned to normal. Yesterday afternoon at the beach, the soulful Rossignol he knew and liked had been very much in evidence, if charmingly uninformed on sexual matters. Still, he was wary of her unpredictability. The best and worst thing about her, he decided, was that she was not altogether civilized.

Alas, he seemed destined to be disappointed by other people. Usually it was not his fault. Sometimes it was, though the mechanism of his role was unclear. Either way, he suffered, for those he loved most had often betrayed him, beginning with Alfred.

"What is this?" he overheard Max ask Joseph. He sat up to see Max leaning on a shovel with a rock in his hand—white granite speckled with black. "Is this anything?"

"Have you found something?" he called out.

Max waved the question away with a hand. "It is too soon to say." He conferred with Joseph. "We think anything of value will be buried deep."

"I wish I could help." Digging was exactly the sort of exertion that might trigger a spell.

"No, don't take any chances," said Max. "Rest and enjoy yourself."

Gustave watched Max jerk the shovel free, then lean hard into it, his foot on the shoulder of the blade. Max was sparrow-thin, like Alfred, and yet robust in comparison. How much he missed his dear lost friend! Sallow, with flabby muscles, Alfred had had the perfect physique for a man who suffered from what he called the malaise of the century—ennui. Gustave had happily adopted Alfred's philosophy, which amounted, in a word, to debauchery. Drink, smoke, and whore yourself into oblivion.

The warning signs of the defection had eluded him. When Alfred finished law school and opened a practice in Rouen, what had he thought? Nothing. He must have assumed that Alfred was stalling until he undertook his real work, which was . . . what? Suave disdain? His trademark contempt for the bourgeoisie? Boredom raised to an art form? He'd always thought that Alfred had abandoned his principles, marrying because he needed someone to nurse him through tuberculosis and syphilis. But perhaps he had changed his view of matrimony, discovering some hidden advantage that Gustave had yet to glimpse. They had never discussed it.

"Voilà!" Max cried. Gustave looked up to see Joseph hoisting a timber from the sand. "Come see what you think."

He laid his book on the blanket and walked over. "A rotten plank," he declared.

"Exactly my point," said Max, nonplussed. "It's definitely not a tree." He wiped his sweaty brow on the sleeve of his robe. "A human hand made this, but whose, and when?" He took out his pocket magnifier.

Journalist, raconteur, photographer, and now archaeologist! Was there anything Max would not take it upon himself to master?

Joseph ran his hand along the rough surface. "It can be a boat, *peut-être*?"

"From the floor of a hut?" Gustave offered.

Max sat down in the sand and studied it with the glass.

"I shall leave you to it," said Gustave.

"Worm holes!" cried Max. "Part of the anchorage, perhaps." He stood and retrieved his shovel, paced off a few meters, and began to dig anew. Joseph followed.

Gustave returned to his blanket and lay with the sun at his back. He paged through his book and closed it. Today he was too introspective for witty aphorisms.

In a delicious irony, Alfred had suggested that he might find a lover at Pradier's studio. And he had duly met and fallen in love with Louise. Another disaster in the inventory of his broken heart. But how he had loved burying his face between her perfumed breasts, the eminently graspable indentation of her waist, the silky rise of her hips. Her taste for foul language matched his own scatological genius. But for all her looseness, Louise turned out to be deeply conventional, hoping to trap him in a settled, long-term affair different in title only from a marriage. Why had he been so blind to her—

Max kicked sand onto his leg, standing above him. "I am exhausted, *mon ami*. What do you say we picnic on the beach?"

Gustave brushed off the sand. "I am ready when you are."

They gathered up their things and headed east, about a kilometer across rocky terrain to the shore. It, too, was deserted.

The clouds had dissipated, the water and sky both bright blue, one glittering, the other still as paint. The three men dismounted. Gustave walked closer to the sea, eyeing the water like a duck as he spread his blanket on the packed sand. He flopped onto it and removed his boots, then pulled off his trousers and shirt.

"You yourself reported that the water was cold only yesterday," Max said, watching him disrobe.

"It's fine." Gustave stuck a foot in the surf. "I'm going in!" With that, he flung his underwear to the sand and charged into the water, diving and surfacing like a porpoise. He floated on his back, bobbing on the gentle waves. When he glanced shoreward, Max was still observing him. "Take the plunge!" he shouted, using his hands as a megaphone. "It will do you good!"

"All right." Max slowly undressed, folding his clothes into a neat pile. He waded in up to his knees, plashing water on his chest and shivering. "I was right. It's frigid."

"It's warmer over here," Gustave lied. "There's a current. Swim out." He lay back and felt the waves lift and pulse through him. He heard Max approach, the sound dulled by water in his ears.

"I'm freezing. Where is this current?"

"The Red Sea," Gustave opined, spewing a little fountain from the side of his mouth, "feels like floating on a thousand liquid breasts."

"Ice water, not breasts." Max splashed him violently.

Gustave retaliated, dashing water into his face with an elbow. "You are just jealous, *mon ami*." He stopped splashing. "Of my new lover"—he caught Max's eye where, to his horror, he saw the truth register for an instant—"my new lover, the Red Sea."

"She is not yours, Short Pants. Or anyone's, despite your pretty description." Max turned to swim to shore. "She is too *cold,*" he called back over his shoulder, already winded.

After lunch, they returned to Old Koseir. On his blanket, Gustave could smell the sunshine drying his hair, warming him through his clothing. As he lay unthinking, a woman's face appeared on the orange screen of his eyelids, like one of Max's photographs developing on the paper negative. It was Harriet Collier! Had she always intended to seduce him? How close he had come, again without warning or insight. He closed his eyes and breathed evenly until he drifted off.

Sometime later, he woke to Max's excited shouts. "A treasure! I have found a genuine treasure!"

"Bring it here, won't you?" Gustave called drowsily from his makeshift bed.

Max nipped over and knelt down. He was beside himself with exuberance. "Look at that!" He passed the object to Gustave. "Gold! I can hardly believe it."

Gustave sat up and held the coin with two fingers. Recto, verso, it seemed to be authentically Roman, with an imperial head in the center and an illegible Latin motto encircling it. It was heavy, still gleaming after centuries underground, probably pure gold. "It's beautiful," he said. "Where was it?"

"Over there." Max pointed to a hole close by. "It wasn't even very deep. All of a sudden it was simply . . . there. I heard the shovel strike it."

Max's enthusiasm was contagious. *"Allahu akbar!"* Gustave cried. "Perhaps there are more."

"There must be." Max hadn't looked this happy since the day he photographed the Sphinx. "I shall keep digging. There might be a whole trove!" Max clapped his shoulder and stood up. "I was worried we'd have to go farther north. Joseph told me there is another ancient port in better shape thirty kilometers away. But now we can camp here and dig again tomorrow."

"We're not going back for the night?" Gustave looked at the sky. It was already getting late to start back. To stay away for an evening would not be rude, but the next day, too? What would Miss Nightingale do with herself? The idea discomfited him. Such a long absence would be an affront to her. He felt a pang of guilt. Why hadn't he considered this before he left Koseir?

"I don't want to lose a minute," Max replied. "And if I explain what we're doing, we'll have a Bedouin gold rush on our hands." He shined the coin on the cloth of his robe. "No, we can camp here and dig all day tomorrow, possibly the next."

Max was right: it would be a waste of time to go back and forth. But it was simply bad manners, Gustave convinced him, to abandon their companions for more than one night, and so Max agreed to return to Koseir on the morrow, even if it meant traveling in the dark.

"I am swearing Joseph to secrecy with baksheesh. At least for now. If he talks after we leave, so be it." Max turned to go. "You, too," he told Gustave, putting his fingers to his lips.

The rest of that day and the next, Max and Joseph dug, riddling the sand with postholes and trenches, but they found only pottery shards, half an amphora, and another timber.

Gustave passed his time at the beach, more resigned to the delay after he discovered a shallow reef not far from shore. He spent hours among its colorful inhabitants—pink and white madrepores, giant red sea urchins, fleshily flowered anemones, and schools of fish like yellow butterflies. When he was not swimming, he lazed on the sand and recorded the exotic new creatures in his journal. Like the strains of a catchy melody, other thoughts drifted into and out of his ken. Thoughts about women. And love. Men and women. Friendship. Men and men. Women and women. The whole bewildering array of potential configurations and motivations occupied him. And what of Louise, whose beauty, even in recollection, still made him weak in the knees? Had she changed? Or had she hidden her true nature for as long as she could, then begrudgingly revealed it to him? And Miss Nightingale: did she want only friendship from him? And what did he want from her?

The sun beat fiercely down. Only a man truly ignorant of women would be so continually baffled and surprised by them. Until now, he had never regarded them as anything but sparring partners in the game of sex, never thought of them the way he thought of men—as people. It seemed only natural that men ran the world and women gleaned their living along the edges. But Miss Nightingale did not fit any familiar category of woman. It was exciting to be with her, but the moment they parted, he felt confused.

At the end of two days among the jewel-toned anemones, brilliantly striped and dotted fish, and waving corals, he felt reinvigorated. In the water, at least, he had seen every beautiful object clearly.

22

ABSENCES

The Frenchmen didn't return that night. The next morning, Flo shopped with Trout and Hakim, who knew enough French to help with the prices. It was market day, the dusty street transformed into a bazaar with shaded stalls and booths offering food, spices, clothing, crafts, and livestock. Flo bought two silver bracelets from Darfur. Trout inspected cheeses, sniffing until she found a lump of salty sheep feta for two *paras*. At Père Elias's instruction, Hakim bought olives and a lamb to be butchered and delivered later.

That afternoon they used the bathtub again, each spending a good hour in the warm, salty brew, comfortable in the silence.

Soaking in the tub gave Flo time to think, which, she knew, was not always a good thing for her. Thinking led to feeling, and feeling, sometimes, to panic or gloom. But no, the water was therapeutic. She was determined not to read too much into Gustave's continued absence, nor worry much either. Though the consul was not in the least concerned for the men's safety, she was a bit alarmed. Anything could befall three Europeans traveling incognito. They were farther from civilization than anywhere else on their trip, and the road might not be safe.

She dipped a cloth into the tepid water and lay it upon her brow.

No. She was not worried so much as disappointed. Why had he left her alone in Koseir? He had been so busy on the caravan, with barely time to chat, avoiding her, it seemed clear now, one way or another. Had her behavior on the beach—her ignorance of sex—annoyed or discouraged him? She had the distinct feeling he was punishing her.

Toward evening, Flo pulled the plug and watched the water coil down the drain and seep through the shells on its return to the sea. A ring remained that Trout tried to scrub using the bar of soap, but without rinse water, couldn't remove.

"Leave it for Hakim," Flo said.

"The consul will think we're dirty."

"No. He'll think we *were* dirty. And now we're clean."

A messenger bearing a bottle of rakı for Père Elias arrived before supper. He reported the Frenchmen would return by midnight and had arranged with the camel drivers to depart for Kenneh the following dawn. The women should pack tonight.

At the dinner table, Flo was obliged to be social, but she could not force her attention to it. Had it been a shuttlecock that must be gently batted back and forth, the conversation would have languished on the floor. Trout, lacking French, had no obligation—as usual—to keep it aloft. Her lack of charm sawed at Flo's patience.

Père Elias looked puzzled and sad, as if worried he were guilty of some faux pas. She wasn't in the mood to reassure him. Her distress must have been apparent, for halfway through dinner, Trout asked in a whisper if she was *quite sure* she was feeling all right. She was. She offered the excuse of being tired, but she was a poor liar, and the blameless consul and maid both seemed miffed that she was not more forthcoming.

She ate little (the lamb still gamboling in her mind), asked Trout to pack up her belongings for her, and went outside alone on the terrace.

Perhaps he'd never return. The rakı might have been a parting gift for Père Elias. Maybe his itinerary had changed. How would she get back to Kenneh? Surely he hadn't abandoned them. No, he wouldn't stoop so low. It wasn't *that.* She had merely misjudged him. He didn't exist as she imagined him—as her spiritual twin—but neither did that make him a villain. It was reassuring to think so clearly, to remain calm.

Perhaps Fanny was right that she placed too much significance on small things and took the world too literally. *The event on the beach* (titled like a song in her mind) might be a triviality to him. She'd never followed up with the hand mirror, coward that she was. She needed to know he was in the next room to go through with it.

The more she thought, the darker her mood, everything conjoining at last into the familiar doom and hopelessness. As when Kaiserswerth was canceled. As when the deaf school refused her. As when she fell to pieces walking with Efreet-Youssef on the beach. As when, as when, as . . . usual.

If he did not reappear soon, she wouldn't be able to face him at all. Her enthusiasm would burn through every pore until she shone like a lighthouse warning him off. She might swoon, or worse, fall upon him like a stray dog upon a scrap of food. Upon his arms, whose curves and angles she knew by heart, almost by touch. No, he had never existed except as an ordinary man, a person of no particular consequence she'd briefly encountered. Nothing like herself. A person who couldn't possibly understand her.

Sometime in the middle of the night, a commotion erupted downstairs. She heard his voice, angrier—or merely drunker?—than usual. Fouler, too. Something about constipation and Max's shitty camera and turds. Then an answer in kind using words overheard only in the roughest quarters. You are an asshole. No, you are. Then you are a bigger asshole. A pause. *Mon ami,* you make my argument for me. I *am* a bigger asshole. My asshole is so big I can eat and shit you out. Therefore, *you* are the turd. Then furniture scraping the floor and muffled thuds followed by a spell of hilarity. She fell back to sleep, content, at least, in their laughter.

At dawn they loaded their luggage and said their good-byes. Père Elias's eyes filled with tears as he kissed her on both cheeks. Gustave, too, teared up as he kissed the consul and gave Hakim a rugged embrace. She liked to see such generosity of sentiment in him. WEN never cried, nor did the Poetic Parcel.

Gustave and Max looked awful. She could almost see their heads thrumming with a hangover. They barely spoke and took only two thimbles of coffee for breakfast.

After their intimate talk on the beach, she had hoped that Gustave would make more time for her. But when he left her in Koseir, that prospect seemed to vanish. Besides, even if he didn't notice them, how would she get over her hurt feelings? If they did spend time together, it would be to chat in the evenings, with Max present. Or perhaps Gustave had formulated one of his plans. For privacy, they could meander around the camp, though it would be dark. Lions and jackals, venomous reptiles. Still, it might be possible.

Minutes from Koseir, the weather turned turbulent, dark skies with ominous winds. Max sighted a khamsin in the shape of a funnel sucking up sand behind them. They hurried on, not stopping to inspect the ancient glyphs on the domed formations of pink rock. In late afternoon, the camel carrying the goatskins stepped into sand riddled with rat tunnels and fell on its side, spilling all the water. Three hours later, they reached the first well, Beer El Ingleez, only to find it had been covered by a rockslide in the few days since they were there.

Sweat dried on her skin in salty patches that pasted over with sand. She was filthy and itched like a flea-bitten dog.

That evening jackals stole the dinner from the fire pit when the cook left to retrieve spices from his saddlebag. They made do with a meal of half-cooked beans and watermelons for moisture, and went to bed hungry. In empathy with the Ababdeh children, Flo used the occasion to imagine what it would be like to go to sleep hungry night after night. This experiment, however, was a failure. She ended up hungrier than before, thought of nothing but food, and felt more selfish than ever. Tomorrow. Tomorrow Gustave and Max would go shooting and they'd be freshly supplied with fowl. They'd find a village and buy goats' milk or water. Even their personal water and wineskins were depleted.

She fell asleep without undressing and dreamed all night of water. Of rock cliffs softening into great gushes, of licking dew cups from leaves. Nightmare thunderstorms woke her twice. She peeked out of her tent to see if it was light. How terrible it must be to die of thirst! Her lips were so firmly stuck together she felt a gluey membrane—or was it skin?—pop apart as she opened her mouth to lick them before dozing off again.

She awoke before dawn, roused by the camel drivers making their rounds with oil lamps. A camel snorted and groaned as it turned in the sand.

Her dress was too stiff to wear another day. She'd ask Trout to help her change into clean brown Hollands. She lit a candle and stepped outside to cold, refreshing air. The stars were out high in the sky. In the near distance, Gustave sat with his back to her on a box, pulling on his boots. Max was pushing his camera cases from the tent, where he insisted on storing them every night lest they be stolen. Lamp in hand, she stepped behind a rock and urinated, carefully lifting her grimy frock. She'd have to throw it away. It would rot before it could be washed.

Skirting the banked embers marked off by rocks, she advanced toward the outline of Trout's tent. Faintly etched against the gray sky, it resembled a small black pyramid. "Trout!" she called. "Are you awake, Trout?" She was feeling cheerful. It *was* a new day. They'd secure water or milk in the next village. Joseph was a clever haggler.

There was no reply. She opened the flap and peeked into the blackness. "Trout, come out, come out wherever you are!"

Which was, no doubt, behind a boulder doing her business. Flo decided to walk around the camp. She trod stiffly, her legs cramped and aching from the night's restless sleep.

"Rossignol," Gustave called out. "*Bonjour.* Where are you marching to?

"*Bonjour,* Gustave. I'm waiting for Trout. Just stretching my legs." Her throat tightened on a strand of unacknowledged worry. Trout had never wandered away. And never would.

"I'll come with you." They linked arms and continued around the campsite, making discreet forays behind boulders. "Halloo!" Flo called each time to give ample warning. "We are looking for you, Trout." At one tall outcropping, a serpent skittered across their path. Mohammed had severed a snake outside her tent the first night of the journey. What if Trout had been bitten, or was ill? Perhaps she had digestive trouble and was vomiting in the desert at a respectful distance.

By the time they'd completed their circuit, the restraint that had kept her walking and talking normally escaped with a sigh. "Oh, Gustave, I think she is missing." She gripped his arm. He placed his hand on top of hers.

"Surely she is just asleep in her tent, *n'est-ce pas*?"

"I don't think so." Trout always woke before Flo. If she had gone to relieve herself, she would have had ample time to return. If she were sick, they'd have to go looking for her.

The thinnest rim of molten gold trembled at the horizon. The colors of the surroundings began to change from grayish black to muted browns and pinks. She felt a powerful urge to pray and closed her eyes for a moment; then she stepped forward and lifted the flap of Trout's tent.

It was dark inside. Dark, and empty.

"We might muck it up anyway," Max said, yielding to Flo as she plunged back into Trout's tent moments later, this time to investigate thoroughly. Everyone had gathered around.

The men naturally hung back, for it would have been indelicate for them to barge in and invade Trout's meager privacy. Besides, Flo was more likely to recognize something amiss among the alien feminine trappings.

The air inside the tent was close as a summer afternoon before a rainstorm. It smelled of camel. She peered about.

Trout's absence was more palpable amid her possessions, as if the expectation of her return added to the oppressive stillness. Her belongings were undisturbed, her clothes folded and stacked inside her portmanteau, her boots lined up alongside the bedding. The dress she'd worn the day before was nowhere to be seen. Perhaps, like Flo, she'd never disrobed.

She picked up Trout's journal, which was lying open, the pages crammed with sloping lines of minute cursive. On the last page, a nib had leaked, leaving a black smear. Nearby, the inkwell had tipped over and soaked the sand. It took a moment to find the pen, which had rolled or fallen far from the book. A chill ran through her. Trout had not wandered off. She'd been interrupted while writing. Tears sprang to her eyes. Kidnapped!

Still clutching the journal, she bent low and exited to the fresher air, folding the tent flap closed behind her. Everyone was congregated, waiting. "She is missing, with signs of surprise." It would be too awful to say "struggle."

They searched the environs, peering behind every rock and dune and into every gully. One of the crew found camel hoofprints—two sets—that seemed fresher than their own from the evening before.

After a brief discussion among the Europeans, Max took charge. He signaled Mohammed, standing apart with his crew, to approach. Through Joseph, he questioned him. "Have you heard anything from your men about this woman's whereabouts?"

"Find out if all the crew are still with us," Gustave urged.

Joseph duly translated both questions.

Stroking his beard as calmly as if it were a cat, Mohammed answered with what Flo adjudged respect tinged with fearful caution.

He gestured with dark, slender hands, his voice solicitous and steady as an undertaker's. But the length of his reply filled her with dread.

Joseph waited for Mohammed to finish, then chose his words judiciously. Mohammed and his men knew nothing of Trout's disappearance, he reported. The crew was all accounted for.

Max fixed Joseph with a stare. "I know he said more than that."

"*Oui, monsieur, c'est vrai.* But he want me to say *con forza* his men all counted."

Flo could not for the life of her remember at that instant if there were five or six camel drivers, nor could she easily distinguish among them.

"All counted," Max repeated, leveling his gaze at Mohammed. "*Charabia evasif!*" He raised his voice. Evasive double-talk. An unfortunate expression, she thought. In it, "Arabia" signified nonsense. She hoped Max had read about how easily the hot-blooded Bedouin with their strict codes of honor were offended.

Gustave added, "Ask if they are all here at this moment."

"Good man," said Max.

A collision of languages ensued as Joseph translated into Arabic for Mohammed and back into French for her, Max, and Gustave, and each one commented in turn. Tower of Babel, she thought. Ripe for misconstruction.

Through her own silence and inaction she felt Trout's absence as sharply as a physical complaint. For the first time since they left Kenneh, she wasn't translating for her. Poor woman! Missing in a vast and hostile wasteland. Flo felt suddenly alone and useless, her chest hollow with foreboding. Around her, the words seemed to boil over, subside, and boil over again as they argued back and forth.

Gustave said, "*Allons! du calme, mes enfants, je vous en prie!*"

Mohammed nodded and, in the ensuing silence, took the floor. Joseph translated. "He say one man comes to him yesterday and ask permisso to leave. His mother very sick. Last night he goes home."

"I knew it!" Max said, pounding the sand with his ivory-topped cane. Startled, Flo stepped back. "Foul play," he continued. "Trout did not vanish on her own." He shook his head. "Foul play."

"Mohammed swear by all holy that man have nothing to do with Trout," Joseph added.

"Il est menteur, le con!" Max cursed under his breath. Joseph let the words pass without the Arabic equivalent.

"Perhaps we should return to Koseir," she blurted, more out of nervousness than common sense. Her first instinct was always to retreat to the place or moment before a catastrophe, as if she could turn back time itself.

"No," said Max. "That will do no good."

Through Joseph, Mohammed proclaimed that they must continue the journey to Kenneh or risk exhausting their food.

He is not the least intimidated by us, she thought. What she had earlier taken for trepidation was something else. But what? Duplicity? Humility? The simple desire to stick to his routine?

"*Inshallah,* perhaps the woman will return to us," Mohammed said. "I remain at your service, effendi." With that, he and his crew turned away to tend to the camels, which had been staked in place since the night before.

Max shouted after him, his cane in the air. "Wait right there! If a Frank is harmed or dies, an Arab, or more than one, shall also die!"

Flo caught her breath. Striking a Bedouin could be fatal. What did insulting or threatening one lead to? To her relief, the camel drivers stopped and listened to Joseph hectically translating. "He say he know the law, effendi, and he and his men are innocent." Mohammed stopped, gestured toward them, and offered a benediction. "May Allah watch over you."

"Et vous," Gustave rushed to say.

"Audthu bilahi min ash shaytan ar rajim," Mohammed intoned, smiling and bowing before turning away.

"What was that last?" Gustave asked. He looked beside himself with worry.

"He say he seek Allah to protect from the accursed Satan."

"As should we all," Max replied halfheartedly. He wiped his forehead on his sleeve. "Tell Mohammed to send out a search party for the next two hours."

The message was conveyed. Mohammed held up his hand and nodded, then sent two men to untether their camels.

Max shook his head. "As Damien said on the morning of his execution, 'It will be rough day.'"

Gustave sat down Indian-style and put his head in his hands.

Flo wondered if the mention of Satan was one of the numberless Arabic proverbs proffered to throttle discussion, or a sly reference to the Europeans as white devils. How could you determine a man's intention if you didn't speak his language or share his beliefs? She'd happily embarked on a study of ancient Egyptian religion but had no curiosity about Islam, which seemed an amalgam of oddities and borrowings. She felt with conviction what she'd written home more than once—that Egypt would be an exquisite country were it not for the Egyptians who lived there.

After sending Joseph to spy on the remaining camel drivers, the three of them gathered in the men's tent, talking and pacing in circles. Flo was feeling more terrible by the minute, knowing Trout must be terrified wherever she was. Which she did not wish to imagine. Instead, she pictured her doll-sized, wrapped in her green plaid shawl in a cartouche with Ramses, her hand securing her black straw bonnet. There she stayed, etched on stone, immobile, safe in the vaults of history until Flo could figure out what to do.

Why, they asked each other, had Trout been kidnapped, but not Flo? Gustave gently suggested she was more vulnerable alone in a small tent, while Flo probably escaped because her tent was large, implying several occupants. Flo's spirits sank at this supposition, thinking it must be true. Max believed there would be a demand for ransom and that the camel drivers were implicated.

How had it been accomplished, especially as none of the camels was missing? They agreed that a person or persons of professional stealth must have crept up in the night. Max again proposed a conspiracy among the camel drivers that would have eased the culprit's way.

I am responsible for her, Flo kept thinking. *I and only I. I should have anticipated these possibilities.* Or was that hubris? Taking responsibility for everything, like God.

The discussion was wearing on her nerves. The obvious horror in Trout's abduction was *rape,* a word she dared not say but found so harrowing that merely to think it produced waves of nausea. Instead, they talked around it, addressing it historically, which was only slightly less disturbing. Max mentioned the long, infamous history of white slavery in the Orient, which traced all the way back to Saphira, the Circassian concubine in King Solomon's court. Beautiful young white women had been kidnapped for centuries, not to mention, Gustave added, the loathsome custom of destitute parents selling their daughters into seraglios. Naturally, some of these women had been found and returned home. If what had happened to Trout was commonplace, might there not be a commonplace solution? But here they reached a logical impasse: since Trout was neither young nor beautiful, why would anyone want her in the first place?

It was unendurable to think of the flinty, middle-aged spinster, so upright in her way, being violated. The cartouche cracked. Trout ran shrieking across the dunes, pursued by turbaned men on camels. Flo struggled not to faint, her face hot, hands cold, and head pounding. She missed Selina and Charles, even the heaving, righteous bosom of Fanny, the speechless awkwardness of WEN. What if Trout were killed or sold into slavery? What if they never learned what happened to her? The tragedy—and her failure as an employer—would settle on her head like a lead weight. And on her heart. She could barely follow the conversation.

Gustave, sitting next to her, seemed to sense her upset, but she made it clear that she wished no affection from him. If Max saw signs of intimacy he might assume that she was Gustave's conquest, not his confidante. "We must *do* something to help the poor woman!" she cried abruptly.

"Yes, yes," Gustave and Max agreed.

At once they decided to send a man back to Koseir to request that Père Elias dispatch a search party into the desert. The messenger took Trout's camel.

Two hours later, the luckless crewmen returned empty-handed and subdued.

After a quick luncheon, the caravan pulled up stakes and continued toward Kenneh. The crew struck Trout's tent and packed up her belongings with Flo's.

The passing vistas merged into a muddy blur. Flo's mind locked onto Trout, her thoughts painfully mixed. Trout had been a good patient while ill and better than no company at all at Père Elias's, where they had enjoyed the tub together even if in a dull silence. Though Flo was desperately worried for her, she could not lie. She refused to be a hypocrite, like the vicars at home, who turned the recently deceased into saints, seconded by parishioners known to despise them. It was only when she allowed herself to imagine danger to Trout's person that her feelings toward her were temporarily simplified—purified—into a singular loving concern. It was so much easier to deal with Trout—to feel genuine affection and sympathy for her—when she was absent.

That evening they camped later than usual in order to reach the well at Hagee Soolayman, where camels were always watered on the second night of a return journey from Koseir. Mohammed explained that they could not alter the itinerary. If they had tried to stop earlier, the camels would have balked, for they knew where the well was. In their blood, they knew, he said.

Flo was limp with exhaustion. It was nearly midnight. She would have traded anything for a bath in the pink tub, and thought longingly, too, of the Red Sea. Just to behold it again would be refreshing.

The crew bought goats' milk from the Ababdeh, whose huts clustered in the surrounding hills. It was too late to go shooting for fowl, so they dined on beans and apricot paste. The tribesmen watched from a distance like vultures about to descend on their crumbs, but only the children, naked and shy, came forward to beg, singing and dancing in the orange glow of the campfire. Flo gave them most of her portion.

At Gustave's insistence, Mohammed posted a sentry outside her tent. With the guard in place, she retired and prepared for sleep. She lit a new candle. The light was hypnotic, and staring at it, she was able to calm herself and collect her thoughts.

She reached into her camel box and retrieved her desk. Touching her writing supplies was reassuring. Steel pen, inkwell, nibs, her diary, and Trout's brown book. She prepared to jot a line or two in *Lavie.*

Wouldn't it be a miracle if Trout had managed a word about her abductor? Or inadvertently noted something suspicious, or had a premonition of what was to come? Didn't the circumstance demand that she peek at the journal to search for clues? Just the last brief entry before the ink smear . . .

25 April 1850

Here is your drudge in the desert again, cold and lonely.

We left Koseer at dawn. I am writing with one hand, holding your key in the other. I like to remember that you kept it in your pocket near your heart.

The wind is howling. So I checked the pole that the natives say will hold up the tent in a storm. Miss N told me the Egyptian name for tent is "house of hair." Goat hair, thick as a doormat and never washed. I think vermin live in it that chew on me when I sleep. I itch and itch.

Flo paused to scratch her ankle. Thinking about a bite always made it tickle.

I am cold. My breath is the only heat. Except for shoes, I am dressed. I won't change clothes until Kenna as there is no water to bathe and no privacy in the desert. Which Miss N calls "solitudinous," as if a fancy word could fill all that emptiness.

Flo cringed each time she encountered her name. It was terrible to read another person's truth, especially when it included one's self.

My eyes stung and hurt all day. I wonder can the desert burn them out. No job fairs for blind maids. I'd be put in the workhouse, caning chairs or weaving on a handloom. Such dark notions I know you do not care for.

It had never occurred to Flo to provide Trout with a green eyeshade. It had seemed a luxury—like good gloves—not a necessity.

I sleep on a rug, but sand works its way through. That is the story of Egypt: one thing after another burrowing into the skin. It isn't a carpet proper, but a saddlebag with the seams ripped open and restitched flat. When we trek in the daytime, it is stored just above the camel's foulest part.

I told Miss N I did not want to be alone in a tent, but she did not answer. She sleeps in a big tent and is not afraid like

Flo cringed with horror. She didn't recall Trout asking to share her tent. She felt a sudden heat, a spreading shame, quickly striped with anger. Question after question tumbled through her mind. Who had given Trout that key and why? Which must be the same one she'd found on the dahabiyah floor and later seen under Trout's pillow. Not only was Trout's disappearance a mystery, the woman herself was.

She slammed the book shut, sick with guilt and worry.

A moment later, she opened it and started at the beginning.

23

"THIS IS TRAUT'S BOOK"

19 November 1849, in Alexandria

The boat from Malta took three days. Yesterday the captain shut off the steam lest we arrive before sunrise and be set upon by robbers and such. We will lodge here a fortnight.

Miss N is beside herself with happiness. She loves the moon and calls it Ices. I call it Ices too to please her. She does have her moods, sometimes sad, sometimes bright as a new penny.

I am homesick. I'd liefer sit twixt your knees and roll cigars while you read me your poems than see the sights. I do miss my Massa.

Polished Miss N's shoes, pressed her bodice, washed and hung her underthings, dressed, combed, and coiffed her, trimmed her nails, rubbed the looking glasses.

20 November 1849

I had a Turkish bath today, washing with palm leaves. I hope I do not get a rash. Then we et luncheon of bananas, dates, citrons, and odd fruits I did not taste. All the servants are men—cooks, chars, and scullions too. The women live bunched up together in rooms. We visited an Armenian church though I do not know what made it Armenian other than the vicar's funny hat.

After church, we called on the Sisters of Charity. Miss N does like her hospitals and diseases. She says these dirty low sons of men are all on their way to perfect truth but it will take them longer than us.

24 November 1849

Today we saw a lot of women in black robes. It is hard to tell who is fat and who is thin with all that cloth.

We rode asses to and fro, such small beasts your feet touch the ground. A man runs in front to clear the way. Bounce and bounce, my bottom was sore as a blister.

I fear I shall have to see every rock in Egypt if Miss N has her way. I did stay at the hotel while the three of them went to see the place where Admiral Nelson beat the daylights out of Napoleon's frogs.

I hope you are thinking of me.

Polished three pairs of boots, washed Miss N's clothes. Scrubbed the chamber pots. Darned holes in her stockings. Cleaned Mr. Bracebridge's pipe and kit for which he thanked me.

26 November 1849

I'd liefer be home where I know what to do and it is always the same. And I can visit you evenings in your rooms at the Temple. When the big day comes to go to Paris together, it will be a hop and skip next to this.

I do not like being a lady's maid, there is too little work. I have no hearths or knives to clean, no fires to lay, no scuttles to fill, no lamps to trim at night. My hands have turned white. You know I like to be in my dirt and then scrub clean, it gives such a feeling of worth. All play's worse nor all work.

28 November 1849

I had a close scrape, thanks to Miss N. She wished to visit a mosk so we dressed in heathen clothes. Miss N said our hands and faces must not show, but I could scarce breathe with my face covered. What is wrong with the human face? said I, but she did not reply. Miss Selina told me the Mahometans reckon a woman's face and hair the root of temptation and sin.

So many red hats I have never seen. They look like upside-down flowerpots. The women wear veils done up with metal rings. If all a man can see of a woman is her eyes, it will lead to a lot of rude staring if you ask me.

We heard the call to prayer. I am getting to like this song caroled five times a day. Everyone washed hands and feet. A priest called out and we pressed our heads to the floor. You couldn't see a patch of ground, just miles of Turkey carpets. When we were outside again, a crone grabbed my arm shouting Frank! Frank! I'd of fainted but for Mr. Charles and Paolo spiriting me away.

I do not think Miss N means to wear me down, but she does. I am only a maid, I want to say. I will comb your hair and polish your boots and lace your corset, but spare me your enrichments. (That is what she calls her wild ideas.) I do not care to see inside a pyramid, for she told me it means climbing through tunnels by candlelight. The thought of all that stone pressing down on me makes me feel I will throw up.

Polished the boots, scrubbed the chamber pots, washed out clothes, swept and polished the floor on my knees, made the beds, dressed and coiffed my lady.

Flo set the diary down. This was a different Trout from the woman she'd slept alongside for the past three months and shared a household with for a year before that. It hadn't occurred to her how often Trout might like to express her opinions or how pointed they were. Such a simple thing, speaking your mind. She took that right for granted, though it was a habit Fanny did not admire in her.

She reminded herself she was reading Trout's *secret* thoughts, but she didn't like it one bit.

And that dutiful list of daily chores! Flo had never so much as boiled an egg. Was it her fault if she had been born into a wealthy family? She felt guilty, always guilty, and yet incapable of satisfying even the few obligations of her privileged life. She trusted that in time her father would settle three or four hundred pounds a year on her so she could live independently of her family. She had only to reach the age when she was proclaimed a spinster without prospects. Then she'd be free, with perhaps one devoted servant, someone nothing like Trout.

She picked up the soft brown leather book and continued reading.

3 December 1849. We are in Cairo now.

I have hardly sat still for a week, running after Miss N.

We were towed up a canal from Alexandria. It was dandy and I worked on my crochet. Then we boarded a crowded steamer. Miss N jumped ashore without so much as a fare-thee-well. I shook like a wet hound until we found her on another boat. I do not care to make history like Miss N, who shows her derring-do at every turn. Nor do I trust her. When she gets an idea in her head, she does not consider anyone else. The second boat was as bad as the first, full of jabbering foreigners and bugs. The children cried all night and there was no room to lie on the floor.

Polished 3 pairs of boots, washed Miss N's hair and combed it dry, washed out her underthings and packed up 3 times.

4 December 1849

There are not enough brooms in the world to sweep Cairo clean. Miss N loves it and calls it a garden. But she hates the desert. It is an abomination, says she, like Sodom and Gomorrah. At least in the desert I would not have to sweep the sand away. Here, that is all I do. But it comes back like black to a kettle.

I saw a baby hippopotamus at the consul's house. It was cute enough to kiss, with big whiskers and pink as a piglet. No crocodiles yet and I hope I never do.

We are lodged in fancy rooms at the Hôtel de L'Europe. Dinner takes two hours, with fancy desserts like Vol-au-Vent of Pears, and Dantzic Jelly. Mr. Charles said it was a capital meal.

Every afternoon I walk at Miss N's side, nodding at the ladies with silk parasols. Remember the night you took me to the opera, and I was proud to be the only servant in the house? I would never wish to pass for a lady. Give me bootblack and soot so I can prove my worth to God with hard work.

We wear veils wherever we go. They keep the sand out of our faces and spare the heathen the sin of looking at us.

Miss N said she will not be surprised if Cook's started tours on the Nile. And isn't it grand to see it before the English middle classes wreck it forever? I kept my peace, as I have never booked a Cook's tour, though I rode the railway third class to Shropshire last year. It was thrilling.

7 December 1849

Mr. Charles engaged a houseboat for the next four months with hooks and cubbies everywhere since there is so little space. The parlor is pretty, with green panels and a divan all around. Miss N is content though she keeps saying Squawk, squawk I am no dahabiyah bird. I am sick of this cleverness and it is only the second day.

We can see the pyramids from here. You know what they look like.

8 December 1849

Miss N used up her petticoat tape to sew a flag that says PARTHENOPE whilst Mr. Charles hung a Union Jack and his family colors. Do you have family colors, Massa, you never said.

Nine crewmen we have, all odd. They are not slaves and not free men either, for each is beholden to another, like a wife to a husband. When the wind quits, they row and sing the loudest song. Otherwise they do not make a peep. We cannot walk the deck where they sleep and eat for fear of catching their fleas. Miss N says the Egyptians are too beaten down to drive the flies from their faces. She is disgusted with them.

9 December 1849

I am tired of Miss N's outings. I am her companion when Miss Selina is ailing. She is a delicate sort, not like your drudge, though lately, I suffer from headaches and stomachaches and pain in my eyes. But Miss N is no coddler and I must go with her.

We visit filthy ruins and temples that all look the same. At one, human bones stuck out. I saw naked slaves in such poverty as breaks your heart. The poor things are humble and do not complain. God will provide, they say. Mr. Charles believes a contented mind is a curse.

I sleep in a levinge to keep the bugs off. It works, but I don't sleep sound tied up like a prisoner.

Here the diary broke off for two pages where, Flo saw, Trout had written and rewritten a letter without finishing it to her satisfaction.

My sweetheart,

I want to post this so you read about my trip before I return. Miss N writes for hours every day. I have heard her read to Miss Selina and seen her letters. Her words are so fine I can see the color of everything and smell its smell. So here is your drudge, writing a proper letter. The moon is like silver, the stars are diamonds. I miss you reading to me so much

Dearest Gilbert,

A letter for you.

We see beautiful skies and here was one. The moon was like a silver platter in need of polishing as I could see gray spots on it. And the stars were diamonds that would take your breath.

I miss you. I wish I spelt better so you would not smile at my words. It is hard to write to a poet and a gentleman such as you are

Flo's face grew warm, as if she were standing near a roaring fire. Apparently Trout had read her letters. Flo often left them lying about, assuming that Trout was bound by honor and devoid of curiosity. She decided on the spot not to mention the lapse, but to keep her papers out of sight in future. The irony of her own invasion of Trout's privacy was not lost on her. She felt herself blush again, this time with shame.

As for the fussy, spoiled, and thoughtless "Miss N," she barely recognized her. What if the rest of the world saw her as Trout did? Surely she would know if she were horrid, wouldn't she? The heat spread down through her torso. She could feel her pulse at her throat and in her chest.

She reminded herself that she was never intended to see these words. Trout was unhappy; what she had written was as much a reflection of her own feelings and flawed character as of Flo's.

Flo blew her nose and sighed.

It was the old question of evil in different guise. Did people intend to do bad? Certainly Fanny and Parthe did not. Nor did Flo believe they were evil. That was the essence of the conundrum that the ancient Egyptians had solved millennia ago: Good came out of evil and evil out of good. She could be both saintly and horrid—like Gustave, who had devoted a book to resisting temptation yet patronized brothels. This unfathomable paradox, this engine of history, seemed an impractical way for God to have fashioned the world. How could there ever be justice if good intentions led to ill? Her head was throbbing.

No, I *am* horrid, she thought. I simply blind myself to it, inured to others' protestations. That is why I cannot bear my family and why

I refused Richard. I am selfish and willful, lacking, *severely* lacking in humility. She put her head between her knees.

She wished she'd never read the diary, and knew, too, that she'd finish it. She had to find out if there was a happier ending for her, as if her actual future depended on Trout's opinion. Had Trout thought better of her in time? She began to tremble. Her teeth chattered and a few tears dropped onto her hands.

She stood, found her hairbrush, and languidly began to brush her hair, establishing a calming rhythm in the strokes. Trout was no icon of perfection. Her secret life did not bear scrutiny. She had an illicit love affair or at the very least a clandestine friendship with a man. Flo tried to form a picture in her mind of Gilbert, but conjured instead Max. Because they both had cameras? But Gilbert was a poet if Trout could be believed. Her lover!

Stunning. Trout led a double life, cavorting in the evenings with a gentleman who lived in the Temple at the Inns of Court, a dignified address on the Embankment reserved for barristers and judges. How long had Trout known him? How old was he, and what possible interest could he have in a servant? None of it cohered. She wondered if he had a wife and whether he and Trout slept in the same bed. If Trout were morally deficient, Flo might be less inclined to credit her judgments.

Shakily, she picked up the book again.

11 December 1849

Miss N is sinking into one of her moods. Miss Selina knows it I can tell from the looks she gives me.

We had no wind the last two days. Miss N found a tomb in the desert and began to weep, saying it was not the lack of life but the death of life that made the desert unbearable. She hates to see skeletons or any sign of a dead thing. I think she is losing her wits, which has happened before. She gave me a petrified shell that looks like a tiny ram's horn. She keeps calling my name, though she does not need anything. <u>Trout, Trout, it is all dead, dead and evil,</u> over *and over. I put her to bed early and she did not read at all and tossed about for a long while as I mopped the floor.*

14 December 1849

Every day Mr. Charles goes ashore with Paolo to shoot partridges or turtledoves. In the evening, we sit on deck and watch the sunset. Miss N keeps saying I must read the Arabian Nights so I will know what I have seen. I am glad she does not have the book on hand.

Mr. Charles likes to visit other English people, for which I am grateful as there is always good wine and clean food. Miss N says she would rather be the hermit, but then goes and charms everyone.

18 December 1849

I am reading Exodus because I am miserable in Egypt like the Hebrews.

Bennysoof, Benny Hah San, Benny-this-and-that. I am weary of ruins and beset with ailments. Sore feet and knees. Itchy rashes. Tired eyes.

The river is wider now, more like a sea. White Horses, Miss N calls the waves. White Horses, I say back. We make a game of it. We have not seen a house for days, only mud huts with people creeping in and out.

I have become lazy. My hands are lily-white and I have lost my calluses. Miss Selina will not let me wash her clothes. I would feel better if I was a help to her. When I am not in my dirt, I feel useless.

19 December 1849

It scares me that I cannot call your face to mind. I was never afraid at home and here I tremble over the smallest things. I wish I'd of quit my job and stayed in London. How can a gentleman like you love me I am such a plain creature?

I am sleeping poorly. Do I snore in your rooms? Miss N says I am cutting wood in my sleep.

There is bad feeling twixt her and me. Words here and there over little things, like one dog snapping at another. My mother used to say to take care when you sew, even a small needle can draw blood. We stay out of each other's way.

12 January 1850

Aswan nearly kilt me.

The first time you asked me to keep a diary I did not want to and wrote only lists. Do you remember? "Polished 40 pairs of boots, blacked the grates and fenders, scrubbed the flags," and so on. Now the diary is a comfort to me, though betimes it makes me miss you so much my chest hurts.

Here is my close call with Death. Mr. Charles invited three chiefs to the parlor. The oldest one said our houseboat was too big to go up the falls. I liked to cry from joy. But Miss N said it was a trick to raise the price. After many cups of tea, they agreed upon a sum to try the rapids the next morning.

I did not sleep more than five minutes that night. Miss N was so happy she bought ostrich eggs to celebrate. Squawk, squawk, we are going upstairs to Noobia. I had no appetite due to terror sticking in my belly like a knife.

The next morning, we moved everything below so it would not fly away. Furniture, pots, dishes. Miss N said I would stay on board with her and Mr. Charles. I was so scared I could not peep.

Up and up we went six different times, the boat almost standing on end. Once we heard a crack and a rope broke. I was sure I'd drown or be beat to pulp on the rocks. I prayed like mad. A hundred men pulled with all their heart as if they loved us dearly. I cannot tell you how it felt to be dragged up those rocks without speaking of things I have never done, such as falling out of a tree or jumping off a mountain. It is a miracle we did not die ten times over. I was sick and throwing up. Miss N was pleased as punch.

Such horrors of travel. I hope this will put you off ever going to Egypt. I'd never go a second time and if you went, I'd worry myself to death every day you were gone.

Flo was shocked. How had she not noticed that Trout had been ill and too terrified to talk? Or had she simply pushed it from her consciousness? How selfish and insensitive she was! But then the next two entries painted a nicer picture:

20 January 1850

Today Miss N was a help to me, more than she knows. I lost your key and she was kind and found it. When she wasn't looking, I kissed it and pressed it to my heart.

I do so miss doing kindnesses for you. Fixing your dinner and petting your face and especially washing your feet. Oh it gives me a chill to write it, but most of all, licking your boots. Which fills me up with love and humbles me before you and God and shows I love you as much as any good Christian woman can.

1 February 1850. Derr

The Nile is skinny now and we travel close to the banks, like English barge-folk.

Miss N is suddenly pert as parsley, speaking French to me and to herself too. Today I heard her laugh while she was writing.

10 February 1850. Aboo Simbell

I feel bad. Shamed and humbled to my bones which is a lot for one who has no puffery. I got stuck in the sand on the way to the big temple. The crew tried to yank me free, but I'd liefer burn to a crisp in the desert than let them touch me.

Miss N tried to lift me, but she is too small. It was Mr. Gustave, a Frenchman, that rescued me. She was so grateful she invited him and his mate Max to dinner. But I had lost my dignity in the sand and was ashamed to see him again so soon. I ate in the cabin.

12 February 1850

Miss N and I had a fight.

I broke the first rule of service, I forgot my place and asked if she knew my name. Oh of course, she says. Troutwine, she says, fidgeting and acting put upon. She blushed and blushed until I told her Christa. I know she would of fired me at home, but she needs me here. We did not go into the spelling of my family name, which I am sure she does wrong—Troutwine like a fish and a bottle of spirits, instead of Trautwein.

She is vexed with me. I think we are not speaking.

I wish I could pick you up and carry you about the room, then set you on my lap to pet. I wish I could wear my chains, that is all I think about.

Flo looked up. *Chains?* Did Trout mean bracelets and necklaces or great, jangling shackles? And why would she treat a grown man like a child?

28 February 1850

We have visited Aboo Simbell every day the two ladies are so taken with it. Miss Selina draws and Miss N studies the pictures. I am bored. I have seen enough of Egypt for eternity. Because a temple is big and old does not make it sacred if you ask me.

Idleness does me no good at all.

7 March 1850

A toothache for days and only now I am strong enough to hold a pen. Miss N cared for me like a mother, holding my head just so, and brushing my hair and putting her fingers in my mouth. She laid hot towels on my face until the pus ran and the swelling went down. She thinks it was an absess in the root. I am lucky to still have my tooth in my head.

The only other lady that ever touched me was Mrs. Hallam the day before she died. I had brought her a pot of tea and she asked me to take out her frocks so she could look at the prettiest ones, and gave me a sovereign from the nightstand. She said she'd grown fond of me, and wanted to give me advice. Be careful who you marry. Then she took my big red hand in her soft white one and held it.

Miss N's mood is gone dark again, I do not know why. I would comfort her, but now that I am well, we are back to maid and mistress. But I do love her better than before. She was angry before, and now she is kind, though fallen back into herself. I pray for her at night.

It is seven years that I am a slave to my Massa and six years of padlock and chain. Dearest heart, I miss you. Your feet will need a good scrub and soak by the time I return. I will bring my soft wire brush for your nails. And the oil and lead to black myself up for you all over like you like.

Black up? Flo set the book on her lap. *Padlock and chain?*

She arranged the puzzle pieces in her mind: hardworking, independent-minded Trout; her gentleman friend or lover; the key, the chains, the lead and oil; her calling him "Massa." All at once it came clear—Trout was dressing up as Gilbert's slave. It was perverse if not downright wicked.

Shocking.

Oh, and that most distasteful detail: Trout licking his boots! But *why* would stiff-necked, pious Trout do such a degrading thing? Why would she black up and wear chains and probably allow him to photograph her doing it? It made no sense.

Oh, no. Of course. There was only one explanation, though Flo hated to contemplate its terrible, *enslaving* power: Love. It seemed that everyone in the world but her had a soul mate.

20 March 1850

Miss N has taken to praying morning and night. She has become fond of her Frenchman, Mr. Gustave, and went for a walk with him. Otherwise, she is miserable. We try to cheer her up with card games and stories, but she will not be jollied. All she wants to do is sit in the ruins and study her books. Miss Selina does her best, but she must attend to the Mister, who does not like to amuse himself alone. They love Miss N like their own flesh and blood.

I think we shall be home in August, five more months. It is easier to endure a thing once you are halfway, which I am not yet and very lonesome for you. When I return, please take me right away to the Marleybone for the pantomimes.

I killed bedbugs all day in the cabin. They climb up the walls and watch me from the ceiling with their tiny eyes. I miss the park at Embley, with nary a deadly serpent or crocodile, just spiders and field mice.

5 April 1850

Mr. Charles is starting to get on my nerves with his jokes. Such as when we arrived in Luxor he bought grapes on the sly and put them up his nose like two big balls of snot and came to dinner that way. Everyone laughed and the grapes went flying across the table. Other times, he makes speeches. I have heard much about the Corn Laws and the Reform Bill. He likes the problems of poor people (not servants) and debtors. Miss Selina cannot control him though she tries. Miss N says he has the biggest heart in all of England.

20 April 1850

I am on my way to the Red Sea with Miss N and the two Frenchmen. I like Mr. Gustave and Mr. Max. They are jolly and act like boys.

We are crossing the desert on camels. They have a hump reckoned to hold water for days. Tonight we had a good supper of lamb and beans. Mr. Max has the best of cameras and wants to make my picture. I shall be the first Christian woman with a photograph in the eastern desert. The picture is for guess who.

24 April 1850. In Koseer

I can smell the Red Sea and from the balcony, I can see it. It is blue.

We are stopping with the French consul.

You will laugh to hear that I spent half the day in water, but not the sea. In a big pink tub. A nice morning with Miss N. But then at dinner she had a bad spell and could not speak. I can never tell when she is going to be wretched, but now I know it is not my fault. So I say nothing and do what she asks and try to show her that I do love her better than before. If she was my kin, I should take her home to Shropshire and feed her good country food and ale to make her strong.

The consul has a servant, a pretty young boy. He stares at me when we are at table which I do not like.

When I want to think of you I touch your key.

That entry brought Flo back to where she'd begun. She laid the book aside.

She hadn't noticed Hakim staring at Trout or anyone. He always looked away or down, like any servant, except when he helped her haggle at the market, and then he had looked *through* her. She could not imagine what it was about Trout that had emboldened him to stare. Simple curiosity? But why stare at Trout and not at her? After reading Trout's diary, the whole world seemed topsy-turvy, thick with intrigue and secrets.

24

LEMON ICES AND RAKI

After Trout vanished, everything went to hell. Joseph came down with a fever. Fearing contagion, the camel guides kept their distance, polite but guarded behind their *kaffiyehs*. Mohammed assured Gustave that, barring further trouble, they'd arrive in Kenneh just one day late. He promised they'd have water by midday on the morrow. However, the next day they found a decomposing camel carcass in the well at Bir es Sidd. Only the caravan crew deigned to fill up their skins. Gustave watched with revulsion as a camel guide lifted a goatskin pissing from many holes and gulped down the foul liquid.

That evening, the Ababdeh, also strapped for water, sold them the dregs of a skin of sheeps' milk, a mouthful for each of the Franks, but nothing for the crew, who vowed to continue drinking the polluted water. They could drink their own urine, if necessary, Mohammed bragged. After a poor supper of apricot paste and gamey partridge, Gustave and company went to bed thirsty, exhausted, and demoralized for the second night in a row.

The morning of the third day, Gustave's mouth was so dry it was difficult to form words; his tongue cleaved to the roof of his mouth. Max proposed a remedy. He claimed to have read that a piece of flint held in the mouth slaked thirst. "Water from a stone?" asked Miss Nightingale, lifting an eyebrow as Max handed the flint to her. "That sounds familiar." But she too proceeded to suck on the mineral. It neither dissolved nor lost its sour taste. Gustave found the rough texture and metallic tang particularly unpleasant. The constant urge to swallow involved removing the flint or lodging it in the pocket of the cheek. "Don't spit!" Max cautioned "Swallow."

Miss Nightingale became so quiet and docile that Gustave began to worry for her. Was she despairing again, or merely disheartened from fatigue? He still had her note to God, which seemed somehow vital, like a chit in a game that could redeem her from any peril. Nevertheless, he determined to cheer up his pucker-faced friends and hit upon a brilliant scheme later that afternoon. "Max," he called as they were picking their way through a rocky gorge, "do you recall the lemon ices at Tortoni's?"

Max sagged on his saddle, his eyes dulled with fever. "Yes."

"If only we had a lemon ice now. Wouldn't you like one?"

Max made no reply.

"Lemon ice, anyone? Gustave called out. "Cold, sweet, delicious—able to quench any thirst."

"You are torturing me," Max grumbled without looking up.

"Torture? Lemon ices? *Au contraire,* I salivate just thinking about it. Surely, if you could—"

"All right, *yes,* I'd like one." Max pulled his kaffiyeh up to the bridge of his nose.

"Do you remember the halo of white frost? It melts faster than the rest. When it touches the tongue, it turns to cold sugar."

"Will you please stop?" Max begged. "You're making me thirstier."

"Wait. Imagine just one teaspoonful in your mouth. Let it melt slowly, from your own heat. It glides over the tonsils. By the time it reaches your stomach, you feel like swooning—"

"Mademoiselle, aidez-moi!" Max cried. "Please, shut him up!"

Rossignol, he thought, had been listening with pleasure. Now she looked pained. "Gustave, perhaps—"

But he continued, swept up in his own obsession. "I love to crush the ice with my teeth. That soft crunching, the coolness against the palate—"

"I am going to kill you." Max withdrew a pistol from his belt. "One more word and I shall shoot you."

What a humorless prick. Max had the imagination of a gnat. Was the gun even loaded? He didn't think so. "Lemon ices! Lemon ices! Lemon ices!" he taunted.

"You provincial shit! Goddamned spoiled brat. Ride ahead. Joseph and I will follow so I don't have to listen to your un*ending* crap."

"All right! I have stopped." He'd never seen Max so furious.

He apologized and pleaded for forgiveness, but it was too late. Max seemed to have erased him. Miss Nightingale, too, was silent.

They were forced to make camp early, before sunset. Not only was Max not speaking to him, he had also developed a high fever and was no more able to sit astride a camel than levitate on a carpet. This development jarred Rossignol from her funk. She tended to Max as he vacillated between delirium and sleep. Then, after another meager supper, she asked Gustave to accompany her on a walk. Looking sad and determined, she trod to the guides' area, halted crisply, and called for Mohammed.

Bowing and bestowing blessings of peace, the guide rose from his bed behind the camels, his demeanor calm, his face expressionless. Pantomiming, she begged him for some of the crew's contaminated water. He shouted something, and one of his underlings promptly handed her a goatskin. Holding her gaze, he shook his head and pinched his nose by way of a warning. She thanked him and curtseyed.

Gustave and Mohammed followed her to Joseph's tent, where both patients were quarantined. She whisked a linen handkerchief from her bodice and, while the men watched, moistened it with the foul water and dampened Max's face and chest. "We must lower his fever," she said to no one in particular, passing to Gustave a palm fan to wave over his friend.

Lying nearby, Joseph roused himself to watch. Rossignol placed her small palm on his forehead and shook her head. "Both of them have raging fevers, though Max's is worse. I believe he may be in mortal danger."

"What else can we do?" Gustave was truly alarmed. He'd never cared for a sick person—only kept vigil, first by his father's deathbed, then Caroline's, and lastly, Alfred's. He'd always left it to others to scurry about with treatments and blandishments.

"We must wet them down, do their sweating for them."

And so he removed Joseph's shirt and sponged his chest with it. When Mohammed muttered to them, they didn't so much as glance in his direction. Soon a second goatskin appeared, as malodorous as the first. Then the crew retired.

It was only after the two patients were cooled and sleeping that it occurred to Gustave that without water none of them might survive another day, perhaps not another night. "We must drink something," he told her as she sat in his tent.

"But there is nothing." She was fanning herself. "Sit closer and I can do us both."

"We shall have to drink alcohol," he said wearily. "I wish I had wine or beer, but I have only raki."

The fanning slowed. "Oh, for a glass of wine."

"We must drink as little as possible, though." With empty stomachs and thickened blood, he explained, liquor would hit them like a hammer. "You'll become tipsy, you may fall into a sleep from which I won't be able to wake you." He wondered if she'd ever been properly drunk.

She fanned his face. When the temperature finally plummeted in the middle of the night, they'd need blankets, but now this moving air was minor bliss.

The veins in her hands were so much smaller than his. Scale, to quote Max—for by now the word all but belonged to him—was an integral part of female fascination. His thumbs were big and meaty next to her small, sharply angled ones. Her fingernails were glossy pink ovals, with lunular white at the cuticle. His own were twice the size, flat and square as stepping-stones. Her wrist was especially alluring—a second pale throat marked beneath its translucent skin with a faint fretwork of veins.

"Have you ever had rakı?" he asked.

"No."

"It's pleasant, made from anise."

"I've seen Charles and Paolo drink it. You mix it with water, don't you, and then it turns cloudy and white? Quite the magic elixir."

"The water dilutes it. It's strong brew, like whiskey or cognac." He looked questioningly at her. She shook her head. She'd never drunk them either, she said, except medicinally, for a quick jolt of warmth after a frigid outing. "And I rubbed brandy on Trout's gums for her toothache."

"La pauvre Truite." He patted her hand, briefly, determined not to make any gesture in concert with the rakı that bespoke a seduction. Women were rightly leery of drinking with men.

She hugged her knees. "Do you think we shall see her again?"

"I don't know."

"But what do you *feel*?" she importuned. "What do you intuit?"

He closed his eyes to subtract her worried expression from his calculation. What did he think? He hadn't a clue. "Her disappearance is a complete mystery."

"Yes." She was wiping her neck. The notch at the clavicle had always seemed to him fashioned for a human finger to press upon. "I'm ready to try the rakı," she said, as if resigning herself to a chancy medical procedure. "But shouldn't we give some first to Max and Joseph?"

"When they wake." Reaching into a camel bag, he pulled out the first of two unopened bottles and filled two cheap glasses. "Drink it slowly," he cautioned.

"I shall."

"And when you're done, I'll take you back to your tent. You'll be safe there, with the guard."

She didn't answer.

He sat down Indian-style, facing her on the rug. "Slowly," he cautioned again.

For the longest time, she sat poised but unmoving, her attention lapsed or wandering. Some epileptics were like that, he knew, carried off by petit mal seizures, physically but not mentally present. His own fits, alas, were of the grand mal sort, and unmistakable. Thank God, the mere fear of having an episode had never triggered one. What a humiliation that would be. Yet another reason not to wed: shame. Shame of a condition equated with madness. Shame at the thought that someone might observe him doing things he himself would never see or remember. Flailing, frothing at the mouth, falling down, convulsing, his hands twitched into claws, face grotesquely contorted. This, too, had driven him into reclusion.

She was staring at him. "I thought perhaps you'd make a toast."

"Yes. Of course." He couldn't say why exactly, but he found this remark so winsome that he wanted to cry. Again! What was it about this English spinster that brought his emotions gushing forth? Or was it simply the trip itself? Every day in Egypt he seemed to have become more sensitive, more easily moved. He lifted his glass. "To Max. To Max and Joseph's recovery."

"And to Trout," Flo added. "May she be unharmed."

"Unharmed!" They clinked glasses.

"It tastes like licorice," she exclaimed. "No, wait!" She inserted the tip of her tongue a second time into the clear liquid and savored it. "Horehound." She didn't know the French word for this candy.

Gustave's first swallow only served to spike his thirst to a more unbearable level. He wanted to down the whole glass, but restrained himself, if only to set an example.

"Let's have another toast," she said.

"Excellent. Your turn."

She took this seriously, ruminating like a child who still believes in the omnipotence of her thoughts, as if the toast might take immediate effect in the world. "Let's drink to Père Elias and Père Issa."

"To the twins!"

With this second splash of stinging sweetness, his tongue came alive.

"I've been wanting to ask you something," Flo said suddenly. She took a substantial gulp of liqueur.

"Please."

The wind began to gust against the tent, its walls ballooning slightly in and out.

"Are the hospital matrons in Rouen drunks?"

"What a strange question! Not at *all.* I never saw drunken women at the Hôtel-Dieu. Only the good sisters."

"That must have been wonderful, to live in a hospital." She took another sip. "I would have loved that. My mother said hospital women were lower than servants, and loose."

He was amazed. He'd never seen anything untoward at the Hôtel-Dieu, but then he hadn't been allowed in the wards themselves. "What do you mean?"

"Fanny said they hang about for immoral purposes. Because, you see, our matrons belong to no religious order."

"Yes, in France they are all nuns."

"I'm starting to feel the rakı," she said. "In my knees. And how ever shall I toddle off to my tent with melted knees?"

He chuckled. "Don't worry—it will pass. And then you'll get sleepy." He decided not to tell her the other possibilities—lewdness, panic, uncontrollable laughter, passing out, throwing up. The less she knew, the better.

"Tell me about your father." Her glass was half empty.

"Have another sip," he suggested. Christ, he was thirsty. "He was a great doctor. My brother, naturally, followed in his path. He, too, has an excellent reputation."

"Bully for him." She dipped her tongue into the glass, a hummingbird visiting a dangerous flower, then quaffed the rakı.

"But he couldn't save our father."

"I'm sorry." She picked up the book he'd been reading, *The Odes of Horace,* then cocked her head and stared at him, waiting for the next revelation.

He didn't blame his brother, he told her. "We're not close, he and

I. We're nothing alike, for one thing. He's far more conventional."

"My sister, too. She belongs in the eighteenth century!" She drank another mouthful. "She lives for needlework and poor-peopling."

"What?"

Both her mother and sister, she explained, dabbled at charity. "But it's an event on their social calendar," she said with a sneer. "That's all. You know, riding to hounds, hunt balls, the London social season. And *poor*-peopling." Her voice rose. "They bring a joint or a bird to the cottagers and think they've saved the world entire. *Aargh!*" she growled. "My bootlaces are too tight."

"Allow me." He loosened them.

Her face brightened, shifting in that way he recognized as the precursor to a change of subject. "May I see Max's photos? Oh, dear Max! We must look in on him and Joseph."

He'd forgotten. They struggled gracelessly to their feet, walruses clamoring onto a beach, he thought with amusement. She laughed at her own awkwardness. They linked elbows and wobbled together to the tent. The patients were sleeping, their heads cooler to the touch than before. "Good," she pronounced. "Perhaps they are past the crisis."

Returning to his tent felt like balancing on a tightrope instead of treading through sand. They held hands. He steered and she followed, each step a challenge in coordination. At last he opened the flap and they dropped down on the camera cases. "Ah," she said, smiling, her eyes half closed. "The photos?"

"Of course, my pleasure."

They were calotypes, he explained, gingerly lifting them from their cases one by one. She wanted to see all of them, dwelling with special interest on the Sphinx and Philae. "Oh, and there is one of your crewman." She pointed to the sweet, one-eyed model. "He's everywhere."

"Hadji Ismael. Yes, to convey the immensity of his surroundings."

She made a game of finding Hadji. Sometimes he was clad in Turkish trousers, a shirt, and a fez or turban. But more often he wore only a loincloth and white skullcap, his suntanned body dark as the cleft rock, and dramatic against the lighter stone of the monuments. He was easy to spot, slouched at Abu Simbel against the royal wig of Ramses, or seated on a ledge in the pharaoh's crown, his dangling feet in sharp focus. "He's as still as the statues," she observed.

Gustave laughed. "Yes, well, Max told him the brass tube of the lens was a cannon that would shoot him if he so much as breathed. He's always terribly relieved when Max finally folds up the tripod."

"That's awful," she protested, giggling. "Would *you* have lied to him?"

"I don't know. But Max is all business, you see. He regards people as instruments in his various plans." It was only a matter of time, he decided as he spoke, before Max cashiered him for a more influential friend.

"But, you see, Hadji's not in all the photos." He handed her an expansive view of Abu Simbel with the Nile flowing past the temples like molten metal. "Max took this one from high on the opposite shore."

"Ah!" she exclaimed. "There's the sand ramp we climbed every day. I had no idea it was so imposing." She sipped at her drink. "The camera sees so much better than the eye, really." She studied a panoramic vista of the cataracts. "For instance, in this one it could be the eye of God."

Perhaps that was why he hated to be photographed. The camera was inhumanly accurate, and, yes, like being seen by God, whose existence he had outgrown, save for the resentment of being spied upon.

"Here's one of you, is it?"

Max had taken the image of him skulking in the garden behind the Hôtel du Nil against his wishes. He was wearing his long white flannel robe with the signature pom-pommed hood. "I detest being photographed," he said.

He topped off their glasses and carried them outside in order to smoke. Following him, she plopped down on the sand without ado. "I'm feeling the rakı more."

"Oh?"

"Things are spinning." She pointed skyward. "The moon. The stars. It feels as if I've been twirling and got dizzy. Not entirely pleasant, I must say."

"I'm drunk, too," he confessed. *"Ivre et heureux, ivre et heureux,"* he sang to the tune of "Frère Jacques." *"Toi aussi. Toi aussi."*

They were silent for a moment.

"I might need to lie down." she said. Which was just as well since the pipe smoke was scorching his already dry throat.

They hurried back inside. "Much better," she said, flat on his carpet bed.

"You should sleep."

"But it's not that I'm tired. In fact, I'm soaring like a bird." Her eyes were fixed on the tent top as if it were a masterpiece. "No wonder the men take brandy after dinner." She laughed. "I always imagined them solving mankind's problems. Wait until I tell Parthe! Oh, you should meet my sister."

He had no interest in meeting the sister. "I'd be honored." He hated to be polite when he was in his cups.

"She's such a prune, no curiosity whatsoever, but very dear nonetheless. They're all very dear, you know? How can I hate people who have been good to me all my life? But how can I love them when they refuse to understand the first thing about me?"

"I love my sweet old *maman*. But when she chatters on I simply close the door." He drained his glass. "Have you tried flattery on them?"

"I don't expect flattery from a woman carries much weight."

He pondered it. No doubt she was right. Though he was naturally suspicious of flattery from either sex.

"I'm so worried." She sobbed suddenly. "Trout, the poor old battle-ax. She never harmed a fly, really, and never would."

As he reached to comfort her, she snuggled her face and fists into his shoulder without protest, rather like a squirrel with a nut. Patting her in a way he hoped was supportive, he couldn't think of anything clever or comforting to say. Drinking could leave him stupid and boorish, inclined to recitations of Corneille, the theorems of Pythagoras, smutty ballads, or the conjugation of irregular verbs. And so he said nothing. Eventually they dozed off, each of them a lump of incoherence.

He awoke to find her beside him, sound asleep. What luxury, what privilege to observe her at his leisure! It felt almost illicit. But since he suspected that a sleeping person could sense another's gaze—the heat of it—instead of staring, he stole long, furtive glances at the individual hairs of her brows, the whorls of her ear, which were less fleshy than his, her smaller earlobes. Her eyelids were shiny and translucent, with faint pink squiggles that were invisible when her eyes were open. A brown smudge in the shape of a pickle covered part of one cheek. Her hands were ravishing, as if a sculptor had idealized them, the fingers slender and tapering, the skin creamy as vellum.

Moving quietly as a breeze, he gathered half a ream of paper and some flour, then crept outside the tent so as not to disturb her. He tore the paper into tiny shreds, added the flour, and reentered the tent to moisten the mixture. It was an act of faith to use so much of the rakı.

Sitting beside her prone figure, he applied the mixture to her hand, molding it to the bones. He worked deliberately, with focus and delight. His head was buzzing. The gluey stuff smelled like a cabinetmaker's shop. Plaster of Paris would have been better, but this would suffice.

"Oh, my." She opened her eyes. "What are you doing?" She sounded drunk, her words slurred.

"Making a model of your wrist. Then I'll have it cast into an objet d'art for my study at home." A sculpture of her wrist arranged on his desk alongside his dictionary and inkstand, his travel treasures—*a mummy, stones from the Parthenon, egret feathers, Rossignol's note to God . . .*

"Mmm," she hummed, closing her eyes again.

He remembered the process exactly, as if no time had passed since he and Caroline fashioned heads for their puppets. The papier-mâché squeezes he'd made with Aouadallah at Abu Simbel had been something of a refresher course, though they'd cracked and had to be redone in the usual way. Max had been displeased. Yes, *displeased* was the word he used, as if Gustave were his employee.

"It feels very nice. Cool." She rearranged her feet and sighed. "Have you noticed that the worst loneliness is to be in the wrong company?"

"True." He could not divide his attention, not when he was on the verge of achieving a perfectly smooth surface. Was this not what Bernini experienced, releasing the figures yearning to be set free from the carrera? Though that was sculpture, of course. So, not freeing a figure, then, but catching one—a living, breathing subject—and fixing it in time.

"You went away," she said vaguely. "People I wish to leave me never do. But I didn't want *you* to."

He was ecstatic, the strands adhered to the pads of his fingers all of a sudden imbued with the spark of life. "I never left you, Rossignol. And never would. We are in Egypt, after all. Where would I go?" Indeed, in this moment, she *was* Egypt. And in Egypt their friendship would likely remain. Any future they had was dim, inscrutable. Letters arriving in the post with talk of Shakespeare.

"You did." Her eyes were still closed. "You went to Old Koseir. And then I lacked the nerve. Though I was *planning* to, thank you very much." She opened her eyes and, with her other hand, moved the lamp closer. "That is *so* kind!" she marveled, her voice high and incredulous. "You are making a squeeze of my hand?"

"Of your wrist, actually. But not a squeeze—a cast." He explained again that he would have it fashioned in bronze, for his desk.

"What a lovely thought." She stifled a yawn. "So full of sentiment. I quite like the idea of my hand being a guardian angel on your desk."

He'd commission Pradier to cast it. No, not bronze. Alabaster or marble—like the bust of Caroline—the veins in the stone suggesting the delicate tracery within her flesh.

"I think you've forgotten about it." She pretended to pout. Whatever her complaint was, it didn't seem serious. She was giving a comical performance of herself. Starring, directed, and adapted for the tent by that master storyteller, rakı.

"I most definitely have not," he insisted, playing along.

"I think you *have*." At this she wagged her finger at him playfully. What a mild inebriate she was.

"Well, then, I apologize if I've offended you," he said, propping her arm on a shallow box to dry.

"*Merci beaucoup*. I accept."

It would be so easy to take advantage of her while she was sauced. He pictured what lay beneath her skirt, another entry in the encyclopedia, a cunt to match her adorable chin and lips. The size of a mouse, he thought, warm and pink and furry—

But no, he knew her too well. Whenever he felt a deep bond, it was impossible to violate it, to inflict harm. For alongside his cynical pronouncements, he was hopelessly loyal, extravagantly forgiving to the point of weakness. He couldn't hold a grudge. Though Alfred had ended their friendship without explanation, he had sat holding the man's hand at his deathbed, and guarded the body all night. He'd never felt a moment's anger either—just grief. To seduce her now would be betrayal. He'd always known that friendship carried a high price. He was glad she had no inkling of her power over him.

"Trout has a lover," said Flo abruptly. She tapped on her glass.

"Good Lord! What makes you say *that*?"

"Promise me you won't tell anyone, though—especially Max."

"I promise, on my dear mother's life." Suddenly he ached for his mother. She must miss him terribly. He'd nearly canceled the journey at the outset, weeping prodigiously on the train from Rouen to Paris, the anguished indecision continuing for hours at Max's apartment. Then he'd written her to tell of his upheaval, and somehow that had helped.

"I read her journal. She seems to have written him love letters she never mailed. I suppose she didn't want to provoke my suspicion."

"What will you do?"

"I don't know." It was clear from her tone that she hadn't yet posed this question of herself.

He blew on her wrist and fanned it. *"Je suis desolé. La pauvre Truite. Et la pauvre Rossignol."*

. . .

Again, he woke first. She lay sprawled on the carpet. The cast had dried. He leaned down, preparing to cut it off, when she opened her eyes and fastened on him. She studied him unself-consciously, indeed boldly scrutinizing his face. It was like being admired, he thought. "Don't move," he said, sawing carefully through the cast with his pocketknife. He lifted the cast off. "Thank you."

Again, that series of shifting expressions that denoted she was about to change the subject flickered across her face. She would have made a terrible liar, a worse card player.

She rose up on one elbow and leaned toward him so close he could see the aura of fine hairs on her cheek in the lamplight. He smelled liquor. Her breath? His? They were besotted with rakı, pickled in it.

"Would you pass me the bowl, please?" she said.

He handed it to her. She picked up the spoon still stuck in the papier-mâché and stirred it halfheartedly. "Do you think it needs more rakı? That is what you used, isn't it?"

"Yes. And yes." He scrambled on his knees to retrieve the bottle and gave it to her. She tipped a few more drops into the bowl.

"I should like to make a mold of your face, Gustave. Would you mind?" Her lips, he noticed, were chapped and starting to peel.

He liked the idea, just as he liked it when she stared at him. "Please do."

Neither of them moved.

Grinning, she said, "I think you should lie down, don't you?"

If she were any other woman, he'd have thought she was seducing him. Which she wasn't, but the thought set him tingling anyway as he reclined on the kilim rug.

Kneeling above him, she covered his face quickly, spreading the mixture in globs cold and slick as *Maman's* cold cream. Did skin absorb liquid through the pores? The mere possibility soothed him; he was parched again.

"I think I shall die of boredom." She smoothed his laden forehead. "Or of idleness."

"Nonsense. You shall live to be a hundred."

"What's the use if I spend it ordering mutton chops and listening to empty chatter?" She tilted his chin up. "Hold still, I'm going to do your nose."

He had no desire to move. Her touch was exquisite, hypnotic. Delicate as baby Caroline's, the sort that relaxed every fiber and nerve. He felt all of a piece, one calm texture, like a bowl of pudding, or the sea.

"But if I don't marry, I have a chance of a better future."

The masque was tightening, making his skin tingle. It occurred to him there might not be a future. They might not live to reach Kenneh. Max and Joseph might already be dead in their tent while he himself was nothing but hardening dust, a man lying on his back while an attentive and lovely woman rimmed his nostrils with glop. Was it a mere accident that they were alone and completely soused? Though he didn't believe in God, he'd always allowed himself a secret, halfhearted faith in destiny, in the dexterity, pointedness, and utter appropriateness of fate. If it was good enough for the Greeks . . .

Perhaps he could allow himself to bed her after all. Orgasm was the only thing that silenced his mind, the closest thing to godliness he knew—each *coup,* Creation repeated anew.

Now there was some gorgeous garbage! *Je mérite le premier prix de la merde.*

She turned and scrutinized him. "One more bit." She reached for something with her hand.

In the next moment, she smeared the mixture over his mouth, blending it into his cheeks and chin with quick, feathery strokes. It felt pleasantly sticky, like jam. Twice, in a gesture he found arousing, she inserted the tip of the spoon to fashion a slit so he could breathe and talk. "There, it's done," she said softly. "Now we wait until you are dry."

"I'll just lie here," he muttered through the mask.

"I'm afraid I shan't be able to capture your eyes or mouth. You'll have holes there instead."

This hardly sounded appealing. Weren't the eyes the portal to the soul?

She wiped her hands on her skirt. "And now I am going to give you my profile."

Did she mean a drawing of herself? Perhaps by Selina? He'd hang it above his desk, near the *mummy, egret feathers—*

"*Look* at me," she commanded.

He obliged. Turned to the side, she sat stiffly erect, her neck regal, only one eye visible, like the jack in a deck of cards.

"I'm looking." Was *he* to draw her silhouette?

"If you wish to talk to me, you must address my profile. This is how Sultan Abdulmecid conducts audiences."

Gustave did not know how to respond.

"I wish I could speak with my family like this," she went on. "You see, a face in profile is powerful because it's inscrutable."

True enough, he thought. It was a wonder the European monarchs hadn't hit upon this trick. Nothing of her affect was revealed. He might as well be talking to a postage stamp.

"Also, the sultan is frequently seated behind a carved screen, making it even more difficult. I know you are going to Constantinople, so—"

"Mmm." He had to mutter like a ventriloquist or risk breaking the mold. "I don't expect to be granted an interview"—he took a breath through his nose—"with the Sublime Porte."

She leaned over him and dabbed more plaster on the rims of his nostrils. "I want to know how it feels to be so superior that one doesn't have to look another in the face."

"That tickles." His eyes watered from the effort of suppressing the itch.

"I'm sorry. Try not to sneeze." She resumed her imperial posture. "You may address me now," she said, with the hard perfection of a struck coin.

"I cannot think what to say." A wave of desire passed through him.

"Imagine that I am your ruler, your Solomon," she said to the side of the tent. "What dispute shall I settle for you then?"

He did have a problem. Suddenly he wanted her. But how to plead his case, how to ask her? *I come to you with a rising cock that all day has wanted to crow.* "I can't think of a thing," he mumbled, taking care not to open his mouth.

"Then I shall question you. But do try not to move your face." She asked his age and height, the names of his parents, how many cousins he had. (He was astonished to learn she had twenty-seven first cousins.) She wanted to know if he'd ever been engaged. She told him she wished he were her brother.

Her mouth was neither full nor meager, with a well-shaped upper lip. He wanted to kiss her, a desire perversely strengthened by his inability to do so from behind his mask. She chattered on without emotional force about her relatives and pets.

He dozed off and woke to feel her working the mask free from his mouth. "I would like to kiss you," he said drowsily.

"My father kisses me on the cheek."

As she popped the mask free, his face felt suddenly refreshed. "Then I shall kiss you on the mouth, Sultan Abdulmecid."

Behind her closed lips, her teeth were a fortification. Obviously she didn't know she was supposed to open her mouth. Drawing back, he lifted her hand and placed her fingers in his mouth. She shivered. Then he reached forward and placed his own finger in her mouth. When he kissed her again, her lips were pliant, her mouth open. She held her breath.

He was refilling their glasses. "I should take you to your tent."

"Mmm. But let me lie here just a little longer." She opened her eyes and closed them again.

"Would you allow me to make another cast of you?"

"I might. Yes."

She turned toward him and drifted off in his arms.

Twelve hours of night felt like a day, a week, a life. Again, they stumbled to Joseph's tent, where they found the patients no worse. They woke and slept, woke and slept, talked and murmured nonsense. He had never felt so comfortable with another person in his bed.

At some point he began quite naturally to caress her, his hand on her waist, then sliding up her ribs, a tidy but exotic landscape of concavities and rises. He kept his eyes closed, seeing only with his hand. She touched his face, tentatively, then with more vigor, stroking his cheeks, feeling his ears, nose, and lips.

But he must not, he reminded himself, could not, for many reasons, the first of which was that at Koseir he'd found a single chancre on his penis. In a matter of weeks, he'd know if it was the pox. He'd bring himself off outside the tent later on, but now he gave himself to the slow pleasure of touch. Alcohol was a beautiful thing. If he had children, God forbid, he would name the first one Rakı. Slowly, so that she would perceive what was happening to her in her fog, he unbuttoned the top of her bodice. And then, in order not to frighten her, he hit upon a clever scheme, placing her own hand on her breast and then covering it with his.

"Oh," she said, gasping. She touched his face again with her free hand and slid her other hand out from under his.

He had felt a staggering number of breasts over the years, all reduced now to zero. This was the first, the only one that mattered. When her nipple hardened in his palm he became light-headed, his cock so hard it was bobbing up of its own accord, practically straining against his shorts. Knowing she'd be frightened if she felt it, he moved his hips back, even now feeling the pressure of his swollen testicles. He put it out of his mind. Her breast, her breast, her breast . . . Her arm. Her neck. He was fading into and out of his body on waves of rapture.

He must distract himself or explode. He reached for the bowl of papier-mâché. "*Wait,* don't move," he said. He added some rakı and mixed it up. "This is going to feel cool."

She opened her eyes to see what he was up to.

He folded her bodice out of the way to reveal her breast. "I am going to make a mold of your heart."

When he next awoke, he wondered if he'd suffered a nervous attack. So complete was the oblivion from which he emerged that at first he couldn't be sure whose consciousness was peering out through his eyes. Was this what animals felt—sensation without identity?

Alone, he sat up and lifted the tent flap, clasping it under his neck. It was light out, the Orient's bellyful of colors faded to a dun expanse. The camels were bunched on the ground, grotesque swans. And there was Miss Nightingale's white tent, medieval-looking with its decorative fringe and flag. Was it morning? Afternoon? No one was about. He closed the flaps and lay back down.

His head felt heavy and swollen, as if wrapped in a ream of sopping squeeze paper, while his mouth was dry as a broom. Thirst. That was how the previous day had begun and ended, with a thirst beyond words, beyond enduring. He recalled a stream of pilgrims on the road, calabashes hanging from the pommels of their saddles, their bad-tempered wives screaming out an unending chorus of disapproval.

Trout. Privately, he had wept for her, though not in front of Miss Nightingale, thinking it would alarm her even more. And Max, seriously ill. Joseph, too. He prayed Max was better, though he didn't love him and never would, he realized hazily—not the way he loved Bouilhet and Alfred. Still, Max was the best of companions for an adventure—fussy and ambitious, perhaps, but never too cautious.

Abruptly, a memory of Miss Nightingale surfaced, her mouth moving quickly, her neck rigid. The word *Abdulmecid. . . . Abdulmecid*, repeated in his mind like the tolling of a distant bell.

Inside a bandbox, he found the two casts he'd made.

Something had been said, not in profile, but looking straight at each other. What the devil was it? It had been, well, poetic. Poignant. He had promised himself to remember.

25

AMONG THE ABABDEH

Never having ridden her camel at a gallop, Flo was amazed at how rapidly the riders she first glimpsed churning up dust flurries at the horizon materialized at the camp: Père Elias and his houseboy, Hakim, both showered with fine grit and wearing kaffiyehs over their faces. The forward contingent of Trout's search party!

Dazed by thirst, her head still throbbing from last night's rakı, she stood up, spilling the last plate of beans and apricot paste onto the sand.

Père Elias promptly ordered his camel to kneel and slid to the ground. "Mademoiselle Nightingale," he cried. "We have found you at last! You are all right, I hope?"

Of course you have found me, she thought. I am not the one who is lost. "Thirsty," she replied. "Have you any water?"

"Plenty." He leaned over his camel. "We carry a full load, six skins each." He hurried to her, kissed both cheeks, and handed her two goatskins.

"It is good to see you. Please, excuse me." She raised a skin above her head and, to her surprise, squirted a perfect liquid arc into her mouth. Hakim shifted on his feet. *"Bonjour,"* he muttered. She acknowledged him by shutting her eyes as she gulped and swallowed, gulped and swallowed.

"And where are the gentlemen?" the consul asked.

She pointed to Joseph's tent. *"Malades,"* she managed, "with fever." Her belly was cramping. She stopped drinking and placed the damp goatskin against her cheek. "All but Gustave, who is inspecting rocks for petroglyphs." In fact, he had gone to relieve himself.

Mohammed and the crew members welcomed the riders, bowing to Père Elias and embracing Hakim. How did they know him? Were they his relatives? she wondered. Cousins?

After another long slug, she began to revive, like a wilted plant responding to water flooding its leaves and branches. While the men exchanged formal pleasantries, she rushed two of Hakim's goatskins to the sick tent. Max was so grateful, he wept as he drank, while Joseph leaned forward on his elbow, his Adam's apple bobbing up and down like a hungry chick as he swallowed. Their fevers had broken. Still, both men were weak and without appetite. They needed to return to Kenneh as quickly as possible to avoid a relapse in the desert heat.

The camel guides were sharing Père Elias's dates and water good-naturedly when she returned. Just then she spied a haggard Gustave plodding back toward the camp. Earlier, when he exited his tent, they'd exchanged the stuporous greetings of the desperately hung over. Now, though pale, his eyes sunken within swollen circles, he smiled at her. She passed him her goatskin, and he drank until he was quenched.

She could wait no longer. "What about Trout?" she asked the consul. "Have you found her?" She was determined to stay calm but felt herself trembling. She feared the consul's presence boded bad news, possibly the worst news. Gustave reached out his hand and she took it, gratified that Max remained in the tent, though she would not, she decided, relinquish this comfort if he suddenly appeared, reputation be damned.

Père Elias and Hakim were conferring in whispers. "Please," she begged them, "we have been sick with worry."

"Mademoiselle Nightingale," Père Elias began, crossing himself,

"I beg your forgiveness for taking so long. Of course, I shall tell you all that I know." He glanced at Hakim, who sat beside him, hanging on his employer's every word like a spaniel awaiting a tidbit. The wind gusted at ground level, an impish, invisible creature that ruffled the hems of the men's robes, her filth-stiffened dress.

"Out with it, *monsieur*!" Gustave shouted. "Is she among the living?"

"Oh, yes, *forgive* me, dear friends. Yes—she is alive." The consul put his arm around Hakim's shoulders. "That is why I—*we*—have come. To explain everything. I beg you only to be patient."

Flo felt her body sag in relief. Thank God. Thank you, *thank* you, God. Gustave squeezed her hand and held fast to it.

Warm and newly familiar, his hand propelled her into a parallel awareness. Comments from the previous night floated like motes in a sunbeam across her mind. *Oui, d'accord. J'aime ton visage.* But a strange fog enveloped her, as if she had kept a secret so long and thoroughly that she herself had forgotten it.

After securing the mold of Gustave's face in a box, she recalled, she had groped toward her tent, acknowledged the drowsing sentry, and lain upon her bedroll without undressing. A moment later, it seemed, the sun was blaring. Peering outside and seeing no activity, she went back to sleep. Shortly after eight—four hours later than usual—the crew roused themselves and she got up for good. It was then that she noticed her unbuttoned bodice and the tatters of papier-mâché clinging to her neck and chest. He had made squeezes of her, yes. And they had kissed. Beyond that, she was sure of only two things: that she would be happy to see him again and that no harm had been done her. Nevertheless, before emerging from her tent, she had inspected her drawers for blood, finding nothing but a stiff patch of cloth where something had dried. Her virginity, that priceless jewel for which she had no earthly use, was intact.

They had talked. And talked and talked. She remembered laughter. Above all, the impression of tenderness given and received. They had been playful, like brother and sister, though not exactly. She felt her face heat up as she remembered the feel of her fingers in his mouth and her will dissolving in a burst of pleasure. And then he had placed his finger in *her* mouth, whereupon the sensation had doubled and trebled until she felt herself purely a body, all thought having vanished for the first time in her life. She had liked that. Very much. Was this what Clarkey called *amitié amoureuse*? Loving fellowship?

Père Elias was nattering on at the edge of her attention, carefully laying the groundwork for his story. The camel guides ululated and hooted as he lauded the Ababdeh women, who were, as everyone knew, blessed with strong feet and lean figures. Their flawless, nut-brown skin was especially glorious against their white shell necklaces.

She returned to her thoughts. They must remain in touch after Egypt. She pictured him visiting at Embley, herself in Rouen or Paris. They might remain friends for years, decades—a lifetime of substantial letters and conversations. She could consult him about her plans to serve God, and confer with him about his writing. They would be the best of companions, like Clarkey and M. Fauriel. Perhaps lovers. Had Clarkey been sleeping with Fauriel all those years? Certainly she must be now with Mohl. She had heard that the French knew how to prevent pregnancy. If anyone knew, Clarkey would. A brutal determination formed in her mind: she would keep him as a friend, whatever it took.

But was this the touted bliss of love that she'd read about in Madame Sand's spicy novels? It was not the crushing sensation she'd expected, but rather feathery and weightless. How lightly his hand had covered hers! And how much it assured: to keep her safe, to guide and delight. Such a simple act, holding hands. We are a pair, it said. Two in harmony against this inattentive, suffering world.

She let out a deep sigh. Whether it was love or not, she couldn't stop smiling, especially now that she knew Trout was alive.

The consul's speech, alternating between French and Arabic, had slowed, as if he were approaching sensitive material. She turned her attention to it.

Not one Abadi in living memory, he explained, had refused matrimony. Most boys eagerly anticipated it as a mark of manhood and privilege. To make matters worse, Hakim's father was a sheik; his mother, a powerful matchmaker and matriarch. Humiliated by the recalcitrant son who would not take a bride, they had disowned him. It was owing to these grave circumstances, Père Elias summarized, that Hakim had hit upon a plan that, alas, had come to involve Trout.

Following the consul's logic, Flo's mind leaped forward. "I hope he does not propose to marry my maid." Snickering and chortling followed Père Elias's translation. For the first time she had the undivided attention of the crew, even Mohammed.

"Non, certainement pas," Père Elias replied. "Although Hakim prefers the company of older women, he does not wish to marry anyone, I assure you."

The crew continued to laugh. Apparently they found the idea of Trout as a wife utterly ludicrous. Flo felt slighted on her maid's behalf. Trout might be forty-three years old, but she was neither infirm nor unattractive. Indeed, she was a person of a certain dignity.

As if reading Flo's thoughts, Gustave stood and called them to order, his hand raised like a constable's directing carriage traffic at Mayfair. "See here, there's no need to mock Miss Nightingale's companion."

"Forgive me," Père Elias said, raising both hands as if to bless the crew, but in fact to silence them. "She is a fine English lady."

Oh, thought Flo, if you only knew.

Grumbling, Gustave sat down again next to her.

"Understand that Madame Trout is safe," Père Elias said. "To my best knowledge, she is perfectly safe and sound."

Again, Gustave jumped up, with more vigor than he'd shown all day. "Will you not simply produce her then?" He sat back down. "These people talk long, but not straight," he whispered. "There is always something hidden in their words." Color had returned to his cheeks and sweat lay in a thin film upon his brow.

She removed her handkerchief and blotted his forehead as she eyed the consul. "Where is she then?" she demanded.

Shaking his head, the consul regarded his sandals. "This will take time."

Now Hakim stepped forward, addressing Flo in frantic Arabic. "I regret the sorrow and worry I have caused you," the consul translated. "*I* am the guilty one." His face reddened as tears flooded his handsome brown eyes. "I beg you to spare me and the men who helped me."

"C'est ça." Gustave clapped hands, looking away with distaste. "The confession."

Things, at last, were starting to come clear. Flo watched as the consul comforted the sobbing, shaking Hakim, and urged him to continue. "I only wished for the forgiveness of my beloved father and mother," the boy finally managed.

The crew clucked in sympathy.

"I had to do something to restore my mother's honor, or she might have died," Hakim explained.

For all his tears, Flo thought Hakim unrepentant, a remorseless upstart of a boy.

"Also," Hakim continued, sheltered by the strong arms of Père Elias, "I did not wish to be an orphan."

"The poor boy," Gustave said meltingly into her ear. Even he, it seemed, was taken in by the sob story.

Flo could hardly credit the sympathy Hakim's testimony had generated. "Oh, I have had enough of *all* of you," she suddenly shouted, rising to her full height and jamming her hands over her narrow hips as she walked toward Hakim. "*Where* in the blazes is my Trout, boy?" she thundered. "I command you to bring her to me at *once,* since you claim to know where she is."

As he listened to the consul's translation, Hakim's eyes appeared to darken, then lighten and glaze over. His face turned waxen. Flo recalled with definite satisfaction that he was said to be frightened of women. This power over him pleased her. All her life, it now seemed to her, she had backed down from those who opposed her, trapped and helpless and despising herself for it. Rarely had she sought directly to exercise authority over anyone, yielding instead to misery, as if that would bring the desired result, as if justice could be achieved merely through patient suffering and the pity of others. Never had she felt power—the raw force of it— possess her being as it did in this moment. Her body jolted into a fine alertness, every fiber of her straining forward with pointed intention. She could smite him if his answer proved unsatisfactory. Yes, smite him!

Hakim's lashes fluttered like a child's caught in a lie. Any second, she expected, he would dissolve into another gushing waterworks of regret.

Instead, he swooned. The guides promptly collected him, fanning his forehead and patting his cheeks. Only Mohammed did not move or show concern, his usual composure prevailing. His lack of sympathy was not, then, the mark of a weak man, as she had thought, but the flimsy mask of power. Max had been right all along, but she had had to be outraged to see it: the guides had conspired in the kidnapping.

Père Elias stepped to her side. "I knew nothing of what I am telling you until you sent word that Madame Trout was missing. Let that be absolutely clear."

"Of course," she replied. Was there anyone in this part of the world who was not fundamentally self-serving, not frightened to death of retribution? Still, she believed the consul, her reasons having as much to do with his bathtub and bonhomie as his declaration. She had observed his kindness and fondness for Hakim—he did not beat him, for one thing. Indeed, the consul was nothing if not brave to inject himself into the tribal dispute. Yet even the consul's good intentions did not soothe her present frustration or allay her feeling smothered by his ingratiating politesse. She preferred to fulminate, to yield to the new energies roiling within her and fly into a satisfying rage.

"Oh, everyone is innocent!" she screamed, throwing up her arms and glowering. "I suppose it's all *Trout's* fault. No doubt she kidnapped herself!" Blood rushed to her face. "You're all liars. A pack of liars!" She felt magnificent, her own heart pounding applause within. Even Gustave hung back, watching.

"Oh, she was kidnapped, that is clear," the consul confirmed, bowing. "But, miraculously, the family is reconciled, thanks to Madame Trout—"

"Is she their slave, then?" Flo pictured an abject Trout hunched over a cooking fire in a shadowy desert cave. She reached for Gustave's arm and found it. Touching him settled her. Her breathing slowed.

Again, the consul begged forgiveness. "Not at all. On the contrary, she has been treated well. But soon you may ask her yourself."

The consul and Hakim were staring at something beyond Flo in the white distance. She turned to see what it was, but had she not known that something was there, she wouldn't have noticed the faint streak at the horizon where the desert melded into the browned blue of the sky.

For an indeterminate time, the streak did not change, though a dusty halo formed around it. Slowly it elongated into three bars, which soon shifted into three ovals. Waves of heat, the watery illusion of a mirage, transected the blur as it approached.

Looking bored, Mohammed sat down with his men, but Hakim and the consul remained standing, arm in arm, watching the distant shimmer. At the corner of her eye, Flo glimpsed the tent flap open as Max and Joseph edged outside to join the spectators.

"Why the silence?" Max asked in a weak voice. "Is something wrong?"

Quickly grasping the situation, Joseph grabbed Max by the shoulders and turned him in the direction of the oncoming visitors, still a faraway smudge.

Long moments later, three camels loped into the camp with three riders in full Bedouin traveling fig—striped woolen mantles and kaffiyehs to shield their faces from the scouring sand. Only the eyes and hands were not covered. While Flo and her entourage waited, two of the figures ordered their camels to kneel, then helped the third down. They approached in a line, the two on either side supporting the third, processing as regally as Victoria through London. Flo heard a muffled "Mum!" escape into the boundless desert air.

"Is it you, Trout?" she cried, bringing her hands up to her mouth. "Is it truly you?" Her chest felt as if it might burst open like a magic trick into a bouquet of flowers—white roses for sheer gratitude.

"Yes, mum," came the quavering voice.

Flo rushed to grasp Trout's hands, then hugged her. They stepped back to arm's length to regard each other, then embraced again.

Weeping, Hakim prostrated himself at the feet of the other two figures, clutching their ankles. Flo watched as his parents removed their robes. The father wore a leather apron; rings bedecked his ears. His hair was stunning. Save for a short tuft on the top of his head, it was dressed in the corkscrew ringlets the Italian painters favored for Jesus. Though age had creased his face like a map folded too many times, his body was lean and muscular. On his arm he wore a leather band in which a short knife was sheathed. The mother was clad in a long white gown secured under her upper arms, while a long wrapper covered her head, one shoulder and an arm. Flo had the unkind thought that it would have taken quite some time for her to starve, as she was not lean like most of her kinswomen, but plump as a pigeon breast, with skin firm and gleaming as a ripe apple.

Everyone gathered in a circle. Flo counted thirteen, including the camel crew, who bunched together in a wide arc, with Mohammed seated at the sheik's right hand, no doubt a position of honor. Hakim's mother removed and folded Trout's mantle and kaffiyeh.

There, at last, and apparently none the worse, was Trout. She stood stock-still, allowing herself to be appreciated. Her face split into an improbable grin.

Gustave kissed her on both cheeks. "We feared you'd been sold into white slavery," he said, nodding at Flo to translate.

"I don't know about that, sir," Trout said.

"It's just as well."

Hakim's mother fussed over Trout, cupping her chin, stroking her cheek with the back of her hand. She offered Trout water and dates, acting, Flo thought, like a body servant. Or, indeed, a parent. Had she in some fashion adopted Trout in lieu of the bride that had been denied her? Oh, the strangeness of it! This would require a longer letter home than going up and down the cataracts had. Parthe would be beside herself.

"I've had an adventure, mum. I do hope you didn't fret for me too much."

"Oh, but we did. We searched everywhere for you. We did not know anything except that you had been taken." Feeling more relaxed now, Flo bit into a fresh date; it was slightly chewy, with cool honey at the center. "I knew you could not have vanished under your own steam."

Flo was wretched at keeping secrets. She hoped none of the guilt she felt for reading Trout's diary colored her voice. She would never volunteer it, but what if Trout suspected once the book was returned to her? Flo recalled the panicky feeling that had overcome her when she realized Trout had read *her* letters. Apparently she had no greater control over her impulses than Trout did.

Trout tugged at her arm. "I shall tell you about it later, mum," she said under her breath. "I don't wish to speak in a language these people can't understand."

"Very well," said Flo, but she thought it odd that Trout should be solicitous of her kidnappers. Perhaps she did not yet feel wholly safe.

The Bedouin couple had brought the makings of a feast: goats' milk, durra cakes, and something resembling clotted cream, churned as they rode, the consul explained, by the rocking motion of the camels.

After the food, Père Elias offered Turkish cigarettes, greatly prized, Flo knew, in the desert. Only she demurred. Even Hakim's father, who had brought his own long pipe, accepted. Hakim's mother passed hers to Trout, who, after a few moments, sat happily wreathed in smoke. Flo could not help staring.

"I always thought smoking a filthy habit," Trout told her between puffs, "but now I've taken it up"—she tapped her ash to one side—"I quite enjoy it."

Soon Hakim's mother rose to perform a dance while his father chanted and the camel drivers clapped. She moved about the circle slowly, rotating her hips to the repetitious melody and flexing her hands into arabesques.

"She is happy," Père Elias explained to Flo and Gustave. "Her honor has been restored and she has her son back."

"How I miss my own dear mother," Gustave opined. He turned to Flo. "Don't you find this reunion touching? Do you not miss your own?" He stopped himself. "But no, I suppose you wouldn't." He sounded apologetic.

"I love my mother. I wish her well," she said. "But *away* from me, or I from her." She felt more determined saying aloud to another person what she had only thought privately. Addressing the consul, she said, "You will tell us more, I hope, when the celebration is ended."

"It will be my duty and my pleasure."

"And, of course, there is the matter of justice to discuss," she added.

"Oui."

Hakim danced at the edge of the circle, by turns catching his mother's eye and then Trout's. The drivers reclined on their elbows or sat cross-legged, contentedly smoking. Indeed, with Trout returned, the scene resembled nothing so much as opéra bouffe, Flo thought, complete with costumes, exotic sets, comic interludes, and a plot of mistaken identity.

Late in the afternoon, Hakim's parents prepared to depart. They had saved the gifts for last, whether by tradition, or in a final attempt to purchase her goodwill, Flo did not know. The idea of justice was, in fact, much on her mind. Punishment. Possibly clemency. Whatever she decided would require a wisdom she wasn't sure she possessed. She was weary, and bloated, too, after so much food and water.

The father withdrew a live kid with hobbled legs from his saddlebags—the animal barely a weanling—as well as a soapstone cup packed with hair grease for Flo. (Trout already had one, she later learned.) Next, he presented a limp bundle of fur with dark, glassy eyes. Despite all the hunts at Lea and Embley, it was the first fox Flo had ever seen. She shuddered.

"What is that, mum?" Trout asked, pointing to another furry offering.

"Merde!" Gustave cried. "It is a dead rat." He poked at the animal, stretching out one of its long back legs. "But a rat from a circus. On stilts. Disgusting."

"No, no!" The consul wagged his finger and moved closer. "It's a jerboa, not a rat. They roast it over their camel-dung fires. It's tasty! Not at all what you would expect."

Removing the knife from his arm sheath, the sheik skinned the animal with a few deft strokes.

Flo felt faint.

"I saw him catch it," Trout said with remarkable equanimity. "Walked right up to the burrow, he did, and pulled it out with his hands."

"The Ababdeh are great trackers," Père Elias said as the sheik proceeded to skewer the animal on a stick. *"Voilà!"* he exclaimed, accepting the kabob and bowing to the sheik in studious thanks. Hakim, observing nearby, looked proud and pleased. Vindicated.

Shell necklace softly clicking, the mother next stepped forward with two bronze rings lying in her open palm. She stared at Flo's nose, visually inspecting it at close range, then pointed to her own nose ring, smiling. Flo felt herself stiffen as the woman grasped her hand and tried to push the ring onto her finger.

"Please," Flo told the consul, flinching. "Tell her no more gifts! They are unnecessary. Besides, how can a *gift* compensate for a kidnapping?"

"It would be a great insult to refuse these last tokens," he cautioned. "This represents most of the wealth of the family. You might undo everything."

At that, Flo allowed Hakim's mother to place the nose ring on her fourth finger. The woman did likewise for Trout. Flo and Trout curtsied. The mother smiled and fired off something in Arabic.

"Tell them how much we appreciate their generosity," Flo urged Père Elias.

Trout settled the ring on her finger and admired her hand.

"What are we to do with the baby goat?" Gustave asked.

"Eat it," Père Elias replied. "You shall need it for the rest of your journey."

"And the fox?" Flo asked. Do we—"

"Yes, that, too."

After the festivities ended and Hakim's parents had departed, the travelers decided that they would not eat again until morning. The camel drivers built a fire and withdrew to care for their animals, grateful for the gift of fodder the Ababdeh had brought—dried zilla stems they'd collected en route.

As the sun fattened on its downward arc through the western sky, Flo, Gustave, the consul, Hakim, and Trout lounged on blankets around the campfire. Gustave smoked his chibouk, making sure, it pleased her to notice, that some part of him—leg, foot, hand, elbow, or shoulder—was always in contact with her. The consul stoked his French briar pipe and drew a long breath. "This is not a simple matter," he warned.

"Fine, but you must tell us everything," said Flo. "I shall translate for Trout."

He nodded.

Hakim might as well have arranged for the sun to rise in the west instead of the east, Père Elias said, for all the confusion he had caused. In the end, only the boy's cleverness had prevented a tragic outcome, for the situation was more complicated than he had yet allowed.

When Hakim's father was unable to convince Hakim to marry, he faced the threat of being deposed by his first cousin. For a while it seemed the father might have to kill the cousin. Later he offered him the dowry of Hakim's sister, though not the girl herself. The cousin refused. Hakim's parents implored him to reconsider marriage, but by now, friendship and employment with the consul had strengthened his resolve. "Though Hakim is an excellent worker, I would not have risked bloodshed merely to retain a servant," the consul said. "It was a matter of the heart for me, too," he confessed, "for I have grown fond of Hakim. To me, he is like the son I never had." The consul's voice was shaky. He stared at his feet.

"I see," said Flo.

"*Enfin,* the father proposed to give the cousin Hakim's sister for a second wife. The cousin promised to consider it."

"Oh, dear," said Flo. She hated the very idea of a second wife. Before Egypt, she could not have imagined anything more limiting than to be bound as a wife. To be a second wife must be a complete forfeiture of personhood.

This broke Hakim's mother's heart a second time, Père Elias explained, for an Abadi daughter, once married, was forbidden ever to see her mother again. "That's when Hakim took permanent refuge in Koseir, with me."

"I still do not understand how Trout figures into it," Flo said.

"I am nearly finished," the consul said. He uncrossed his legs, stretching them out in front of him.

"So the daughter was taken away weeping, and the mother could not be comforted. It was just then that you and your party arrived in Koseir. Hakim had never before met an Englishwoman. He hatched the idea to arrange a gift for his parents that would redeem them in their clansmen's eyes: a visit from a great English lady. Something like a state visit, you might say," he added. Apparently the Ababdeh knew well the power of England, having ushered soldiers and diplomats across the desert bound to or from India by the Red Sea route. And so the visit was arranged.

The consul's voice dropped to a whisper, as if Hakim might suddenly grasp his French. "I wonder if he told them he was considering marrying Madame Trout."

"More likely," Gustave said, "he simply let them arrive at the idea themselves, without contradicting it."

Flo completed the thought. "That way, the parents could hope for the unthinkable and settle for the merely fabulous—a visit from a fine English lady."

"What a clever lad," Gustave noted.

Flo glared at him.

"Genius put to bad use, though."

"I knew nothing of this plot," the consul insisted again.

"So you have said. Do you think Hakim was aiming for Trout?" Flo asked.

"Aiming?" The consul tapped his pipe bowl onto the ground beside him. "I don't think I understand."

"Did he particularly wish to kidnap Trout?"

The consul paused. Clearly, if he knew what answer she desired, he would have supplied it. "I don't know," he admitted. "I don't know if he understood that she is your servant."

"Oh, my."

"Do not upset yourself," Gustave said, patting her hand. "What's done is done."

"Yes." But she felt the terrible certainty that it was her fault that Trout had been taken, her fault for consigning her to a small tent alone.

"You must trust to fate, to destiny, is what I mean," Gustave said, "not that you should put the incident from your mind, but that everything is not under your control—or anyone's. Do you see the difference, my dear?" He put his arm around her while the consul continued.

Gustave's remark astounded her. For some reason, she had never truly believed in accidents until now. She'd always thought that if a person were paying attention, there could be no accidents. His reasoning provided enormous relief. For at least the moment, she felt both innocent of and forgiven for Trout's abduction.

"Hakim enlisted his cousin, one of the caravan guides, to assist him. It's likely they all knew of it." Père Elias coughed and muttered sotto voce, "Of course, I know none of this part firsthand, you understand."

"Yes, yes." The consul's insistence on his ignorance—and thus his innocence—was vexing. What possible point did it serve?

"The visit was a great success," the consul went on. "All the clan came to meet the great English lady in the family hut and lavished food and gifts upon her. Hakim says that she bestowed favors and privileges in return."

"What privileges?" Flo asked.

"Did they even share a common language?" Gustave added.

The consul shook his head. "I don't see how. Nevertheless, Madame Trout reciprocated. So Hakim said. He was there."

"Is it true?" Flo asked Trout, who startled upon being addressed.

"I did talk, mum. I could not be silent amidst all that gabble, so when they spoke, I spoke. I never understood more than a word or two."

"Perhaps Hakim will elucidate," Gustave said.

Hakim was blushing again. "It was all harmless lies, happy lies. My parents and I are reconciled, my father's power is secure, and my mother is eating again. All is as it was before the trouble began. No harm has been done." His eyes were welling up again.

"Except that your sister is wretchedly married," Flo said.

"A minor point in the scheme of life," said the consul, lighting his pipe anew. "She would have been sent away eventually."

Trout raised her finger tentatively, like a schoolgirl who wants a second chance at the correct answer. "When I saw they meant me no harm, I talked to them. And I gave them things I had to hand." She looked stunned, like a person shaken awake from a dream. "From my chatelaine." She reached into her pocket and withdrew it. "The thimble and beeswax—"

Flo took the chatelaine in her fingers.

"The black and white thread."

The chatelaine was almost empty. Only the needle case and the black key remained. Flo felt like crying at the sight and heft of it, so reduced, so much lighter in the hand. The gratitude she felt for Trout's safe return overwhelmed her with a great wave of relief and then, abruptly, like a cloud obscuring the sun, exhaustion overcame her.

Total darkness of thought and feeling. It was the fatigue of confusion, of too much information and too little sense. She might not be able to reach her tent unaided. And there was still the matter of justice. Père Elias and Hakim planned to leave shortly; she would start for Kenneh with two sick men before the sun was up. She couldn't wait any longer to resolve the matter.

She turned to Trout. "Do you wish these people punished?" Her voice was hoarse.

Trout did not react. Flo repeated the question.

"Is it up to me, then, a mere servant?"

"Not entirely." Flo stretched out her aching legs. "But you are the party most injured."

Trout thought for a time. "What would the punishment be?"

"Death, most likely."

"Death?"

Flo nodded at the consul to expand on the point, and feebly translated as he did.

"Yes," he confirmed, "that is the penalty for abducting a European in Egypt, though it is not so straightforward with the Ababdeh, as they are not subject to most Egyptian laws. You would have to present your grievance to the Bedouin sheik. But in all likelihood, the penalty would be death. The Ababdeh are sworn to protect all travelers in this desert." He exhaled a long curl of smoke. "They both rule this wasteland and are its hostages."

Flo thought it useless to bring a case before the Ababdeh prince. It would take weeks, for one thing.

"Nothing, then," Trout said. "*No* punishment."

The consul didn't look surprised. *"Très bien,"* he said. Upon learning the verdict, Hakim wept and spewed thanks to every quarter.

"Good," said Flo, rising wobbily to her feet. "And now I'm afraid we must retire." Gustave supported her unsteady frame.

Once more, Père Elias bid them a poignant adieu, kissing them on both cheeks and weeping, as he had in Koseir. She watched the two men mount their camels. From atop his beast, Hakim saluted.

With Père Elias leading the way, they vanished into the pink twilight at a canter. Venus rose above the diminishing figures as Flo watched the already darkened eastern half of the sky absorb them until all that remained was a wisp of dust kicked up by the camels' long, ungainly legs.

Encircling Flo's waist, Gustave shepherded her to the tent as if helping a wounded soldier from a battlefield. "Trout," she whispered, "must sleep with me." The sentry opened the flap, and she collapsed onto her knees.

She slept, she knew not how long, awakening to Trout staring down at her. It was still dark. Their ruined dresses lay balled up in a corner of the tent. She dimly recalled Trout helping her into a nightgown over her objections, saying work made her feel better.

Trout was holding the hairbrush and comb from Flo's camel box. An oil lamp burned nearby. "Yes," said Flo.

Trout sat down behind her and began silently to brush out her matted, grimy hair.

"Thanks to God you are safe and sound," Flo said. She felt refreshed after sleeping. More blessed yet was it not to be thirsty. "I couldn't have borne it."

"Yes, mum. Thank you."

Flo felt the tug of the boar bristles mediated by Trout's steadying touch as she parted the hair into small sections. After a time, Trout rose and returned with a pair of embroidery scissors.

The brushing was soporific, and Flo willingly drifted off. Periodically, she jogged herself awake to enjoy Trout's tender ministrations. The lamplight was lovely, glimmering in the satin ties of her gown, darting off the scissors in golden splinters. As Trout snipped through the unassailable knots, a fine shawl of sacrificed hair collected over Flo's shoulders.

"You will have quite a tale to tell your nieces and nephews," Flo said drowsily.

The brushing came to a halt. Trout lowered her hands. Flo sensed them behind her, motionless on the blanket. "No, mum. I don't think I *shall* tell it."

Flo turned around. "Why ever not?"

"No, I am sure I never could."

"But, Trout—why in the world not? You are fine, after all. And it is a tale deserving to be told in detail, to be passed down—"

Trout began to sob. "That was the consul's story you heard, mum, but . . ." She broke off, racked by crying.

Her ease giving way to fear, Flo swiveled completely around. "But *what*?"

"Even if he *is* telling the truth." Trout blew her nose and dabbed at her eyes. "He wasn't *there,* mum. He was not me!" A look of arrant terror had seized her face.

Flo patted her tensed hand. "Of course, you are right. I am sorry. It must have been fright—"

A piercing cry issued from Trout, so shrill it raised gooseflesh on Flo's arms and neck. She had never heard such a sustained and unnerving noise. It was the sound of agony, of butchery—a death cry—Trout's mouth a rictus of recollected terror.

Immediately the sentry burst into the room, dagger at the ready, two cohorts not far behind him. "Get away!" Flo screamed, grabbing the hairbrush and waving them back with it, at which Trout's cries abruptly ceased. Utterly bewildered, the man retreated, the tent flapping shut behind him.

Trout started to weep again in sustained and heaving waves, a tidal bore of tears. "Oh, mum," she gasped between sobs, throwing herself across Flo's small lap, "he doesn't know what it felt like to *me*!"

26

FEVER

The caravan departed for Kenneh early the next morning, the trek that day bland and uneventful, with fewer travelers on the road. Perhaps the pilgrims had already reached Jeddah and thence to Mecca. They would not travel again until after the inundation subsided the following winter. Last December, Gustave and Max had delayed the Nile trip nearly a month to see the weary throngs return to Cairo. He imagined the faithful slowly circling their immense black stone. Clockwise or counterclockwise? He could not remember if he ever knew. By evening, he couldn't remember much of anything and ached all over. A great lethargy descended upon him. He'd caught Max and Joseph's fever.

Pleading exhaustion and lack of appetite, he excused himself from dinner. Miss Nightingale offered to nurse him. When he refused, mostly to avoid Max teasing him afterward, she insisted on brewing tea and delivered it personally. She tried to engage him in conversation, but her words vanished in the heat between them like melting snowflakes.

The next evening, she sent Trout with a pot of tea and a note. *We missed you again tonight. Max says you are no better. Please keep me informed. Your, R.* He threw the note away, but committed the three staccato sentences to memory in the process of appraising what she must have felt composing it. It smacked of restraint, that particular

English trait. It flattered and troubled him, but he could not think why. His brain was soggy, steeped in a bottle of India ink, and as devoid of color. Abstractly, he mourned the absence of sensation: the green of desire, the purple of rage, joy's cool blue undulations.

Earlier that day, he'd glimpsed her, occupied with Trout. Though he hadn't understood what they said, he observed a change: Trout was no longer sullen and silent. She spoke, and Miss Nightingale listened. Once, he heard them laughing together.

For sheer mystery, only his nervous episodes matched this sudden, stuporous malaise. When the fever waned, the lethargy waxed, as if it fed on the fever. Nothing pleased him. Food lacked flavor; sleep was not refreshing, though he slept at every chance, nodding off in the saddle until a stutter in the camel's gait or a voice awakened him. He developed distaste for everything, like a man who opens a door expecting a restaurant and finds instead an abattoir, the saliva gone foul and bitter in his mouth.

On the last evening in the desert, she approached him as he exited his tent for some air. "Are you improved?" she asked, touching his arm, her hand lingering. They stood waiting for the crew to fetch dinner. He smelled the goat on the brazier. Or was it the jerboa?

"No. I am not yet myself." He hadn't been able to look into her eyes. He knew he was a disappointment to her. He was a disappointment to himself, unable to muster a shred of enthusiasm.

"I am sorry."

"Thank you." He hadn't thought to ask after her, though later he recalled she looked wan and tired, a little sad.

"Gustave?"

"Yes."

"Shall we see each other again?"

The lethargy dissipated like a mist burned off in the radiance of her regard. "Of course we shall, Rossignol. Yes."

She looked away for a moment. Tearful, or marshaling her courage? "When?" she asked. "And where?"

His dear Rossignol, speaking Louise's words. *When* and *how soon* and *not soon enough*. But she was not Louise, nothing like her. He peeked at her face. How completely guileless she was, unself-conscious as a plant leaning toward the light. Of course he would see her again. He wanted to, he must. He *should*. No, he *wanted* to. Certainly he owed her an explanation out of kindness, lest she be crushed, expecting more torrid encounters, more kisses. *There is nothing wrong with you,* he wanted to say. *It's me, Rossignol, I think I am infected.* Or was that also an excuse not to pursue the friendship—

"Gustave?"

"Yes?"

"You were saying?"

"My mind wandered. Forgive me." He was tired, his will as vaporous as a cloud. His knees buckled.

She caught him, gripping his arm. "My dear Gustave! Come sit down." She guided him toward a camera case outside his tent. "Rest."

"Thank you, Sweet. You are so kind to me." He hung his head between his knees and waited until his heart stopped thudding. "I am all right now." He stood and began creeping toward his tent. "In Cairo. We should meet in Cairo. That will be best."

"Where are you going? The food is nearly ready."

He forged ahead, muttering *sleep, must lie down*. The prospect of eating was nauseating.

She followed him, her steps halt, then hurtling, like Bambeh's polka-dotted lamb. He remembered the adorable bend of its knees as it trotted behind her, the clatter of its hooves on the dock at Esneh.

"Cairo is fine," she said agreeably. "We shall both be collecting ourselves before heading home."

"Home?" He stopped and turned to her. "Home for you, but not for me. Remember?" His voice was louder, more emphatic. "I am headed to Palestine. After that, Syria, Turkey, Greece, and Italy."

"Yes—"

"Perhaps Persia." That was a lie. Because he'd overspent in Egypt, they'd already canceled Persia.

"Yes, of course." She blushed furiously.

He was inordinately annoyed, the place names a docket of his grievances, indictments against her for forgetting their journeys didn't match, for daring to think that they could. He was bound for more exotic ports, not home, and certainly not England.

"Cairo, then." She folded her hands. "Shall we write in the interim?" She'd recovered nicely, he thought.

"Yes, I would like that."

They settled on the last week in May, which would allow enough time to finish their visits on the Nile. He reminded her that he dare not kiss her even on the cheek because of the fever. Instead, he kissed her hand.

As soon as they parted, the lethargy returned, heading toward dejection. One thing he hated about being ill was how vulnerable he felt. And how inclined to introspection he became. His feelings for Miss Nightingale were a puzzling amalgamation of contrary impulses. He admired so much in her—candor, passion, determination. But he found most women charming, irresistible. There was almost nothing about them he objected to. He liked them skinny; he liked them fat. Smooth or hairy, fair or dark, he found them endlessly enchanting. The housemaid at Rouen, the grisettes of Paris, the whores of Esneh. He loved them all. But did he love her? Given his appetites, he wouldn't be able to disregard her sex forever. Further, he genuinely wished he could give her a taste of the sensuous life, of the pleasures the body offered. Considering her natural depth of feeling, what greater gift could he offer her? On another evening—a dinner in Paris or London—they would drink too much, or he would comfort her and feel again the soft roundness of her breasts . . .

His melancholy was now so profound that something might have curled up and died inside his chest, leaving a ruined place like a patch of contaminated soil where nothing would grow.

The next day, when they reached Kenneh at noon, the sun was thrumming inside as well as upon his head. He hadn't eaten solid food for two days, was short of breath at the slightest exertion. That morning Max had remarked on his haggard expression and shrinking paunch.

Word of their arrival spread to the river from sentries posted outside the hamlet. The Bracebridges were waiting on the deck of the dahabiyah; the crew of the *cange* jumped to attention as he picked his way along the beach. Miss Nightingale fell into Selina's arms. Charles greeted Trout, his jolly, stentorian voice resounding across the sand.

Max had hurried ahead to explain that he was ill. "Please, come aboard!" Charles shouted to Gustave. "Brandy. Luncheon. You must be starving."

As he limped along on the crutch of Joseph's arm, he gauged from their assembled faces how awful he must look. Selina, still embracing Flo, paled. *"Pauvre homme,"* she cried, *"venez ici!"* She conferred briskly with Max. "We wish to take care of you, dear man."

He preferred his bed in the shaded fug of the *cange,* where he could sleep naked, vomit, fart, and curse without regard for etiquette. He whispered to Joseph, who called back, "*Monsieur* say he too sick."

"Demain," Gustave croaked. "I shall see you tomorrow."

As he stepped aboard the *cange,* Hadji Ismael reached up a hand to steady him. Of all the crew, Hadji Ismael was his favorite, the sweetest. How many times had he repeated that supremely soothing gesture—reaching up to help him mount and dismount his horse or donkey. And just before the caravan departed, he'd handed up a blessing with a goatskin of wine. *Peace be with you. May Allah protect you.* It was, without doubt, the most poignant gesture in the Orient, an act of love even if it were purchased, like his whores.

Two days later, pasty and withered, he emerged on deck. There was less of him in every sense—flesh, appetite, ambition, and will. Though no longer feverish, he felt like a sack of shit and wondered if his malaise was related to the sore on his prick. That possibility boded ill.

The *cange* rocked gently as a cradle. In the curve of the beach that served as anchorage, he saw two fishing vessels, and beyond them, a felucca sitting low in the river with a cargo of burlap sacks. The *Parthenope* had sailed.

27

BEAUTIFUL CAIRO

A vertiginous cliff with a stray goat glued to the rocks; fields of barley; water wheels pumped by oxen: sailing with the current and a south wind, the river flew by in vignettes of Egyptian life, as if Flo were watching a magic lantern show. Then the wind reversed, blowing from the north, and they lay about, unable to make progress or tie up. The temperature dropped. Paolo said that in twenty-five trips on the Nile, he had never encountered such frigid weather. Scoured by sandstorms, Flo's lips blistered and her face peeled. Unless securely pinned up, the women's hair whipped into Gorgonian tangles. Charles was seasick off and on.

Between Kenneh and Cairo, there was nothing on the scale of Abu Simbel that they hadn't already seen. Only Dendera, just outside Kenneh, and Memphis, far to the north, promised new antiquities. They reached Dendera on the first day of fair weather. It turned out to have a crude temple that dated to Roman times. Flo found its miles of sculpture and bas-reliefs inauthentic, like trying to fathom Greek sculpture through Roman copies.

After Dendera, for more than four hundred miles Arab hamlets dotted the riverbank: Girgeh and Asiyoot, Manfaloot and Benisoof, their minarets visible like hat pins through the felted air of constant sandstorms. It took three days to put ashore at Girgeh, the wind was so severe. Not a single candle was to be had in the entire town. A Coptic father supplied them with a small cache of church votives. Each city, otherwise, was the same: a market, the ubiquitous water-wheels, buffaloes, and ibises, and beneath it all, brutalizing poverty. She hungered for a real city, for Cairo.

Memphis, however, was inspiring. Though fallen into a reflecting pool, its single most beautiful statue was of Ramses. Again that serene face! She strolled through a palm forest, retracing in her mind Moses's tribulations, for this was his city. His tribe never forgot the story of their exodus. In every generation, Moses warned, they must behave as if they had just gone forth from Egypt. Memory was sacred, part gratitude, part scar. The cooling of the fires of suffering into history. She, too, would never forget Egypt, she promised herself as they struggled northward against the cold windings of the khamsins.

At Giza, just south of Cairo, a storm prevented them from disembarking for the pyramids for two more days. The pyramids! It was time, at last, to tour them. Selina remained shipboard, too infirm for the arduous climbing required.

In England, people regarded Egypt as nothing more than a tray to hold the giant monoliths. If you went to the East and missed them, you hadn't "done" Egypt. A simple formula applied, like something out of Euclid. *Egypt = Pyr and Pyr = Egypt.* Aided by guides up and down the face and through the passageways, Flo compared herself to a rat navigating the drains at Embley. Yes, exactly like a rat sniffing through the maze of a bigger, more important rat. They were, she reported afterward, monomaniacal tributes to tyranny, amazing only for their size and expense.

On May 16 they reached Cairo and sadly prepared to leave the boat that had been their home for four months. The farewell to the crew brought an inundation of tears all around. Even the stodgy rais wept. Two days later, to everyone's surprise, the crew appeared at the Hôtel d'Orient for a second round of good-byes. This was an occasion of deep sentiment, since they had already received their baksheesh. Again, a flood of tears. Each sailor gave her the Arab salute, grasping her hand, kissing it, then pressing it to his heart and head. She wept profusely and without illusions, moved, she knew, not only by the pitiful Egyptians, but also by the prospect of seeing Gustave within the next two weeks, and the fainter prospect, too, of never seeing him again. She didn't like to ponder what and where *their* last adieu might be, or have been.

Cairo was the end of Egypt, for to her mind it was not Egyptian but Arabian. She took her leave of the magnificent land of Ramses, Abu Simbel, and Philae. *Farewell,* she wrote in *Lavie,* blinking back tears, *dear, beautiful, noble,* dead *Egypt.*

Cairo was even more splendid than Flo remembered. By May there were extra touches of color, the dun city like a pavement in spring when rain has driven the tender new leaves and flower petals to the ground. So much loveliness! Bright rugs on clotheslines exhaled glittering motes with each thwack of the rug beater. On the avenues, mimosa trees sprouted tufts of pink swansdown. The carob trees with their sweet-smelling leathery pods cast a reticulated shade to complement the wooden grilles of the balconies and harems. But what pleased Flo most were the skyline views, the domes of mosques rounding upward like earthbound clouds, the minarets at dusk pointing to the first stars.

The desert dashed relentlessly against Cairo's gates, a petrified sea waiting to flood it daily, but by the time she arose at seven, the sand and dung had been swept away. Without vigilance, Cairo would have succumbed to the dunes on which it perched like a faerie kingdom. She wrote to Parthe, calling it *a jewel that rose to the seventh heaven* and *the most gorgeous of cities.* With Trout and an efreet, she wandered the streets, slipping into tiled courtyards and dark bazaars. Repeated visits to her beloved Sistine Chapel had added the beauty of familiarity and made it more like home. But she didn't repeat any of the tours of her first Cairo visit. The new vistas and thronged intersections were freshly exhilarating. She had the easy freedom of a person with a pouch of gold in her pocket and a secret she could choose the exact moment to contemplate or reveal.

On the third day, with Trout, Selina, Charles, and their efreets, she went to the street of perfume sellers and silk mercers to buy gifts. She and Trout rested in chairs while the merchant unrolled fabrics. Bolt after bolt spilled onto the cobbles in sumptuous layers—translucent voiles, iridescent organdies, heavy damasks threaded with gold and silver. She could nearly taste the purple haze of plums, the chalky pink of a petit four, billows of white silk lustrous as boiled icing. She wished to clutch them in a giant bouquet, fling them like streamers into the street.

But she didn't buy a single yard, suddenly aware that her own eagerness had exaggerated their beauty. The possibility of impending bliss had made her generous, willing to grant a greater splendor than before. The mosques struck her as especially majestic not because they brought her closer to God, she now realized, but because she imagined herself walking with him there polished by moonlight in another week, two at the most. The prospect of happiness had painted the city exquisite.

Should she mention this odd effect to him? If they did speak of beauty—she felt the blood rush to her cheeks just pondering this—they would be talking about themselves. About their *happiness,* a word she rarely allowed herself to contemplate. She was prepared to answer any question he posed, thrilled at the prospect of being known to her depths. She might rally her courage and speak of the night in the tent, if only to say how much it had meant to her. And that she did not care if it was repeated.

The next two days, rains came, heavy and incessant, the streets gushing into brown creeks. The Cairenes threw ashes and rubbish to dry the mud and make it passable, trampling down another layer of refuse the way the Nile deposited soil. When the sun returned, there was no sign of what lay buried.

On the river, when she had no word from him she hadn't troubled much over it. He had been ill when they parted, barely able to stand upright. He was a lively, loquacious man; at some point, a letter would arrive.

After a week in Cairo, when his silence grew louder, the city was still a lovely consolation. At the same time, she began to worry about him and secretly to steel herself against desolation, in case their friendship had ended at Kenneh. She had been awkward and self-conscious; so had he, unable to look her in the face. Only the mention of writing letters had heartened them both.

And yet, silence. He must be ill. Or delayed. Another week and she would be gone.

Selina periodically caught her eye, an invitation to confide. Otherwise she stole glances, appraising Flo's face for distress the way you cup a child's forehead for fever. Flo hated denying her information, but if she spoke to Selina, she would have to acknowledge the possibility that he had vanished without explanation.

Selina suggested they tour the tombs of the viceroy. They had already visited his mosque, begun before his death as a place of worship and a shrine to his life.

Unwilling to dress in mufti and risk another probing, Trout stayed at the hotel.

Flo took a strong and immediate dislike to the tombs. They were an insult to the memory of the beloved viceroy, whom even the British called the father of Egypt. He had planned to be buried in his alabaster mosque, but when he died a year before, his grandson and successor, Abbas Pasha, had consigned him to a garish vault at Hawsh al-Basha instead. It was there that she began to see the ugliness of Cairo.

She had glimpsed Abbas Pasha on his houseboat at Esneh, where he had ordered a man to be lashed five hundred times. The English consul called him an indolent degenerate who openly tolerated corruption and cared more for horses than for people. In the past year, he had fired every Christian in his employ.

The tombs, a discordant mishmash of European and Oriental styles, fit this cruel tyrant to a tee. She was bored when not disgusted as she toured chambers tricked out like dance halls, the walls painted in bright colors and jammed with Greek, French, and Egyptian molding and cornices. Shrouded in dust and grime like a thousand dirty windows, the crystal chandeliers struck an especially hideous note. If the mausoleum had been modeled on a Neapolitan bordello, it could not have left her more displeased and irritated.

When she returned to her rooms in the afternoon, she found Trout sitting motionless, barely registering her arrival as she entered and clicked the door shut. "Are you all right?" she asked.

Trout sighed and nodded. "And you, Miss Florence?"

"Fine." She removed her gloves. "You look quite strange."

Trout stood and straightened her apron. "Do you imagine I shall continue as lady's maid when we return, mum?"

No matter how far she and Trout progressed in their relations, Trout's precipitous beginnings and endings always threw her off balance, even now, when she was feeling kindly toward her. "If you are wondering about an increase in wages—"

"No, mum. Not an increase."

"Well, then," Flo said. Trout might as well have thrown a cold glass of water at her.

"Mum?" Trout was nothing if not persistent.

"Yes?"

"Will Mariette be your maid in future?"

"I am not prepared to discuss this at present." Had Trout misconstrued her kindness, thinking herself a pet, or her favorite? In fact, Flo did want Mariette to resume, but it was none of Trout's business.

"I am not asking for the job, mum. That is my point. I'd rather be maid-of-all-work when we return."

"I shall remember that when Mrs. Nightingale and I speak of it."

"Thank you, mum."

Flo moved toward the bedroom, gathering her gloves and veil from the foyer table.

"There is another something, mum."

There was no way to gauge the importance or nature of a topic from the way Trout raised it. Flo had learned to be apprehensive from just such vagaries. She froze.

"About the caravan."

Flo sat on the nearest chair. It was French, a relative of Père Elias's gilt Louis XVI lugged to the shore. "What about the caravan?"

"I don't know as they understood, but when they tried to marry me off—"

"Who? What do you mean?"

"I think that's what the primitives were up to. They brought one bearded fellow after another to me. What else could it have been?"

"I certainly don't know."

"I told the mother I was to be married, mum. It was none of her concern, but I was afraid, so that's what I said."

"And you are worried about having lied?"

"No, mum. No, it made me feel bad as I had not yet told you or Miss Fanny. It was a secret, but now the secret is out. I thought the consul might of told you."

"No, he did not." Flo was getting more confused by the moment. "How would he know what you told them? As you yourself said, he wasn't there." She wasn't at all certain she had grasped Trout's point. "And why would he tell me if he did know?"

"I don't know what anybody told anybody else in all that babbling." Trout's voice warbled with pique. "I speak only the Queen's English."

Flo had allowed repeatedly that it was impossible to be lucid if everyone around you spoke blather, reducing you to pantomime and grabbing at words like rags to stanch a bloody cut. How had the Ababdeh understood anything Trout told them? It made her head swim to imagine the scene. "None of this is clear, Trout. But it's not a sin to lie to save your life. Anyway, it's done and over. And besides, you say you weren't lying."

"Yes, mum."

"Whatever passed in that tent," Flo said (*tent* triggering a flood of associations that made it difficult to stay on track), "is none of my business." His soft lips, her skin flushed from the rakı, his fingers sticky with papier-mâché. "I am only glad you were not harmed. I was very worried, you know." Above all, his gentleness. She remembered exactly how she felt when they kissed—

Trout dropped to her knees and scooted in front of her. "Oh, mum, I am so happy to know you. You are the finest of ladies."

"Goodness," Flo said, "we all care for you." She knew Trout loved to hear this, and though it was true, she felt guilty for resorting to a sentiment that had been truer—more spontaneous and heartfelt—at the time of Trout's return. To repeat it now was a cheap trick, especially as she'd snooped in Trout's diary and entertained unkind thoughts about her. "We were all worried—myself, Max, Gustave. Joseph, and Père Elias. We would have gone to great lengths to find you."

Trout began to emit the high-pitched mewling of a sick kitten. "Oh, mum," she squeaked, "if only I could describe what it was like to be whisked away in the night by heathens."

"There, there," said Flo, lightly patting Trout as she grasped both elbows and helped her to her feet. They moved to the sofa, arms still interlaced.

"I am so grateful," said Trout. "How can I ever repay your kindness?"

"No need. You would have done the same for me, I'm certain."

"And here am I," Trout's voice quavered, "saying I do not wish to continue as your maid!"

How like Trout to point out baldly her own infelicities. It was almost endearing.

"You must think me an ungrateful wretch." Trout blew her nose and tucked her hankie back into her apron pocket, where her chatelaine, diminished by the dangles she'd given the Ababdeh, still rode. "So you don't mind?"

"What?"

"That I am to be married?"

A dozen questions rushed into Flo's head. "I am quite amazed by your news," she said, her voice lacking in wonder. How could she subtract what she'd read in the diary from her mind? If Trout ever found out, her humiliation would be total. "Will you stay on at Embley? I imagine, like Mariette, you shall wish to live apart."

Trout shook her head. "Oh, no, mum. I don't hold with living with a man under one roof. It makes for bad feelings." She leaned closer to Flo. "But we are going to Paris together for a honeymoon, next December. Gilbert has it all planned. He is keeping it a secret, too. His family are quality people and would not approve of such as me."

Trout's gentleman poet, it seemed, was ashamed of her. "And that doesn't trouble you?"

"Oh, no, mum." Looking down at her lap, Trout shook her head.

Flo was growing impatient. "But if he does not respect you—"

"Oh, he does, mum. But his kin would not understand, him being a gentleman and me not being a lady nor wishing to be one or act like one." Trout looked her in the eye. "He says it is an ordinary miracle, me and him. But that most people don't credit miracles."

Would Trout allow herself to be gulled in the name of love? Flo could not abide such drivel. "What in the world do you mean?"

"I know Gilbert's heart. I knew it before I ever met him."

"How is that possible, Trout?" Flo sighed and leaned back on the sofa. "Listen to what you have said." Trout was the last person she would have figured for a romantic sop.

"I don't rightly know how it's possible, mum. I only know it's true."

"I see." Flo looked around the room for a distraction. "Do you suppose we could have some tea, Trout? I think there is time before dinner." Did Gilbert have honorable intentions, or was he taking advantage? She felt protective of Trout and abhorred the idea that a smooth-talking, educated man might casually misuse her.

"Yes, of course, mum. I should of thought of it myself."

Trout set the kettle to boil on the potbellied porcelain stove. She removed dishes from the buffet and laid the table opposing the sofa with napkins, spoons, cups, and saucers. "You see, mum, I saw Gilbert's face before I ever met him."

"Was it one of his photographs?"

"Oh, no, mum, nothing like that."

Trout told the story quickly, without embroidery. Seven years before she came to live with the Nightingales, she was working at a lodging house in Grosvenor Street. The kitchen chimney was greasy, and the sweep had missed his appointed time. Late that night, while everyone slept, she undressed, climbed the rungs, and brushed the chimney herself. She liked drudgery, she said. To be covered with soot and char and lead, too, from blacking the grates gave her satisfaction, she explained.

She had laid a fire to warm herself, washed up in a basin in the kitchen, and fallen asleep. Most unhappy she was, she added lightly, though Flo thought this might be important. She hated where she was working; the maids had stolen from her, and the house was not completely reputable. The owner was a vulgar woman to boot, Trout said, and she feared a character from her would tar her good name by association, though without a reference, finding a new position would be difficult.

Trout paused to pour two cups of tea and then set the teapot to rest on a trivet.

In the middle of the night, she continued, she heard a sound and woke to see a man's face complete with beard and mustache in the fire, formed from flames. It changed expressions, as if they were conversing—smiling, laughing, thoughtful, etc.

A man in the fire. That was familiar. Flo was sure she'd heard those words before from Trout.

"The very next day," Trout continued, "I went down the road to buy a pitcher of ale for the house and passed a man in the street who was the image of the face in the fire."

"That is strange," agreed Flo, not sure what to think. Hallucinations? If Trout could unwittingly invent bodily illnesses, might she not also conjure a face from a blaze?

"I watched him go into a tavern and waited for him like a dog until he came out. I was ashamed, but I could not help myself."

"Then what happened?" Flo could hardly imagine stern, flinty Trout in the throes of an infatuation and servile as a dog.

"I introduced myself and told him the story. From that day to this he has not left me." Trout added a lump of sugar to her tea.

"And that was your Gilbert?"

"Yes, mum. That is my Gilbert. Gilbert Pennafeather. He is a known poet." She sat back, teacup in hand.

As Flo drank her tea, she wondered if the story of sweeping the chimney had anything to do with Trout's custom of "blacking up" for Gilbert and calling him "Massa," as if she were a slave on an American plantation. But, of course, Flo only knew about those details from the diary. Oh, and the chains and lock. And the iron key, which still hung from the chatelaine, as incongruous as ever. "And what do you make of it all?" she asked.

Trout regarded her big pale hands. "I don't rightly know, mum. It was a long time ago. I never could abide a man who interfered with me." She laid her spoon on the saucer. "Gilbert lets me be. I clean for him sometimes. We play that I am his maid and he is my mister," she said, smiling. "He's offered to keep me, but I have refused. I like to come and go as I please." She gulped her tea to the dregs. "And I like to work."

Flo was silent, afraid to say anything lest she give herself away.

"Gilbert is my sweetheart. He reads to me and I write to him. He likes to know how I spend my days."

Blacked the grates, scrubbed the flags. Why would a poet care about such banalities? Then Flo remembered that disturbing line in the diary—*but most of all, licking your boots.*

"I do remember feeling I was not in my right mind waiting outside the pub that first night, not knowing if he would speak to such as me."

"But now you are in love."

Trout grinned but did not answer. She stood and collected the flatware and cups.

"Thank you for the tea." Flo was anxious to rest before dinner, a formal affair at the Hôtel d'Orient. She had had enough of Trout and especially of her unquestioned happiness.

28

CROCODILE GODS

After Kenneh, Max dithered over the list of monuments remaining to be photographed. More agitated than usual, he kept adding and subtracting names. Gustave was grateful—*so* grateful!—that they'd already finished with the necropolis at Giza, the Sphinx, and the pyramids. He lacked the strength to crawl through those dark tunnels now, or scale the meter-high blocks to the apex of Cheops's pyramid to watch the sunrise. Miss Nightingale might be viewing it at that moment. He pictured her twisting through the passageways in her blue dress, hugging a small notebook to her chest. The graffiti might not amuse her, he thought. The name of the singer *Jenny Lind* scrawled repeatedly on an arch, apparently by a fan. And on the top of the great pyramid, a certain Henri Buffard could not resist advertising his goods. Nor could Gustave wash the useless information—*Constructeur de Papier Peint, 79 rue St. Martin, Paris*—from his mind. As much as Europeans loved Egyptian antiquities, they loved defacing them more.

He glanced at Max's list on the table between their beds. *Grotto of Samoun (Crocodiles)* had been added. Gustave had never heard of it. Perhaps Joseph had suggested it while reminding Max yet again that he had journeyed up the Nile sixty times.

He was in a foul mood. The suspicious chancre that had appeared at Koseir was now characteristically painless, smooth, and hard as a button. *Please God,* he prayed, *let it not be pox,* though he was almost certain it was. He avoided looking at his body because next, if he were right, a rash would erupt on the palms of his hands or the soles of his feet, possibly the backs of his legs. Syphilis could mark a man almost anywhere. Perhaps this was Kuchuk Hanem's true keepsake. He remembered the delicate blue Arabic script tattooed on her arm. He had his own translation now: *Love killed your sister and it will kill you, too, but slowly.*

He went on deck. Aided by a stiff breeze, the *cange* was skimming along with the current, sails furled. The sight of the passing shore dizzied him. It took a moment to get his legs under him.

Except for a man at the rudder, the crew was relaxing—smoking, sleeping, playing backgammon. He joined Max and Joseph chatting with Rais Ibrahim in the shade of a canvas awning.

"It is hardly worth the time to see it," Rais Ibrahim said.

Joseph demurred. "But *messieurs* wish to take mummy home."

Max noted Gustave's arrival. "We're discussing whether to visit the Grotto of Crocodiles," he explained.

Red vest, note to God, Dacca cloth . . . mummy! Until that instant, he'd forgotten the shopkeeper in Kenneh who'd promised to inquire about mummies. Surely the man would have tracked him down if he'd found one. The whole town knew of his return.

"How long would it take?" asked Max.

"Half a day," Joseph said. "Perhaps one day."

The captain pursed his lips and sighed histrionically. Accustomed to slapping his crew when they displeased him, he plainly wished to pummel Joseph for contradicting him. And just as plainly, Joseph's opinion rested on the hope of a fat baksheesh if he succeeded in finding them mummies.

"I do want to bring a mummy home," said Gustave from his fog. The sound of his own voice startled him, as though he were hearing it amplified through a pipe or megaphone.

"I am puzzled," Max said. "Joseph says one thing, the guidebook and the captain another."

"Do you have it here?" asked Gustave. "The book?" Rais Ibrahim shot him a penetrating glance.

Max removed it from his pocket and passed it to him.

The entry was brief and dripping with disdain, written, as Bouilhet liked to say, from a very high horse. *Not worth visiting,* the guidebook said, unless you wished to bring home the charred mummy of a crocodile. *Difficult climbing* also was noted. Apparently the grotto had emitted suffocating fumes for years and was highly flammable.

"Listen to this," Gustave said. " 'Fragments of Homer and the lost orations of Hyperides of Athens were discovered there in 1845.' "

Max's eyes widened. Gustave continued reading to himself. Nothing else valuable could have survived a fire that broke out in 1846 and burned for more than a year.

How could a fire burn for more than a year? A tiny asterisk led his eye to the bottom of the page. The grotto had heavy deposits of bitumen. Pitch. Essentially, the cave was a tar pit! That meant no photographing and no squeeze-making. "I vote for going," he announced, closing and returning the book. "I think we should take Joseph's advice. We both want mummies."

"So be it," said Max. "A search for buried treasure."

Rais Ibrahim, also highly flammable, excused himself and sulked on the deck with his back to them, dangling his feet in the spray of the keel. The excursion would lengthen the voyage by a day, one additional day until the captain could screw his new wife. They hadn't challenged him before. Max had been right, Gustave realized, to insist on withholding half his fee until the end, ensuring that he kept his foul moods to himself. Max usually was right about money. When Gustave paid Kuchuk Hanem twice her fee, he had disapproved, and clearly, on the second visit, Gustave did not get his money's worth.

Rais Ibrahim had hired two guides from the village of Maabdeh as well as donkeys to ride and haul their provisions and swag. The next morning they disembarked south of Manfaloot at el-Cheguel Ghil, where the desert and the fertile delta met, and where, Joseph said, there had once been crocodiles in the millions. These days the animals were a rarity in Middle Egypt because they had all been mummified. He and Max soon would see for themselves.

The riverbank was high, blocking completely views of the land beyond it. They ascended on their donkeys, tacking single file. It was a bright, sunny day, not yet too warm.

The top of the embankment overlooked a wide plain planted with corn, barley, and flowering fava beans, their scent sweet on the air. Between the rows, in ragged pink patches, clover bloomed, and lupine, in a scattered purple haze. In the distance Gustave spied a herd of black goats or sheep that dotted the ground like ants on a cloth. Just beneath him, on a ledge, two donkey foals gamboled, braying and tossing their gray velvet heads. He and Max smiled at each other. What a good decision to venture through lush and little-known lands!

They soon reached Maabdeh, a cluster of mud hovels surrounded by a brick wall. Pointing to it, a guide explained that it had been raised against Bedouins, who routinely pillaged the livestock and crops, and sometimes abducted women and children.

Threading along the edge of the plateau to another steep hill—five or six hundred meters, Gustave estimated—they passed a limestone outcrop with clear chisels marks. Giant blocks had been quarried willy-nilly, leaving what appeared to be a deranged staircase. No one, Joseph remarked, had worked this stone for a millennium.

As he zigzagged steadily higher, Gustave avoided looking down, observing instead his donkey's muscles twitch under its hair coat as it leaned into the trail. Twice it faltered, terrifying him, rocks falling away in a miniature avalanche. Difficult climbing, indeed.

At the next precipice, he was mystified to see the Nile again, winding after him like a thick green serpent. His sense of direction was muddled. Max proudly pointed out Manfaloot, crowned with gray minarets, on the opposite shore, as if he had placed it there himself to further addle Gustave's bearings.

Below lay a veritable panorama of Egyptian agriculture on another vast plain. Or was it the one he'd seen earlier? For the first and last time, he reconsidered filing a report about the abundant crops to honor his government commission. But if he wrote one, he'd have to write several. None, then. Villages tufted with palm trees came into view, and beyond them, like a dreamscape rendered in pastels, the soft pink and lavender outline of the Arabian hills. He memorized the view. If Max had taken a photograph, it couldn't have captured the subtle colors, the shapes as luscious as an odalisque's curves. *An odalisque's curves:* he liked it.

As they turned right (what direction would that be? he wondered), the guides galloped past him, shouting. He followed, lurching forward like a boy on a hobbyhorse. His mount had a ball-crushing gait, as bad as a camel.

For the third time, a rocky prominence blocked the view. Beneath it, the trail glittered miraculously, paved with crystals.

"Talc," Max cried triumphantly. "They mined talc here, but no longer."Had Max memorized the entire guidebook? His flaunting of details, his heedless glee, galled him.

After twenty minutes in the sparkling dust, Gustave saw a dark cleft in the rock like a gaping mouth painted black. The entrance to the grotto. "We are here," he announced before Max could speak. "Are we not?"

"Obviously," granted Max.

They dismounted and tied their donkeys to shrubby trees. With Joseph bringing up the rear, they entered the opening single file.

As Gustave bent into the darkness, a sickening stench assaulted him. Breathing through his mouth, he followed the back of Max's blue jacket for three or four meters. Abruptly the tunnel enlarged, the line backed up and all seven men crowded against the slippery black wall where the crevasse ended.

"And now we enter!" cried Joseph. Before Gustave could make sense of this remark, the first guide, lantern in hand, disappeared down a smoke vent at the base of the wall. Max scrambled after him, whooping with delight.

About a meter tall, the tunnel was unpredictable, narrowing and widening as it bored through the earth. He crawled on his knees, he wiggled and slid. One vertebra at a time, he inched forward on his back, snakelike, propelling himself through the turns by digging down with his heels. Several times he scraped against treacherous spikes overhead. Had he not lost weight, he thought, he might have debrided his skin against the stone—*dégoûtant!*—or been stuck in the passage for the remainder of a short life.

The bad odor strengthened, along with the heat. Drenching sweat ran in runnels down his belly and back, his groin and armpits. In front of him, the worn-down soles of Max's cavalry boots dragged lightly along the ground, like the feet of a marionette. Behind him, the guide shouted out encouragements in Arabic and butted him with his head.

After several insufferable minutes, the tunnel flared into a gallery where he was able to stand. He yanked out the hem of his shirt to use as a mask.

What exactly was that rank smell? Not shit. He knew the smell of shit all too well. As a child in diapers, his mother liked to recount, she had found him carefully dabbing it on himself and the walls of his room. *You were painting,* she'd said with a laugh. He begged her not to tell the story to friends, but she did, especially after baby Caroline came to live at Croisset. So, not shit. Shit didn't frighten him, but this odor did.

Before he could see much in the cavern, Max pulled him aside. "This is why I took precautions," he whispered, "why I told the guides no exposed candles." He pointed to his feet. Gustave followed a wan light to the floor.

Mummies. They were standing on mummies. He recalled the drifts of dead cicadas he'd seen as a boy encrusting the streets of Rouen. He'd be thirty-two when the next swarm hatched. Four more years.

He stepped forward and heard a crunch. Then another. Then a sifting sound like rats scurrying through litter. He froze and shouted for a guide to bring his lantern.

"Many rooms like this," Joseph said, rolling his hands to illustrate iteration. "My last *monsieur* spends five hours in the grotto and never finds the end of it."

Pitch dripped from the ceiling, forming stalactites that hung down in ravaged partitions. Eight months and three thousand kilometers and here he was at last in the heart of the heart of ancient Egypt. Or in the heart of its death. Mummies covered the floor. They *were* the floor. It felt like standing on a stack of mattresses. Death, usually so invisible, so quick to vanish once it struck, was preserved here in a stinking pile, and he was the fortunate fellow balanced on top of it. But would he never stop noticing the stench? Shouldn't his nose have acclimated to it by now?

He picked up a crocodile and sniffed it. The distinctive odor of active decay was unmistakable. Though the bodies had been preserved, dried to the lightness of husks, in the dampness of the cave something continued to rot. Hair? Nails? Bones? The leathery skin that remained after natron had extracted all the fluid from the flesh?

Besides the large crocs, there were pointy mummified eggs and baby crocodiles with elongated bodies and snouts easily recognizable through their bandages. All of them, he knew, were sacrifices to Sobek, the crocodile deity, to keep the real crocodiles at bay. His worshippers had not stinted. The hoard contained thousands of crocodile and human remains. Tens of thousands. Perhaps hundreds of thousands, he revised, estimating the depth of the piles. Millions, if you counted all the caverns in the grotto.

He'd watched the fearsome reptiles slicking through the Nile at Aswan. No one was safe near a croc, even if it appeared to sleep as it basked on the muddy bank.

Why *not* make a god of the thing you feared most? In which case he would have numerous deities: the butcher, with his sharp knives and dull brain; the grocer, with his palette of vegetables and colorless imagination. Professionals, too—lawyers and doctors (including his brother), and all proper dames. Only artists, a few teachers, and whores were exempt from his pantheon.

A sound like claws on pavement interrupted his reverie. He lifted his lantern and shined it on the brightest objects in the cavern—Max's hands, rending a crocodile mummy. Twisting off the legs like drumsticks and tossing them into a corner, Max broke open the torso and plunged into the gut cavity, pulling out blackened gauze.

"What in the world are you doing?" Gustave asked.

"Looking for treasure. Gold or jeweled scarabs." He crushed a tiny crocodile underfoot and lifted a bigger one. "They're so light," he said, tearing off its limbs.

From each animal Max disarticulated, noxious odors rose in fresh waves. Sick to his stomach, Gustave moved to the next gallery, trailed by a guide.

Everywhere lay linen, scorched or reduced to cinders. That was part of the odor, too—burned cloth. A stockpile of small charred packets leaned against a wall. Organs? He knew the Egyptians mummified them separately. Hearts reduced to crumbs? Brains withered to walnut shells?

He decided to look for a human mummy and located two right away. But they had already been pilfered, their wrappings in disarray. After half an hour of kicking aside one crocodile mummy to find an identical one beneath it, he settled for the charred foot, still attached to the ankle, of the first mummy. This would do well enough. How could he transport an entire mummy anyway? They were as delicate as butterfly wings. Everywhere he stepped, he heard and felt them cracking. Yes, a foot made a fine memento—of the arduous climb, of trampling mummies. He returned to the first gallery.

Max was kneeling over something, his guide standing alongside, arms heaped with booty. He straightened up and wiped his brow with the filthy sleeve of his jacket.

"What do you have there?" Gustave asked.

"No scarabs, but wonderful stuff." Max delved into the farrago of the guide's bundle. "A crocodile mummy, of course." He held it up briefly. "Also, a bird mummy—"

"Really? I didn't see any birds." He felt a tiny bit envious.

"Also a snake. And yes, here"—Max withdrew a wafer-shaped object—"a fish. And we found a cat mummy."

Now Gustave was jealous. "Let me see it."

Max dug it out of the pile and passed it to him. He studied the shape. The ears were missing or had been flattened in the wrapping. It could have been a loaf of rustic bread.

"These are my favorites," Max said, sorting through a second lot arranged on the floor. He withdrew two gilded feet—*two gilded feet! That son of a bitch*—then a pair of blackened hands, and finally an entire head, its long tresses intact in an unnatural shade of red.

Was it possible the second room had been more plundered than the first? Gustave wondered. That made no sense. He must simply be unlucky. His souvenir foot was so meager by comparison.

He spied something on the floor and picked it up. "You've forgotten a trinket." It lacked wrappings and felt leathery and velvety by turns. "What is it, anyway?" he asked Max.

"Give it here, and bring the lantern closer."

Gustave watched Max turn the thing in the light. A tiny face appeared, then wings and little claws. "Ugh!" Max shivered, revolted. "A dead bat!" He flung it high in the air. For a split second, a rustling like silk rubbing on silk issued from the reaches of the ceiling.

In the next moment, bats rained on them, swooping and diving from every direction, a hail of creatures. Colliding in midair, some of them tumbled to the floor and hopped like crows. The cave echoed with their piercing whistles and squeaks. "They are attacking us," Max cried, covering his eyes with his hands.

"No, *monsieur,* they no attack," Joseph offered calmly. "You attack. They run away."

Unconvinced, Max huddled on the floor.

In their panic, some bats escaped through the passage the men had entered; others fled through narrow ledge gaps. Most returned, chirping, to their sleeping nests, vanishing into the dark vault of the gallery. The air was suddenly clear. Stunned bats lay throbbing on the floor. He could see them floundering about in the shadows, like broken umbrellas.

"Little bastards," said Max. "They scared the shit out of me."

"Yes, they did," remarked Gustave. He wasn't afraid of bats, had trapped and killed stragglers in the chimneys at Croisset. "They're only dangerous if they bite you, and they only bite when they're rabid, which is why if one does bite—"

"Enough!" Max stood. "We should go." He brushed off his shoulders. "Are you finished? Did you find anything worthwhile?"

Gustave showed him the foot. "For my desk."

Max nodded, unimpressed. "I am ready to leave when you are." He withdrew a white cloth from his pocket and gently placed his loot on it. *He had brought a cloth and yet not advised him to?* After Gustave added his mummy's foot, Max folded the cloth and tied it up like a picnic lunch.

"You'll need a wooden chest for all that stuff," Gustave said.

"I have a wooden chest. Two, in fact, packed inside the trunks." Max paused thoughtfully. "In the meantime, I shall wedge them into the camera cases if I have to."

The climb into the cave had been wearying, and though they'd been in the grotto for only an hour, the air was execrable. Watching Max think and move so spryly, he felt asthmatic.

After securing their lanterns, they lined up and descended into the passage; Max went in front of him and Joseph behind. The second guide went last, dragging the plunder with him, out of everyone's way.

Halfway along, Max shouted that he had made a discovery. He sounded excited, but then he was more easily excited than ten men. Another of his bothersome qualities.

The stench Gustave had first encountered assailed him anew. He gagged, regretting he hadn't thought to cover his mouth with a rag. This odor was different from the one inside, he noticed, and far worse.

"It is so grotesque as to defy description," Max called out, delighted, it seemed, in the very repulsion he felt. "How did we miss it on the way in? Oooo! It is ghastly!"

"What is that dreadful stink?" Gustave asked.

"This! This is the dreadful stink." Max coughed, italicizing his words. "*Sacré nom de Dieu,* it is terrible when you get close."

"*Y'allah!*" The guide in front shouted.

"*J'arrive!*" Max shouted. "*J'arrive tout de suite!*" To Gustave, more quietly, he called back, "The poor bastard is having a fit. I'm going ahead."

Now on his knees, now on his belly, Gustave edged forward. If memory served, he was approaching the part like the neck of a bottle. Surely he'd have noticed anything freakish in such a confined space. Whatever it was, Max had missed it too. He wondered about the guides—did they know it was there?

Turning on his side, he squeezed by an especially bulbous crag. Behind it, in a cranny at an acute angle to the main passage, he saw it: the head, torso, and arms of a man wedged behind a curtain of glossy stalactites, like an actor waiting in the wings to spring onto the stage. The legless corpse without wrappings was not an ancient Egyptian but a modern one, an obvious victim of the grotto in which he had, it seemed, begun naturally to mummify, for the face was shriveled and flat as a plate. Within it, the mouth had contorted into a circle where an agonized scream had been preserved for the ages. Chills rippled through Gustave's shoulders, into his belly.

He screamed. He gagged. He pressed his hand to his face to filter out the odor, but the sleeve of his shirt was sticky with resin. It, too, stank.

If fumes or smoke had overcome the man, where was the rest of him? A gruesome scenario took shape in his mind—a later explorer severing the legs to get them out of the way.

The eyes were half open, the sockets empty beneath the lids. He expected to see an insect crawl out, daintily place each of its legs on a clean patch of flesh, and wash itself like a fly. He stared at a stalactite to annihilate the image.

As he stole another look at the face, the tendrils of a profound dread insinuated themselves into his very being. He tried to back away, but without room to rise on all fours and crawl, he succeeded only in squirming closer. He shivered and groaned in revulsion.

Complaints beset him from behind and in front. "Go," chided

Joseph, knocking at the soles of his shoes. "Too hot for sightseeing in this here."

"Gustave, where are you?" Max yelled. "Say something."

Ahead of him, the light of a lantern faded. He hadn't wanted to carry one himself. *Abu Muknaf,* the Father of Thinness, could have doubled his girth, carried a lantern, and still slid through the shaft like a greased hog.

"I am coming to get you!" Max's disembodied voice promised.

Joseph jerked on his left foot. "*Monsieur,* you are all right?" he asked. "Have you faint?" In his poor French it sounded like *Have you daydreamed?*

He closed his eyes and silently invoked the beach at Koseir—*cool turquoise water rushing around my ankles, Rossignol sorting shells on her lap, the breeze like . . . like . . .* A black wave of tar and rot.

Max's arms snaked toward him. He must have turned around. "Give me your hand," he urged. "I'll unstick you."

"No. I shall come out by myself." Fuck shit, fuck shit, fuck fuck fuck! he cursed under his breath. "I am only resting."

"Resting, my eye," Max said with a sneer. Joseph continued to push at his leg. In a moment of terrifying clairvoyance, he saw his own amputated foot on some future tourist's desk.

"I'm trying to help you, asshole."

"*Va te faire foutre*. I'll be out when I'm ready."

When Max reached for his hand, the iron lethargy that had weighed him down for days lifted all at once, as though yanked free by a pulley. "Do not touch me, I warn you," he growled. He felt his terror altering into a new shape, like liquid left on a stovetop that suddenly solidifies into a nasty, inedible bolus.

"A couple of minutes more and you'll be out," Max reassured him. "Courage!"

The new shape was fury. At that moment in the stuffy shaft, Gustave struck a vein of pure hatred for his companion. He hated the way Max talked—too confidently. He hated his planning, the way he burped, the smell of him every night in the next bed. The way each time he blew his nose, he inspected his handkerchief afterward. He *hated* that. He detested Max for being skinny and eating enormous portions without gaining a gram.

"Stop being foolish," Max said, clawing at his hand.

"*You* are the fool," Gustave replied, retracting his hands into knobs under his chin. "Did anyone ever tell you that you laugh like a jackal? You fuck like one, too."

"*Calme toi.* Let me help you, *mon ami,*" Max coddled in an oily and patronizing tone that outraged him even more. He was indebted to Max for convincing his family to let him go, and for taking charge of the trip, but not enough to tolerate his acting the nursemaid.

"You and your shitty ambition," he spat. "You fart higher than your asshole."

"Give me your hand and *shut up*."

"Am I disrupting your almighty schedule by pausing for two minutes?" The disgust he had felt for himself while ill was misdirected, he saw that now. In fact, he was disgusted with Max and hadn't wanted to acknowledge it. Their friendship had soured, like a marriage. Without the novelty and color of the Orient to distract them, it would have soured sooner. After eight months the bloom was off the rose, leaving only the thorns. This burst of understanding, like most knowledge, did nothing to mitigate his wrath.

"The delay is beside the point!" Max said. "You are using up the air in the tunnel. Think of the poor sods behind you and give me your hand!"

Hypocrite! Max didn't give a shit for the other men. For all his wealth, he was not a generous person. He was a tightwad and a measly tipper. Even drunk, he'd bestir himself to calculate the tip to the last *sou*. Or *para*. Or *piastre*. Calculating, that was Max, with his industrious lists. Always thinking and planning his life, never just giving in, following the impulse wherever it led. Was that why he fucked so ceaselessly? How awful it must be to live from the neck up. The closest Max came to pleasure lasted only the few minutes he fucked, when, instead of feeling his brain, he felt his prick. Gustave was the true voluptuary; Max, no better than an aging delinquent with a bit of philosophy under his belt. It followed that Max envied his own easy sensuality. Who wouldn't envy a man who conjured a thousand liquid breasts while floating in the Red Sea? How had he ever trusted his opinion on *Saint Anthony*? He'd have no need of Max's advice in the future.

It would be impossible to travel with him for another year. "You know nothing of pleasure," he blurted. "You are a fake, pretending to be enjoying yourself when you don't know how."

"Move, move, move!" shouted Joseph. The guides conferred in rapid Arabic, their voices ricocheting in the passage like scattershot.

"One way or another you are coming out of this cave, *Garçon.*" Max had reached his head, and was pulling him by the occipital knot, a six-months' growth of ponytail.

He bit him on the wrist.

"Goddamn you!" Max screamed. "*Fils de putain!* I should leave you to die in here." He sucked noisily at his hand.

"Maybe then you'd begin to take life seriously."

"You think I don't take it seriously? Am I the one who is ignoring a commission that could set me on the path to the Legion of Honor?"

"You can't take life seriously if you can't enjoy it." It had never once occurred to Gustave that the commission might actually be important, that it might impress people in Paris.

"You are mad, you filthy cunt licker!"

"Shithead!"

"Asswipe!"

Max slapped Gustave's head so hard it stung. His skull vibrated like a cello string.

"Shit-eating bourgeois bung hole." Gustave swatted at him. He would have killed him if he could, he thought with the stirring clarity of rage.

He felt his left shoe pop off. Joseph ran his thumbnail down the sole of his foot, the same way his father used to check reflexes. The foot jumped. He lurched forward involuntarily.

"Enfin!" Joseph cried. "Keep going, *monsieur.*"

Max grabbed both arms and pulled. "You accomplish nothing but jackassery," he said, grunting. "You have squandered your money and opportunities. And I am the one who pays for it, you idiotic prick." Holding fast to Gustave's arms, he paused to catch his breath. "Because of you, I have lost Persia."

Gustave yielded against his will, dragged toward the corpse's face, that mouth through which every iota of human strength had been mustered in a final cry of pain or plea for help. The mouth would swallow him whole! He bumped along the sharp stone floor, bruising and scraping himself.

"No, the great Flaubert is too refined!" Max shouted. "You whoring wretch! You wanker! If only you would write some reports for the Ministry of Agriculture"—he paused his tirade to pull once more, like a midwife helping to birth a child—"then at the right moment, you could trade your commercial reputation for something more literary. One must make a name. It doesn't matter what *for*!"

What if Max were right? What if writing well were not enough to ensure success? If the salon were more crucial, if social demerits outweighed the fruits of his desk? "All right!" he muttered. "Enough. I am coming out."

Max let go of his arms. Joseph released his foot. He looked at the wall; the dead man was behind him.

The guides stood to one side, hawking up brown phlegm.

The sun was high in the sky, heating the barren cliffs. Gustave, Max, and Joseph lay flat on their backs, unmoving, until vultures began to circle overhead.

"Jesus Christ," Gustave muttered after a long time. "That was as bad as the night in the wagon with Achille. Worse, because I remember it all."

Max sat up. "You were scared shitless in there, goddamn it. Just admit it."

Gustave sat up, too, resting his arms and head on his knees. "Shut your mouth, will you?"

Joseph pricked up his ears. "*Messieurs,* no more. *Je vous en prie!*"

"He is right." Gustave said.

"Just admit your were stuck. Be humble for once in your life."

"About my commission," he began, getting to his feet.

"What about it?"

He sensed Max's eagerness. "Did you actually expect me to go from city to city, asking 'How much oil do you shit out here? How many potatoes do you cram into your trap?' You have a legitimate project of interest, while I—"

"While you were treated like a king because of your commission? Did you keep that in mind when you decided to do nothing in exchange for the protection and largesse of your country?" Max stood and brushed off his trousers with no effect. The dirt was oily and ground in.

Watching Max's futile gestures, it occurred to Gustave that his friend was even stupider than he'd allowed. Suddenly he found himself succumbing to laughter, shrieking like a maniac. "My commission?" he finally managed. "No one cares about that, you idiot. We were treated well because we are *French,* not because of a wad of paper. Have you never noticed that the Egyptians revere Napoleon like a god?"

Joseph stepped between them. He came up to Gustave's nose. "*Messieurs—*"

"Must you always bellow like an ox?" Max asked, plainly at his wit's end. "You are a bumpkin, and you will always be a bumpkin." He scuffed at the gravelly ground. "Anyway, this is not about our commissions," he added cryptically.

Gustave couldn't resist. "Then what is it about?"

"Here's a hint," Max said, dripping contempt. "What is the one thing that can ruin the friendship between two people?"

Two's company, three's a crowd. Wasn't that the old saw? It had no bearing on their situation, though. Not wishing to venture a stupid guess, he waited for Max to answer his own question.

"A third person. Particularly a woman." Max glared at him. "You have been distinctly selfish about the lovely and lonely Miss Nightingale. Am I blind? What in Christ *is* it? Are you, perhaps, taken with her? Have the lovebirds had a spat? Did you fail to fuck her?"

Gustave's fist was five centimeters shy of Max's jaw when Joseph's forearm intervened. The guide screamed in pain and clutched his elbow. Gustave immediately apologized to him. Glowering, Max mounted his donkey and started down the trail in a silence broken only by the clatter of hooves on rock.

That night on the *cange,* Gustave and Max slept like a young couple feuding after their first fight. In their separate berths, they turned their backs to each other and hugged the walls, pulling up the covers around their ears.

Max was right about one thing: he had certainly not shared Miss Nightingale with him—not one word of what they had discussed or written, nothing about their walks on the beach at Koseir, at Philae, at Kenneh, and nothing of what transpired in the desert while Max was ill. But the source of the venom he regretted spewing at Max, was, he realized, much simpler: he hadn't the least desire to be with him, in the grotto, even on the *cange*. He would have preferred to spend his time with her, as ridiculous as that was. A woman never could have squirmed through a tar pit, nor endured his lubricities when the spirit moved him, nor accepted that lasciviousness was merely beauty with a hard-on. Though she was neither an entry in the *Encyclopedia of the Cunt* nor a potential reader for it, at the moment she, not Max, was his closest friend. He could say things to her without being attacked or made fun of. He thought she understood him, and he was beginning to understand her.

The question was whether he should make the effort to continue their association. And if he did, what would be the result? Even with the mercury treatment, the syphilis might preclude a normal sexual bond. He couldn't stand the thought of passing her the disease. On the other hand, he couldn't bear the thought of *not* seeing her again. And if he saw her once, he'd want to continue seeing her, talking to her, reading to her, receiving letters, replying to them. Could he control his desire as well as flaunt the proscriptions of the civilized world? There would be so much to explain, so much to overcome. The task would never end or it would end badly.

Debauchery, which he had practiced so assiduously, was not always satisfying. Perhaps that was why one of the things he liked about her was the way he was in her presence. Not that he was smarter or more high-minded, but he was different—more trusting, more trusted. Still, he couldn't always be the sensitive soul she found so endearing and that was such a refreshing change for him. What if she began chattering again, for example? One way or the other, she would wear him down. He would hate himself for disappointing her, and yet it seemed inevitable that he would.

First Kuchuk Hanem, now this. He was sick of romance. Love, he reflected abruptly, seemed to be a form of perfection akin to art and, therefore, largely unattainable. Indeed, rarity was essential to its power and appeal. This thought had vast ramifications, he realized. For one thing, his second visit to Kuchuk Hanem appeared in a new light. He could actually *relish* his bitterness now without feeling like a fool. Every love he'd ever known, beginning on the beach at Trouville, pointed toward it: love was something to anticipate and recollect, to aspire to, but not to expect or rely on.

The rest of the Nile trip passed quickly: Hamarna; then Antinoöpolis, a city reduced to a few ancient marble columns where he made squeezes; then Asiyoot and Benisoof, where Joseph presented a final letter from his wife for translation. Gustave took his time mulling it over.

"*Vite, vite,* read her to me," Joseph urged.

Unlike its fellows, it contained no mention of money, but rather a list of what she wished to do upon Joseph's return: take me to hear music, take me to Stars and Moon, the new café in the Greek quarter. Did you buy me any gifts?

"I am a bit embarrassed," Gustave said, "it is so personal, so intimate."

"Just read to me, *monsieur*. I excuse you."

"She says she is going to fuck your brains out when you get home."

Joseph shrieked his happiness.

"And she asks you to please burn her letters."

Joseph's eyes glittered as he dutifully lit a small bonfire on the brazier that evening after dinner.

On the twenty-fifth of May, Cairo glimmered into view. As they glided past Giza, the pyramids seemed to float, suspended in the clouds. They reached the yellow walls of Solimon Pasha's garden and the Grande Princesse's palace, then docked at last at Bulak, the westernmost fringe of the city sprawl and home to most of the sailors.

Breasts, thighs, scented hair: Cairo, he mused, meant a return to the world of women. Miss Nightingale was not the only one awaiting a man in the glorious city. In rooms with carved wooden grilles beyond the grimy harbor, freshly depilated wives, daughters, whores, and mothers awaited the crew. Plots would thicken, pleasures and problems bubble up. Daily life could resume in its endless chain of caprice.

In Bulak the first evening, they dined with Rais Ibrahim's uncle. Bad news, however, greeted the captain. The new wife with whom he'd so ardently anticipated reuniting had tried to murder his younger brother by secreting a needle in a piece of bread. His uncle had sent her packing to the house of her father. After dinner, the captain decided to divorce her.

The next day was taken up with pay calls on the *cange* and gut-wrenching farewells to the crew. To Hadji Ismael, Aouadallah, and Rais Ibrahim, Gustave gave big baksheesh. He wept, knowing he'd never see them again. The crew scattered, some bound for home, others for drinking, whoring, and gambling binges while the two Frenchmen set off on donkeys for Cairo proper.

29

CALL FROM GOD

Nearly the end of May and still no word from him. Charles was kinder than usual, so solicitous he embarrassed her. Such a public event, her disappointment. But she would be strong; she would not succumb, she had promised herself. It was just a trial like all the others. She never expected to be happy, like other people. Did God even *care* about happiness? She thought not. What was love anyway but a frivolous yielding of oneself to another, just half a step from willing ignorance!

Three days before her departure for Greece, her dreaming returned with a vengeance. She lay abed, lost in her reveries, which negated utterly her situation. Her dreams were not of her storied greatness, or her desire to be of use in the world, but of *Mme. Florence Flaubert*. No. Not that, not marriage. But they did meet again. And after that, there were many trysts, twice a year in Paris alone, where Clarkey was an accomplice or, alternately, a married matron who, regressing to her Scottish roots, betrayed a newly happy Florence. Cut dead by the blood mob, Flo took a position in Margate as a governess, an even more embittered Miss Christie. And crueler, it turned out . . .

No. No! In Paris, they ate at the best restaurants, joking and plotting over wine. By then they had their own private and sophisticated language. They'd invented an entire culture! *We are the Floflau tribe,* giggling behind everyone's back. He introduced her to clergy, which he had no use for, but was acquainted with from writing *Saint Anthony.* She visited convents and spoke at length with nuns and mothers superior, picking their brains for projects to secularize or, more accurately, Protestantize.

His mother, conveniently, soon died, and she took up residence in Croisset. They engaged a nursemaid for baby Caroline and she became the dead Caroline, not to the child, who had never known her mother and thus had no expectations, but to Gustave, who still mourned his best playmate. Now he had Rossignol instead. They had separate apartments with separate bedrooms: *amitié amoureuse.* Each afternoon he read aloud what he had written while she had slept the night before. And each evening, after dinner, she shared her schemes to improve the world, though these remained vague, overshadowed by their consuming friendship, by love. Sometimes theirs was a bodily love; at other times it remained platonic. This was the most perplexing aspect of the lives she lived, lying abed at the Hôtel d'Orient.

Would she become as precious to him as his whores? Would she overcome her bodily discomfort and shame? Their relationship was easiest when the night in the tent was not repeated. But in sweeter dreams, they lay in bed together as he gently stroked every inch of her, fondling her hair, tracing her eyebrows, her umbilicus ("Yours is folded like a camellia bud"), examining the inside of her mouth, the bottoms of her feet, places she'd never seen or wondered about. She loved it when he studied her as closely as a jewel, when he called her his most precious artifact from Egypt. One day he shyly asked if he might look *there. Oh dear God.* Coyness did not suit her. She hadn't pretended not to understand, but turned her head, pulled down the cover, and parted her knees.

Then his desire asserted itself, and . . . what happened next? She could easily evoke his chest, arms, legs, and back because she'd seen some part of them. (Never his underarms, it saddened her to realize.) She liked all of him—the way he walked, rolling slightly forward on the balls of his feet, as if he were excited to see where they led him; his hands, with their no-nonsense fingers and powerful wrists. Yes, she enjoyed the *thickness* of his body, his meaty calves, the curving and angled planes of his knees glimpsed only through his trousers or robe, like a piece of sculpture under a drape. He kept his beard scrupulously clean even when the rest of him wasn't, not like those men whose whiskers bore a scrapbook of the week's meals. But the parts of him she hadn't seen frightened her. They might be ugly, if nephew Shore were any indication. Two sacs like a bull's. A flaccid hose without symmetry, nothing to admire from the point of view of pure *form*. She tried to imagine seeing it for the first time, before it engorged. (She knew the technical terms, had seen the farmyard examples. They were not reassuring.) Would it pale as it stretched or flush a dull purple with the added blood? Or was the adult penis sheathed and bright pink when it emerged, like a dog's? It might not match the rest of him, the way some black-haired men grew auburn mustaches. It was all so horrid, so irregular!—at odds with the rest of his beauty and yet, she knew, the most important part. His maleness itself. His . . . *member*? Such an odd appellation. If only she had a brother, she'd know so much more about the mysterious thing. That was what she and Parthe called it when they were younger: the *thing*. Baby Shore was cute except for his little *thing*. Was WEN's thing long and slender as he was? Small or large, fat or thin, she wouldn't care. It was not the part of Gustave she loved most, merely the part she would have to tolerate. If he chose to parade about naked in her presence, which she imagined he would do quite naturally—she'd look elsewhere. But oh! Ugh! The thought of them joined by this finger of flesh, of the grunting urgency that would overtake him, turning him into an animal, every bit of his finer self subsumed once they were doing it—

"Flo, dear, it is past noon." Selina's voice. Flo opened her eyes. Apparently Trout had shown her back to the bedroom. "Will you not come down with me for lunch?" Selina looked worried.

"Is it? Already?" Flo reached back and fluffed her pillow under her head. "I am not particularly hungry."

Selina stepped closer. "But you've eaten nothing today. No breakfast—"

"I know." She wanted Selina to leave. She wanted to return to her dreaming. "I'm thinking about Kaiserswerth." She folded her hands together as if to pray. "And my family."

"Are you all right?" Selina sat down on the bed. "Charles and I were wondering if you would be well enough to travel in two days."

"I'm fine." As if to prove it, she turned back the covers, swung her legs over the bed, and sat up. "Trout?" she called into the sitting room. "Could you fix me some tea with milk?"

Trout called back that she would.

"Silly me," Selina said. "I feared you'd be moping. I thought how I might behave in your circumstances." She smiled at Flo, her eyebrows sympathetically raised in a question. "Romance is such a mystery. You shouldn't trouble yourself too much to solve it." She took Flo's hand.

"I know. Or rather, so I've heard." She would not easily return to the dream now. "But he might still appear."

Selina looked at her lap.

She pities me, Flo thought. She assumes he will not come. How could she? How dare she! The time had not run out. They weren't to be towed up the canal to Alexandria until the thirty-first, and it was only the twenty-eighth. He'd be in Cairo by the end of May. He would.

Selina looked straight at her now. "I think not, my dear."

"Why?"

Selina hesitated for so long that Flo realized Selina knew something she didn't know. Oh God, she thought, sickened, he has died! He has died and they were waiting to tell me until I got home. He is gone forever in some nameless grave on the Nile. *If only I had been with him.* Had she said that aloud?

Selina finally raised her head. "I hadn't wanted to tell you, dear Flo."

Oh no. Oh please, God. Florence felt a pain in her chest as if someone had thrust a spear there. The room began to dissolve. He was gone. And she had selfishly worried over a letter while he lay suffering in some putrid mud hut.

"Paolo saw him here in town," Selina said plainly. "Spotted him, I should say, for they did not speak."

"What? *What* did you say? Then he is not dead?"

Trout entered with the tea, shakily set it on the nightstand, and hurried from the room.

Selina's expression hardened. "He is very much alive, I'm afraid. At this moment, I wish he *were* dead for breaking your heart so cruelly."

"When?" Flo clutched the sheets in her hands. She couldn't move, might never move. Each of Selina's words nailed her in place. "But when did Paolo—"

"Three days ago, I think. Paolo approached him to ask how he was faring, but he disappeared with his dragoman into a tobacconist's."

Flo sagged forward in a heap. "Oh dear God," she wailed. "Oh God!"

"There now," Selina cooed, enfolding her in her arms. "Oh my poor darling Flo." She patted her and rubbed circles on her back and clutched her to her bosom. "Oh my poor dear."

Heartbroken and humiliated, Flo plunged from one feeling to its opposite, now crushed or furious, now pathetic, listless. She had known sadness and disappointment most of her life. This was utterly different. She hated herself and him. A storm swirled around her, *through* her. She felt quite mad.

Determined there must be some mistake, she questioned Paolo against the advice of Selina, who said it was but pulling a fresh scab from a wound. Was he certain it was M. Flaubert? How had he looked? Was he sure it was Joseph, no chance of his having mistaken both men for a similar pair? Paolo was firm; it had, indeed, been M. Flaubert and his dragoman, Joseph, and they had evaded him.

Selina was adamant that Gustave did not intend to see her again.

In the kindest way possible she urged Florence to excise him from her mind. Together, Charles and Selina pronounced him unworthy. Florence had been no more than an amusement, one of the Nile's passing attractions.

Flo secretly hatched the notion that if Gustave missed her in Cairo, he would catch up with her en route or in Alexandria. In this scenario, every corner of the tugboat, and then the steam packet through the Mahmoudieh Canal, would flicker with his shadow. In Alexandria he might stalk the hotels and docks. No, it was more likely that he would surprise her as she climbed to the upper deck or seek her out among the women on the lower, causing a commotion—shrieks of indignation from the harem wives followed by awed silence as he lifted her hand to his lips and she melted into his embrace.

Outside of this fantasy, she existed in a state of abject anguish. He had betrayed her trust, trampled her feelings. Had she more experience with men—other suitors, another serious beau besides Richard—she might have taken it in stride. She was naive, everyone said so; she agreed. Florence the idealist, the innocent. That was how they had raised her. Virginal. Untouched. Good bridal material, but ardently uninformed as required. And so naturally she suffered not just a broken heart, but a broken spirit, too. She blamed herself for talking to him in the first place. Ridiculous. Had God appointed her to safeguard every road in Egypt from Frenchmen bearing firearms? She despised her naïveté far more than she hated him. Him, she missed. *Still.*

She could have loved him, she was sure of it. This admission, in the second week, made the pain of his rejection excruciating. She could not imagine her future except as an extension of her miserable present. If she continued in such an agonizing state, WEN might not settle an income on her, worried that she was too weak to live alone. She would simply give up, living at home under Fanny's rules, pleasing her as she had during Miss Christie's reign, when she would have done anything to secure her mother's love. She would at least have that—her mother's love, for Fanny, whatever her flaws, loved her. She would become her mother's doting daughter. And a faithful sister to Parthe, never again leaving her alone. She had learned her lessons. Home was safe. Fanny was right: men were brutes. She'd have no more adventures. She'd plant a garden, play with the animals at the Hurst, take up tatting, tiny tiny tatting with its minuscule loom. Collars, gloves, camisoles, pillowslips—the list of items she could tat was satisfyingly long! She'd surround herself with people who cared for her even as they did not understand her, people who would never leave her. Milder and more obliging (broken!—why not admit it?), she might eventually wed. Perhaps an older man—a widower—who had no expectation of children (he might already have them) or of what it took to produce them. She must plan, for eventually WEN and Fanny would die, and then where would she be? She could not live with Parthe, even in this sorry state. Yes, she would wed. Late, to a man who'd respect her bedroom door. They would love each other, but without the passion. She wanted nothing now but to be protected. If she allowed herself to be loved for traits she did not much admire, she might cease hating herself, and her monster might disappear for good. She'd replace the brown Hollands, then, with a corset. A narrow world was better than no world at all.

He infiltrated her sleep with nightmares. Thoughtlessly, he left her on the beach as the tide rushed in, and she barely managed to outrace it, doggedly retracing her steps to Père Elias's villa. At Philae they had an argument over a squeeze and he yelled at her and that was the end of that. She returned to the houseboat in tears and never saw him again. In every dream, he did something so awful that she had no option but to leave him. Her heart was still broken, but her pride was intact when she woke in the morning. Then all day, it eroded until she detested herself with the same fury and fearful despair.

On her last morning in Cairo, she felt her eyes open, sticky as usual with grit. It was not yet light out, and not exactly dark, but that indeterminate time before dawn when one can sense the impending sunrise physically, like the first awareness of fever—the little ache in the wrist, the heat in the dry eyelid. She could not bear another day. Not another moment. She was utterly spent in body and mind. In spirit.

Lying exhausted in her hotel bed, a memory surfaced of another time when she'd been in the grip of a desolating weariness, when her limbs were too heavy to move, as if they'd fossilized to stone. It had happened twelve years ago, when she was seventeen.

There had been an epidemic that winter. In Wellow, two corpses had been laid out in the street. Only she and cook had escaped the influenza. For two joyous if grueling weeks, she had run the household while caring for her parents and Parthe, not to mention fourteen bedridden servants. She had a gift for the bedside; even Fanny said so. But when it was all over, after doing so much, *inhumanly* much, WEN said, she was completely drained.

The first morning after the crisis passed, she had felt leaden, as paralyzed as now. The servants had begun to return to work. Only Old Gale was still bedbound. Flo's life was about to return to normal, to make-work instead of real work, to boredom. She had dragged herself from bed. Then, after breakfast, the sun had come out—just for her, it seemed—and she decided to walk as she'd done a thousand times before down the drive and across the rise of the nearest fallow field. She could see herself clearly in memory, wearing her old green gabardine dress and Scotch cape. She carried a basket; one never knew what one might find on the heath and in the forest.

The grasses and weeds, just beginning to send forth the year's new shoots, were springy underfoot. She picked out buttercups and dandelions, barley and wheat escapes and nameless smaller grasses with tan tassels. The outdoors was always a balm, especially that day. Near the hedgerow that divided the field from its neighbor, she often picked wild blackberries and raspberries, not caring if the thorns ripped her skirts or tore at her arms. Fanny did not approve, but as Flo had no clothes more practical for this or any physical task, there was nothing she could do about it. Besides, Fanny always tucked into the berries as heartily as the girls.

A wind chuffed up from the east, sweeping her uphill. It was an altogether lovely morning, the sky a bright Delft blue streaked with the faintest white herringbones. She liked to listen for sounds out of doors, enjoyed the way they fell upon her ears—shyly at first, then louder the longer she listened. Near the hill's crest, she waited for the sounds to clarify and separate, like objects gradually distinguishable in a dark room. Behind her, the trees lining the drive to Embley shushed in the breeze. Closer by, a bird—a chaffinch?—sang *pink pink* while sparrows chittered as they reconnoitered for insects among the privet's dense weave. There was no such thing, she had learned, indoors or out, as absolute silence. Late at night, houses creaked and groaned as timbers, floors, plaster, and paint cooled or heated according to the season. *Housetalk,* she and Parthe called it when they were young—her coinage, she was pleased to remember. The name rendered it less frightening, the natural resettling of inanimate objects, instead of the stealthy movements of evil spirits.

At the top of the hill, just as she picked out the call of a honey buzzard, the strangest thing happened. All sound ceased, turned off like a spigot. She shook her head to shatter the silence and thumped her temple with her wrist, as if to unclog water from her ears. The quiet thickened and constricted, pressing against her like wet cotton wool.

Around her, branches still swayed in the wind, and birds zipped back and forth, noiselessly. Her heart began to race. The basket fell from her hand soundlessly as a feather. She clapped her hands. She screamed three times and heard it not.

Had she gone stone deaf, in an instant?

Sinking to the grass, she couldn't hear her dress rustling as it ballooned around her. Yes, deaf as a doorknob. A chill seized her spine, fanning into her limbs and torso. She closed her eyes, counted to five, and opened them again.

The sky had shifted to a deeper hue, not the indigo of night, but the violet-gray of twilight. Home—she had to get home to Fanny and WEN and Parthe. No—WEN had gone down to London. Home, then, to her mother and sister . . .

A saving thought came to her: she must be dreaming. She had only to awaken and she would be safe in her bed, alongside Parthe, drowsy Parthe. Yawning, yawning, it took Parthe forever to wake up. . . . *Yes. This is a dream and I shall wake up at home in my bed.*

A mighty thundering, like an avalanche, threw her flat on the ground. Or was it only the sound of blood rushing in her head? She had heard that once when the doctor plucked a leech from her stomach and blood—*her* blood—had spurted out. But this was louder. Louder than lions, louder even than the looms at the Arkwright Mills. And plangent, like the sea. Advancing and withdrawing, roaring and subsiding, a ferocious and magnificent sound, as if the ground itself were alive. Yes, it *was* the ground. As she lay in the weeds and dirt, the giant soughing moved through her body. It surrounded her, everywhere at once, with no point of origin. *Oh please,* she prayed, let it be my own panicked chest rising and falling and not some monster inside the hill, preparing to erupt from the earth.

In the next instant, the sound gathered her up as an eagle plucks a hare from the cornrows and bears it away in its talons beneath the wild shade, the *whoosh whoosh* of beating wings. It carried her dangling midair, powerless, over the crazy quilt of crops and pastures, forests and fens. More fields and valleys whisked by beneath her, all the way to the rocky coast of the channel, then out over the ocean, to the deep pelagic whites and blues thrashing. And all of it was breathing, and she was breathing with it.

And then there was something—not words in a human language, but a *voice*. The sound reverberated, rooting itself inside her, *becoming* her heart, liver, spleen, intestines, brain, lungs—every part that pumped and spilled and flowed within her. It was the thrilling voice in the tree that lives on in the cello, the useful voice of the iron tongs upon the anvil, the voice of the plumb bob saying *here, here it is straight,* of milk shooting from the cow's udder. Not words, but pure meaning, as when the heart aches in the body, broken from grief or despair.

You are Mine, it said.

Mine like the corn in the fields, like the animals striving without thought or complaint. All work, it said, *is My worship. All work,* it said, *is praise.*

And she knew it was the voice of God, calling her to His service. But how? How was she to work?

Wait, it said.

At 9 A.M. on the thirty-first of May, Florence stood in the hotel lobby with its checkerboard marble floor, a pawn, she thought, in someone else's game. She was watching the porter attach straps to the luggage when Joseph burst through the door and past the potted palm, nearly upsetting it. Rushing forward, he bowed and, with eyes downcast, handed her an envelope.

Even before she opened it, a new question entered her mind: what if meeting Gustave were part of God's plan for her?

30

THE RITUAL OF TREADING

Fortunately for Gustave, he could avoid staying at the Hôtel D'Orient, where Miss Nightingale would be, without explaining himself to Max. He and Max had lodged there when they first arrived in Cairo and quickly denounced it as a citadel of porcelain and plate. With heavy drapes and furniture completely unsuited to the desert, it seemed designed for travelers who had no wish to leave the comfort of their homes—merely to change the view through their windows.

They took rooms instead at the Hôtel du Nil, a boardinghouse for Europeans of moderate means. It was simple, verging on shabby. The proprietor, M. Bouvaret, a retired actor from the provinces by way of Constantinople, was obliging enough and could be bought with small tips as necessary. Joseph supposed him a Turk whose family had assumed a French name during the brief Napoleonic era.

Avoiding any mention of their argument, he and Max conversed easily. It was the manly thing to do. Women, in his experience, often harped on painful subjects, threshing them like grain until only hulls remained, and then only dust, and still they prodded, poked, hypothesized. Instead of incessant wounding, he and Max posited theories of art, history, and the future of the world.

He began another long letter to Bouilhet by describing the brownish-red rash that had appeared in irate blotches on the backs of both legs. *My bodily doom is sealed,* he wrote. *I suppose it was just a matter of time until the disease caught me out.* But his mind, he told Bouilhet, was brimming with ideas, and he had begun furiously jotting them down, along with character sketches. Spurred in part by Rossignol's aspirations and Trout's secret love affair, he'd been thinking again about a female protagonist. It rankled to admit it, but Max—damn him for a perspicacious critic!—was right: there was much to explore and even exploit in an ordinary female. He sent one scenario to Bouilhet:

A Young Unhappy Woman

> *A provincial who has read too many romances, she expects her life to resemble them, full of galas and velvet gowns, champagne toasts and steamy love affairs. In short, she is bored. She must select her lovers from among the locals (the druggist, doctor, blacksmith, grocer, etc.) or from travelers (a merchant, soldier, veterinarian, notary). The best she can hope for is an illicit liaison with the son of the richest landowner in the county. Once a year he throws a ball at the manor for his poorer neighbors, a scattering of crumbs that she mistakes for jewels . . .*

In a real bed for the first time in months, he closed his eyes and drifted toward somnolence, oars dipping in water just beyond the walls, his mattress steadily rocking as the blue *cange* sailed on in his landlocked body.

When he wasn't sleeping or writing letters or postulating the future of humanity, he contemplated Miss Nightingale, though he delayed writing to her. It struck him as odd that in her absence, she was *Miss Nightingale,* but in person, she was *Rossignol.* Though she, too, had renounced marriage, *Miss Nightingale* embodied all that he despised about convention. But *Rossignol*! She was a rare creature—an Oryx, a black leopard, a vibrantly plumed parrot from the Amazon who spoke multiple languages while retaining the ability to sing like a bird. And like an exotic animal, no one knew her mind. That was what he had come to desire as much as her body—to know her mind. For it was the mind of a man in the body of a woman. *Wrong,* he corrected himself. It was not the mind of a man; he would have recognized that. It was the mind of a rebel, a revolutionary.

He tried to imagine her as a wife (not his), and immediately sensed it would ruin her. The institution would chafe at her until she either surrendered—not likely—or was eroded to a bitter nub of a woman. Her sharp intelligence must be kept occupied, or like a surgeon's scalpel, it would grow dull and dangerous with disuse. Even friendship would be beyond the capacity of Rossignol the bored and bitter wife. No. They had no future together except as Egyptian adventurers, and that chapter, sadly, was nearing its end.

Cautioning him to be less noticeable than a shadow, he sent Joseph to inquire at the Hôtel d'Orient. She was indeed registered there, scheduled to depart within the week. He vowed to write to her. But not yet. He could not approach her yet.

His legs, his poor legs! He hid them from Max, could barely tolerate seeing them himself. The scourge had spread to the soles of his feet, a leprous bloom of white and red patches. Otherwise he felt fine, his mind supple and clear after weeks of lassitude.

Tanned by the desert sun and dressed as natives, he and Max passed for Mahometans to visit Mamaluke sites where they made more squeezes and photographs. The city seethed with feral cats. Early summer was their breeding season, and their near-human cries in the alleys and gardens at night sounded like torture.

At the end of the week, Max got bad news. The graphic letter he'd sent to a lover in Paris had been intercepted by her husband, who had thrashed her and banished her from the house. Max moped through the rooms.

"Will they divorce?" Gustave asked.

"God, I hope not!" Max paused his pacing. "Married women make the best lovers. They are more experienced and less demanding."

Gustave nodded, agreeably, to this platitude, though his history with Louise contradicted it.

Of course, Max said, he loved her.

Gustave discovered his sympathies lay not with Max but with the ruined wife. What would become of her if the husband refused to reconcile? Max would not step in. For a woman to have a love affair was far more dangerous than Gustave had realized. Yet, to his mind, it seemed the only way a sensitive woman other than a crusader like Miss Nightingale could assert her independence.

After a day, Max dropped the subject. Rogue. Bastard. Yet who could blame him? Why was sex such a boon to men, and for women, such a disgrace? Surely, mankind had erred, configuring sex as a commodity, a matter of ownership and property instead of simple delight. The premium on virginity sentenced every woman to just one lover. He couldn't imagine living with this restriction.

Joseph's wife, whose desperate pleas for money had filled her "love letters" for months, met him at Bulak in a new dress and hat, though the cupboard was empty and she had not prepared dinner. Joseph appeared at the hotel the next day in a fog of jasmine and sandalwood. He had bathed. "She is ruin me!" he told Gustave proudly.

On May 29, Gustave and Max decided to extend their stay in Cairo to attend the Ritual of Treading before heading north to Alexandria, where they'd catch a packet for Beirut the second week of June. Joseph was glad to have a few more days of work.

That night, Gustave wrote *her* a lengthy letter. He'd settled on "her" and "she" rather than *Miss Nightingale* or *Rossignol* until she was replaced by the next fascination, should there be one.

He decided to tell her everything, to make a clean breast of it. Indeed, it was an autobiography of sorts, tracing his life back to age nineteen. Surely if anyone could understand his obsessions, she could.

It was a loving letter, without a return address. When he finished it, he sent Joseph to deliver it by hand.

At dawn on the third of June, he perched atop a wall on the Street of the Faithful alongside Max and Joseph. By eight an enormous crowd had gathered, milling about like angry bees.

Doseh, or the Ritual of the Treading, was performed in Cairo several times a year to commemorate a miracle. A Mahometan saint had once ridden his horse through a street filled with clay jars of food without breaking a single one. Strangely, over the years, the ritual had modulated into a menacing key. It was no longer a celebration but a test of faith, with lives instead of jars at stake.

With every minute that passed, the crowd enlarged. After two more hours, a sheik clad in dazzling white robes appeared on a black mount with a lavish saddle and bridle embellished with gold tassels, bells, and embroidery. At his signal, the crowd arranged itself in the street to form a thoroughfare of flesh—men prone on their bellies in ranks so close together they looked like herrings packed in a tin. Not a brick of the street was visible. Locusts and mummies, Gustave thought. Now living men.

Wild music commenced, played on flutes and drums. It drove the spectators to a frenzy. Eunuchs beat the crowd back in a storm of cudgeling unlike any he'd seen for speed and vigor. When they were done, the river of bodies was immured by a wall of spectators, both eerily silent. Gustave trembled with expectation and dread.

It was trial by happenstance. An injury in the treading was a reflection of sin. "Why not throw them in the river to see if they float?" he asked Max.

Max lit his pipe, puffing until the tobacco glowed. "I don't think injury is the idea but the power of faith." He exhaled a long plume of smoke. "Of the *mind.*"

"Or of the heart," Gustave added, genuinely glad for Max's company just then. He could not have attended so strange a spectacle alone. For a change, he found Max's detachment, his coolly dispassionate powers of observation, calming. Since a benevolent crowd was a rarity anywhere, he felt safer with Max, too, though his fear was nothing compared to the excess tenderness and empathy. He suspected that the almost paralyzing vulnerability he felt was not the result of his own pain and sadness, but of Rossignol's, at his hands. How she must have suffered when she received the letter! He dreaded the coming days for her. He felt sad, he felt guilty, he felt sorry. He felt altogether too much.

At noon the sheik entered the street. His mount was so spirited, prancing sideways and backward, skittering with high, dressage-like kicks, that the rider had to restrain him. Either the beast simply wished to have his head, or the sight and smell of the helpless men had spooked him.

It was not the first spectacle Gustave had seen in Cairo. Eight months earlier, he and Max had watched magicians and mountebanks perform tricks and snake charmers tempt vipers from baskets. Fortune-tellers in varied guises had promised him a hodgepodge of fates: wealth, health, many women, and an early death by water. Most impressive were the spinning dervishes. They had plunged spikes through their chests and mouths, then affixed oranges on the sharp end and continued to whirl, their long, tan skirts floating up in perfect disks. Surely that had been a clever illusion. A man would perish on the spot from such an insult to the body. And he did not believe in miracles.

The sheik began his passage through the street. A deafening cacophony of cheers and songs erupted from the spectators as the steed picked his way on skulls, smalls of backs, tender napes, the thin-skinned backs of knees. From the flattened men a cataract of anguished excitement issued in the form of prayers and ululations.

He couldn't bear it, even with Max beside him, meditatively puffing on a short-stemmed meerschaum. "I am leaving," he cried out, hardly audible over the throng. He leaped to the ground on the other side of the wall.

"Wait!" Max called to him. "Wait for me." He and Joseph dropped down and caught up with him.

"Surely some of them will die," said Gustave, walking rapidly away from the scene. He began to cry.

Max put his arm around Gustave's shoulder as they entered a quiet lane shaded by plane trees with their trunks painted white. "If that is true, they knew the risks."

"Still."

Max felt his neck for heat. "Has the fever returned?"

"No. I'm just feeling sensitive."

"Could you be coming down with something else? Perhaps it's a simple case of exhaustion." He patted Gustave's back.

"No, I am well." He was. He was more himself than ever, a sensitive fellow with a big bluff. Max, he knew, grasped this, but it was not in his nature to speak of it. Instead, they continued back to the hotel arm in arm.

The next morning, Joseph reported that there had been no injuries from the *Doseh*. Gustave hoped he was telling the truth. He was dead tired, having spent much of the night imagining himself flat on his belly while a hoof hovered above, threatening to smash his neck. He wished to be like a plant, existing without awareness of the past or future, simply breathing in and out, feeling nothing.

The next day, still hollowed out, he rambled with Joseph through the bazaars one last time, without desire: perfume sellers, chandlers, goldsmiths, olive and date vendors, spice merchants, booksellers, bakers, tailors. He engraved the scenes in his mind against the likelihood he would not return. When tradesmen approached, he held up a weary hand and they retreated to their covered booths like a sea to its depths.

The next morning, the last before they left for Alexandria, he indulged his nostalgia once more—for women drawing water and *fellahin* from the countryside selling grain in their distinctive long blue tunics and white turbans.

On the day of departure, he gave a big gratuity to M. Bouvaret, who had helped twice with the luggage and generously drawn maps to sites in and around the city. His most painful farewell would be to Joseph, loyal, love-besotted Joseph. He would hold off until the last moment, when he and Max boarded the ship for Alexandria.

"Wait," said the innkeeper, pocketing his baksheesh. "You must not depart yet." He followed them out the door, helping again with their possessions.

Moments later, he returned, lugging a large tin pot. *"Y'allah,"* he said, urging them toward the street. "Now, *messieurs,* this is how friends say good-bye in the Orient." Beaming, he pitched the potful of water at their feet.

"What?" exclaimed Gustave. He checked his valises. Not a drop had touched them or him despite the big splash.

Bouvaret clapped the pot. *"Revenez avant que cette eau ne sèche!"* he shouted. Come back before this water dries.

Once again, the dam broke and tears rolled over Gustave's cheeks. He had to stifle himself. To be so easily moved was unnerving. First, the men at the treading and now a little water. A rainbow on a strand of hair. Or the memory of Trout holding her hat atop the dune while Max gathered moonlight into his lens. The whole evanescent display of life in all its depravity, all its glory. Because the water had been, above all, *glorious* as the sunlight sparked it. It had hung in the air like a liquid marquee announcing, *anointing* the moment with a homespun grandeur. Water from the Nile, no doubt. He wanted to embrace the innkeeper for the aptness and sweetness of the gesture, but the man had already turned toward the door.

31

THE TWELFTH ROOM

She recognized the birdsong—redstarts, thrushes, finches—that punctuated the cool air. Bordered with tall cedars and thick-boled pines, the grounds were orderly, with gravel paths and flower beds, not a profusion, but enough to acknowledge that beauty had a place among the poor and sick. Flowers, in good measure, promised a future, added hope, though a superabundance of blooms could deny suffering, enforce a rote cheerfulness. At home they often had just this obliterating, chastising effect: how dare you be ill or poor when the snapdragon and lily of the valley lift their perfumed throats and offer their silent bells to the wind? No, Kaiserswerth was a practical place, she saw that right away—and her true destination after eight months of wandering. For the first time in her life, she was on her own—no family, no chaperones or maid.

She did her best to put Egypt behind her. On a good day, it was as if she had never been there—never walked along the beach at Aboukir Bay, where Lord Nelson vanquished the French, or saw the ships left to rot, their hulls bleached and bitten like the bones of giant, mythical birds. A different Flo had struck up a conversation with a stranger thoughtlessly discharging a gun in public. Better not to remember any of it.

Here is what I most wish as I write this, my songbird—that I could be with you in Cairo.

Her first impulse was to throw his letter away, but she relented and read it, then reread it, first to freshen her grief, and later for comfort on the long journey from Egypt to Prussia.

Please forgive me for the silence you have had to endure; I know that from silence, as from pain, one can make nothing. I have been ill in various degrees since we parted, often too ill to write. For days, I was quite delirious; I remember only Joseph bringing me tea and brandy with soft, tasteless bread.

A trove of letters had accumulated in Cairo during the remainder of Flo's Nile voyage—ten in all, five from Parthe. The voices of loved ones from a distance constituted the best sort of homecoming. They professed to miss her, and she believed them. But she was no longer the person they missed. After knowing Gustave, she realized that she was not the singular freak it had suited them to believe. There were other monsters. Even two made a group. Two made her almost . . . ordinary. Run-of-the-mill Flo.

After Cairo, the family scanted on letters. Parthe claimed to have posted letters addressed to Trieste, Poste Restante, and to Flo's hotels in Dresden and Berlin. They never reached her, while Selina and Charles received packets without interruption. Was the blood mob punishing her in advance? Had they guessed her secret plan?

The trip to Greece was improvised and panoramic. They stitched a crazy quilt through the Mediterranean and Adriatic on a thread of bad weather, with delays for quarantine and diplomatic disturbances. Twice they set forth from Trieste and were refused entry at Grecian ports. Remarkably, it took thirteen days instead of three to steam from Alexandria to Corfu, and ten days from Corfu to Patras. *We are going to Greece by way of New York once the isthmus of Panama is cut through,* she wrote WEN in a rare moment of jocularity. At last, they traversed the Gulf of Corinth and reached Athens, where the Bracebridges had a villa.

Dear Selina, determined that Flo love Greece as much as she did, insisted she wait for a sunny day to view the Acropolis. Yet even under blue skies Greece was a disappointment. Abu Simbel had evoked God for her, while the Parthenon deified man, its stone divinities poor facsimiles of the great philosophers and dramatists. Her hopelessness persisted.

Charles was ailing. Egypt, he claimed, had induced neuralgic headaches along with accumulations of phlegm and coughing spells. She applied leeches to his forearm with her customary care, glad for a task to divert her from dreaming and panic. He booked a reservation at Bad Pyrmont, in lower Saxony, for three weeks in the baths and vapor cave, first in salt, then in steel. On July 2 they departed for the north.

The meander through Europe was a revelation. Everywhere, from Vienna to Prague and on through Germany, tempers were flaring after the clashes of 1848. Berlin and Prague were in shambles, with soldiers garrisoned in civilian homes. The scent of gunpowder stung the air with the threat of armed confrontation. In every crowd, Flo saw flashes of steel and the dull glow of military braid, reminders of the fragile truce.

But O, her *désespoir*! The only way to fight it was by doing. Something. Anything. She visited galleries, churches, and museums. She walked and tended Charles. Sundays at unfamiliar churches anchored her, though expatriates latched on like hungry fleas.

In Prague she began to improve. The best distraction of all turned out to be hospitals. The Brothers of Mercy and Sisters of Mercy ran two exemplars of hygiene and compassion. Protestant establishments, they proved that women could serve like nuns outside a monastic order. In Berlin a trio of progressive institutions inspired her: the New Model Hospital; the Elizabeth Hospital; and most amazing, the Rauhe Haus, where delinquent boys apprenticed in the trades lived in cottages with deacons as a kind of family. The kindness wealthy Germans bestowed on their poorer brethren lifted her mood.

The second-best distraction was making Fanny squirm with letters that pretended to innocent motives. She pointedly described the new hospitals, contrasting them with one in Hamburg run in the English style by dissolute doctors and therefore full of bad women. From Berlin she lauded spinsters who had founded charities. With her private fortune, Mlle. de Sieveking had established a home for fallen daughters, and Mlle. de Bülow, an infants' hospital and school for scrofulous children. Though the implication was clear, Flo spelled it out: if they were serious, WEN and Fanny could undertake genuine charity instead of hunt balls and poor-peopling. If Florence had funds, *she* certainly would.

She let drop that the women in Berlin were more liberated than their English sisters. Solitary fraus and fräuleins moved through the streets without risk to reputation. They shopped alone, spent afternoons reading in the free libraries, and attended evening concerts unescorted. "I have just turned thirty," she wrote her mother, "the age Jesus was when he began his real work, and I hope to become useful in the world." Though Fanny would be outraged, Flo knew she would not respond to these gibes.

While Charles recuperated in the spa, she and Selina sauntered arm in arm, companionable as ever. To Flo's relief, Selina correctly construed Flo's silence on the subject of Gustave as a large red KEEP AWAY sign. Otherwise Flo would have borne the untenable burden of defending the man just when she was trying to forget him.

She had less time to brood because her mind was working round the clock, absorbing information, formulating schemes she might undertake at home. Her Ragged School teaching, the work closest to the German mold, must certainly continue. But what of England's major wasted resource—the indolent upper-class women who counted their lives in cross-stitch and bore children in a world teeming with orphans merely to keep occupied? What if they could make their way without footmen and chaperones, unencumbered by hooped and trained gowns too voluminous to pass through a gate or doorway? Fashion was nothing more than a pretty cage.

These women were bored, whether they knew it or not.

It rankled to think of how much suffering they could abate, were it respectable to do so. She began a tract called *Cassandra,* about the oppression of daughters. *The upper-class English family uses people. If it wants someone to sit every day in the drawing room, she must comply, even if she may be destined by God for science or education. This system dooms some minds to incurable infancy, others to silent misery.* In a renewed frenzy, she filled the pages of *Lavie* with daily notes and tirades: *July 20, Berlin: Suppose we were to see a number of men in the morning sitting around a table, looking at prints, doing worsted work, and reading little books. How we should laugh!*

Despite the displacements of travel, time passed rapidly. The German trains were efficient, with private sitting rooms in addition to sleeping cars in first class. Best of all, she dreamed less. Somewhere north of the Alps, the anticipation of Kaiserswerth began to outweigh her sadness.

Max was sure I'd recover, and ordered the cange *to Beni Hasan, but the winds had curled up in their caves. Every day we were becalmed he ranted.*

But no, it is foolish to delay what I wish to say with journalistic ramblings.

Let me begin again.

Three weeks by herself. No maid to launder or lay out clothes, dress her hair, or keep her calendar. Her own labor, she saw immediately, was the price of freedom, which was fitting, as Kaiserswerth was an experiment in communalism, with identical privations for all.

What did Kaiserswerth not grapple with? Infants, orphans, troubled adolescents, the old, the ill, the criminal, the homeless, the *hopeless*. Pastor Fliedner and his wife, whom she was asked to call "Mother," were the epitome of methodical devotion. Familiar to them through Baron Bunsen and her own enthusiastic letters, she was welcomed as one of their own. Language was no problem: she spoke German, but wrote notes in French, which they read with ease.

Did she wish to be treated like a visitor or a probationer? A probationer, she said. She roomed in the dormitory, expecting austerity, but finding instead utilitarian plenitude: simple furniture, latchhooked rugs, kerosene lamps, and books. Books everywhere—medical texts, proposals for legal reform, reports from the Kaiserswerth colonies abroad. Manuals on teaching the deaf and blind and reforming delinquents. *Accouchement for Midwives.*

With Pastor Fliedner's approval, she decided to write a pamphlet about the deaconesses for an English audience. If she penned it anonymously, WEN would print and distribute it.

> *First, I want to tell you something that only one other human being, my dear friend Louis Bouilhet, knows. (If you ever saw him, you would be struck by our resemblance. We are doppelgängers of each other. This was our first bond, not enough to sustain a friendship, but later, a constant emblem of our shared love of literature and writing.)*
>
> *It was to Bouilhet I confided when I was nineteen that I was considering castrating myself. No doubt, you will find this idea* engoué, *if not horrific. Surely you must be thinking, "Why is he telling me this? And why has he broken his word to me?" Bear with me, Rossignol.*
>
> *You see, I am an epileptic, though my family won't admit it. They treat it as a dark secret, like a murder among the ancestors. I thought if I gave up gratification, I might be free of seizures. The idea appealed to me for another reason—the purity of renouncing the pleasures of the body. If I had done it, I believe I would have become a religious man and—dare I say it?—in that regard rather like you.*

The probationers numbered one hundred and twenty, most studying to become deaconesses, a smaller number, nurses, like Flo. Nursing was a decent profession at Kaiserwerth, with standards of deportment and actual techniques to master. The hospital's one hundred beds were always full. She learned all manner of care—bandaging, applying tinctures, the treatment for burns, for suppurating infections, for whatever wounds a body could sustain and survive. A man's horse had crushed him; an aged deaconess was dying of tuberculosis; a child had almost frozen to death in a pond. A doctor from the village prescribed the protocol, and the nurses and probationers carried it out.

Real work, every day. She was so occupied and met so many people that her brief notes in *Lavie* did little more than track the blur of activity. *Walked the bad eyes and the bad chest along the Rhine. An itchy family was admitted. Poison oak?* Each morning she awoke eager for the day's accomplishments.

> *Not that we are so different in other ways. Everyone thinks that only women are hysterics, while I believe that men are, too. Myself, for example! Often, for no reason at all, my heart beats like a tribal drum. I become emotional over trifles. Sometimes I begin to choke, or odd pains shoot through the back of my head. Other times I am in a state of exaltation. As for boils, I could write a book about the way they come and go like demons battling for my soul. In this intensity of feeling, we are, I know, alike. (Not that you suffer from boils!) Everything troubles and agitates me. A zephyr to others is the harsh north wind to me. I have become more* vache, *more beastly and yet more sensitive, more capable of torment. (Does this sound familiar?) Also, it goes without saying that the characters I create, such as Saint Anthony, drive me crazy. I live inside them and they in me. I suffered every agony Anthony did, but mine were self-imposed. Do you see this, dear Rossignol—that the same bells call out to us?*

The Fliedners allowed her to assist at a major operation, a leg amputation set for August 1. The day before, she met the patient,

Herr Fuer, a carpenter with sugar in the blood. A nail puncture on his shin had festered into gangrene. He was forty-five, with thick blond hair that stuck out from his head like shocks of wheat, giving him a clownish demeanor at odds with his grave condition. "I am frightened, fräulein," he kept saying. "I need to pray." She prayed with him. She wrote two letters for him and sang hymns. He joined in, his voice quavering with anxiety. Pastor Fliedner stopped by to pray with him, too, though Fuer was a Catholic. *What higher purpose,* she wrote that night, *can there be than saving a life or a soul?*

The next morning, she impatiently rolled bandages until summoned to the surgery. For the next five hours, she and Sister Sophie attended the surgeon in the small, brightly lit operating room. Using a circular saw, the doctor removed the leg as high as possible to forestall spread of the poison. The cutting was grisly but brief.

She hadn't expected beauty—there was no other word for it—in such a dire circumstance. The reek of rotting flesh, the gore, even the patient's suffering mattered less than the continual awe. Awe for the incision, the steel blade entering the flesh with an unparalleled and godly presumption of intimacy. Awe for the beautiful taking up of the blood vessels. She watched the arteries flex like molten canes still hot from the glass furnace. When they straightened, filling up with fresh bright blood, the surgeon tied them off with seven waxed threads. The room was a slaughterhouse, but she paid no notice. They packed the wound. The white gauze bloomed and bloomed, not sapping Fuer's vitality but stanching the spillage as if with a crafty abstract rendering of bouquets.

In the afternoon and evening, Fuer suffered greatly. She prayed with him when he was conscious. What made the operation so arduous and prolonged, the doctor said that evening, was the insufficiency of healthy skin to fold over the wound. They dressed the stump a second time with collodium strips, but they proved too small to be protective. The surgeon removed them and she helped stitch up the wound with black silk, then put on a Maltese cross bandage. *Cold water compresses every five minutes, one of us always with him. Flower-pots on the windowsill from Sister Ernestine.* She fell asleep with her pen in hand.

• • •

Friday, 2 August 1850

12–12:30 Took my place by Fuer, who was going on well. In the afternoon I read to the dying man and the disfigured man in the garret, who are not allowed to join the others.

2 P.M. Cupped Margareta.

3–4 P.M. Making up powders, decoctions, infusions, etc., under Sister Ernestine's direction at the apothecary.

6 P.M. Men's ward. The amputated man.

7 P.M. Pastor's class with the seminarists. They practiced telling him the story of Isaac and Elisha and the angels, which they will relate to the children tomorrow. He teaches like Socrates. Questions and answers, never outright lecturing or correction.

Early the next morning, while scrubbing glass vials at the apothecary, an extraordinary paradox about Abu Simbel occurred to her: at the heart of Ramses's monumental splendor was complete anonymity. The pharaoh who ruled for sixty-six years would never be forgotten as long as his name, Ramses or, in Greek, Ozymandias, issued from the lips of the living, which his monument at Abu Simbel ensured. But he, too, like Osiris and the primeval traveler before him, the dying sun, had passed through the twelve rooms in the hours between sunset and dawn. He'd sailed the infernal river, past ogres and tormentors, ravenous snakes and crocodiles, while priests made sacrifices and recited spells from the "Book of Going Forth by Day." At the Hall of Two Truths in the seventh room, Osiris weighed his heart against the feather of truth while the monster Ammit—she loved that name, which meant "bone crusher"—waited to devour the failures. Presumably the golden scales had balanced, and he rejoined Ra in the Barque of Millions of Years, sailing toward the glorious dawn of eternal life. But *none* of it was possible without the multitude of nameless artisans—the jewelers, cooks, embalmers, priests, stonemasons, bricklayers, painters. Their names, Bunsen said, survived more quietly, not in the mouths of people like her and Gustave and Selina, but buried with them, inscribed on parchment and protected by the magical rope of the cartouche.

She'd written a *third* note at Philae, she suddenly recalled. Not a plea to die, but a bargain offered to God. *I am prepared to serve without reputation.*

For a dozen years she had clung to God's words. But what were these words anyway? Inventions of the brain, proximate fruits of intention. *Wait,* the Voice had said. And she had always understood that meant to await further instructions. But what if the waiting were *part* of His bidding, imposed not to humble her but to effect a sustained alertness, a sharpened attention to whatever happened? The eye of the falcon, the sun god's eye, watching over everything.

By now her note, retrieved by the wind, would be nourishing rice stalks or lotus leaves. The notion pleased her. Perhaps His long silence was like that, not an absence but a slow fruition, as of the pale yellow, plate-size lotus blossoms that swayed over the sodden expanses of Nile silt.

I know how sensitive you are to words from our time together at Koseir when you forbade me to speak the name of a certain part that I later told you against your will. But in addition to my epilepsy, I have contracted an unspeakable disease. I am loath to write this word, but I must; otherwise, nothing I say will make full sense.

Pox.

She found it puzzling that the deaconesses had sprung up in Germany and not in England, both being Protestant. In England, the rural poor and the new industrial class cried out for such an institution. If she studied the Kaiserswerth methods, she might transplant them and start her own institute at home. Women not married to God, but to society, in His name.

Have you heard the old joke: One man to another: What is the price of love? Second man: Ten francs or marriage.

The true answer is pox.

What is a man to do who harbors this disease? I shall be lucky if I do not go mad. The cures are problematic. Valerian root is inexpensive and often prescribed but does not work. Gum from the lignum vitae is expensive and unproven. I shall try the mercury cure ("A night in the arms of Venus leads to a lifetime on Mercury"), which is what my father would have prescribed. The treatment must be repeated periodically, as the disease is thought to remain in the body until death.

I wanted to tell you this in Kenneh but lacked the courage. Even to speak of it is a great dishonor to you, for which I apologize.

No, she'd never gone to Egypt. Never set foot in the sand or sat on the shore of the Red Sea. It was not she who wished to die at Philae and instead was rescued by a man who became a friend, unlikely as that was.

And so, Rossignol, I want to say that you are beautiful. I wish that I had told you this before, but you are. Your mind is likewise beautiful. I have never met your like. I would say you have the mind of a man, but that would not suffice, either.

I know that marriage holds no appeal for you, but what else is there between a man and a woman that would not provoke the condemnation of society, that would not be considered an abomi-

nation, that would not cause us pain? I had hoped we could be lifelong friends, but alas, I am drawn to you in the way that men are drawn to women. I began to love you—it was so easy and natural. But how can we have a future with my illness?

• • •

Saturday, 3 August 1850

Walked the bad eyes and the rheumatism in the morning. Lunch with the infant schoolmistresses. Reading Bible with penitents at evening—a new group of ten women fresh from prison.

In her heightened existence, responsible for prolonging lives, it seemed natural to entertain opposing feelings, to be what she would have once called confused, though now she did not feel confused. She felt capacious. On the one hand, she suffered the scarifying sorrow of loss, and on the other, she was proud, filled with an immaculate and pure joy. For this was love, or had been.

No more love, no more marriage. When she had refused Richard, those words had been as much a judgment on herself as on him. She had pitied herself, as though her hands had been severed before she had touched a single thing on earth—not a leaf, not the honed blade of a knife, or the silky hand of an infant. Now she had. They had touched like God and Adam on her beloved Sistine Chapel. No longer a stranger to love, she had set it aside. Rushing between patients, measuring elixirs or sitting in a profound quiet with the dying deaconess, she felt joy and grief and had no need to distinguish between them. Like the good and evil in the temples at Abu Simbel, they flowed together. They were one.

The next Thursday morning, a week after the amputation, she was alarmed to find Fuer, who had been steadily improving, stuporous and hemorrhaging from the nose. The doctor visited three times that day. She followed his instructions, placing a bladder with artificial ice on Fuer's head, renewing it every two hours, applying cold-water compresses to the back of his neck and temples. His moistened hair looked like the feathers of a molting bird. She washed his hands and chest frequently and checked his pulse every half hour. By 10 A.M. it had risen to 130. She and Sister Sophie put leeches on his temples as he drifted into and out of sensibility. She offered to stay the night with him, but Mother ordered her to her room.

She barely slept. Vigilance had rooted in her, her schedule shaped to his. She woke at 5 A.M. and found him bleeding at the temples. She held dry compresses against his brow, pressing upward with her hands flat on the cloth. Fuer stared at her so resolutely that she knew he was trying to communicate. His eyes rolled back in his head.

She called for a priest to administer extreme unction. While the old cleric prayed with enough heart for the three of them, she held the patient's hand. After that, the room quickened with activity. At nine, the doctor arrived, examined Fuer, and declared it was typhus. Mother appraised the scene to determine who should care for him in his final hours. She chose Flo.

By evening, his teeth and tongue were black, the rest of him gray. Every half hour, per the doctor's orders, she put thirty drops of ether on his head to assuage the pain. His hair was straw now, trampled and lusterless. She continued to refresh the ice bladder every other hour, and hourly applied strong chamomile tea compresses to the stump, which was pink and healing nicely, like the one healthy tree left in a forest decimated by fire. Through his coma, she sensed his fear, which had been the worst aspect of his suffering all along. *Strong steel and acids every hour internally and as much water as he can drink, mixed with raspberry vinegar. All day I held dry cloths to the bleeding, pressing down with my hands. This it is to live.*

She slept on and off at his bedside and awoke disoriented at 8 A.M., two hours later than usual. He was still alive. At nine the doctor came but did not dress the stump. He listened to Fuer's heart and chest without ever looking at her, not wishing, she sensed, to convey emotion. After he left the room, she sat holding Fuer's damp, clay hand. He was breathing, just breathing; it was all he could manage. And then, in a few minutes, without any struggle, he died. Gone in an imperceptible instant. And *where* had he gone? Where did they go when they left the body?

The job was not finished. She fumigated the room with vitriolic acid and supervised the removal of the body to the chamber of the dead, where it was sprinkled with chloride of lime and no one was allowed to enter. That afternoon his sisters came to call on him. She had to turn them away weeping.

Selina came to the institute for an afternoon's visit. She noted what a rough place it was, lacking in the usual amenities: no hot water for a bath and very often no cold water. Flo bathed, she explained, when she swam in the Rhine with the orphans. Selina was glad that Flo's family had not accompanied her. They would have been alarmed and disapproved. And interfered, Flo added.

That evening, after Selina left, Mother Fliedner asked her to accompany Deaconess Amalia the next day. They would be selling lottery tickets at the village inn to raise funds.

"What is the prize?" Flo asked.

"Money, just some money," answered Mrs. Fliedner. Flo had never heard of such an undertaking. She wondered if it was better to award a gift. Perhaps chocolates or some other delicacy?

Mother said they hadn't time to shop for chocolates and the people of the village were content to win a small pouch. Flo thought it undignified, but agreed.

The next morning she set out with Sister Amalia. Stationing themselves at a rickety table in the porte cochere where the carriages collected and deposited guests, they sold a small roll of chances. At lunchtime they picnicked by the river on bread and cheese. Sister

Amalia returned to the hotel and retrieved the table and chairs. She asked Flo to help her set up outside a restaurant down the street.

"But we have sold all the tickets."

"Yes," the sister agreed. "Now we beg. People will throw in their change from dinner."

"I see. And they do not expect anything for it?"

"It's just small change," the deaconess replied, "like the poor plate at church."

They had no sign, no booklet or prospectus to distribute, Flo pointed out. The deaconess said everyone in town knew of the Fliedners' institute. But Flo felt the need to identify herself for each customer who tarried at the table. "I am Florence Nightingale," she recited, "asking for your generosity for the work of Pastor Fliedner's Institute for Deaconesses." The sated diners did not meet her eye or acknowledge her. She shortened her speech, mumbling "for the deaconesses" and looking down as she offered the bowl Sister Amalia had brought for the purpose.

In her boredom, she imagined people she knew exiting the restaurant. The Poetic Parcel and his new wife, Annabelle, arm in arm and deep in conversation, Richard tipping his hat, then scurrying away upon recognizing her. Parthe, flustered as usual, shifting from foot to foot as she chatted. Max, tripod in arm, to capture the event for posterity. WEN, in his silk top hat, and Fanny, swathed in fur, speechless before this beggar, their splendidly brought-up second child, who was pleased as Punch for them to see her.

They collected a pathetic sum. Flo guessed she'd been asked along as a test, to be mortified or shocked. If so, she had passed with high marks. Begging for alms did not bother her; she was not asking for herself, but for God.

That night she went home deeply contented. *I have found my destiny,* she wrote in *Lavie, and it is so blindingly bright that I might have removed from a darkened parlor directly to a lakeshore in a single step and there seen my own reflection. At first I was a fractured and jagged rippling, but I have smoothed and settled into a trembling liquid whole.*

. . .

Perhaps it is cruel to be so candid. If so, I send you my deepest regrets. You see, though in my heart I am a red romantic, I know how foolish the pursuit of romance is. The only cure for it is celibacy, at least in the ideal case, for there is no way to protect oneself from love. I shall have to settle for the friendship of other cynics like myself.

I am honored to have known you as my friend.

I cherish you. I embrace you and beg your forgiveness with a thousand tendernesses.

Gve

No, she had never been to Egypt. Never stroked his shaved head, mapping the tender bumps, placing her fingertips on his lips and eyelids. She had never entered his tent, been kissed and touched *there* and *there,* her body a night sky pierced by stars.

. . .

Saturday, 10 August 1850

8–9 Apothecary

2 P.M. A fever patient came in; longed to nurse him. Itchy family discharged.

4:30–7 P.M. Writing out receipts, etc, longed to be with the severely sick.

8:30 P.M.: Walked in the moonlight along the Rhine with Sister Sophie. Death is so much more impressive in the midst of life.

The last week was difficult on many counts, not least being the sadness of imminent departure.

On the wards, the patients worsened. Three were bedridden and three more she had to lift into and out of bed. What gainful experience could there be after Fuer? Nothing; only making beds and dragging the invalids out to bathe.

In three weeks they buried four patients, not unusual, Mother said. People tended to be very ill by the time they went to hospital.

On her last day at Kaiserswerth, she breakfasted with the probationers and deaconesses, bathed the infants in the river, and said her farewells at the hospital—all distressing, as these people felt like family now.

At four o'clock Trout and the Bracebridges fetched her in a coach. They'd taken rooms in Cologne, where they drove posthaste. Flo was anxious to draft the Kaiserswerth pamphlet. She wanted to finish it while things were still fresh in mind—her practical little room, the songs the orphans sang, everywhere the healing odor of iodine and disinfectant. She promised the Fliedners she'd return within the year. *My home, my heart's home, my salvation.*

Saturday, 17 August 1850. Cologne.

Selina and Charles sightseeing all day and Trout here at the hotel with me, both of us glad for the leisure. Long letter home to Parthe explaining the blessed institute. She will not oppose me if I can win her over first. I know she will show it to Fanny. My happiness graces every word. The letter sings! I send her my sincerest love, for I do love them all and have missed them in my own way. Even the fighting is part of my care, I say.

In truth, her family had less power over her now that she had settled the question with God and met another monster. It was only a matter of money now, and time. Time until WEN surrendered to her will.

She had thought of Trout often at Kaiserswerth, not missing her assistance, but marveling at her situation, and at her own blindness to it. To be with her again at the hotel was comforting.

Though it was too personal and ephemeral for display, she would keep the cast of Gustave's face. In every other way, it was a perfect souvenir, blank as the desert and the paper from which it was made, and yet as shapely as any object willed into existence. What had passed between them was just as unique and private. She felt no need to speak of it. Nor could anyone guess it. He was part of her now, and she of him. She had his face, not just in papier-mâché, but also in her mind, in her fingertips. And no one could fathom any of it simply by *seeing* her. Just as she had looked at Trout without seeing Gilbert, who was a part of her. When she looked at another's face, she must remember this—that no one was strictly singular. A person was more than herself or himself. She determined in the future to imagine that every face she saw was illuminated that way, lit by something continuing to shine inside, like a sun that had not yet risen but would as it had every day since Creation.

ACKNOWLEDGMENTS, SOURCES, AND A NOTE

Perhaps because it is my first novel, this book has had many friends, which I am pleased to acknowledge here. I am thankful to the Virginia Center for the Creative Arts for residencies that allowed me to complete this work surrounded by peace and beauty and nurtured by the fellowship of other artists. At the Florence Nightingale Museum, the archivists and curators, in particular Caroline Roberts, extended friendly as well as helping hands to me.

I am especially grateful to Anika Streitfeld for her Solomonic book sense. Nirah Shomer, Michael Nowak, and Francis Gillen all read an earlier draft and made crucial suggestions. John Giancola, Kathleen Ochshorn, and Julie Raynor offered unflagging support.

It is also my pleasure to thank the team at Simon & Schuster: in London, Jessica Leeke; in New York, Michele Bové; Emer Flounders; Nina Pajak; and especially my editor, Anjali Singh, for her brilliance, passion, and diligence. Thank you, as well, Jonathan Karp, for your strong support of this book.

Gillian Gill, who does not know me from Adam's off ox, generously advised me about biographical sources and corrected my clumsy nineteenth-century French. Any remaining infelicities or inaccuracies are my own.

There are not enough words in the English language—or any other—to express my gratitude to my agent, Rob McQuilkin, who understood this book at every step and whose enthusiasm and confidence in it never wavered. His wisdom informs every page.

Margaret Joan Libertus, one of my dearest friends and staunchest supporters, died as this project was drawing to a close. May her name live on in the Field of Reeds.

SOURCES

Within the weave of language in this novel, scholars of Flaubert and Nightingale will recognize phrases and sentences familiar to them. For example, I use some of Nightingale's actual diary entries verbatim, most famously the "no more love, no more marriage" excerpt that here, in her fictional life, she shows to Richard Monckton Milnes. Likewise, I have sometimes deployed genuine Flaubert quotations among the thoughts, writings, and remarks that I have invented for him.

Though I have relied in large part on primary sources—the letters, journals, and books of Flaubert, Nightingale, Du Camp, Mary Clarke Mohl, and others—I have also benefited from many secondary sources, including Gillian Gill's *Nightingales: The Extraordinary Upbringing and Curious Life of Miss Florence Nightingale* (New York: Ballantine Books, 2004); volumes 1, 4, and 7 of Lynn McDonald's definitive *Collected Works of Florence Nightingale* (Ontario, Canada: Wilfrid Laurier University Press, 2001, 2003, and 2004; vol. 4 edited by Gérard Vallée); and Mark Bostridge's *Florence Nightingale: The Making of an Icon* (New York: Farrar, Straus and Giroux, 2008).

Of the many French sources I consulted, one of the most useful was Michel Dewachter's and Daniel Oster's facsimile edition of Du Camp's original travelogue and photographs, *Un voyager en Égypte vers 1850: Le Nil de Maxime Du Camp* (Paris: Sand/Conti, 1987). Also invaluable were Frederick Brown's *Flaubert: A Biography* (New York: Little, Brown, 2006) and Francis Steegmuller's *The Letters of Gustave Flaubert, 1830–1857* (Cambridge, MA: Belknap Press of Harvard University, 1980). Finally, Trout's relationship with Gilbert

Pennafeather is closely modeled on Hannah Cullwick's relationship with Arthur Munby as described in *The Diaries of Hannah Cullwick, Victorian Maidservant,* edited and introduced by Liz Stanley (New Brunswick, NJ: Rutgers University Press, 1984).

Websites devoted to Flaubert, Nightingale, Du Camp, and almost everyone else in this book appear on the Internet in an ever-widening tide. For the eternally curious, a little googling will yield fascinating information, such as Flaubert's response to the government charges of obscenity against *Madame Bovary;* a photograph of "La Poétesse," the marble statue that Louise Colet is sitting for in James Pradier's studio when she meets Flaubert; and the round-robin pornography that Richard Monckton Milnes penned with Sir Richard Burton and other literary luminaries. Our knowledge of the Victorians continues to grow, providing us an increasingly rich portrait of their age and a mirror for our own.

A FINAL NOTE

This is a work of fiction inspired by real people. Though I have hewed close to the facts, I have also taken liberties with them. For example, Nightingale attended an amputation at Kaiserswerth, but a year later, on her second visit. The Baedeker that Flaubert drops in the Nile was in truth not yet available in a French version. Flaubert and Nightingale did indeed tour Egypt at the same moment with nearly identical itineraries, but as far as we know, they never met. However, the historical record does suggest that they glimpsed each other in November 1849 while being towed through the Mahmoudieh Canal from Alexandria to Cairo to that place on the Nile where still today one may engage a dahabiyah or *cange* and see the sights.

ABOUT THE AUTHOR

ENID SHOMER won the Iowa Fiction Prize for her first collection of stories, *Imaginary Men,* and the Florida Gold Medal for her second, *Tourist Season,* which was selected for Barnes & Noble's "Discover Great New Writers" series. She is also the author of four books of poetry. Her work has appeared in *The New Yorker, The Atlantic, The Paris Review,* and many other publications. As Visiting Writer, she has taught at the University of Arkansas, Florida State University, and the Ohio State University, among others. She lives in Tampa, Florida. *The Twelve Rooms of the Nile* is her first novel.